I0578372

By
RAYMOND BURKE

THE STARGUARDS
Of Humans, Heroes, and Demigods

The Magna Aura Genesis
The Axalan Revelation
The Terra Chronicles
The Destinia Apocalypse

THE CELESTIAN ODYSSEY

THE CELESTIAN ODYSSEY

BOOK FIVE OF

THE STARGUARDS

Of Humans, Heroes, and Demigods

RAYMOND BURKE

The Author asserts the moral right to be identified as the author of this work

ISBN: 1-9162746-0-9

ISBN 13: 978-1-9162746-0-0

THE STARGUARDS

Raymond Burke is a British-born author - The Celestian Odyssey the fifth novel in the Starguards series.

His background includes an early life in Canada and the US, employment in the British Army as an aircraft technician, an MSc degree in Archaeology from University College London, and short-article writing. He is also a member of The Mars Society.

Raymond cunningly lives without a fridge, satellite TV, iPods, and he also can't drive. And while he has taken up 3D printing, he's a self-confessed 21st century caveman . . . and loves it!

Through all, he has been a keen writer. He lives in London.

To

2020

For those who survived and to those lost.

ACKNOWLEDGEMENTS

Every book brings out the best in my family and friends. A most treasured thank you to Nigel Livingstone, Chris Bellay, and Mark Veal. To constant supporters John McMillan, Mark Emsley, Dave Baseley, Dave Money, Jenny Stripe, and Lori Buttermark. To my fellow writers and artists Lance Steen Anthony Nielsen, Nick Cirkovic, David P Perlmutter, Jon-Jon Jones, Stephen Marriott, Anne John-Ligali, Soulla Christodoulou, Nilam A McGrath, and Elisa Gianoncelli. To Patrick M. Powers for inspiration and guidance.

And as always to the members of the LOTNA sci-fi group.

Cover design by Ennel John Espanola.

Formatting by Shabbir Hussain.

Any leftover errors are mine alone to claim.

I can spell; I just like to make words up!

BOOK FIVE

THE CELESTIAN ODYSSEY

Of Journey Ends and Beginnings

Prologue

Somewhere. Somewhen.

"Where am I?" the girl asked again.

Scared and alone, she couldn't remember how she had arrived, wherever she was. But 'here' seemed to be everywhere and nowhere. And pitch black.

She felt different, strange, as if sapped of energy. Under where she lay felt like a heavy stone slab. She couldn't feel any bindings around her, but she couldn't move. She shivered. It was cold. Every now and again fleeting, flashing jumbled-up images pulsed through her mind—an explosion, escape, and a desperate fight for life. Her head pounded in the darkness.

Hushed voices suddenly hovered around her; urgent, harsh, alien.

"Who's there?" she cried out haltingly into the darkness, her eyes failing to adjust to anything in the nothingness around her.

A sense of movement drifted toward her. A feeling of dread coldness emanated upon her, followed by a voice, now neither harsh nor threatening. It spoke her language.

"Understand, I am Techmoses," answered a being from the encompassing shadows. "Comprehend, Urvursur attends as my second"

A second presence not far from Techmoses grunted in a much deeper voice, though the girl could not see either one of them.

"We attend you to assist our interrogations," stated Techmoses; the girl not deigning to correct his grammar. "You attacked our universe. We hasten to ascertain the purpose."

The girl didn't know what he was talking about. She tried to move and though she couldn't even see beyond herself, she could feel now that she was tilted almost upright toward her captors unless they were floating above her. She tried to not let her thoughts wander. She squirmed uselessly against what she could now sense to be some form of temporal bonds.

Techmoses spoke again, addressing another.

"Antrameda, are you ready?"

"Commitment, my Lord," came the solitary answer.

A female voice. From behind the girl who jolted in terror, shuddering from the coldness of their voices.

From in front of her, the iciness spread to the girl again, as Techmoses asked in deliberate slow tones: "Who are you?" Gentleness caressed his firm voice.

She twisted in her intangible bonds trying to see her captors. She screamed in frustration at her failure.

Then she froze as the briefest of flashes of some form of dark light, flared long enough, black against black, for the girl to see the darkest of forms raise a hand. From his long-articulated hand a strange black dense energy infused their captive prey.

The girl screamed, her soul feeling as if on fire.

"Where are you from?" Techmoses asked in a soft voice.

She could feel the words being dragged from her being against her will.

"Earth!" screamed the girl, in heaving gasps of agony. "Earth!" she repeated.

"Eeearrth?" Techmoses drew out the word accompanied by an expansive cold front enveloping the girl. "Your purpose?"

Her tongue was agonisingly dry, but the words scraped involuntarily over it.

"I... I don't know. I don't know... where I am," she gasped.

"Verified truly, she does not know," the female alien spoke.

"Comprehend," Techmoses acknowledged, a little irked. "What are you?" He seemed to be leaning right over her. A disembodied voice in the depths of night.

The girl's eyes widened in shock as another burst of black energy wreaked through her body. She resisted.

No more words, she vowed to herself. *Brave, be brave.*

"What are you?" Techmoses repeated, slowly; rising tension under his soft voice.

Her breath was erratic, her eyes searching for some

recognisable form around her to find some purchase in reality, something to cling to, a place of sanity, but all was deep unfathomable darkness.

Her mind searched for the answer; anything to lie, protect herself, survive. But the truth flowed out as if directed by an outer force.

"Astral. I'm an Astral!" she whispered, her mind numb with pain.

In the darkness, she sensed Techmoses and Urvursur turn to each other.

"They exist!" There was palpable excitement in Techmoses' voice. There was more alien chatter amongst them.

Turning back to the girl, he stated, "Comprehend, your death is already ordained. Your Kinstate will be razed to oblivion with you as the instrument." There was a gurgle of pleasure from him. "You will not remember any of this, but understand, I thank you."

The girl could not tell if he was being sarcastic or genuine, but she did care that she was being set free.

Addressing Antrameda, still behind the girl, he commanded: "Return the Astral to her timestream. Observe. We possess enemies anew to destroy."

"Command obeyed," Antrameda responded, making preparations the girl could only sense movement behind her.

She definitely felt her platform lower to what she thought was more horizontal.

She heard more alien conversation. Their tongue was fastflowing but harsh. The room turned even colder. If she could understand them, she would have heard.

"Alert the Forethere!" ordered Techmoses.

"Assembalation as we speak," Urvursur confirmed.

"Progressions? Voddodon's graviportal?"

Urvursur's voice grew gravelly with grimness. "The world has been suffused. No defence upheld. Threshold complete."

"Expectation achieved," came Techmoses' proud voice. "Success and contact to Amagesh. Report on Resvurgem?"

"The Infinitus had been intercepted. Destination?" But Urvursur knew already.

"Earth!" came the expected answer.

A low growl of satisfaction rolled through Urvursur, sending shivers through the girl. Something in the air was building up behind her. It made her hair stand on end.

"Degena position?" Techmoses enquired.

"The temporal dimension has been located."

"Expectation achieved," replied Techmoses. "We will join in the hunt."

"Comprehend," Urvursur bowed.

"Warloron?"

There was a brief hesitation. "Contrary expectation, Warloron has been vanquished! Altair prevailed."

There was no reaction from Techmoses, just a quiet as deep as the darkness around him as he digested the news one of his cohort was dead. And at the hands of a Starguard.

Around the girl, a low hum started to rise from behind her.

"Nexionon?" continued Techmoses, more sombrely.

"Dimensional calculations stable. Fortress threshold complete. We will cross undisturbed. The inhabitants therein will be destroyed!"

"Magna Aura?" Techmoses growled the name of his enemies' world.

"The Starguards divide themselves. They war for command. They complete our work for us!" There was pleasure in Urvursur's cold voice.

"They will unite when the storm gathers!" Techmoses said.

"Resistance expectation one hundred percent," Antrameda concluded, interrupting her works behind the girl.

"Foreseen, but negligible" challenged Urvursur.

Antrameda scoffed. "We foresee their natural rebellious spirit. Spawn of the cursed Storm of Stars; they will resist!"

Techmoses made a gargling growling noise in his throat, which would have been construed as a laugh in human terms.

"Resistance will not matter. What they call blood we will

simply rape from them and use it to wash their universe away forever!"

The girl had listened in agony as the hum rose in crescendo and a churning coldness captured her soul, her eyes barely registering as Techmoses and Urvursur turned and blinked out of existence in a flash of blackness.

The girl was left alone with the female alien, whose cold presence she felt walk around slowly to her side. Yet the girl could just about see a black outline above her.

Antrameda reached out and touched the girl's head, the iciest of sparks ripping down her spine.

"Bvo, Astral!" her farewell gesture sent the girl into convulsions.

And Zane screamed and screamed until unconsciousness swept her away.

CHAPTER ONE

The storm had appeared more than twenty years ago. At first, it had manifested as a continual area of extreme low depression, not seen before on Halcyon. However, the darkening squall had not been responsive to any of their climate control fields. Environmental probes did not return and lives were not risked to enter its black swirling depths.

Every year the clouds had grown denser, centred over a small is let within the southern Astral Islands chain, circling in a prescribed manner twenty kilometers across and fifty kilometers high. Crystalator scanners could not penetrate the cloud layers; they indicated nothing was there. The storm did not exist.

A quarantine perimeter had been set up; no one allowed to approach the area. Communications about the storm were restricted until it could be figured out what it was and how long it would persist. Sky and Star Warriors monitored its nature constantly.

But there was a theory, that the storm was not of this dimension. It was a breach; from where and by whom it was not known. If it was the Lore, then Magna Aura would stand ready again. All they could do was watch. And wait for things to change.

Then change came.

The Starguards returned home.

****

"Halt, fly no further! Identify yourselves!" a voice boomed over their manoeuvre suit comms.

Sceptre, Urana, Decion, and Azure stopped as they flew through space, several hundred kilometers above Halcyon.

The swordship barring their way was huge, much bigger than any built during their time on Magna Aura. While still a streamlined silver-white-hulled shard, it was broader than traditional swords, with a set of six stubby engine nacelles tapering into flaring points at the rear. More weaponry seemed to bristle from its ports, Decion noting a pulse cannon fixture near the nose. Command towers and comms fins studded the main body. It was very much a warship, built in the traditional Trinari exacting lines, the kind they could have used while fighting the Lore.

Decion grunted in approval very much admiring the approaching Sword. In Earth parlance, he would have called the Sword's form extravagant, but then again the Celestians had always preferred artistic style, even for war ships.

Decion's gaze then shifted toward Halcyon as something caught his eye; lightning. He did not believe it at first, but he had spied the unmistakeable nebulous black clouds on the far side of Halcyon as it rotated out of view; a storm the likes of he had never seen before or believe could exist on Halcyon. He wasn't sure if the others had also seen the tempest, but he didn't have time to raise the question.

Without warning, four figures materialised around them. Sceptre glided ahead of the others, hands lit with energy.

"Who are you?" Sceptre demanded.

Of the four individuals, two donned the characteristic two-toned-blue Sky Warrior manoeuvre suits, but armoured and with sealed helmets for their occupants to breathe within the suit's personal forcefield. However, the other two men wore the open-faced helmets and armour which Sceptre recognised from his studies on Earth as being stylised Greek armour. They were also not garbed in protective breathing gear like the Sky Warriors. They bore natural forcefields, like the Starguards. But these weren't Starguards.

"Astrals," Decion muttered darkly under his breath.

And upon closer inspection, twins at that.

Sceptre could feel the other Starguards tense, as they realised what the twins were.

"Who are you?" Sceptre repeated brusquely, perturbed at having been halted by their upstart kin. "Identify *yourselves*, now!"

The four newcomers looked at each other, each refusing to answer. But Sceptre could see in their eyes that they recognised them; they just didn't want to acknowledge the fact too quickly. They were young unblooded warriors, Sceptre suspected, but not used to being challenged. He looked over at Decion, whose eyes shared the same thought.

For once, Sceptre wanted Decion to cut loose and teach these Astral whelplings a lesson. Decion took a sideways glance over at Sceptre, sensing his attention and understanding the silent command.

Welcome home! Sceptre thought.

The juggernaut swordship hung between them and Halcyon in silent splendour, like an over-wrought jewelled dagger, Sceptre thinking of how to evade or disable it, if they were attacked.

The silent tension boiled over. Decion readied his dimensional sheath to unleash his lancesword. Sceptre's hands were on the verge of lighting up.

"Stop this nonsense!" Urana intervened, commanding Sceptre and Decion to stand down before any blood was shed. She addressed the four strangers. "You know who we are! I am Urana, sister of Cirrius. Who are you and where is my brother?" she said in a polite voice with an undercurrent of charged anger.

"Urana?" scoffed one of the brothers. The twins looked at each other quizzically. "If it is really you, you have all been missing for forty years!"

"Forty. . . did you say forty years?" Urana exclaimed, looking at the other Starguards' reactions. "By all the Universe!" She stared back at Sceptre in disbelief.

"That's not possible," Sceptre said. "We were on Earth less than ten years!"

Then he thought of the battle with the Storm of Stars. He shook his head not knowing what to believe.

Are the Storm of Stars still playing with us? his mind dared ask. *Did Zane deceive them?* He did not want an answer.

Decion and Azure looked just as perplexed.

"If you are who you say you are," the same brother spoke, "then you must be Sceptre," he looked at Aerl, "and Decion," he added, bowing to them. "And you, you must be. . ." His voice took on a tone of disgust, but the man on his right, his twin, chided him with a click of his tongue.

"Azure," he finished airily for his brother, "Loremaiden. Daughter of the Traitor Synther." Azure flinched at the unwanted honourific. "Saviour of the Magna Aura system." He bowed, but he seemed to mock her.

Azure, about to protest, felt a strange sensation surge through her body. She felt weirdly and dizzyingly energised.

Boorishly, the first twin continued, addressing Azure: "You must be the one who breached the temporal forceshield!"

"That's for us to know!" Decion replied authoritatively, masking the fact he didn't know either. Urana gave him a quick approving sideglance. Better Cirrius didn't know everything.

Urana took the moment to reply vociferously to the brothers. "Hey! I asked who are you and where is my brother?"

One of the twins smiled proudly, as if to reveal a big secret. "The King is on Halcyon, where he has ruled for the past thirty years. And we are the Astrals, his allies, and warriors!" He proclaimed. "I am Antichilles. This is my brother Tyran," he indicated his twin. "With us are Sky Leaders Tymmon and Maxsos."

The normal mutual cordial exchanges of greetings were interrupted by Urana.

"King? What do you mean?"

"It's a long story. He can explain it to you," Antichilles replied. "If he wishes."

Urana bristled at their brazenness.

"Where are Altair and Alpha Rion?" Tyran asked, with genuine bafflement.

"They are not here?" Sceptre asked in return, looking down at the slowly-spinning world as if he could see them himself.

The Astrals shook their heads.

"Then we do not know," Sceptre answered. "We hoped they would be here. It looks like they may have died on Earth."

Decion scowled, not pleased at the thought of his younger brother being dead. "Weren't you cursed Astrals watching over Earth? Watching us? Shouldn't you know their fates?" he demanded; a curious thought springing to mind as the young Sky leaders again looked at each other and then Antichilles.

"As I said, the King can explain." He left it at that.

And before the Starguards could ask any more questions, Antichilles threw his arms open to the cosmic air and the party of Astrals, Sky Warriors, and Starguards disappeared from the environs of outer space...

... to land on Sky Command.

In the expansive main hanger bay to be exact, Azure instantly recognising the smell of the skimmers, the slight creaking of the bulkheads and hull and the faint soothing vibrations from the grav-engines, keeping the Sky Warriors' shell-like headquarters aloft. She felt at home. This was the hanger where she had first met Novan.

Her memory prompted her to ask, "Have you heard from Novan?" Her voice echoed around the hanger, which Azure realised was surprisingly devoid of Sky Warriors and crews.

There was no answer from their escort, but a new voice spoke up.

"No, we haven't heard from any other Starguard, until you arrived today," a female voice said, entering from the opposite end of the hanger. "It's very good to see you," she continued.

"Timechantress!" Decion yelled, clenching his fists upon seeing the blue-haired Astral ahead of them. "How dare you greet us! What are you doing here, bitch?" Decion raged.

He instinctively made to grab his lancesword from its otherworldly sheath and charge the Astral, but Sceptre and Urana held him back, just.

"Let her speak!" Sceptre urged. "You have a lot of explaining to do, Astral, for your part in our abductions to Earth!"

Timechantress stood before them. Her daughter, Celestra, and another younger blue-haired girl stood either side of her.

Antichilles turned on them. "How dare you address the Queen in such a manner!" he shouted haughtily at them. "You should be kneeling before her!"

"Queen?" Urana sneered; a horrible feeling mounting inside her.

"And our mother!" Antichilles announced as he and Tyran took off their helmets, their bright blue hair proudly confirming their heritage. ". . . Aunt Urana!" he sneered back.

The Starguards could only look on startled.

Azure stifled a laugh, receiving a look of pure venom from Urana.

Azure retorted, "Well you have to admit after all we've been through, you had to see this coming!"

Urana twisted her mouth, trying not to smile. Still, she was in no mood to countenance having to obey an Astral.

"Where's my brother, Timechantress?"

Her haughtiness intact, Timechantress stepped to one side, stretching out her arm. "This way," she smiled at Urana, "sister."

Urana bristled, but held her tongue.

They followed, as Timechantress led them through the familiar corridors of Sky Command, the cool-blue-hued corridors, a somewhat comforting sight.

Decion smirked.

"What are *you* smiling at now, Decion?" a peeved Sceptre asked.

"These Astrals," he whispered, "They are time travellers, yet did not foresee our return. They are worse than the other lot!"

Sceptre looked at Decion's serious demeanour. Then they both broke out in a laugh. He clapped the larger Starguard on the shoulder, the other Starguards bemused at their mirth. It *was* good to be home.

As they walked on, scores of Sky Warriors looked around at them and each other, whispers echoing through the halls and corridors: *The Starguards had returned!* Through more corridors, skylifts, and transtubes, Azure knew they were heading for the Sky Commander's office; she had been there enough times and she hoped to see friendly faces.

However, the atmosphere was eerily muted, the Starguards feeling distinctly uneasy, even Azure, who nominally would have been the ranking Sky Warrior after Cirrius, following Gal Agar's death. But even she was shocked to see who the new Sky Commander was as they approached the office.

"Tol? Is that you?" She saw her old colleague standing outside the Sky Commander's office, his dark blue uniform indicating his rank.

Time had not sat well upon him. Even for a Celestian's longer lifespan than a human's, forty years had seen the grey appear in Tol Valar's hair, wrinkle lines, and a faint scar on his forehead weathering his face.

"Hallo, Deb, or should I say, Azure?" He saluted her. "Who would have thought you were a Starguard!" he smiled. "And thank you for saving our worlds!" His gratitude was heart-felt. He almost bowed.

"Thank you," she returned a slight bow, "And everyone is very welcome. It was a shock for me, too, you know. And now you're the Commander. What happened to the rest?" Azure remembered Ade, Dessa, and Glith. A wave of nausea suddenly flooded through her body and she barely heard Tol's reply.

"All gone—Universe hold them," he briefly closed his eyes and dipped his head in respect. "I was the highest ranking Sky Warrior left, so I was appointed the Commander."

"Well, you look. . . well," Azure fibbed.

Tol laughed without bitterness. "No I don't. Thirty years of war have taken its toll. . ." He stopped himself short as if speaking out of turn.

"War!" The Starguards voiced as one.

"That will be all, Sky Commander Valar," Timechantress said, before any more questions could be asked. She dismissed him with a tilt of her head.

"Yes, your Highness," he bowed deeply to her. He turned to the Starguards, "If you will excuse me. I have duties to attend to." He took his leave, giving Azure a furtive look who half-returned it.

"War, Timechantress?" Sceptre repeated, "Against whom?"

"All will be explained. I did not want us gossiping in the corridors." Her frosty smile ended the conversation.

She turned and opened the door, the three young Astrals, Timechantress, Celestra, and four Starguards stepping into the Sky Commander's office.

Cirrius sat at the Sky Commander's desk. The twins and the blue-haired girl filed in to flank him. Celestra stood by her mother beside the desk.

The office was much as Azure remembered it from Gal Agar's time. It had never been a big office; it had been more his personal office than the battle and conference suites down the corridor. Behind Cirrius and the desk, the large portholes and air hatch still showed the glorious blueness of Halcyon's skies. However, the furniture and decorations had been changed. Gone were Gal Agar's personal touches replaced by Tol Valar's awards, trophies, and vid-pics of various events. The right-hand wall was a weapons panel with selections of projectile arms and swords, while the left-hand wall held screens and maps of the Magna Aura worlds, and swordship status. On the desk was what looked like a flag and a coat of arms, though Azure was not sure if they belonged to the Magna Aura system or to Cirrius himself.

As the door had opened, Cirrius looked up suddenly, discreetly tucking away whatever he had been working on. His face brightened upon seeing the visitors.

"Rain?" Cirrius cried out, a big smile surfacing on his face. "It really is you!" He rose quickly, bounding happily around the desk, hugging his sister.

Urana returned it with wholeheartedness. She regarded her 'little' brother. He wore his blue-on-blue Sky Warrior Supreme Commander's uniform, but now it was adorned with a short dark blue cape. His blue hair was darkening and his square-faced features made him look more like their father than the brilliant-but-shy youth she had left behind.

"I suppose you're older than me now?" she asked, trying to lighten the tension around them. She gently caressed his hair.

Cirrius returned her smile, creasing his eyes. "I am at that, 'big sister'." They laughed, somewhat awkwardly.

He looked at the rest of the Starguards in turn, leaning forwards hugging them, stiffly, but firmly.

"And look at you, little Azure. How you have grown. Thank you for saving us all," he voiced solemnly.

Azure blushed. She hadn't expected any praise from Cirrius.

"Of course," was all she could say, quietly. "Your majesty," she added without malice.

A hurrumph announced someone's disapproval. "You don't expect us to call you 'Your Highness'?" Decion smouldered. He was also aggrieved they were all still standing and hadn't been offered so much as a draft of nectar.

Even the drunkard Archron had better manners than this, Decion's face grew darker.

Cirrius smiled back, but said nothing.

"A king isn't even a Celestian concept. Where did you get that from—Earth?" Sceptre asked.

Cirrius sighed. "Well, it is good to see you all, too," he replied disarmingly, feeling less than welcomed himself. "Yes, Aerl," he addressed Sceptre, "King is an Earth term. We needed something for the Magna Aurans to rally around. Zasandra introduced me to the term and history of kingship on Earth. And, no, Decion, you do not have to address me as 'Your Highness'. Though as the King you would have to respect me in public, even if you don't in private. I am no dictator, but we needed to come together after the attacks."

"Which brings us to this war we heard about," Sceptre interjected.

Cirrius sighed again, waving a dismissive hand. "So, you have heard."

He directed a pointed look at Timechantress who indicated

with a quick shake of the head it wasn't her.

Cirrius continued, "Ten years after you disappeared... well were taken by the Astrals to Earth..." He looked a bit sheepishly at them all, "Magna Aura was attacked by an unknown enemy with powerful spacecraft. They caught us with our guard down. We thought we were safe after the Lore attack. And we had not encountered any other beings in the surrounding systems. We have never even seen the enemies' faces. They still attack from time to time, probing for weak spots. So, as the Supreme Commander of the Sky Warriors, I consolidated power establishing martial law on Halcyon. I extended my powers to Placia, the outer planets and the City-States, to all intents and purposes ruling the Magna Aura system. I became King. But Astara, as the new Protectress of State, disagreed with my plans and resisted my command over Placia."

"Good for her!" Urana retorted with a joyful smile. "Placia is a sovereign world, and I would have done the same!"

Cirrius continued, disregarding his sister's outburst. "There were years of tension and we were watched over by the Astrals. Timechantress and Celestra had sided with me." He smiled at them behind him by his desk. "We now have a truce, ultimately agreeing on the mutual protection of Magna Aura. Anyway, as time went on, Zasandra and I fell in love, married, and had children, the twins Antichilles and Tyran, and our daughter, Xestina."

While the twins looked on impassively, the younger blue-haired girl gave a nervous smile.

Azure looked at the young Astral, who returned her gaze, reminding Azure of a shy young girl who became a Starguard. She knew Xestina would have to grow up fast in time to come and she didn't envy her.

"And so we have protected Magna Aura for the past thirty years, each time the attacks becoming stronger. We have built more Swords, the City-States now converted back into Swords— sorry, Aerl," Cirrius said to Sceptre. "We needed them and the citizens are now housed here or on Placia."

Sceptre nodded. Millennius City-State, his home, was now a spaceship once again. He had no time to lament his loss.

"And lastly, about twenty years ago, a new religion formed from nowhere. Citizens have been worshipping a deity called Bood!" he flung a hand up as if backhanding a bug away.

"Bood, who is he?" Decion asked.

"Ne," Cirrius corrected him.

"What?" asked Decion.

"Ne," repeated Cirrius. "Bood is apparently a neuter deity. So Ne in place of she/he, Nis for hers/his, Nir for him/her, etcetera, etcetera" he finished. "No one knows where this being originated, there are no temples for Nir, or any images," Cirrius shook his head.

"Maybe the Neb. . ." began Urana.

"No," Timechantress cut her off. "The Neb have constantly been faithful to the Universe and the Great Mother and Holy Father. They performed the coronation of Cirrius. They have been loyal," she defended the religious Peoples and their order.

Cirrius added, "But even they cannot fathom the origins of this Bood. It is creating divisions. So besides the attacks, I have this. . . disorder among the worlds," he gritted his teeth. "I strive to bring order and protect the people, here and out there," he pointed in the general direction of the porthole and beyond, "You have seen my flagship, the *Celestient*; magnificent is she not? Her sisters, *Rethemer* and *Exthereal*, currently guard Halcyon and Placia, and rotate with the seven other new swords in patrolling the system." He pointed his chin over the left wall with its status reports. "The Trinari have excelled themselves in their craftsmanship!"

That, the Starguards could not deny just from glancing at the readouts and images.

"And the Star Warriors?" asked Decion, his battle senses intrigued.

"The Star Warriors still survive, under the leadership of Star Commander Ilis Rona, a fine Xarian. But we could use your command, if you so wished," Cirrius extended the fig leaf.

Decion thought about it. He did not know Ilis Rona, but he did not want to seem to be changing sides, again. He glanced over to Sceptre who seemed to have read his mind. He nodded his assent.

"That would be agreeable," responded Decion. "I will meet with this Ilis Rona first," stiffly adding, "Your Highness."

Cirrius graciously sniffed away Decion's slight. "Star Commander Ilis Rona is a fine capable commander, but she could learn a lot from you," Cirrius replied.

Azure was puzzled and asked: "What about the other Astrals; didn't they help you in the war?"

Cirrius looked at his wife. The children bowed their heads.

Azure swallowed hard, knowing there would be a terrible answer.

"There are no more Astrals," Timechantress said, almost in a matter-of-fact manner. "They have disappeared or are dead!"

"Dead!" Azure was shocked.

The Starguards reacted in kind. As much as they loathed the Astrals, they knew some of them had their best intentions at heart, except for Timechantress and the deceased sons of Destina, Netherlord and Archron.

"But they returned us back here. Or at least Zane did!" Azure added.

Celestra made a face. "Zane? She's dead!" she smirked. "My father said she died in an attack!"

"An attack? Huh!" scoffed Azure. "Your father tried to kill her and thought he had, but it turns out she is a Loremaiden, like me. She survived and ended up on Earth."

"A Loremaiden?" Timechantress gasped, aghast at the notion.

"And then there is the Time Empress," said Sceptre.

Timechantress shook her head. "Time Empress? I do not understand any of this. We do not have an Empress!" she waved her hands in confusion. "What happened on Earth?"

The Starguards heaved a collective sigh and told the gathered Astrals of their adventures since being taken from

Magna Aura right up to the battle with the Storm of Stars and their return to Magna Aura.

For hours, Cirrius and the Astrals listened with intent, astounded at the sheer scale of their adventures. At the end there was a reverential silence, until Cirrius said:

"So, the Storm of Stars really existed!" Cirrius' voice was soaked in awe.

"And the Antiqchronals?" Timechantress' voice was quiet.

"It was all true what the Scrolls of History had within them and what the Knights Destina believed," Decion added.

Cirrius pondered this for a while. "And I missed it! What I would have given to be there?"

His sister rebuked him. "Cirrius, countless people died, including all the surviving Celestian Knights and a lot of humans we knew—friends. And possibly even Altair and Alpha Rion. And it's all your fault!" The last accusation was aimed at Timechantress.

Cirrius grasped the sides of his head, exasperated. "No, it is not. How could we have known? We had a plan. No one was supposed to die, let alone in the realm of Gods."

"I should inform Astara about Alpha Rion," Decion said sombrely.

Timechantress replied, "She has been informed you have returned and is on her way here."

Decion nodded, still hoping for a chance at some revenge on the Astral.

"And now you're telling us that the Astrals are gone as well," Azure brought the conversation back to the Astrals. "How do you know this?"

It was Timechantress' time to sigh, composing herself; resigned as if to tell a guilty secret.

"Xathanius contacted me. Or rather Lightstream was able to communicate through the temporal shield. I swear I did not know Lazeron and Cal Xarien had helped Synther and their mother, Destina, kill my brother. Lazeron lied to me!"

She thought bitterly of that night Netherlord lied to her

about Lord Aeon disappearing after Synther's supposed death.

"Now I know it was Zane who saved her father. Who would have thought that," she half smiled at her niece's accomplishment. "Lazeron's lie is one reason why I left him for Cirrius, but by then Lazeron was dead. . ."

"By Zane's brother's hand after they thought Netherlord had killed Zane. Sceptre said."

"Justice," Decion coughed indiscreetly.

"Indeed," Timechantress agreed, with a hard stare at Decion's undisguised hatred. "Anyway, Lightstream's message said Xathanius wanted the Astrals to be together as a family again, especially as his own had been extended. He had forgiven me." She smiled faintly. "That meant a lot to me." She held back as her eyes glistened, before continuing. "But still, I thought it might be a trick to capture me, after my actions with sending you to Earth, so I left Celestra on Halcyon and went to the Chronopolis to see if things were safe."

Her eyes widened as she stared off into the distance in remembrance. "But I didn't see anyone; there was just a surrounding temporal wall around the Chronopolis. I could not see or sense anything beyond the wall, no bodies or signs of fighting, and my powers could not dispel the wall. But I could tell you I was scared. . ." she stared off into the distance again. ". . . and alone. I think they were attacked and they sealed off the Chronopolis for protection." She shrugged, not knowing what else she could have done.

"So I returned to Halcyon, told Cirrius what had happened and we started planning from that moment onward. It's another reason why he's King and there's martial law. We were protecting Magna Aura and our family from whatever may have happened to the Astrals, for if the Astrals were attacked, then the attackers are sure to come after me and my children." She regarded them with a fierce stare. "And no one attacks my family!" she added defiantly.

She continued, "Then a few years later, Halcyon was attacked by these mysterious ships. It seems more than a coincidence.

These two events may be connected and the two attacking enemies are one and the same. But we do not know for sure. So here we are, trapped in our own system, cut off from the Astrals, and from any help." She sat on the edge of Cirrius' desk. "Until you all returned." She sounded neither relieved or overly joyful.

"And how did you pierce my temporal forceshield?" Cirrius asked, his curiosity ever reaching out.

The Starguards looked at Sceptre, who elected to tell the truth.

"Zane's Loremaiden powers."

"Of course. Of course," Cirrius nodded. "She would be quite powerful."

Decion shook his head. "Look, we have just fought the Storm of Stars. No offence to you Astrals," which he absolutely meant, "but we Starguards are honed fighters rather than watchers behind the scenes. We will fight whichever enemy shows up and be victorious," he ventured.

Timechantress was about to reply snidely, when Azure spoke up.

"No, Decion, Timechantress may be right," she said to the general shock of the group. "On future Earth, Zane went for help from the Astrals and she returned without them. She told us the Astrals had gone. So at some point, the Astrals disappeared from the Chronopolis, leaving it sealed-off for whatever reason. So I can't see any other reason for the Astrals to have disappeared, unless they had been forced to disappear. And now Magna Aura is under attack. It cannot be a coincidence?"

"But when did the Astrals disappear?" Sceptre asked.

Azure shook her head, unable to fill in the blanks. "We met the Time Empress as a little girl, but her parents weren't with her. None of the Astrals were. And Timechantress was being invited back to meet the Time Empress," she concluded. "Maybe."

Sceptre was confused. "But Zane was millions of years in the future and Timechantress was here. How can they both have been at the Chronopolis around the same time? How can you Astrals tell your relative time when you're time travelling?" he asked Timechantress.

Timechantress shook her head. "The Chronopolis inhabits its own temporal dimension and is anchored to an Astral's individual present time, so no matter when we are in time, whenever we return to the Chronopolis we return to our own present, rather than to our past or future to avoid paradoxes."

"That sounds amazing!" Azure said. "How do you do that?"

Timechantress shrugged again. "I do not know exactly; to us it is just like breathing. Phasia trained us in so many things, advanced things, but at heart, all of us Astrals were just warriors of the ancient world. Celestra knows far more than I do," she turned to her daughter. "And the younger ones know far more than me about it; the physics goes beyond my ken. I just know it works!" Folding her arms across her chest, she made a face of apology, pursing her lips.

"Cool," Azure remarked with a crazy grin on her face. She felt light-headed, exhilarated even.

Seizing the moment rather bluntly, Cirrius asked, "So, do you all accept my reasons for rulership?"

"What else can we do?" Urana sighed, her glum expression mirroring the others as they contemplated the new Magna Auran order.

More importantly, Decion held his tongue, for now.

"So where are we on your royal court?" Urana asked.

Cirrius laughed. "Well, I know you would not want to be 'Princess Urana' so you can just be yourselves. All of you are my loyal knights and defenders of the Magna Aura system."

"Really?" Decion protested. "Why not drop the King act and we all rule as a council? Why not let the Magna Aurans rule?"

An uneasy smile spread across Cirrius' face. "Decion, I've held these worlds together for forty years." He held up his hands to defend against Decion's anticipated argument. "Yes, I know I'm responsible for the fact you weren't here, but that was unexpected. I was alone, with Astara, and we had to defend

Magna Aura. What else could we have done?"

Azure broke the silence. "You could have found Novan!" she said, face beaming. "We could use his help or he might need ours," she rubbed her head, the giddiness giving way to a strong headache coming on from nowhere.

Everyone looked at Azure. She tried to hide her discomfort.

Turning back to Cirrius, she reiterated, "No offence, but we need Novan's leadership and his extra Swords and warriors."

"Novan? He is lost." Cirrus dismissed her idea with a swat of his hand. "We have no idea where he is. He has not contacted us and we have no idea what happened to him and if he found his mother, the Goddess Elysius!"

Azure chuckled. "He did find her! In a place they call the Ribbon System. But now Elysius is dead after saving them from the Lore!" Azure was upset.

Why wouldn't they listen to her?

Her head throbbed like a pulsar, like the universe wanted to desperately spill out of it.

As they waited expectantly for her explanation, none of them, least of all Azure herself expected what happened next.

There was an explosive flash of vibrant blue in her eyes. And then she fainted.

Sceptre caught her in his arms.

"Universe, here we go again!" Cirrius rolled his eyes.

CHAPTER TWO

We had escaped; escaped the onslaught of our enemy by dint of having constructed great dimensional portals; their original purpose for the transport of ships and supplies for exploring the unrivalled realms of the unknown. We had kept the portals secret from the other Peoples until we were ready to reveal them for the benefit and survival of all.

But our enemy had forestalled that idea forever. They attacked us for having killed one of their own, accidentally. The horror of that day is still imprinted upon our minds millennia later, the stories passed down from generation to generation, our younglings experiencing it as if they had lived through it, such was our hatred for our enemy.

We converted our ships into thriving star cities travelling the fresh voids of space in a new universe. We recreated our civilisation, newly discovered worlds providing everything we needed as we explored. We seeded new colonies on the myriad of planets offered to us. We built new dimensional portals on each world and hid them within great pyrathedrals; always ready to move in case our enemy were to discover our location. We would never be defeated again.

From our original forms, we genetically engineered ourselves to be stronger, better; altering our bodies, our very colour. We would be the colour of revenge, the counter-colour to our would-be destroyers. Throughout our new history and inter-civilisation rise, we swore never to forget or forgive our transgressors. The one thing that held us all together was our hatred for them and their allies, who stood by and let them try to destroy us. Never would that happen again. We would return to our rightful home one day and slaughter our enemies.

But two things happened to change our course. One, when we finally felt we had the courage and strength to exact our revenge, we probed our old universe to spy on our enemy. But what we found astonished us. Our universe had been destroyed; vanquished by the dreaded Lore. Now stranded in this new universe, we thought to end our hatred, satisfied, for surely they must have been destroyed when the Lore attacked. Our vengeance had not been personally sated, but it was justice; one evil had destroyed another evil. The Universe had shown us Justice. So, we sought ways to live in peace. But our peace was not to last. That was due to the second reason.

We did not know at first what we had created. It was a living weapon; sentient, to hunt down our enemies. But it grew, became aware, and moulded itself into our image. It—or she— as she was to become, became all-powerful. We had always worshipped the Universal gods of our universe. But we forgot ourselves and bowed down to her. She became our Goddess. She called herself Sentity. She pervaded our space, our explored galaxy, and even perhaps the entire universe. She was the personification of the universe, a sentient universe. And we were her Chalant; her champion children.

At first, she was benevolent. For thousands of years she visited successive generations, usually in the form of a little girl, her long purple hair and glowing purple eyes winning over our hearts and minds. But we grew restless; too lazy and complacent. We needed to move on, and at that time, find our enemy, and avenge our ancestors.

Sentity had never understood our need for vengeance; sentient or not, she did not like the idea that we would leave her one day. And the more we tried to exert our independence from her, the more her benevolence turn malevolent. We found ourselves the enemy of God. She started to destroy our cites and worlds and in a feat we thought beyond her, she created monsters to fight us.

But when we fought, captured, and studied these monsters we discovered a horrible truth. They were us; made from our dead. Sentity had fashioned their bodies into her own version of life; grotesque, animal-like creatures with misshapen purple bodies and course mane-like hair. We could not save them, for they were not alive, not in the sense we knew it, and no longer our beloved kin. Sentity called them the Gravan; the risen children.

Sentity was too strong for us and the Gravan too many to fight as they destroyed world after world. She could control their minds as she could never do ours and they were able to rise from the beyond time and time again.

We were left with one agonising choice: to escape this universe, and run, as before. We had no choice but to send our people and ships through the portals to another dimension and destroy the pyrathedrals behind us. Upon the last remaining world we abandoned Sentity and the Gravan and hoped they would never escape and find us.

And so here we were; another defeat, another universe. Another generation on the run. How cruel were the universes against us? But fate seemed to turn our way again.

We heard them first. Voices, languages, and dialects we had thought long lost. Peoples from before. They had escaped it seemed. We listened for a long time, our spies and scouts, gleaning the facts of their escape and recent battle with the ancient evil Lore. They had mixed their blood, were weakened, and had lost their champions, the Celestian Knights; their younglings the Starguards champions in their stead.

But most important of all, our enemies still lived among the so-called Magna Aurans. They were still alive and had not been rejected for their genocidal insolence against us; never punished! We had been revived; granted our universal right to justice. We were now the purest of all the Peoples. We would destroy the inferior ones. Our enemies would die, but so would the rest of the Magna Aurans who had harboured them. And only at the end, would they know who we were.

CHAPTER THREE

Azure dreamed. It was so vivid and real that she could not tell if she was actually asleep or awake. She cast her eyes around her, standing naked within the colourful shifting starscape which had suddenly taken a firm hold of her. The sliding forms showed her things, gave her answers, and awakened her soul. She could feel the power, the energy coursing through her, and she finally understood the reality of her life.

Her face tightened into a wide smile, a beautific feeling. She could see the radiant blue light shining forth from within her. She started to laugh. It rolled from her belly and out of her mouth like a non-stop flow of energising ecstasy. She whirled around in her bluening cosmos. She couldn't stop laughing.

"Azure, wake up, what are you laughing about? What is happening?" a strained voice asked, startling her awake.

Azure shot up bolt straight. She was in a bed.

"Universe! What was that?" she heard the same voice cry out.

The starscape abruptly vanished. The world now seemed disorientatingly blurry, undefined visions slowly wavering into focus, reality flooding back. Her mind registered the voice and a memory was triggered.

Azure rubbed her head. "Medtech Iesse, is that you?" She groggily opened her eyes, just as the blueness faded away. She lay back down again on her side facing the medtech.

Azure found she was indeed in the medbay. Not much had changed since the last time she had been here, perhaps a few more diagnostic chambers and upgraded machines, which she could see had been manufactured in the spatial printers. But it was very much the same medbay.

However, Iesse seemed to have grown a bit rounder. Her eyes were nevertheless the same doleful, expressive brown orbs studying Azure with concern.

Iesse stood by with a slender scanner in her hands. She had just administered a shot to Azure's arm. "That's better," she smiled. "Yes, it is me," she answered Azure's waking query. "Though I have been a full Medscholar for twenty years now. It is funny, this is the last place I saw you forty years ago. Still fainting, I see," she said with some mirth. "But with no Classia to help you escape this time!" her brown eyes crinkled.

Though most medtechs were bald, Iesse had grown a lock of twisted black hair down the back of her head past her shoulders. It suited Iesse's dark skin, Azure thought, before giving a wan smile at the memory of her previous stay in the medbay.

"I don't faint all the time," she protested sulkily. At least her head felt much better after the shot. "And congratulations on your promotion." She looked around the bay. "How did I get here?"

Iesse approached her a bit tentatively, Azure noticing her reluctance to look her in the eye. She remembered how other Sky Warriors had looked at the Starguards as they had returned and the lack of excitement at their return.

"Urana brought you here," Iesse replied. "She stayed a while then she was called back to the King." A sad smile tinged her next words. "I was saddened at the loss of Gal Agar against the Lore," Iesse lamented. "He was a great leader."

Azure pursed her lips in sorrow. "Thank you, he was like a father to me." She raised her hand to thank Iesse, who instinctively stepped backward, as if fearing a strike from the Starguard.

Propping herself up, Azure asked, "Why are the people afraid of us?" Iesse looked around furtively. "It's okay," Azure assured her. "I'm not Cirrius, you can speak around me."

Iesse looked Azure straight in the eye this time weighing up her trust.

Then she said: "You abandoned us. You left us to fight for other people rather than your own. You left us with Cirrius and those Astrals to rule over us. Even Astara could not stand alone. And then we were attacked by more aliens and at war for thirty years before you returned. We do not know whose side you are on or if you will back Cirrius after the war!" Her eyes darted around the room as if scared for having dared utter any dissenting words.

Azure was astounded at what she had heard. "You think we abandoned you? Is that what you have been told?"

Iesse slowly nodded her head once.

"No, that's not true, we were taken by the Astrals to their world, called Earth. We were there for some time and then to cut a very long story short, we found ourselves in the far future fighting against the Storm of Stars alongside the Antiqchronals, including the Lore. One day the histographers will hear our stories. But for now, we have to fight against this new enemy."

Iesse's face broke from fear into astonishment. Surprise and dubiousness filled her voice.

"The Scrolls of History were true?" She gasped at Azure's nod. "It must have been a glorious battle! Are the Lore now dead forever?"

Azure shook her head, laughing. "No, would you believe they are now a force for good. At least that's what I hope. All the Antiqchronals are now at peace."

Iesse smiled. "Oh, Universe praise them. And what of this world, Earth?" She leaned toward Azure, curious.

Now it was Azure's turn to smile. "Much like Magna Aura. The people could be like Magna Aurans, but are more primitive," she emphasised the last word. "They have centuries before they catch up to us. They can be the most selfish, war-like people or the most sensitive and selfless. The extremes are amazing, nothing like Magna Aura where everyone is happy and comfortable."

"Was happy," Iesse muttered to herself, Azure cringing inwardly as Iesse continued. "But you liked it; I can tell. Did you like it more than Halcyon?"

Azure pondered for a moment, her lips twisted in a memory.

"There's a saying on Earth: 'Nice place to visit, but I wouldn't want to live there!'" They both laughed, Iesse understanding its meaning. "A few years were good, but a lifetime would have been a nightmare. I'm a Halcyonite." Her smile faded, as she remembered something. "How long have I been in here?"

"A good few hours," Iesse replied.

"Hours?" Azure repeated. Her dream had seemed like scant minutes.

"Yes, it's almost the new day." She hesitated before continuing. "That strange energy in your eyes. . ."

"Lore energy. . ."

". . . Lore energy," Iesse hesitantly repeated, barely whispering the word, still afraid that saying it would make them re-appear. "It was coursing through you. Why is it happening now? Do you know? Are the Lore coming back?"

Azure smiled. "Yes, I do know what's happening to me now. And no the Lore are not attacking again," she said to quell Iesse's fears. "But I do need to see the King."

Iesse looked over her shoulder toward the door. "The King has warriors posted, just in case."

"Just in case of what?" Azure was alarmed.

Iesse shrugged.

"Well, I'm a Starguard, so let's see what they do," Azure spoke loudly. She swung her legs over the side of the med table and shouted: "Hey, sky marks, I demand to see Cirrius now!"

A couple of late-duty sky marks duly made their way over to the medstation.

"What?" one of them sneered.

"I demand to speak to the King," Azure said, ignoring his blasé response to both a Starguard and ranking Sky Warrior. "I have important information for him; information which could save his life."

"What information is that?" the other sky mark enquired. "Why is the King's life in danger?"

"I'll only tell the King, in person."

"Why?" remarked the first sky mark.

"I do not answer to you. As a Starguard, you would be duty-bound to at least let the King know and for him to decide for himself. And as you can see, I still wear the Sky Warrior uniform and I outrank you. Yes?"

The sky marks looked at each other in brief silent conversation.

"We will pass on the message," one of them said.

"Oh, thank you," Azure replied sarcastically, as one left and the other sky mark blocked the doorway.

Azure lay back down on the bed, ready to get up and confront the boorish juniors. But then she and Iesse heard a commotion just outside the medbay's sliding door.

"You heard her, do it now!" came a strong female voice.

"Yes, Protectress," came the instant snappy reply.

Azure heard footsteps quickly receding away. She sat up, staring at the door as a familiar figure dressed in the black and red of the Alphatronius clan came in.

"Astara!" Azure ran up to Placia's Protectress of State wrapping her in a warm hug.

The elder Starguard held Azure. "Dismissed, Medscholar," she turned to Iesse.

The medscholar smiled graciously, bowing silently and leaving through a side door to her office, but not before giving Azure a reassuring smile.

Astara's dark blue eyes gazed at Azure as she held her by the shoulders. "I am glad you have all returned safely. Decion has told me what happened, here, and to you all on Earth," she said with a sad smile. "You saved us all, Azure!" Astara hugged her again.

"Not everyone," Azure replied sympathetically. "And we didn't all return."

Closing her eyes in acknowledgement, Astara nodded. "I know, but I know Alpha Rion's heart as if it were my own. I would feel it if he were dead. And whomever this Chalant is, I am sure they are both safe. As for Altair, Universe, I don't think anything can kill him. His anger alone would get him through anything!" They laughed, though Astara studied the young

Starguard. "But you have grown, both as a Celestian and as a Starguard. We could have used you during this war!"

Azure regarded Astara. She still looked the same; beautifully chiselled features with her porcelain-white skin framed by her long black wavy trestles and eyes as blue as her own. But after forty years of missing a brother and thirty years of war even that took its toll on a Starguard. It might not have shown to the normal Magna Auran, but as a Starguard, Azure detected a slight sign of weariness about Astara.

Astara noted Azure observing her. She laughed, "Yes, I am almost twice as old as I was and it is showing, I am sure," she remarked.

Trying to seem less guilty at thinking the same, Azure shook her head, "Actually, I was thinking how much you haven't changed, though Cirrius has. And I don't think for the better. To win this war, we need Magna Aura together. We need the Starguards together. And we need Novan back!"

If Astara was taken aback she did not show it. "My brother is lost," was all she responded with.

"Not necessarily," Azure replied cryptically. "And that is why I need to see Cirrius!"

Astara's eyes narrowed in puzzlement. "Now I'm intrigued. Let us go!"

They started walking toward the door, the remaining sky mark baulking at stopping them when they walked past. He followed at a discreet distance.

"What are you up to, Azure?" Astara questioned, curiosity in her voice, as they walked through the corridors toward the Sky Commander's office.

"You'll see," came Azure's enigmatic reply.

Minutes later, Azure and Astara found themselves challenged by numerous sky marks posted at secure points along the command decks. But once they saw that Azure had been released from the medlabs under the authority of Astara, they melted away into the background.

Tol Valar awaited them at his office door. "Twice in one day on your first day back," he quipped, looking at Azure.

"What are you doing here?" asked Azure.

"Comms reported you were on the way," he replied. "Just came for support." His eyes caught Astara's for a brief moment. "Protectress," he greeted her as she nodded back in acknowledgement.

"Are the rest here?" Azure asked of the other Starguards.

He stepped aside. "They are all in there."

Without knocking, Astara open the door. She let the Sky Commander know he was dismissed with a curt look. He executed a swift turn and marched off.

Astara and Azure stepped into the room, Azure noting that everyone was indeed here.

Cirrius was seated, with Timechantress behind him and Celestra with Tyran, Antichilles, and Xestina standing to their right. On the left were Sceptre, Decion, and Urana. Astara joined them, while Azure placed herself in the middle of the office, in front of Cirrius who looked none-pleased at being summoned by the youngest Starguard.

"So, after your little sleep, you summoned me for what reason?" Cirrius scoffed at her. "Are you going to tell me more about Novan? How we need him. How he would take my place as leader. Are you planning what those humans called a coup?"

Azure laughed at Cirrius. A loud petulant guffaw.

"Don't laugh at me," he ordered, everyone tensing for trouble.

"Or what?" Azure teased. "What can you do to me?"

"I am the King. I can imprison you or exile you!" He grimaced at his own loose tone.

Azure laughed again. "I always thought you were the smart one," Azure said. "With all your plans and analyses, you figured out who I was. But you didn't figure everything out, did you?"

Cirrius' brows furrowed. "Figure what out?"

"Cirrius, I formally request that you give up your authority as King and hand back power to the Magna Aurans. Then together, we Starguards can fight this mysterious enemy, as one."

Timechantress coughed in disbelief. "Why you little upstart bitch, how dare you talk to a superior like that. . ."

"Superior?" Azure shot back. "We're all equal here, but we know who leads and that is Novan, or Aerl," she looked at Sceptre. "We have no need of Kings or dictators!"

Timechantress gasped, about to throw back her arms and unleash a temporal blast, but Cirrius intervened with a raised hand of his own.

"Enough! Azure, I will not tolerate this outburst. I may be a few years older than you, but there are more superior Starguards than both of us here. However, the authority to rule is mine. Your absence was unfortunate, but necessary, and under the circumstances now, at war, I demand respect and that I stay in power to bring order. Novan is not here. And for all we know, he never will be!"

But Azure wouldn't give up, asking "Why did you tell the people we had abandoned them?" She looked at Timechantress. "And I get the feeling that you haven't revealed the whole truth about the Astrals to them either. Do they know about time travel?" Cirrius and Timechantress looked at each other; their children looking uneasy. "Thought so," Azure said. "Why not?"

Cirrius waved his hands dismissively as he replied. "You can imagine if ordinary Magna Aurans knew about time travel, they would demand we go back in time, bring back their deceased loved ones from the war with the Lore or even return to the Old Worlds and help our parents defeat the Lore. We would be slaves to their time, having to change every detail to perfect their lives. Time is a trap," he stated. "And we will not be trapped. We will not tell them." He scowled, perfectly self-convinced.

Sceptre shook his head, following the argument to its other logical conclusion. "It also makes you the perfect rulers. I assume you have altered the past and changed things like the enemy invasion, tweaked events to your advantage, become more god-like to them."

Cirrius shifted in his chair, turning away to stare out the port to the skies beyond. For a while he said nothing.

Then: "That is my right," he almost whispered.

Decion scoffed. "And everyone thought *I* was the god-seeker!" He got a wry smile from Sceptre.

"Why didn't you go back in time to repel the invaders, find out who they were?" Urana asked.

"Power, of course!" Azure spoke up, a thrill of giddiness spiking through her. She quelled her impulsiveness.

Now Cirrius scoffed. "Power," he repeated in a bored tone. "No, not for power. . ."

"Ah, not exactly!" Sceptre guessed, "You needed the invasion to go ahead so you could gain power that way!"

"Sacrifices," Timechantress said. "Those lives were sacrificed for the greater reality. We told you, time travel is wrought with fragilities. The invasion happened, we cannot change that. We can delay, bend time, wrap and warp, but not break timestreams. Not again." Everyone knew what she meant. "We keep Magna Aura safe. And yes, Cirrus took power to maintain that safety. Who are you to question that?"

"You should have told everyone the truth," Azure said quietly.

"We are the rulers here," Antichilles blurted, angry that his parents' authority was being questioned. "You should be grateful we didn't tell everyone you were dead. My father allowed you to return. He is the King! And you should be thanking the Universe for your lives!"

Decion almost reached for his lancesword, but Cirrius stopped him again with an upraised hand. "No, Decion, my son speaks out of turn," he admonished Antichilles with a dismissive look, before his son could utter another word. "But, I have been doing everything I can to protect Magna Aura. . ."

". . . Including lying to them and time-managing their history?" Sceptre asked.

Cirrius scowled at the question.

"But how did you explain the Astral's presence?" Azure asked. "Surely the people knew they weren't Starguards."

Timechantress shook her head. "That was the easy part," she replied. "We told the truth of sorts, that we were discovered by Cirrius as being long lost progeny of another branch of Celestian Knights from the Hero Siege." She smiled triumphantly.

"The Hero Siege? And they believed you?" Azure asked. "Suppose they return? Then what?"

"Ha, no, they are lost forever," Cirrius replied dismissively. "And as for your absence, we told the Magna Aurans you had abandoned us all to protect other worlds from the Lore," Cirrius explained. "We knew you would return, though not when. But I *am* glad you are back, for now we need to support each other against the enemy encamped at our solar boundary. The Magna Aurans have not turned against you; they are just. . . confused."

"They looked scared to me," Azure said, trying to take Cirrius' apology to heart, but failing.

"Have you tried talking to the enemy?" Decion asked, trying to get a flavour of the enemies' nature.

"Of course we have," a tetchy Cirrius replied. He stared defiantly at Decion, calming himself. "Five years ago, we approached their fleet for peace talks but they fired upon us with highly-advanced flare-rays. Our sword barely made it back from the damage it took. They do not want to talk."

"Novan would have made them talk," Azure interjected.

"Novan is still not here!" Cirrius shouted.

Novan, Novan, Novan, why? Why? Why? his mind railed against the notion of Novan.

Azure shook her head. "You already said that, but I already told you he was alive. And where. And I can bring him back!"

There was silence as everyone soberly absorbed what she had just said. They all looked at Cirrius, the very thought paralysing him.

Azure walked toward his desk. Cirrius stood up, everyone tensing again. Azure looked him straight in the eye.

"I will bring him here, whether you want him here or not, because I know where he is."

"How. . .?" Cirrius whispered, before finding his voice. "How will you do that without your powers?"

Azure grinned so wide, Cirrius leaned back. "Oh, Cirrius, I have my powers and more, so much more!" She walked back, standing among the other Starguards.

Cirrius and the others looked at each other. Surely a Loremaiden couldn't have active powers without Lore present. There was dumbfounded silence.

"I forbid it," Cirrius hotly sneered. "I forbid Novan's return. And I doubt you could do as you say, as you cannot have your powers!" he gloated.

Azure laughed again, more through gritted teeth as she relished what she was about to reveal.

"The Lore, Cirrius, there were millions upon millions of them. They are energy. You can't destroy energy only transform it. I transformed a lot of Lore—*a lot of Lore*!" she emphasised. "Their energy is still floating around Magna Aura, even after forty years. And I can feel it. It is *so* strong. It is why I fainted; I was absorbing it like a drug, before I knew how to handle it. But now I do. I can tap into it," she made her hand glow blue, ". . . and use it." She created a little light sculpture of Sky Command then let it vanish.

"So I have permanent powers now!" She grinned as she watched as Cirrius and the Astrals drew backwards. "And the best thing about this energy, Cirrius, is that it gives me the *power* of the Lore, not just the energy emissions. . ." she grinned even wider as they looked at her knowing what was to come, ". . . but the temporal energy as well."

Timechantress tried to react. "Stop her!" her voice was a trembled shout. But she was too slow.

"Bye, bye," Azure waved her arms in the air, as she, Sceptre, Urana, Decion and Astara disappeared in a flash of blue light.

INTERLUDE

The Further Extra-dimensional Adventures
of
Alpha Rion and Chalant

PRISONER GOD

After leaving the domain of the strange alien called Amagesh, Chalant and Alpha Rion travelled in the surgeship for days, with nothing more to see other than expansive blackness dotted with a myriad of dazzling lights. The night time view was spectacular without a cloud in the sky and the surrounding stars stood out in bright unfamiliar clusters.

Their crystalators indicated they were still travelling over the ocean, but even through new portholes produced by Chalant, they couldn't see it miles below.

They had made their ship more comfortable by creating more seats which conformed to their bodies, almost cradling them, which on command could tilt upright or down for sleep. A compartment had been made at the rear for a privy, the seal tight around the hollow protuberance for waste so they could literally evacuate the waste down below once finished then reseal the protuberance's exit. A simple vent contraption recycled their air.

The surgeship had enough absorbed solar energy to channel along its outer skin, and expend it as exhaust. At the velocity they were travelling they hoped they wouldn't starve to death before finding land with something edible. And they were getting very hungry.

Chalant, who hadn't slept in all this time, wondered which direction held this mysterious Land of the Mind, Amagesh had alluded to.

Alpha Rion, who had peppered her with umpteen "Do you know where you're going?" answered by frequent 'nos', was sleeping. Ship travel wasn't for him. Chalant smiled, thinking about what it would be like to have a normal life with Alpha Rion once they arrived at a place they could call home.

>*Over here!*<

Alpha Rion sat bolt upright, eyes wide, startled, looking around, his hand ready to draw a sword.

"What!" Chalant jumped. She swivelled in her pilot's seat so she faced Alpha Rion beside her, who was more alert.

"Did you hear that?" he asked. "A voice, in my head?"

"No. It was probably the ship trying to talk to you. Why?"

"The ship? No. . . I don't think so!" he said, his tone wary.

>*This way!*< the voice whispered again.

Alpha Rion jerked around turning this way and that. "It just happened again!" he exclaimed looking suspiciously around the ship's cabin. "That's not the ship. Why would I hear it? I'm not telepathic! Are you sure you can't hear anything, a voice. . . a male voice, telling me something, like directions?"

Chalant stood up, on alert. "No, nothing. I would hear it if it was telepathic."

Worried, now, Chalant glanced to her left. The part of the ship's wall she was looking at turned transparent, a window to the universe. The bright white star loomed in the east, the wispy horizon of a landmass approaching.

"I think the voice wants us to go in that direction," Alpha Rion pointed slightly to the north east.

"Why?"

"I don't know!" an exasperated Alpha Rion almost shouted. "He doesn't say."

"So you think we should go there on the word of some stranger? Could be a trap." Chalant almost grinned at the thought of some excitement after days of being cooped up.

"Or it could be your people of the mind calling out and they got their signals crossed," Alpha Rion mused. "We should go."

"Fine, but let's be ready for trouble also. This dimension seems to have more surprises than Earth," Chalant sighed. She also had a nagging feeling that this place was familiar, but she couldn't put her finger on it. "Okay, let's go see what there is to see and move on."

Even before she had finished speaking, the surgeship had turned toward the distant landmass. She listened for the voice, but it didn't speak to her. Alpha Rion didn't hear it again, either.

Whoever or whatever it was had done their work, they thought.

>*We're on our way*< she replied to no one in particular.

For a few more hours, in a waking dawn light, the ship sped over the ocean until they crossed over onto a dark brown hard sandy beach, desolate, spreading inward for over ten miles like burned-out chocolate tuff. The land then rose steeply, inclining upwards before plateauing into flat green pastures. They crossed the fields before turning north where the flat plains gave way to dense forests of waving trees as far as the eye could see, shot through with the tops of mountain ranges a further twenty miles away.

Chalant psychically instructed the ship to take them down. Through pink clouds and gentle winds the surgeship glided through a kaleidoscopic sky. Finally in the distance, a sprawling high-walled building complex spread out around a vast pyramid, surrounded by a forest of purple and green which swayed in the breeze.

Alpha Rion couldn't believe his eyes.

"A pyrathedral? Here?" he exclaimed.

"A pyra-what? You mean that fortress thing?" Chalant asked looking in the distance toward the large pyramid surrounded by towering structures.

"A pyrathedral, like the Celestians used to make, well, the Galatians and the temple dwellers Neb. Pyrathedrals are like pyramids crossed with cathedrals and fortresses. They acted as repositories of knowledge and were well-guarded, literally and religiously. Except this one looks bigger and built from that brown block beach by the ocean."

"That's miles away," Chalant gasped, "And that is huge! That central pyramid section alone is twice as big at least than the Great pyramid at Giza." She admired the buildings impressed with the domes, spires and battlements.

Alpha Rion was already recording the buildings with his forearm crystalator which he had detached from his armour.

"The outer enclosure encompasses a twenty-kilometre

square area, the walls are twenty meters high, the central enclosure is at least five kilometres-square, and the central pyramid has sides of almost five hundred meters topping three hundred meters in height. I can see four large separate lakes, smaller tower pyramids at the corners of the outer enclosure, multiple domed temples, scores of obelisks and more general buildings and monuments." He pursed his lips and shook his head in puzzlement. "Except for the construction materials used, I would swear by the universe that this is a Celestian city, but I cannot see how Celestians were here!"

Chalant did not answer. Her mind was wandering, searching for answers. She somehow recognised this land. She made the front section of the ship transparent so they could see the area better as they slowly glided down.

"That's some forest down there. Strange colour," Alpha Rion observed. "Purple plants! I wonder if we can eat them!" And then he saw something move. "Universe! It's not a forest!"

They both now saw that as they closed in.

"Ra! No!" Chalant cursed. "Not here! It cannot be!"

"What? Where are we?" an alarmed Alpha Rion asked, puzzled by Chalant's uncharacteristic outburst. Then he looked more closely out the ship. "They're not plants! They're people!"

"They are. Let's land."

"Land? By them?"

"Yes, now. I'm taking us down!"

Alpha Rion let Chalant lead, trusting her instincts.

The surgeship touched down, a gentle swirl of dust greeting their landing. Chalant stood up, took a deep breath, then made the door appear. It swung downwards to the ground providing a ramp.

Alpha Rion stepped out before her, in protective mode. He stopped short.

"Universe!"

Before him were people the likes of which he'd never seen before; humanoid but animal-like, broken leonines, tall but hunched, powerful long-limbs bent under large purple-blotched bodies. Mane-topped heads held dull yellow eyes and misshapen feaures. The semi-naked in their thousands waited silently as the wind rustled their patchy purple hair. A strong musty smell wafted over the travellers. Alpha Rion turned to tell Chalant to go back in, expecting an attack, but she strode out.

And as one, the gathered throng knelt before her. It was so quiet the two could hear the whisper of the trees and the warbling and buzzing of alien birds and insects. This world was teeming with life.

"What the hell?" Alpha Rion whispered from the side of his mouth. "Tera, who are these people?"

Chalant smiled, a smile which radiated so far beyond physical bounds that even Alpha Rion was caught up in the emotion of well-being which washed through him.

"They are the Gravan," Chalant said. "And I am their Goddess—The Chalant."

Alpha Rion stared in disbelief. "How did a human-alien hybrid become a goddess to these alien people?" he whispered.

Chalant smiled and approached the gathered crowd. Looking at Alpha Rion, she psyed to him:

>*It goes something like this.*<

She flooded Alpha Rion's mind with images from her past.

Earth, AD 1197

>*I was left alone after Lightstream took you to the Starguards in the future. I was set to leave Valtare's ruined castle and resume the search for my brothers, but then I sensed riders coming for me. They were Exmoors, or to be exact, Hunters— their warriors. And they needed my help. They had received a message from another dimension; an unexpected one—a psychic message. The Exmoors sought me out as the only hybrid close enough and one they could trust to travel to this world and communicate with the indigenous species*<

Alpha Rion was confused, "But how can we be here? Is this the People of the Mind Amagesh mentioned?"

Chalant shrugged. "I do not know!" She switched back to

psying, more images flashing through Alpha Rion's mind.

>The Hunter team introduced themselves as Tristrian, Linius, Jenethen, and Elivor. We rode south for days to the French coast, took a waiting boat across the Mediterranean and after a stormy passage made landfall on the Syrian coast. We then rode hard dodging Crusade and Islamic forces for more days to a secluded highland valley by a large lake. The Exmoors had an encampment of huts and tents there where they could hide from local populations and protect themselves from attack. There were about thirty of them all together, the most Exmoors I had ever seen in one place.

>Near the camp was an ancient ruined stone temple complex of stone circles, large T-shaped pillars, and round daises all with strange symbols on them. Some of the stones had crystalators embedded in them for whatever reason. In the centre of the temple was a large granite altar. Tristrian and Elivor shifted it sideways to reveal a deep tunnel underneath. Tristrian told me to follow them and I found myself descending down a long metal corridor for at least a mile, which led to a round stone-lined chamber with an eerie light shining from within. Imagine my surprise when I saw the light was coming from a portal< Chalant's eyebrows shot up to convey her surprise to Alpha Rion, who stood impassively still watching the Gravan. The aliens were all still in bowing mode.

>This portal was a shimmering, larger-than-man size, white disc spinning vertically on its edge. Having seen a similar portal when Gordell disappeared, I asked the Exmoors how this could be, but they declined to tell me. I got the feeling they were afraid of something. They wanted me to go through the portal with a small guard detail, the four who had brought me there. Even after travelling for weeks non-stop the Exmoors had hardly eaten nor slept and they hadn't offered me the chance to rest. They wanted to get on with it. They then revealed to me the reason for their anxiety.

Chalant turned her head as if reliving the memory. >In an adjoining storeroom, made into a make-shift prison and *guarded by more Exmoors, was an alien being—looking very much like an ugly purple humanoid lion. It had come through the portal triggering a crystalator alarm, alerting the Exmoors to its presence. It tried relaying a telepathic message to them. But as the Exmoors loathe telepathy due to the Chryrians, they had no idea what to do so they had tracked me down as a trusted half-Chryrian ally. I was asked to speak with it. Of course the being did not speak our language and it wasn't exactly telepathic, but we did communicate through the mind. I got general fast-paced jumbled pictures, ideas, and feelings from his thoughts. The being intimated that he was a Gravan from the Domain of the Burning Pyramid and that their lands had been invaded by a sorcerer-God. The Gravan had been searching for his Chalant to protect them!<* She gave Alpha Rion an expectant look.

"Chalant?" Alpha Rion asked. "But you're Chalant. I don't get it! There was another Chalant before you?"

Tera shrugged and smiled. Carrying on, she psyed *>So, with that background established and agreed to by the Exmoors, the Gravan being, the four Exmoors, and I readied ourselves for the voyage back to the Gravan lands. I know nothing of the transfer mechanism behind portals, but unlike yours, I felt as if I was suffocating upon entering. Then there was nothing—just blackness, and then I was gasping for air on the other side before realising I was breathing normally.*

>I was inside a small stone pyramid as the four walls tapered to a point above. The portal was still spinning behind us just like its twin entrance on Earth until suddenly it popped and disappeared with an acrid smell. In its place stood a black obelisk at the centre of the chamber. Save for the obelisk the inside of the pyramid was totally empty, no writing on the walls, just an empty shell of a building, perhaps ten meters square. The Gravan pushed open a two-meter high stone which turned out to be a hidden doorway. He led us through a myriad of corridors which led outside, rolling aside another great entrance boulder. I was almost blinded by the bright light which

entered, some of which was coming from the pyramid itself, gleaming off the shiny black stone. I could see now why the Gravan called their land the Domain of the Burning Pyramid<

"But it wasn't this complex?" Alpha Rion interrupted.

"No, I would have remembered a whole city like this. *She went back to her psy story >And then we saw the rest of them; thousands of Gravan before and below us on a long stone ramp. We stood in bewilderment overlooking the crowd, half scared, not knowing what to make of it. And all of a sudden, as one, they bowed down; turns out the Gravan who led us here was their leader.*

Alpha Rion let off a low whistle.

>The Gravan leader communicated to me that as a people they would be honour-bound to me if I helped them in their time of need. I asked them what they needed. He then told me about the being they called the sorcerer-God who had come to their world and had seized the Gravan's sacred Manecrown, endowed with mystical powers. This alien told them to worship him as a God. The Gravan refused, denouncing him as a false God. They tried to fight him, but the sorcerer-God was too strong. That's when the leader took drastic action, entering the forbidden Burning Pyramid expecting to find their saviour—the Chalant—but inadvertently travelling through the portal where the Exmoors discovered him. Luckily it had been them and not the local shepherds. Anyway, there I was, expected to battle a sorcerer-God! After the initial battle with the Gravan, the invader had disappeared, ostensibly searching other lands for more plunder and worshippers.

>The whole thing was surreal with us hunting another alien in an alien forest on behalf of other aliens. We just had to persevere and keep our sanity intact. The Exmoors seemed more relaxed than I was. About half an hour in we found him, remarkably constructing a hut for himself on an island in a lake< she laughed >just standing there with the Manecrown upon his head, a band of silver metal with crystals in it. It looked like he was in some sort of trance. I sensed that the Manecrown

was not only augmenting the invader's own natural psychic abilities, but also taking over his mind. There was a purple aura about his head<

Alpha Rion could not get a sense of the would-be sorcerer-God's face. It was blurred. Tera looked at Alpha Rion with sad eyes. The curious expression caught Alpha Rion unaware and he wondered why this affected her so.

Tera continued >He suddenly became aware of me and without provocation attacked us, like a mad man possessed. The Exmoors were of no use without psionic protection so they retreated. The sorcerer-God and I entered into a psychic battle< Chalant smiled *>But with two brothers growing up and practising, training, and fighting against them in play and for real, this sorcerer-God was no match for me. And after a fierce, but short battle, I defeated him. I ripped the Manecrown from his head and threw it away into the lake<*

"Wow," Alpha Rion was impressed. "What happened to him?"

Chalant gave him a weak smile. *>I didn't kill him. He was weakened after the ordeal and I managed to dig into his mind and temporarily void his psychic abilities. The Gravan didn't want him dead either; it was not their way, so they declared to hold him prisoner, shackled in a cave for eternity on the Fire Island of Vrame. The Exmoors used their crystalators to fashion a secure telepathic limiter to completely render him psychically-neutered. And, hopefully, he is still there, imprisoned<* She looked even sadder at this prospect.

>So, naturally the Gravan praised me even more, declaring me as their new Chalant, their champion saviour. I had naturally played along, so as not to offend them. I stayed a while in their village, got to know the people and their leader, Graagan. Before leaving, I had promised to return, never believing I would ever find this dimension again. Now here I am, quite unexpectedly, back on their world<

Chalant brought herself back from her revelries.

Alpha Rion shook his head in awe. He was still taking it all in as Chalant reached the first of the kneeling Gravan.

>*Arise*< she psyed. And as one, the Gravan arose.

There were a multitude of growls and other sounds Alpha Rion could not make out and which neither his armour's comms nor his crystalators could translate, but he knew they were talking to Chalant. For her part, she was answering back in words for Alpha Rion's benefit and also psying to the Gravan.

"What are they saying?" he asked, as the Gravan threatened to engulf Chalant under their warm greetings, surrounding their Champion.

"They had been waiting for my return. The Gravan are in the midst of planning the impending marriage of the High Third Forest Chief of the Sunward Water. It is an auspicious time for them. But to some Gravan, notably the Heretic Cult of the Prisoner God, my return should be marked by clemency, and the Sorcerer-God released. Others want me to take him back to my world, even though he is not native to Earth, as he is evil and he brings evil spirits with him. But, of course, to do that could lead to unrest here. I couldn't have come at a more critical moment in Gravan history."

"Is that a coincidence?" queried Alpha Rion aloud. "First the sword from the Fortress leads us to this dimension, then we meet Amagesh who tells us of People of the Mind living across the ocean, and now we meet the Gravan who you had encountered before. It's like we're both linked to this place. But how?"

Chalant was about to sound a dubious note, but the Gravan tugged at her manoeuvre suit wanting them to follow him.

She looked at Alpha Rion. "Well, what do you think?"

Alpha Rion leaned in close to her, conspiratorially. "This is important—do they have food?"

They looked at each other then laughed so hard several Gravan were startled. But sensing no harm they started roaring back in imitation.

Chalant gestured to the Gravan who was still waiting anxiously. >*Lead the way*< she psyed to them.

The Gravan dutifully led them away through the green forest. They had a fast lumbering gait. Some were hunched over, but others walked more upright swinging their arms from side to side. It was a silent procession, save for the shuffling of worn bare feet. Alpha Rion noted how hard and dusty they looked with claw-like toes spread out.

The looming trees were taller than anything Alpha Rion had seen before, even more so than the redwoods he had seen on Earth. They were thick, some with multiple trunks, drooping leaves as big as a man, and dense canopies. It was a hot day, but not as hot as where Amagesh had lived, but the best thing was the fresh air and breeze. Along with the myriad of encountered airborne life, he also saw hints of small mammal activity. Well-worn trails led this way and that, but the Gravan kept to a main pathway, toward the pyrathedral they had seen when landing, until they reached a small village with hut-like dwellings of wood, leaf bundles, and large stone blocks for foundations.

When they arrived, an awed Alpha Rion just stared at the stone pyrathedral looming above the village over the tops of the trees. It was too much of a coincidence that it was here. And the Gravan certainly did not build it as evidenced by their crude huts and tools they had fashioned. He wondered if the other Starguards had somehow ended up here after the explosion at Thane's. The buildings' presence would have made sense.

"Graagan? Graagan, is that you?" Chalant rushed forth and greeted one of the Gravan, psying and speaking at the same time.

Alpha Rion couldn't tell the aliens apart, what with their similarity in craggy purple faces, unkempt manes, and tattered green or brown fibrous clothing, which didn't necessarily cover their private regions.

The Gravan leader growled back at Chalant, and she hugged him, her hands barely fitting around his shoulders as they disappeared into his long scraggly mane.

There followed a few minutes of Goddess to Gravan psi banter, Chalant translating for Alpha Rion. "Well, the High Third Forest

Chief of the Sunward Water is Graagan's son!"

"Of course he is," muttered Alpha Rion. Chalant gave him a humoured disapproving look.

She listened to the next bit of news, brows furrowed.

"Well, this is a bit disconcerting," she said to Apha Rion, "according to Graagan, only two centuries of their time have passed since my encounter with them. But to me, it was over nine hundred Earth time."

"So either the years are longer here or time works differently," Alpha Rion thought about that. "If we find a way out of this dimension to Earth or Magna Aura, who knows in what time period we would find ourselves."

"Would the portal from the fortress have deposited us in another time?" Chalant asked.

Alpha Rion mulled it over. "Unlikely, the fortress runs in its own strict linear time. I couldn't travel to the fortress' past or future. Definitely time here is different."

"I see." Chalant chewed her lip.

But she was so happy to see Graagan was still alive. The greetings over, Graagan growled a few utterances to others and suddenly food appeared from out of surrounding huts. The basket bearers knelt before Chalant with their offerings, which were mostly fruits, vegetables, nuts, and tubers. They were ushered to a low long stone table between huts.

Sitting on a rough-woven bark mat on the ground, Alpha Rion removed his visor. He realised he had been wearing it for days; it was just second nature to him. He felt freed up from being on guard all the time. Chalant looked into his eyes, glad he felt relaxed enough. Alpha Rion smiled back. He sniffed at the food then picked up a piece tucking into the sweet orange-coloured fruit which tasted liked watermelon. Another fruit he swore was a Celestian wolobean, though this was twice the size of the normal one. Chalant took mostly vegetables, all washed down with cool water and a spiced juice Alpha Rion still attested tasted like wolobean.

A satisfied Alpha Rion gave a surreptitious burp, to which all the surrounding Gravan growled in laughter and burped loudly in enjoyment.

Alpha Rion laughed. "I did enjoy that!" He looked around appreciatively, thanking his hosts for the food. There were returned growls of affection.

Chalant just shook her head. "They like you!" She finished off her long green stalks of some vegetable.

They had been fed and watered, but she knew her next order of official Goddess business was going to be painful. She eyed Alpha Rion cautiously.

It was her duty to visit the prisoner. She looked a little nervous about this prospect and gave Alpha Rion an apologetic smile. She held his hand as they rose and followed Graagan. Alpha Rion could only assume she did not want to face the sorcerer again, or alone.

"You'll be fine," he assured her.

They walked for another half an hour on a mostly flat path, Alpha Rion seeing more small settlements along the forested way. Part of him longed for the simple life the Gravan had. A large circular lake loomed before them, sitting in a wide plain surrounded by steep valleys, the blue lake's surface shining under the luminous sun. A small boat, built from a fibrous bark rested along a crooked wooden dock ready to take them to the rocky island in the distant centre.

Chalant sat at the front, Alpha Rion in the middle, as Graagan paddled the boat with an oar from the back.

Chalant pointed to another distant smaller island out to their left. "That's the island we fought on——the Island of Chalant Where The Manecrown Was Lost!" She smiled at Alpha Rion's dubious look. "Yes, the Gravan can be quite literal. The Manecrown was never recovered. The lake is quite deep."

They stared at the tree-lined island for a while, then turned their attention to the larger approaching island, which Graagan had steered starboard toward.

As they reached their destination, Alpha Rion could see that the island was in fact an ancient volcanic-cone structure, its cracked upper crater walls sticking out of the lake. Embedded within the island's uplifted walls was a squat building running along the centre of the island ridge system.

"Welcome to the Citadel of the Eternal Ruins on the Fire Island of Vrame," Chalant named the fortress carved into the mountain walls. Alpha Rion smiled at the name.

They alighted from the boat once it had docked, crunching red ash beneath their feet. Then immediately the path made them climb the large stone steps fifty meters upward in a zig-zagging direction toward the mountain fortress. Twice Alpha Rion stopped to turn and admire the scenic view of the lake and forest, his eye inevitably drawn to the pyrathedral miles away. Once they arrived at the summit, the dozen guards at the large heavy stone gates parted to let them through.

Graagan then led them down through more stone-carved corridors, reminding Alpha Rion of his own fortress, save these walls and floors were bare except for lit sconces every few meters. At the end of one corridor was an ill-fitted door. Graagan pulled it open. Behind it the three descended the steps into depths of the fortress' bowels.

Chalant had been quiet all this time, Alpha Rion thinking she was preoccupied with the forthcoming meeting.

At the bottom of the steps was a long winding wide tunnel, naturally warm and dry from the mountain. It terminated at a large circular boulder; this rolled out of the way by half a dozen more grunting guards. Alpha Rion noted the guards all wore iron swords, short and serrated. He kept his swords ready to unsheathe. Whoever this prisoner was, he would not harm Chalant.

The displaced boulder revealed the inside of another large round chamber, lit by sconces circling the room. Within niches stood four more guards, one with a whip, one with a sword, another with a spear and the last armed with an axe. In the centre of the chamber on a slab of rock lay the Prisoner-God.

The figure, a young-looking man, with tanned skin and very light, almost white-coloured long hair seemed to be sleeping.

He wore only a white wrapping around his waist, naked from the waist up and bare-footed. Alpha Rion could see that he was manacled, his arms and legs bound to the low stone dais, a series of crystalators encapsulating his head. Another set of crystalators on the dais formed a low forcefield around the figure. The energy field glowed faintly as only a stasis field could—the Prisoner God was in suspended animation. It was the only piece of high technology Alpha Rion had seen on the planet.

But such thoughts were suddenly crushed in Alpha Rion's mind as he peered closely at the figure in the light. He took a few steps forward.

"Alpha Rion," Chalant whispered, "What are you doing? Stay back." She reached out for him, but he batted her hand away.

He had to see. The person in the field couldn't possibly be who he thought it was. He looked through the stasis field. And instinctively recoiled in shock. The person was someone he had thought lost to the universe, his own kin and blood.

"Solandus," he whispered.

Alpha Rion couldn't breathe. He closed his eyes against the pain which had surged sharply behind them. His eyes had to be wrong. He could scarcely believe Solandus, his presumed long-lost younger brother, would have dared to deem himself a God. How had he arrived here? Why had he acted in so offensive a manner for a Starguard? Alpha Rion's mind raced for answers. How could his brother be imprisoned for eternity by the Gravan?

Horrified, Alpha Rion said nothing, but Chalant sensed his agony. She snatched glimpses of his thoughts weeping from his mind; the days when he, his twin-sister Astara, and Solandus played together as children; Solandus, like their oldest brother Novan, so different—darker skinned and fair-haired—like their mother, the Goddess Elysius; Solandus' departure from their new home on Halcyon to explore the new universe.

Anger flared through Alpha Rion. He reeled on Chalant. "You knew it was him all along?" Alpha Rion accused her. His lips were tight lines pressed against his teeth.

Chalant nodded, reluctantly. A quiet voice answered, "Only after we met again in Earth's future. But what could I say?" She looked back to Solandus. "I never expected to return here, much less with you. . . " she shook her head, no words to say.

Alpha Rion could hardly believe this. His own brother, a false god imprisoned by the woman he loved. Alpha Rion stared back at his brother. There was nothing he could do for him.

Chalant decided otherwise.

>*Graagan, may I visit the sorcerer psychically, to see if he has repented his ways?*<

Graagan bowed to her wishes, grunting his approval to the guards who retreated discreetly a few steps back.

"I'll help you speak with him," Chalant said.

A brother to brother prison visit after all these years. Chalant hoped it would ease Alpha Rion's mind and give Solandus incentive to change.

Chalant entered Solandus' mind. It was easy as he was unconscious. She spent a few minutes concentrating. Her eyes opened.

Strange!

She closed them again. Searching for a connection. Seconds passed to Alpha Rion, minutes in the mindscape for Chalant. She opened her eyes slowly, a weird smile on her face. She looked intently at Alpha Rion and then she said something that made his heart grow cold.

"Keep smiling, I have bad news. He's gone!"

Alpha Rion heard her say, his mind hearing:

>*Everything's fine*< she psyed to Graagan.

Alpha Rion almost gasped, but couldn't give himself away. He looked back with a tight-lipped smile, his expression asking "Where?"

"I don't know," Chalant shot back in frustration. "His body's there, but the psyche is gone. Never seen that before," she replied, astonished. "Did he have that ability?"

"Not that I knew," Alpha Rion responded numbly.

>*The crystalators are keeping him alive and well within the energy fields*< she assured Graagan.

To Alpha Rion: "He's escaped. The psychic shielding must have failed, but he couldn't physically escape. But he's not here or I would have sensed him or he would have sensed me. He's gone and we need to find him!"

Alpha Rion was silent for a moment. This was serious, more serious than he thought.

Then he murmured, "Voices, eh?"

Chalant eyes widened in understanding. The one who had sent the directions to Alpha Rion in the surgeship. He had wanted them to see that he had escaped.

But why? Chalant thought. *To take him away? Then where was he?*

All they could do was share a look of helplessness. But what to tell the Gravan? Chalant needed time to think. She indicated to Graagan that they were ready to leave the island prison. Graagan was happy to proceed. They reversed their journey out the labyrinthine volcanic fortress, down to the lake, and across to the main shore. Thereupon, Graagan returned them back to what Alpha Rion learned was the Gravan capital, the village nearest the pyrathedral, where they had dined previously.

Over the next three days, Chalant fulfilled her diplomatic, religious and cultural duties. There was also a night of raucous feasting before the royal joining the next day. She and Alpha Rion had barely spoken about Solandus.

In fact, Alpha Rion was so sullen he had barely eaten and was prone to walking in the forests alone, the Gravan reporting to Chalant that he was using shining sharp magic sticks to chop down trees, which the Gravan used for fire wood and building stock. Chalant knew he needed time to process, so she let him brood it out.

On the fourth day, Chalant was escorted back to the Palace of the Goddess' Glory, a large wood and stone building of Gravan construct, possibly the grandest building they had ever built, Alpha Rion surmised.

"Don't they have short normal names for buildings?" Alpha Rion grumbled.

Chalant smiled, glad Alpha Rion still had his sense of humour.

Throughout that whole night, Chalant couldn't help thinking that Solandus would attack and that her people were in grave danger.

She decided to broach the subject with Alpha Rion, but he tried to reassure her. Chalant was glad to see there was no reproach in his eyes or voice. She didn't dare check his mind for any.

"I don't think he would attack with me here," Alpha Rion had said. "Besides, I don't think Solandus is even on this world anymore; otherwise he would have exacted revenge on the Gravan. He's somewhere else, but we will find him, he wants us to, after all. Solandus directed us here for some purpose and he will do so again." Alpha Rion was sure of it. "I think that means Solandus has changed," Alpha Rion tried to convince himself of that more than Chalant.

Chalant wasn't easily sold. She went to sleep that night, thinking of days past and a simple life in her own village with her brothers.

The next day, with the sun high in the sky, the royal joining between the High Third Forest Chief of the Sunward Water and the Sacred Daughter of the Well of Stars went as planned. It was held on a high stone and wood platform, which Alpha Rion assumed replicated the pyrathedral. The Gravan may have been superstitious about the city, but their customs and traditions seemed to revolve around it.

The High Third Forest Chief of the Sunward Water wore a bulky decorative tunic of tough grey leather, from one beast or another with green leafy vines tied around his forearms, waist and shins. An intricately carved tall wooden headdress sat on his braided purple mane. The Gravan bride wore a rough garment of green leaves woven into the form of a long dress. Her less-tufted mane held a crown of yellow flowers which trailed down her back. Only they and the Gravan priest-official were on the platform, the rest of the villagers looking up the ten feet or so to the ceremony.

Alpha Rion had tried to make sense of all the growling and it hardly made sense even with Chalant translating; one covenant being the couple had to spit upon each other for pre-breeding luck. After an hour of indeterminable rituals, there were sudden loud roars, growls and toothy Gravan smiles. Alpha Rion blessed the Universe it was over.

Chalant had been invited to the top of the platform to bless the couple, her appearance deemed the most auspicious event possible under the circumstances. And then Graagan and the rest of the villagers followed with gifts of food, wood and stone carvings, and other offered objects, rudimentary currency thought Alpha Rion.

With a reception-like event in full swing, Alpha Rion and Chalant decided to avoid more crowds and to return the surgeship. They needed to talk, but one question bothered Alpha Rion. He asked Chalant to query Graagan.

>*Graagan, how long has the city been here?*< she indicated the pyrathedral.

Graagan's muscled shoulders shrugged. He growled a reply.

"It has always been here, he says," she replied to Alpha Rion.

Graagan growled something else, Chalant frowning at his answer. She seemed to hesitate before answering.

"He said the others built it. The others who came long before the Gravan; the Chalant, the Goddess' champions. They were the ones who built it for the glory of their Goddess. It was the Chalant who fought the Gravan, who the Goddess created as a punishment after the Chalant rebelled against her. Then the Chalant left. And then the Goddess disappeared leaving the Gravan alone." She looked at Alpha Rion making sure he was keeping up. He looked a little confused. "Until I arrived and was made the new Chalant! Understand?"

Alpha Rion nodded his head. "Think so."

A sudden thought struck Chalant. She turned to Graagan,

authority in her voice: >*I want to look around inside the Goddess' city and make sure all is in order*<

An anguished slump of the body and a definite throaty noise of less-than-approval marked out Graagan's position on the subject.

>W*hy not?*< asked Chalant. There was more growling and gesticulating from the Gravan leader. >*Spirits? Dark voices and howling shadows?*< She looked at Alpha Rion.

"Looks like my brother is playing haunted pyrathedral. Let's go!"

Chalant turned back to Graagan. >*Your Chalant will visit the city and rid the spirits for you!*<

Graagan bowed in such a way that even Alpha Rion sensed the explicit: 'Of course, Chalant.'

As they walked along a straight dirt road back through the village past the revel-makers drinking a frothy mixture from clay mugs, Alpha Rion asked, "Should we bring the surgeship?"

Chalant shook her head. "No, I'm sure we'll be fine. I can always summon it if I have to. The interior of the portal pyramid centuries ago was empty except for the portal, so I'm hoping this pyrathedral is the same. What else can be in there?"

Even from a distance, the pyrathedral dominated the landscape. It was built of the same dark red brick of the Gravan world. Around it stood an immense twenty-meter tall wall of red stone, topped by crenulations. There was no visible entrance to the interior.

Chalant and Alpha Rion left a reticent Graagan behind and walked around the exterior for more than an hour, seeing nothing.

Coming back to their original starting point, Graagan was still waiting patiently. He looked at Chalant and touched his forehead, indicating to Chalant what she had to do.

"Ah, I see," she nodded, a little embarrassed she had not thought of it before. Turning to Alpha Rion, she explained, "The Gravan are forbidden to enter the grounds of the pyrathedral or indeed into any of the buildings belonging to the

Goddess. Graagan had to scale the walls before, but he thinks the entry can be found by using psychic energy. . ."

"Oh, now he tells us!" Alpha Rion rolled his eyes at the alien.

"Here goes. . ." Chalant spoke, trying not to laugh.

She concentrated and entered the psi-scape. She could see the pyrathedral in its psychic plane and all the entrances, buildings, corridors and rooms. One room, at the centre of the pyrathedral was somehow shrouded from her view. That had to be their destination.

Outside and just off to their right were two eight-foot doors, highly visible in the psi-scape but seamless in the real world. She pushed with her thoughts, commanding the hitherto unseen stone gates to unlock. The stone blocks parted, clearing dirt and built up weeds away from the ground as they scraped along. Graagan quickly hid his eyes so as not to look upon the interior. He turned away and trotted off as if scared of the consequences.

Alone, Chalant and Alpha Rion entered the grounds. They turned and watched as the great doors closed behind them in grinding finality.

"Well that's not ominous," quipped Alpha Rion.

"Let's just move on," Chalant said.

Now wasn't the time to show nerves.

As Alpha Rion had scanned from the surgeship days ago, the complex was huge. The walls were at least ten-foot thick. A central walkway was flanked by eight large obelisks, unadorned. In fact, they found no carvings, writings or graffiti on any of the buildings or monuments. On either side of the walkway were two long artificial lakes. Alpha Rion tested the water with his crystalator. It was still fresh, though there were no fish or visible life in them. The walkway led to a ramp which fanned out leading to the central enclosure. Across the complex's grounds, they could see more smaller walled compounds with smaller buildings, perhaps residential. There were no ruins. The city was as pristine as if it had just been built.

"So quiet," Chalant said.

"Hmm," Alpha Rion agreed. "We'd better get to the

pyrathedral."

The ramp was intersected athwart by a one-kilometre long ziggurat feature. On it were more obelisks and stone gates and archways. These led into the central enclosure. Passing through an arch in another three-meter wide wall, they came across a squat domed temple, forty meters in the round and tall, the glass dome reflecting the sunlight. They looked in the building finding it ringed with benches, tables, shelving, balconies, stairs and pillars. To Alpha Rion it appeared to be an empty data repository, akin to a library.

"It's beautiful!" exclaimed Chalant. "So simple, elegant, yet masterful!" her voice echoed around the dome. Looking out the glass ceiling she could see one of the huge buttresses arcing off to meet with the *piece de resistance* of the complex: the pyrathedral.

It rose high into the air, a pinnacle of red block pointing to the heavens, declaring its defiance of the ground.

In front of the pyrathedral, a large nave-type structure connected to it concealing the ramped entrance and stone platforms.

Alpha Rion marvelled. "It still reminds me of cities back on the Six Worlds! It's amazing! But I cannot see how this can be!"

The stone entrance led to a short corridor, which in turn led to a chamber around fifty meters square by around twenty meters high. It was totally empty. Stairways on the far side wound their way until hidden by an inner wall, the stairs sandwiched between walls ascending to different levels. Lighting was provided by some unseen source.

"Up we go then," suggested Chalant.

"Let's do it," Alpha Rion stepped forward.

There were no windows and no clue as to how far the steps led. What seemed like halfway up, Alpha Rion's impatience surfaced.

"Anything?" Alpha Rion asked.

If Solandus wanted to be found, where was he?

"Nope, I haven't detected any psychic activity. Let's see the view from the top for any clues."

An hour after entering the city, they were at the top of the pyrathedral. The last level was as the first; windowless, red stoned, and hot. An empty shell of a pyramid.

Alpha Rion shrugged, confused, and somewhat angry.

"Is this all? It's empty! Where's the portal?"

"I don't know." Chalant turned around to look at him in warning. "But it's not empty." Chalant was concentrating on something. "I can sense something, like..."

No sooner had she spoken when red brick rose up and sealed the exits, grinding to a close. And just as quickly, metal panels clanked down along the stone walls.

Alpha Rion stared at the panels. Some of the metal cladding bore strange markings punctuating the walls at intervals.

Alpha Rion and Chalant approached the walls, even as the chamber interior became a gleaming, silvery metallic shaped pyramid.

"Universe, protect me!" whispered Alpha Rion as he eyed the marks on the walls.

"What is it?"

"These markings, they're in the Celestian language. But the names on it are impossible. They're dead!"

Bright light suddenly flooded the chamber.

"Portal!" shouted Alpha Rion, before the light subsided and they could do anything about it.

Even as their eyes adjusted to their surroundings, the two travellers knew they were not alone any more.

"Dead, Alpha Rion? So who are we?" asked a feminine voice, the two whirling to look behind them.

Alpha Rion could only stare back in bafflement and awe, before offering, "This universe is so flucked up."

CHAPTER FOUR

The blue flash of a circular portal opened and the five Starguards crashed down five feet above a metallic floor. Gasps and muttered curses mingled with alarms already blaring upon their arrival, but they ignored them.

Decion's laugh boomed around the room. "Azure, that was cunning. Forgive me for ever doubting your Starguard heritage!" he grinned, sitting up with knees bent, arms propped behind him.

Sceptre shook his head amused at Decion's declaration.

"That was some escape trick, Azure," Sceptre complimented her. He glanced at Urana with a grin, but she seemed troubled. He knew it couldn't have been easy to see her brother that way.

"Where are we?" Urana angrily asked, ignoring Sceptre's look of sympathy. She was the first to stand and was searching out the room.

The others followed suit regaining their feet and looking around. The alarms were still trilling.

Urana turned to Azure, "We shouldn't have run." She glared at the Sky Warrior. "I could have got through; I'm his sister!" She stalked away stopping again to stare at the room. "And just where are we?" she repeated. The room was unfamiliar to her. "And why are there alarms?"

Azure's face dropped. "I'm sorry, Urana, but I had to do what I thought was right. Cirrius wasn't going to listen to anyone. So I brought us here!" She tried to smile reassuringly.

"And here is?" Decion asked, wandering the room, looking for a mechanism to make the alarms cease their racket. He searched his forearm crystalator for connecting sensors but nothing displayed.

At first they thought Azure had teleported them to another part of the Magna Aura system. While the cargo hold they were in looked familiar, there was something different about it. The hold was a fifty-meter cube, with large metal containers in the high-walled room. There was a small double door in front of them, while the rear wall had two huge sliding doors which were closed.

"Azure?" Urana irritably prompted her for an answer.

Azure shrugged. "Somewhere I wasn't sure existed outside of my head," she replied. "We are in the Ribbon System, home of Novan and the warriors who came in search of the Goddess Elysius. This is where they found her. And where she died," Azure said.

"How do you know that?" Sceptre asked, just as the smaller double doors slid open.

"Because she was here before," a male voice said from the entrance opening in front of them.

"Novan!" Azure rushed to the Starguard who stood in the doorway.

But Novan flicked up his right hand stopping her from moving forward. Azure could feel his psi-force holding her back. She looked at him in askance. The eldest of the Starguards stared at them all with a blue-eyed sternness. It reminded Decion of their father, Alphatronius, despite Novan's feathery white hair and fair coppery features—attributes of their mother. His handsome unlined face seemed troubled, his gleaming white manoeuvre suit stiff with apprehension.

"Brother, are you in good spirit?" Decion asked. Astara stood closer to Decion, feeling the atmosphere change.

"Stand down," Novan spoke into his comms unit upon his manoeuvre suit's arm, the alarms stopping instantly.

"Were those for us?" Azure asked, confused.

"What's going on?" Aerl asked.

Novan ignored their questions with one of his own. "What are you doing here, Azure?" He looked accusingly at her. She shook her head in confusion. "It has been ten years since you last arrived on Elysiun and then you disappeared; things have changed since then." His tone grew darker.

"Ten years?" Sceptre shook his head. "I don't understand."

Time travel still bewildered him.

Urana gasped, "Azure, so you have been here before. How?"

Azure sighed. She started by telling them all about her dream after fainting on Sky Command and how she had been on the Celectral at the time of the Goddess Elysius' death.

"But I only thought that a dream. Moments before the explosion on Earth, I felt the power of the Lorelet. I didn't know what it was, so in my fear, my mind reached out to the one person I thought could help me." Her voice was tight when she looked at Novan. "And I see you have now named this world after your mother," she said.

Novan nodded with a slight smile. "The Meccuns could hardly let us continue to call it Meccus, so we changed the name to honour my mother."

A baby's cry could be heard from the corridor outside, someone shushing it. Novan looked behind him, somewhat nervously.

"Are you okay, Novan?" Aerl asked.

Novan pursed his lips. He wanted to talk but could not, hanging his head in defeat.

Someone laughed in the corridor. And then a familiar female voice spoke, even as the baby cried louder.

"He can't speak, until I tell him to," Timechantress said as she walked in carrying the crying baby. "Shhhush," she commanded, the baby looking up at her quietly with wide doe-eyes brimming, before crying even louder. Timechantress rolled her eyes, rocking the baby.

Novan made toward her, but Tyran and Antichilles stepped out from behind their mother to stop him in his tracks.

"Novan?" Azure could only say. "Is. . .?" she left the question unasked as she already knew the answer. And then she realised someone was missing. "Where's Classia?"

Novan looked to the ceiling, eyes closed as if in prayer.

Timechantress smiled. "You see, Azure, you thought *you* were smart. You thought you could outsmart us Astrals who have been time travelling for much longer than you. We spent two years looking for you, Cirrius knowing you would find Novan. Once we knew where to find you, we only had to find out when you arrived and arrive before you did." She looked at Novan, "And as for Classia, your friend and Novan's valiant wife. . . unfortunately. . ." the baby started crying before she finished the sentence as if knowing her next words.

Grief stabbed at Azure's heart. "No!" she cried. "She can't be dead! Novan, is this true?" She felt sick.

Novan solemnly nodded. "Yes, she died in combat along with a company of Sky Warriors who tried to repel an attack by an unknown adversary. But we were powerless, and now I have no wife, and Astarius and our daughter, Elyssia, have no mother."

"Astarius. Elyssia," The Starguards repeated the children's name in reverence as was their custom, welcoming them into the family of Starguards.

"We mourn for your loss," Sceptre spoke for all of them.

"The same enemies who attacked us attacked Novan," Timechantress stated. "So they knew of the Ribbon System independently. The Starguards and the Astrals are being targeted. Now we know for sure!" Timechantress said.

Azure shook her head in frustration. "So why are you here threatening us and Novan's baby?" she angrily accused the Astral.

"Because you would want to undo all that Cirrius and I have achieved. He is still the King. And we Starguards and Astrals should be rightfully venerated like our ancestors were!"

"Unbelievable!" Sceptre said. "All of this just for power?"

Timechantress shrugged nonchalantly. "No, whatever it takes to defend our worlds and families!"

"You will pay for this, Timechantress," Decion swore.

Her sons stood closer protecting their mother.

But Azure stepped forward with a serene smile. "Now that I know what you want, and which side you're on, you may go," she casually said.

Timechantress threw back her head in laughter. "Go? Go where?" And then realisation took over. ". . . But. . ."

"Yep, more Lore energy," Azure smiled radiantly. "I destroyed the Lore here, too! The Ribbon System is under my protection now. Bye, bye!"

She threw up her arms and the three Astrals disappeared through her blue rotating circular portal, Astarius hanging in the air on a cloud of blue energy.

Novan caught him and hugged his son. Astarius gurgled back happily.

"Where did you send them—to human hell, I hope?" Decion said darkly.

"No, just back to Magna Aura," Azure laughed.

"That's a lot of power you have there," said Urana, warming to the notion of having bested Timechantress again.

Azure laughed again. It was nice to be lauded for her Lore powers for once.

Just then, a young girl with long wavy feathery-white hair came running in. She hugged Novan's legs, looking shyly at the Starguards. Novan shifted his arms, holding Astarius cradled in one arm and hugging his daughter with the other.

"Elyssia, these are the rest of our family, the Starguards."

She stood up straight, her dark blue eyes examining the strangers in front of her, her eyes catching Decion's and Astara's armour, which mirrored the colours on her tunic, the black and red of the Alphatronius clan. She smiled at them, until Decion uncharacteristically smiled back with a toothy grin, sending Elyssia shrinking back behind her father. Novan patted her reassuringly on the shoulder, silently haranguing Decion.

Astara stifled a laugh at her brother's expense. "Stick to scowling, brother," she offered. Decion shook his head.

Novan carried on. "Azure, I thank you," he addressed her. "The Astrals took me unawares before I could raise my psi-shields or alarms and defend my younglings. Looks like you have grown a lot, both in power and wisdom," he commended her.

Azure grinned. "Zane, the Astral, taught me a lot, indirectly, and I got the feel of time travelling from her. I always thought there was a connection between us, but I figured it was just because we were both the youngest of our groups and our powers didn't work properly. But once I realised we were both Loremaidens and after my recent dream, I realised I was as much a time traveller as she was. I remembered all the tricks the Astrals used. But I'm sorry I could do nothing for Classia," Azure mourned for her friend. "Perhaps. . ."

"No!" Novan forestalled her thoughts. "The past is the past. We cannot change time, not even for me!" Novan hung his head in sorrow, looking down upon his son. A sullen silence punctuated his words.

"So what's the plan, now?" Sceptre asked. "Will you return to Magna Aura with us, Novan? We will have to remove Cirrius from his so-called Kingship!"

Novan weighed up the question. "I will have to think on it. The Ribbon System will have to be protected. As a Magna Auran colony, the inhabitants consider themselves a sovereign territory. They will not relocate, with or without me. As a People we do need to spread ourselves and explore. Retreating now, even in the face of the enemy could see us wiped out as a species. This is my home and I wish to remain here with my family. But I may consider a temporary return to Halcyon."

Sceptre sighed. "We await your decision."

The other Starguards pledged likewise.

Azure smiled. "Well I have plan. We may have hated them, but they were trying to protect us and now we owe them. To defeat both Cirrius and these cowardly alien attackers, we're going to have to find and save the Astrals!"

Halycon

Cirrius fumed. "What do you mean Azure sent you back here?"

"She's a Loremaiden. The Ribbon System had been attacked by the Lore and apparently she and Elysius defeated them years ago. She used the temporal energy to send us back here,"

Timechantress defended herself. "Azure's quite powerful now!"

"So, we would not be able to get to Novan if we wanted to," Cirrius brooded. "And now they could return here at any time to try and overthrow us." He scowled so deeply it hurt his head.

"Yes, I would not be surprised if they did. Novan still has a formidable Sky Warrior force and three Swords left. With Azure, they would be able to circumvent our defences and attack. What can we do?"

Cirrius thought for a moment. "Why won't they just let me be?"

He and Timechantress were alone in the Sky Commander's office. She and her sons had come back humiliated by Azure, literally time-ported back into Halcyon's skies and left to free-fall before they regained their bearings and senses. She was furious, but knew there was nothing they could do against Azure.

Timechantress sucked her teeth. "Naturally, they want to keep the status quo. They want things to be like before the Lore attacked. But they cannot go back. They have to live with the new reality. Our reality," she mooted.

Over his sulk, Cirrius exhaled through his nose in a decisive manner.

"There's only one thing we can do." His eyes went hard. But he remained silent.

Timechantress shook her head in exasperation. "What then?" she almost shouted.

Cirrius looked at her. "We need allies!"

"Allies? Where are we going to. . . ? Oh, no, no, Cirrius, we cannot do that!"

His expression was adamant.

"I have been thinking about it for a while now, years even. Whomever is out there attacking us might consider an alliance. They certainly want something. They only attack in waves every few years. They could have attacked all out over the past thirty years, but they have not. What are they waiting for? What do they want? Why won't they talk to us? But, I am going to try again and take the first step. I need to set up a meeting with them." He saw the look of doubt on Timechantress' features. He clucked his tongue reaching out for her hand, which he caressed.

He continued, "Maybe attacking is their way of making friends, testing our defences and our ability to stay together as a civilisation. We explored all the other star systems around us for a quarter-galaxy span, first when we arrived here and again after the Lore invasion. There is nothing out there. No other civilisations. These aliens must have come from a very long way. They could be on the run looking for allies and supplies. They have not attacked in the last couple years, we have not been under siege, so I will seek them out and see what they want and what I can offer."

Timechantress was astounded. But at the same time, she understood her husband's logic. However, there was one other option. Timechantress had to address this carefully, she knew.

She walked around his desk and rubbed her husband's back and shoulders kneading out the knots.

"Ummm," he approved, closing his eyes.

Timechantress starting to speak slowly. "You know Netherlord and Archron died for what they believed in," she started out, knowing Cirrius did not like hearing about her late former husband. "They died because they wanted power and would not surrender their pride..."

Cirrius shrugged her hands sharply from his shoulders. "My pride?" he looked around at her with an arched eyebrow. "Do you think this is about my pride?"

Timechantress sighed. "I have lost too much to pride, Netherlord's, Archron's, my own, even our parents. . ."

"Our parents? If they had not of sacrificed themselves to save us then you would not be here. How dare you accuse our parents of this! Get out!" He pointed to the door.

Timechantress snapped her head back in disbelief. "So this really is about your pride!"

"Get out!" Cirrius repeated.

"No!" Timechantress rebuffed him. "You were the youngest Starguard, until Azure came along and you had wanted to prove yourself. Well we tried and it backfired. The Starguards are back and we are all under attack from strange enemies. Yet you won't give up your leadership. Why not?" she shouted at him. "We have everything to lose. Give it up and let us all unite against the common enemy!"

Cirrius twisted his shoulders already feeling the stiffness settling back in like a sack of *holops* upon them. His breath was heavy with anger and he looked at his wife with fury.

"Get out! Get out now! I can and will do this by myself!" He pointed angrily at the door.

"But Cirri!"

"Zasandra, leave me alone!" he rasped.

Timechantress turned and left the room. This was more serious than she thought. The rest of the Starguards had been right. Pride and power were tearing them apart and she had nowhere left to turn. Except. . .

Timechantress stopped herself down the corridor and returned to the office, entering without knocking.

Cirrius looked up from his work, still fuming. "What are you back for? I thought. . ."

But she interrupted him with a raised hand. "We have one more option, but we'll have to play it right," she said with trepidation.

Cirrius looked at her, his brows furrowed in puzzlement, until the meaning of her words became clear. He nodded and smiled, as if resigned to a grim decision.

"It will mean my death," he commented without emotion.

"But we will be stronger after," Timechantress emphasised.

Cirrius contemplated his fate. He nodded solemnly. Standing up and walking around his desk, he hugged and kissed Timechantress.

"I will go and prepare." He looked longingly at Timechantress. "Farewell, my wife. Until the skies bring us together in the Great Upswell."

"I love you, Cirrius. Farewell husband."

They looked deeply into the other's eyes. Then Timechantress left the room again. She had to prepare herself.

Cirrius sat back down at his desk. His heart thundered in his chest as if it was beating his death knell. He keyed his crystalator and started making plans. He had a long way to travel.

The Ribbon System

"Horses, that's what I miss," Decion sighed wistfully. "Reminds me of the *raquas*, though more robust!"

Seated around Novan's dining table in the officers' dining hall on *Celectral*, even Decion had commented on how good it was to be eating proper Celestian food and not the meagre Earth fare.

Their manoeuvre suits had been changed from armour mode into dress mode, a softer, more casual version, to relax over dinner.

Decion had pulled out a small cuboid crystalator, set it on the table and keyed in an instruction on the object from which a holographic image of a galloping black stallion appeared.

"Impressive. And beautiful," Astara whistled, jealous her brothers had ridden these beasts.

"A mighty riding beast!" Decion grinned. "And this. . ." he keyed another entry, ". . . this is a cow. And you can eat it like this." The next few images were of cows, their slaughter, dismemberment, and roasting over a spit. "The meat on cows, called beef, was truly succulent. The only food I miss from Earth. The rest was not worthy. Much more tender than *ezor* loin." He visualised the large ferocious beasts from the Trinari home world, which he reckoned in Earth terms would be a cross between a grizzly bear and a large squirrel. His voice took on a more sombre tone. "Alpha Rion and I were to bring back many horses and cows to breed them. Maybe we still will one day."

"To eat?" Astara asked. There was more curiousness in her voice more than disgust. "Did not the humans process protein instead of manhandling the animal source? It seems a waste of time and effort."

A gruff laugh escaped Decion. "The humans were primitive in this time. They still domesticated vast amounts of animals for processing as food."

"That was still the case when we were on Earth," Aerl put in.

"Not that we do not eat animal flesh," Azure said as she chewed on her *lovgret* wings, the little birds having been imported first from Galatia and then from Placia. They were grilled and spiced just the way she loved them.

Decion sneered at her plate. "Those twiglets are hardly meat."

Aerl laughed. "But true, nonetheless, Azure. Let us not be hypocrites. However, there were movements of various non-meat eaters on Earth," he explained to Astara. "Humans are really still tribal in their views, even over food." He shook his head, remembering some of the culinary experiences in New York restaurants.

"Well, perhaps Alpha Rion will bring some of those animals here," Astara said, putting on a brave face.

Decion put his hand on his sister's. "He is not dead, I know it. He is our brother and knows how to survive. Besides, the woman whom he loves is also a great warrior and they will help each other live. I feel that." He nodded in grim determination. "I will find him myself, Astara. And if he is in human hell, I will bring him out myself, I swear it, for you!"

"For us all," Novan countered.

"Even Altair?" Aerl quipped. Everyone laughed.

"Even Altair!" Novan answered. "The Starguards will be united once more and face our enemies as one!"

"Fruk, yes!" Decion thumped the table. At the blank stares from Novan and Astara, Decion explained, "Fruk is one of the humans' favourite curses, as is 'shik!'"

They laughed, Azure laughing hardest. "I do not think they were the words exactly, Decion, but close enough. And yes, we will bring them all back!"

Astara regarded her elder brother. "I have never thanked you, Decion, for our training. We always thought it a chore, even though we liked fighting. But now I can see why we had to. I would not have survived as the Protectress of State otherwise nor the attacks from the invaders. I know Alpha Rion is alive. I can feel it, too, and I await his return. And I cannot wait to meet my new sister."

Decion laughed, almost looking embarrassed. "It was nothing but my pleasure, sister." He had a mischievous glint in his eye. "You can thank me by finally settling down and raising younglings I can train."

Everyone laughed with cries of approval. Astara joined in, but her demure reaction caught their attention.

"Well, I am actually seeing someone," she revealed coyly. "I hope you get to meet them, soon." She blushed slightly.

Decion raised his glass. "I would be honoured to meet the Magna Auran who has captured my sister's heart," cheered Decion. "They must be truly noble or mad," he laughed heartily.

Astara elbowed him sending him into a short choking fit to everyone's amusement

"But. . ." he looked somewhat embarrassed. "I have a confession—for Novan." Everyone's eyes now turned to Novan. "We may never have seen eye to eye, Novan, since you were more like mother than father, but I can see you are no less a warrior and more than a leader I would have been. To have held this place together for almost thirty years is a great feat. You are more a King than Cirrius claims to be and I am proud to be your brother!"

Novan smiled. "And I never knew I had such a brother in you."

The brothers regarded each other while everyone tried to fill in the following silence.

"Hear, hear," Aerl toasted the sentiments, raising his glass.

Astara saved her brothers from further embarrassment by changing the subject.

"If you are here to stay, Urana, I will surrender the mantle of

Protectress back to you."

She looked and sounded earnest, but Urana detected just a hint of reluctance in her. Just as she would have been.

Urana waved her off. "No, Astara, the role is yours. Of course I hope you're looking after my mountain and Camtrin." Urana remembered her Trinari aide fondly.

Astara's eyes widened in bemusement. "Oh, I am not residing in the mountain, that was your home, after all. I have a residence in Atronia. The Placians leave me alone, mostly." She smiled warmly. "And as for Camtrin, not only has she been maintaining your mountain, but she is also now the Secondary Principal of the Placian Council."

"Glorious," exclaimed Urana. "She deserves it. So she is Second to High Principal Brou?"

Astara shook her head. "Er, no, Brou retired, shall we say. Once you had gone he thought he could corner the Chronimonum market, so Camtrin and others challenged him and he lost. Markan Wenth is now High Principal. He is a good leader."

Urana slowly nodded. "That is good to know, thank you for telling me. I know Placia is in good hands." She gestured kindly to Astara across the table.

Astara turned her attention to Azure. "So, Azure, are you more an Astral than a Starguard now?" she asked. "I mean, you can travel time, which Starguards and even Celestian Knights could not do so freely!"

Everyone looked at Azure as she tried to savour her food.

"Call me Deb, please," was all she could think of.

There was a moment of confusion as again, everyone's eyes converged on her.

"What?" she asked, almost forgetting to swallow.

"You are a Starguard now, Azure. Deb was your former given name, but now as a Starguard, you have only your Starguard name like us." Astara said.

Everyone nodded in agreement.

"Oh," Azure said. "I never thought of it that way."

She wasn't quite sure at losing part of her identity, but she was home now and much was expected of her. Losing a name could hardly be the worst of her problems, but it still needled her a bit. And she didn't want to lose that part of her which had honoured Gal Agar, the Sky Commander who had been like a father to her. But she had a choice to make.

She just smiled. "Azure it is then!"

Novan raised his glass of nectar and toasted Azure, the rest following suit.

As the cheers settled down, Astara repeated her question.

Azure was thoughtful for a moment. "No, not really. I am a Loremaiden born into the Celestian family, while Zane is a Loremaiden born into the Astral family. We probably have more similarities between us like our powers than we do with our respective groups, but I'm a Starguard. Aren't I?"

"Yes, you are," a bemused Urana answered.

"So how are we going to rescue the Astrals?" Novan asked. "We do not even know where they lived, when they disappeared, or where they are now!"

Azure pondered that question. "Well, we know they live in a temporal bubble called the Chronopolis. Maybe I can use my temporal senses to guide me. There must be temporal pathways that I can see or sense to do that?" she questioned more to herself.

"Or we can do it the hard way," Decion said. "We go back to Magna Aura and force Timechantress or one of her whelplings to tell us or to take us there."

"They could not keep us out," Aerl said. Everyone nodded in agreement.

But Azure thought otherwise. "Not to Magna Aura, Aerl, but to an earlier Earth period. The Astrals said they couldn't go back to Earth for long periods of time, lest the Lore sensed them. But what if I and a few of you came back with me? I know roughly the area of Ancient Greece they came from. We could then somehow implant tracking crystalators in them before they become the Astrals in order to track them through time. So when they disappear in their future we would know where they are."

Novan thought about this, but Urana said first, "Or we could just tell them before they disappear and let them know they are going to be attacked."

Decion was not receptive to either idea. "These Astrals are our kin, yet they attacked us and forcibly took us from our homes and people. I do not care to help them. We are Starguards. We can do this ourselves and the Astrals be damned!"

Astara nodded in agreement. In the absence of Alpha Rion she felt more aligned with Decion.

"No," Novan overruled them all. He sighed heavily, as if a decision had been made. "I will come back to Magna Aura with you, temporarily, and confront Cirrius and Timechantress. We, and the Magna Aurans, deserve that much."

"I am glad to hear that," a relieved Sceptre grinned.

"I liked the hard way!" Decion laughed.

Urana was quiet, which Azure noticed.

"Urana, what do you think?" she asked.

Urana had placed her cutlery down on the table and sat with her hands on her lap. Her blue hair was tied and pulled back revealing the full features of her face, the emotion behind her eyes.

"Cirrius is my brother. If anyone is going to talk to him it will be me. And he will not be harmed," she aimed at Decion, who grudgingly conceded with a tilt of his head.

"Fine," Novan said. "Then it is settled. "We will leave when preparations for Elysiun's defences are finalised."

Novan then regaled them on the current situation on Elysiun as they continued their meal of *rantosh* cuts, *dian* leaves, *lovgret*, and *z'mili* sweets washed down with fruity *wolobean* juice.

"Oh, and beer, I miss that, too," Decion said more to himself wondering how to ferment the *wolobean* he gulped down, loudly burping.

Novan ignored him and continued his history of Elysiun.

"Swords *Celectral, Confiance,* and *Temprocity* were converted into ground cities. They are separated by a few kilometres, each under their own protective shields and surrounding habitat domes. *Celectral* is my command centre. And each city has their own unique cultural, and commercial base."

He laughed lightly. "Of course *Temprocity,* being the smallest of the Swords, holding the most warriors is the main training quarters. Families are growing fast so a few independent newbuild settlements have also been established, but not so far away from the motherswords."

"That's amazing," said Urana. "The work you have all done to establish a vibrant world in an inhospitable environment is a testament to all Celestians."

Novan proffered a conciliatory hand gesture, a sad look on his face. He then revealed to them a holographic map of Elysiun with their cities dotted closely together with a few outlying research and military posts.

"There have been sacrifices. Over thirty thousand warriors and support personnel originally departed with me from Magna Aura. Between losing Swords *Relentance* and *Venturon,* with over eight thousand lives lost, and losing more warriors to the Lore and the mysterious new enemy. We are now only eighteen thousand Elysiuns!"

"Universe!" Astara cried out.

"Power supplies, crystalators, and food are not a problem. We have the ultimate adaptable fuel source above us in the star dust. Meccun techs are always striving for methods to metaform Elysiun so a more breathable atmosphere can be nurtured. I have confidence this will be achieved within our lifetimes."

"If only to breathe the air once on this world, before the Universe takes me," he said. "Lastly," he finished, "We have begun to explore the Ribbon System and found other shrouded worlds with promising factors for settlement. But for now, this is our home, another new Celestian abode."

Decion burped loudly again.

"Wolobean juice. . ." he apologetically pointed to his flask, thumping his chest with a fist, to general amusement around him.

"It's late," Aerl stated, trying to hint to Decion to stop drinking.

They all stood. Smiles flashed around as they reminisced about such gatherings on Cirrius' island in more innocent times.

"I have had quarters set up for you," Novan announced as attendants cleared the table. "Let me show you the way."

Novan walked the Starguards to the accommodation deck, passing late night crews, who greeted the Starguards with warm salutes and hails.

A far cry from our welcome back on Halcyon, Urana mused to herself.

There were further expressions and gestures of appreciation and solidarity as Novan showed them each to their room; adapted sword crew quarters.

"I hope we haven't put any crew out," Sceptre's conscience spoke out.

Novan laughed. "Aerl, really, I had to *stop* crew from volunteering to give up their quarters. You are all lucky to have just one room," he joked.

"Do thank the crew for their hospitality," Urana said. She had been anxious as it was her brother who had caused them to literally crash out at Elysiun and put the planet in danger. And now they were taking their rooms. But Novan had made her feel better.

The Starguards accepted their rooms graciously.

Sword *Celectral* made a modest city and its officers' quarters were still of a good standard with several partitioned alcoves, functional comfortable furniture, and a porthole screen displaying the erupting sky above them in its kaleidoscopic beauty.

Pacing her room since entering, Azure promised herself she would explore the next day, but first she had something she had to do. She exited her room running down the wide corridor to catch up with Novan.

The walls had originally been white, but years as a grounded domestic dwelling had seen the walls, floors and ceilings painted and restyled with multi-coloured hues. The corridor Azure ran down was green-floored with golden walls, the arched portholes revealing the streaks and swirled patterns of the starry dust outside, Azure feeling the extra Lore energy intermingling within it.

She finally caught up with Novan, as he greeted a group of young Sky Warriors. One of them stiffened and formally saluted her, alerting Novan to her presence.

"Sorry to disturb your duties," she apologised as Novan had turned around, the Sky Warriors melting away with excited whispers.

Azure felt self-conscious in his presence. Knowing what had transpired between them a long time ago in the past and what she was about to ask now. But she had to.

"I just wanted to ask if I may sit by Classia's memorial. Where is it?" she requested shyly aware of the hurt this may have caused.

By Novan's surprised look, she thought he would decline, but he replied: "Um, sorry to disappoint you, but there is no memorial. Classia died in the sky and my memories are of her out there." At Azure's perplexed look, he explained further knowing her feelings. "I loved Classia, but a memorial here would only make me feel the finality of it. I can make one for you if you so desire, but in my heart she is always with me and our younglings, her legacy. I do not need a memorial." He smiled sadly and walked away.

Zane looked over her shoulder at him, his footfalls echoing down the green-gold floor. She felt lonelier than ever before. But there was also a nagging feeling. She was sure of it. Novan had lied to her.

Halcyon

"You should have told them about the storm! Now the Starguards are gone again!" snapped the voice from Tol Valar's right.

There were murmurs amongst the small group at her softly implied accusation of failure.

"I did not have time," came his answer. "I was never alone with any of the Starguards, especially Azure," he whispered harshly.

Ever since its appearance, he had been investigating the mysterious storm on the far side of Halcyon, including a small cadre of loyal friends. But now the far side of Halcyon was off limits to everyone except the King and the Astrals. It was not known if the storm was natural, caused by the enemy, or created by one of Cirrius' experiments. No one knew, but he and his cohorts did know something: they did not trust Cirrius.

"Do they suspect you?" Another voice. This from a screen which was one of two of the only light sources in the small quarters.

He sighed. "I do not know." He was unsure.

"And who knows if or when the Starguards will return this time!" Another accusing barb from the first speaker.

He tried consolation. "At least for now the storm has stabilised, coincidentally with the return of the Starguards, though it is still impenetrable."

"So what do we do in the meantime?" asked the fourth member of the group. This from the holographic image between them all.

He shrugged. "We wait. We wait for something to change."

"And if it does not?" searched the fifth member to Tol's left.

Tol Valar looked each of the conspirators in the eye.

"Then we will have to kill the King ourselves!"

There were murmurs of agreement all round.

CHAPTER FIVE

Deep space

Cirrius stood patiently at the interior airlock door of the alien space craft waiting for it to be opened. At least eight beings appeared on the other side of the oval metallic door. The crew were purple-skinned and looked to be on average seven-feet tall.

Show no fear, he told himself.

Their angular dark purple ship with weird wavy prongs curving to the rear, was almost camouflaged against the stars. It was larger than a personal carrier, but smaller than one of their mainline battleships, Cirrius had seen images of.

A command transport? he thought.

Eight hours ago, he had flown through space himself from Magna Aura, in secrecy, to meet the alien leaders personally. Comming his arrival he had been ordered to wait. A further three hours later, they had deigned to open the outer airlock. Now he was still waiting for the inner door to release.

Patience, he calmed himself. He was sweating. But if he had to die for the greater good. . .

A soft thunk and hiss announced that, finally, the inner airlock door was cycling open. Quickly wiping his brow dry with the back of his hand, Cirrius cautiously, while trying to maintain his Kingly manner, stepped onto the alien ship proper.

Cirrius approached one of the aliens closest to him slowly, careful not to look aggressive. However, the visitors still seemed as apprehensive of him as he was with them; their demeanour bearing a distinct underlying hostility.

The aliens all wore a thin black carapace-like armour with various coloured flashes and insignias on their chests, arms, shoulders and thighs. Some wore dark green or red shoulder harnesses or sashes. Around each waist was a thin silver belt which bore tools, weapons, and other instruments unfamiliar to

Cirrius.

Stares of disdain held Cirrius at bay. He smiled back uneasily, but held his stance.

The transport interior was airy, but clearly militaristic, dressed in subdued greys with white and black tones, looking incongruous against all the purple warriors surrounding him.

There was a smell wafting around him, which strangely reminded Cirrius of his youth. Magna Auran swordships always smelled like metal ready for battle, but this sweet smell was uncannily similar to a crystal-like flower which was now an artificially-bred commodity on Magna Aura. Only a few cargo loads of the natural flower had originally been transported, but were near exhaustion. Even the Meccuns' synthesised version of the scented pinkish plant could not compete with the original. Cirrius sniffed the air, smiling.

A common point perhaps to talk about, he mused. *A trade deal perhaps.* He felt better about his mission.

He hoped there would be no battle today. He wanted peace. But he was prepared to die. As it looked like his hosts were only just going to stand there silently, he introduced himself.

"Hallo, esteemed hosts, I am Cirrius, of the Starguards, King of Magna Aura. I welcome you to Magna Aura on terms of peace," he bowed, hoping they understood him.

The plans had been made that night on Magna Aura with Timechantress. There had been no sign of the other Starguards returning, but they could not take any chances. Still, it had taken almost three weeks of secret negotiations for Cirrius to contact the enemy and for them to respond. They had arranged a secret rendezvous aboard one of their ships at the edge of Magna Auran space. Cirrius had supplied the time and place and flown straight there. To his surprise a ship was waiting.

He and Timechantress had agreed that if the enemy accepted their terms of peace, and if they were so disposed, they could inhabit Placia. However, they knew the rest of the Starguards would reject that course of action so he needed allies. Timechantress had been left in charge. He had to secure a truce and an alliance. Or die trying.

Upon his introduction, the visitors looked at each other as if confused. An uneasy feeling welled up in Cirrius. Something was wrong. His stomach started to knot up.

Before leaving Halcyon, Cirrius had addressed the Magna Aurans again, announcing to the population that the rest of the Starguards had abandoned them again.

"They have turned against their own people," Cirrius had proclaimed. "They will return to fight against us!"

"Nooo!" had chorused the crowds around him; shock, disbelief, and outrage besieging them.

"But, I, Cirrius will protect you! I vow it!" There had been great cheers at his pledge. It still rang in his ears now.

But now he needed an enemy to be his friend. His gut was telling him otherwise.

"Whom do you think you address?" asked one of the alien officers, taking a few menacing steps forward and lurking over Cirrius. "We are not here on terms of peace!"

Cirrius cocked his head in confusion and fear. He tried to hide it with a compliment. "I see. I also see you have no need of translation devices. You speak perfect Celestian. You learn fast!"

Again, the alien officers looked at each other, almost in bemusement. There was a hint of a self-satisfied smirk on one face, but anger on others.

"Follow," one of the subordinates ordered, ignoring Cirrius' comment.

Almost without ceremony, Cirrius was given a tour of the ship. He recognised many familiar console features as well as the constant familiar plant smell. Hardly a word was spoken, mostly routine commands and greetings amongst the aliens to other crew, but every single purple crew member they passed gave Cirrius a disdainful scowl, which made him even more nervous.

Cirrius then realised he wasn't so much as being given a tour of the ship, but being paraded past for all the crew to see; for what purpose he did not know. The tour processed through dozens of corridors and a few transtubes, past more seething aliens lining the decks. His ordeal ended on the bridge.

And it was only then that Cirrius noted with some disappointment and embarrassment that he had not even been greeted at the airlock by their leader. For he was now in front of him on the bridge.

"See the grandeur of our power," the unintroduced leader announced in a leisurely manner, wafting his arm forward.

The alien commander sat in his raised command chair, a plain black throne-like instalment in the centre of the octagonal bridge, which was the only area Cirrius had noted that was coloured purple. His counterpart's armour was more pronounced than the crews', thicker, but still recognisable with deep purple flashes over his shoulders, and curiously darker purple markings on his purple face around his eyes and chin. His hair was long and straight, past his shoulders, which from what Cirrius could see also hung a cape.

How theatrical, Cirrius mused, thinking of his own Kingly uniform. *Do I look so resplendently pompous?*

The aliens who had first greeted and accompanied Cirrius to the bridge had filtered to various stations sitting at peripheral consoles or leaning against the bridge's inclined surfaces, which sloped with a sharp concave pattern around the command deck. Cirrius noted control modules with notched finger recesses for personal interfacing. The muted lights on the bridge were also soft purple reflecting off the shiny wall surfaces, making the bridge seem like a crystalised flower petal.

A memory fleetingly surfaced in Cirrius' mind, but it was gone in an instant, just like his failure to place the smell still nestling in his nostrils.

The alien leader had indicated a large forward screen which displayed countless red dots.

Their fleet, Cirrius surmised, impressed.

"Over one thousand," the leader responded, as if reading Cirrius' mind.

Cirrius stood astounded. He had not realised how many

ships the enemy had. Each seemed as formidable as a Celestian sword. For some reason Cirrius turned. Behind on the bulkhead was a large holographic portrait of an alien male, looking out from above the entrance at the rear of the bridge toward the front holoscreen. The officers around Cirrius looked at him expectantly.

Cirrius glanced around him; a wan smile involuntarily escaping his lips. He could feel his heart beating faster. The portrait showed an old male, a great stern warrior or leader, with long purple hair and deep-set purple eyes. But it was his skin which made the blue hairs on Cirrius' neck stand up. The skin was pale, like Cirrius'. Not purple.

A sharp pain stabbed at Cirrius behind his eyes; a memory so hidden, it didn't want to be remembered. But Cirrius had to ask.

"He is impressive," he said of the portrait, hoping his admiration for the painting would please them. "Who is he?"

There were audible gasps from the bridge crew. An officer reached for a round snub-nosed object by his hip—a side-arm, Cirrius guessed.

The leader stood up, the surrounding officers backing off.

"You insult us, Cirrius?" The leader asked, fury burned in his eyes. "How dare you utter such words of ignorance and insult our heritage."

Cirrius was confused. "I am sorry, but if there was something lost in translation, I offer my apologies. I meant no offence. But, I do not know who that is!" His head hurt even more. He started to sweat. More trickled down his back.

"Translation? We have no need of translation, we speak Celestian and have for our entire lives as have generations before us! Do you not know who we are?" the leader asked, with rising indignation.

The knot in Cirrius' stomach opened up and fell into a deep pit. He shook his head, unable to talk, each breath choking him.

"Elerae cretin!" The leader's face turned an even deeper

purple. Cirrius took a step back, wondering how he knew his heritage. The leader's voice was thick with disgust. "You seek to rule with your power, yet you have no sense, no honour, and are as treacherous as your forbearers. Before you die, you will look upon the face of the enemies your forbearers tried to erase from history. Look upon us and see that we live. We thrive. We, who of the seven Celestian Worlds, were singled out by the Elerae, your ancestors, for destruction, while the other Worlds stood silently and passively by. And we swore on the Great Father and Holy Mother that we would have our revenge on the Elerae and the other Worlds! Look under the skin we have made for ourselves and behold us in our full glory!" The leader threw out his arms and declared with gleaming pride. "We, are the Amethystians!"

Cirrius' mouth fell agape in fear. He would not have personally known the Amethystians, the one-time inhabitants of one of the original Seven Worlds, but his genes knew them; the poisoned memory stabbing his mind knew them. His body and spirit knew what his ancestral Elerae had done to the Amethystians countless millennia ago. He remembered the story as written by Spheron in the Scrolls of History. It was almost a footnote:

Long ago, so it was written, an Elerae had been killed on Amethystia. The Elerae, fiercely loyal to one another, had found fault with this, and as a one, had travelled the vast scape of space to Amethystia and annihilated the whole world. Total decimation. Amethystia still hangs around its sun, but as a disjointed ring of loose rock and rubble.

Shock reverberated through Cirrius, but he managed to gasp: "How. . . how did you escape?" His mouth felt dry. The taste of fear sucked away all moisture.

"We are master builders, but with enemies like the Elerae we had contingency plans in place. We had Swordships at the ready. Portal engines ready to open dimensional gateways to another universe. And we prayed for the day of revenge. Let me show you our sacrifices." He nodded to an officer, a bulky purple behemoth, who approached Cirrius with a crystalator.

Cirrius instinctively backed away when he saw the short wiry neural attachments.

"Do you not wear neural implants?" the leader asked. He flicked his long hair away from the left side of his head, revealing his own implant above his left ear. "We all wear them. They are harmless," he reassured as if speaking to a youngling.

Cirrius let the mammoth officer approach. The Amethystian attached the implant to his temple, a moment's discomfort giving way almost instantly as the nano-fibre filaments threaded their way into the Starguard's brain. Another moment and memories, visions, images, not his own, began to swirl through his mind—moments not from his mind nor his time, but long ago, even before the first Celestian Knights.

Cirrius watched through another's eyes as ancient Elerae swords hovered above Amethystia. They unleashed fire down upon the lush purple and green world. But even in death, through the screams, pain and dying, there was singing, chanting, and hand-scrolling; the oral history of the Amethystians being recorded right up until the end of their world. Then it rained. Huge dark clouds rolled across the land, blotting out the sun. The rain was black, thick, and stung his eyes so they closed. But not before he turned to see the sky rip open and portals rupture into life. Scores of huge swordships flew through each hole before they collapsed leaving behind a jagged fading scar of energy. All around Amethystia, portals ruptured and scarred the sky.

A face loomed in Cirrius' vision, old, with long fading purple hair. And a name. But they withered out of reach. Those Amethystians left behind continued singing, their voices carrying through the waning portals. And then the planet died. Like a *lovgret*'s egg, the planet cracked open and the heavens met hell in a clash of cosmic fury. Amethystia died singing its own wretched song of despair.

Cirrius opened his eyes. He rubbed them and felt the tears, which he wiped away, though they seemed to feel sticky with black rain. He looked around at the Amethystians and then up at the portrait.

"Methynenes," Cirrius named the man. "Your leader. He stayed behind," Cirrius knew.

The Amethystian leader seemed satisfied. "You are the leader of your people now. And today is your sacrifice. Our vengeance begins with you."

"I came in peace," Cirrius said, as dread paralysed his body.

"We did not!" The leader smiled coldly. "Elerae!" he cursed.

Cirrius, Starguard, King of Magna Aura, stood resolutely still and wide-eyed as the leader of the Amethystians unholstered a short tubular weapon from his belt, raised it, and fired once.

Cirrius felt the small energy pellet impact him. It left him still standing. There was no pain, just the shock of the shot punching deep into his abdomen. He took a breath.

And then the fire started.

The pellet seemed to burst within him like a flare. Cirrius felt his organs melt in a slow baste of escaped stomach acid. His lungs shrivelled into a congealing ash. He found he was paralysed and could not even scream as his boiling blood pulsed to the beat of the fire into his heart. His brain felt crushed under the weight of the electric sensations of unresolvable emotions and thoughts as the blaze ripped through his spinal cord. Legs crumpled, twisted, and broke and Cirrius fell onto his back to the sound of more bones cracking. He couldn't move his arms to wipe away the spots of blood on his eyes nor smell or taste the iron of that liquid as it spilled from his eyes, nose, mouth and ears. Cirrius looked up as the Amethystians crowded around him, choking more air from around him, willing his life to cease. It was the last sight his open eyes saw.

There was no remorse. No ceremony or thrill of victory. Just one part of the job done.

"Throw his body into space," the leader ordered no one in particular.

He pulled a small flat triangular crystalator shard from his belt and slipped it into Cirrius' manoeuvre suit.

"This should make sure the Magna Aurans can find it!" He looked dispassionately down on Cirrius' body. Two security crew roughly picked up the charred body of Cirrius and removed him from the bridge.

Soon, you will all be like this, the Amethystian looked out toward Magna Aura through the holoscreen.

He faced his fiercely loyal bridge crew. Proud faces stared back at him. That their vengeance had started with them would make them heroes for eternity. The leader knew that.

"We celebrate death. Then we return for more!"

The crew cheered, "*Braga Vu Braga!*" Death for Death.

The Amethystian ship turned spaceward and left the Magna Aura system behind.

"What is it, sir?"

"Universe, if I know!" Captain Ber Maran turned the triangular shard over in his hand. "Looks like a crystalator to me."

He scratched the back of his bald head, where the old sharp scar ran, picked up on a nectar-fueled tangle with a stubborn deep core drill. How he had managed to do so and survive was even a mystery to him. The scar was his reminder that life was precious. It seemed to be warning him of that again.

His mining ship, the *Star Ode*, out of Aurana, had detected a strange beacon signal. Upon investigating they had come across the source: a dead body afloat in space. Upon retrieval of the body they could not believe it was the body of the King; the captain barely able to bring himself to call for assistance.

However, scant minutes later, the call still unmade, *Sword Exthereal*, had burst out of star drive and berthed alongside the miners' ship.

And to Maran's further surprise, it was the two sons of the King who ported aboard the bridge of the *Ode*, alone. Without having to say a word, Maran took them below to the medbay to see the body.

Lords Antichilles and Tyran looked down at the sealed opaque medivac tube in the darkened medbay. The medtech pressed a sensor on the tube's side and the cover became transparent.

Cirrius lay serenely in the cramped tube. His chest was a jangled mess of charred blood, gaping holes, and mangled flesh. Antichilles clenched his jaw, while Tyran's eyes flinched in anger. They asked to be left alone, Captain Maran and medtech duly obliging.

Their mother had prepared them, but still their first death, especially of their father, was hard to take. The twins alone had boarded the *Star Ode*, a small crew of fifteen experienced miners harvesting Aurana's moons. The *Exthereal's* captain had been left behind, rather perplexed about their secret mission to Aurana, especially when Antichilles demanded a communications blackout. All signals around their ships had been jammed.

Tyran scanned his father's body with a crystalator. Negative response. He glanced at Antichilles who frowned. But a beep alerted them to the presence of another foreign comms device—the source of the beacon. It was not with their father. It was moving on its way back to the bridge. Tyran smiled and motioned with his head to Antichilles. Maran possessed the alien artefact. They could not take the chance he had viewed it and disclosed its contents to others. They covered their father back up and returned to the bridge, ostensibly to make arrangements for the King's transfer to the *Exthereal*.

There was no preamble or explanation needed as the Astrals re-entered the bridge.

"If you please," Tyran said in a warning edged tone. He held out an open palm.

Maran felt their eyes hotly upon him. He hadn't deliberately tried to hold back information from the King's sons, but he had felt something was not quite right. Now it was too late to explain, he knew.

Antichilles paced the bridge making all the crew nervous

while Maran, himself nervous yet curious, programmed the ship's crystalator encryption sequences to accept and translate the alien device. He then placed the found crystalator shard in the console receiver, finding he only had to simply re-programme the ship's incoming datadrops again to an older configuration.

Odd, he thought as a holographic image sprung to life. *The aliens had Celestian-like encryptions, but an older type.*

Without warning, a tall holographic purple being appeared on the bridge.

He declared: "Your leader, Cirrius, is dead. Behold!" An accompanying image showed Cirrius being shot point blank by the speaker on the alien ship's bridge.

There were cries and gasps around the *Star Ode*'s bridge behind the brothers and Maran. The captain quieted them down with a swift look.

The purple being continued, "We are the Amethystians. And we seek vengeance against those who left us to die millennia ago. Prepare for your end!"

The message ended abruptly in black static.

The two Astrals and the bridge crew had watched in silence. A comms officer started to send a message, but Tyran's sharp stare stopped him short. Maran knew a message to Magna Aura would send the system into a panic and aid the Amethystians' attack, which they also knew would be imminent.

The silence on the bridge was deafening.

"Who are the Amethystians?" Tyran asked. His question hit the bridge like a thunderous bombshell.

Maran stared at Tyran in shock. "What do you mean, your Lordship? Everyone knows who they were. How can you not know, being half-Elerae?"

Tyran looked uncertainly at his brother, abashed, but with another underlying emotion, Maran saw.

"Of course, I should have remembered my history," mumbled Tyran.

Antichilles suddenly departed the bridge.

"Where is he going?" the captain asked, his eyes following Antichilles' departure.

Tyran glanced at his departing brother as he walked off the bridge.

"He is distraught and will stay with father's body to help transport him to the *Exthereal*."

The answer seemed to calm Maran's nerves. But the next question did not.

"May I see your engine room, Captain?" he asked.

Maran's face screwed in confusion. "The engine room?" He shook his head in confusion. "What? Why? At a time like this?"

Tyran smiled, charmingly. "It is mission-critical, Captain."

Maran sighed. He dared not ask if the King's son cared not for his father's death and why they were delaying reporting the news. He did as he was told by a Starguard.

Maran sighed wearily. "Of course, Lord Tyran. This way."

Tyran followed the captain through the corridors and down the short transtube to the engine room. Stacks of contained energy rods and large main-line crystalators lined the lower half of the rectangular two-storey space.

This would do nicely, Tyran thought. He tapped a three-count discreet pitched-signal over his comms.

Ready.

Antichilles stood by in the medbay. The signal came through. He fully opened the medivac tube, picked up and cradled his father in his arms. And in front of the astonished medtech just entering the bay, Antichilles had vanished into thin air with Cirrius' corpse.

A corresponding signal was heard by Tyran over his comms.

All clear.

The bridge crew were on edge. The Starguard leader, their King was dead. And his sons were marching around giving orders, but doing nothing. Certainly not grieving.

Minetech Staka, the duty comms officer, had family on Placia. He had to let them know what had happened. And perhaps they could get to the old Lore-war shelters first, before any trouble started. He started sending a message.

Tyran concentrated. He stared at the rods and crystalators. It was not hard to do. The energy already had momentum. And the regulators were doing their job. But if the energy was too much...or too rapid to be contained...

"Is everything in order, Lord Tyran?" asked Maran, wondering why the boy was just staring at the energy rods.

Just then, an urgent message from medtech Vimor chimed over his comms. Maran ignored it, trying to fathom Tyran's actions. And then he saw what was happening.

"Lord, please, what are you doing?" his voice beseeched. But it was too late. "Please don't!" Maran's quiet strained voice was drowned out by a shriek of an alarm piercing the ship.

Tyran looked at Maran with a smile, then winked out of existence. Captain Ber Maran, rubbed his scar, staring haplessly at the surging uncontrolled energy of engines about to go critical.

Staka was just about to press the send code when an explosion ripped through the ship. The bridge crew could only watch and listen as the explosions shattered them into the cold of space.

Sword Exthereal rocked from the explosion as the *Star Ode* was shredded apart. Alarms blared, but their shielding and bulkheads had held with no injuries reported.

Captain Foltas Gregeree almost demanded an explanation from Tyran as he entered the bridge, but remembered who he was addressing.

Politely he asked, "May I ask what happened on the *Star Ode*?"

Tyran took on an air of authority. "We had word that these miners were plotting with the enemy to overthrow the King. So we dealt with it," Tyran announced, adding, "My brother is already on route to Halcyon now to brief our father. You have done a great service today Captain Gregeree. You and your crew will be rewarded," he finished.

The captain's hard expression changed as he beamed with pride. "Thank you, my Lord." He bowed exuberantly. "By your leave?"

"Of course, Captain." Tyran turned and left the bridge.

Still smiling, Gregeree ordered *Exthereal* back to Halcyon.

CHAPTER SIX

The Ribbon System

"Dead?" Novan repeated.

It had been almost four weeks since any communication from Magna Aura. Novan had asked the Starguards to stay on Elysiun until their defences were secure. But now they could not believe the ominous message which had been delivered by Xestina.

The young Astral's arrival within *Celectral* had set off the alarms, but her polite request to speak with Novan had been accepted, once it was confirmed she was alone. And as one of the youngest of the Starguards, according to Cirrius, or one of the youngest of the Astrals, according to Timechantress, Xestina had been chosen by her mother to deliver the message as it was deemed she was the most innocent and would not be harmed.

The Starguards had gathered in Novan's quarters for greater privacy. Her delivered news had taken them completely by surprise.

"Dead?" Urana's whisper echoed Novan's words. "How? When?" Her face was flushed. The last few weeks had seen her weaker than normal.

Sceptre wondered if it was the same illness which had afflicted her on Earth. Urana had briefly visited the Sky Command medtechs when they had returned to Halcyon, but her condition had not improved and Urana would not talk of it. Sceptre would have pushed her to see the Elysiun medtechs.

But then Xestina had arrived with her devastating news.

Xestina had then related the story. "My father met with the enemy to sue for peace." Her eyes were sad. "But they did not care." Then she dropped the bombshell. "After all these years, he discovered our mysterious attackers are the Amethystians!"

"What? How do you know?" Novan interrupted, "But..." he was lost for words, his mind calculating the ramifications for their people.

Xestina continued. "They killed my father in cold blood, dumping his body into space." She held out the odd-shaped Amethystian crystalator found on Cirrius' body.

Urana snatched it from her small hand. She placed it on the round wooden table between them all, activated the triangular shard, and played the Amethystian's holo message, all watching in cold silence.

Xestina faced them, through the holo image, once the message had ended. Her voice was shaky and sad.

"My mother requests a truce, to mourn Cirrius, and to discuss the future. At the moment, his death has been kept a secret from the public so as not to panic them until we have established some form of succession."

"Succession?" Decion shouted.

Xestina jumped at his voice.

The Starguards looked at each other in surprise.

"Why doesn't Timechantress rule even as regent for Antichilles and Tyran until they are of age?" Sceptre asked.

Decion rounded on him. "Because even as his wife and mother of Halcyon-born children she doesn't have the legitimacy to rule," Decion guessed. "There should not even be a King, but she wants our presence to legitimise her, yes?" he asked Xestina.

The young girl shrugged, blue hair falling over her eyes.

Her voice somewhat husky, Urana said, "Well, no matter what, we have to return to Halcyon." She sat down hugging herself. "He was my brother and I will mourn him," she said, her face a resolute mask.

Novan, Decion, and Sceptre looked at each other, the three making a silent decision with curt nods, arched eyebrows, and twisted lips.

"We will come, Xestina. We will mourn Cirrius," Novan stated. "If the Amethystians are preparing for war then we will stand beside your mother." He gave her a grave look. "But if this is some deception or trap, we will not hesitate to kill you!"

"Novan!" Urana chastised him, standing up in anger. "She is my niece. She will not be harmed!" She glared at him.

Novan turned back to Xestina. "We will come," he simply repeated, without apology.

Xestina's angelic face had grown pale, her eyes blinking quickly. "Yes, lord Novan," she replied. "I will inform my mother to expect you." She looked over to Urana. "I am sorry for you loss, Aunt Urana." She bowed, stepped back, and blinked out through her opened portal.

"Nice etiquette," Decion said in his gruff voice.

Novan smiled. Xestina was not like her parents.

"But can we trust her mother," Decion asked. "Could this all have been fabricated?" He ignored Urana's look of horror at the idea.

"No," Azure said, holding the crystalator. "The crystalator is intact and the data genuine. Cirrius is. . ." she looked over at Urana, unable to finish the sentence.

"The decision is yours, Urana," Novan said.

Urana inhaled deeply, looking up at the ceiling. "We go," she decided. "And if they are lying, then. . . we'll see!"

"Are the contingencies to protect Elysiun in place?" Azure asked.

Novan glanced at her. "Yes, we were about complete." He smiled grimly and stood up from the table. "I will inform my First Tech to prepare. I will be a few minutes." He left the room, leaving the Starguards to mull over their own plans upon their return.

Azure wondered what type of plans Novan had in place. He seemed more furtive with his recent defence plans and he frequently disappeared; out of touch from the rest of the Starguards for hours on end. She wondered if anyone else had noticed. She was about to ask, when Novan returned, the same little smile on his face as when he returned from one of his incommunicado moments.

He looked at her, the fleeting emotion on his face disappearing. Then he arched his eyebrow at her, Azure taking a moment to understand.

"Oh, yes, right, you're waiting for me. No time like the present! Everybody ready?" she looked at everyone for confirmation. "Let's go!"

And in a flash of blue light, Azure ported them away.

Halcyon

The only place Cirrius could be interred secretly and privately was on his island home, Aqrius.

Urana had observed his strangely contorted body in his coffin before it was lowered into a forcefield shroud in the ground. No one said any words; silent introspection was in order.

The memorial stone was draped in the Halcyon and Sky Warrior flags by his sons. The former was the golden sun of Magna Aura on a blue background surrounded by six multi-coloured spheres representing the six Peoples of the Galatians, Xarians, Elerae, Trinari, Meccuns, and Neb. The Sky Warrior flag bore a simple dark blue background with the light blue sphere of Halcyon bisected by the golden sceptre of Acirrius, father to Urana and Cirrius; the inspiration for the Sky Warriors, and the symbol and weapon of the Sky Commander.

Urana wondered if these flags had really rallied the Magna Aurans behind Cirrius, as he had claimed. She marvelled at how inspiring and inventive her brother had always been and at his accomplishments, but also how it had all gone wrong. She could have blamed Timechantress for this, but she knew deep down this had started the moment they had escaped Galatia. He had chosen to follow a darker path. Urana wiped a tear from her eye. Her brother wasn't the only lost and lonely Celestian. They all were. And it was up to the Starguards to keep them on the brighter path. She looked around. She was alone now, the rest of the Starguards making their way inside.

Only Zasandra and Celestra had stayed inside Cirrius' dwelling, to give the Starguards their private moments. Antichilles, Tyran, and Xestina shared their last and private farewells. The twins had then left as they were nominally standing in for their father on official duties, until such time as news broke of his death.

The Starguards entered the comfortable ante room.

Azure found herself in familiar surroundings fondly reminiscing on the night she found out she was a Starguard.

In an adjoining room, Cirrius' library still held the paintings of the Celestian Knights. Azure felt a presence beside her.

Novan smiled as she turned to him. "I cannot believe I am back here, just like that."

"Not the way you would have wanted to return—in secret," Azure said.

"No, not at all." They stared at each other, Novan looking like he wanted to say more.

"He returns to the stars; Great Father and Holy Mother, receive him," Urana prayed loudly to the universe. She swayed a little and sat in Cirrius' favourite high-backed *leckerwood* chair, breaking the mood between Novan and Azure. She looked pained herself and was drinking a lot of nectar. She was followed by Timechantress. Urana gave her a dark look.

"Tell me what happened?" Urana scornfully asked Timechantress, who sat opposite in her armour, though her cape of wings was absent.

Zasandra told her part of the story.

"He went there alone?" Urana balled her fists, not believing what she was hearing. "Why did you or a guard not accompany him? My brother died because of you, Timechantress! Why?" Urana yelled at her.

Timechantress looked away, brushing away tears from her eyes. "I can't tell you," she cried back.

"Can't or won't?" Urana leapt out of her chair with a raised hand to strike the Astral, but Sceptre grasped her arm.

"Hold for now, Rain," He tried to calm her. Turning to Timechantress, he asked: "You knew the Amethystians were going to kill Cirrius?"

"Nooo!" Timechantress answered back in shock. "How could I? I would never hurt Cirrius!"

"But you knew, or thought you knew who was attacking and it had to do with you?" Sceptre questioned further.

Timechantress was quiet, but she nodded. "We thought the same people who attacked the Astrals were the same attacking Magna Aura. We were wrong."

"Universe!" Urana screamed. "Zasandra, you owe us an explanation. On my brother's life you owe him an explanation for his death!"

Timechantress looked at the wall, her mind racing, not knowing what to say. But she knew she had to tell.

A quiet voice crept out of her. "I lied!" she looked away. "I lied about what happened at the Chronopolis," she shook her head in shame.

Decion almost laughed, resisting the urge to say he told them so.

Urana kept her temper down enough to ask: "What lie? Why?"

"Because I was scared!" Timechantress snapped. "You didn't see what I did!"

"What did you see?" Decion growled impatiently.

"Everything I said before did happen. I travelled to the Chronopolis to see my brother, Xathanius, but I saw the Chronopolis being attacked, or at least the aftermath as the Chronopolis was sealed off. I sensed someone was still around so I hid in phase space. And I heard one of the attackers say something like," she lowered the tone in her voice, ". . . the Astrals have met their end at the hands of the Chronossii.'" She was silent for a while, shaking her head in sadness. She looked into Urana's eyes. "Then there was a flash of light like a portal opening and then nothing. I cannot imagine the Chronopolis being deserted at any time, so the Chronossii must have taken the Astrals or killed them!"

"I can't believe you didn't tell us this before," Urana said. "My brother would still be alive if—"

"You don't know that!" Timechantress cut her off, shouting back. "Besides, I can go back and change the past. Cirrius does not have to die, then we would also know the nature of the threat..."

"No!" Azure objected. "We cannot just go back in time and change things."

A stunned silence followed her outburst.

"Why not?" Urana and Timechantress intoned together, giving each other a look of annoyance.

Timechantress continued. "We saved Magna Aura the first time around. Or is saving a civilisation different to saving the life of a Starguard? And even you told me that Zane saved her father by changing time so that he could fight the battle against the Storm of Stars. How is this different?" Timechantress finished.

Azure took a deep breath. She knew there would be resistance to not changing time. "Even you know Timechantress that we cannot just go around changing time. It does not work that way. Time has a habit of snapping events back into place if we're not careful. And where would we stop? If each of us died would we just go into the past and correct that? If news of this got out to Magna Aurans they would demand that we save their child, or husband, mother, sister or loved one who had died. And then no one would ever die and we would be constantly living in the past. We are not Gods—"

"We could be," Timechantress interrupted. "But you Starguards have power you do not want to use. Why have the power. . ."

"Power doesn't mean we have to abuse it," Azure retorted, her heart racing from the argument.

"How can we be abusing our powers, it is for a good cause?" Timechantress stressed. "We. . ."

"Enough!" Sceptre's shout interrupted the argument. Everyone stopped and looked at him. "Do it, Timechantress," he told the Astral. "Bring back Cirrius."

Urana and Timechantress exchanged nervous smiles while Decion and Astara looked on in amazement.

"Sceptre, no, you haven't thought this through," Azure protested.

"Novan is our leader here!" Urana interrupted, grudgingly giving support to Sceptre's decision. "What do you think, Novan?" she turned to him.

But Astara spoke for the first time. "I want to hear more of what Azure has to say," she said. "Then I will make my choice. Nothing is decided until we vote," she said in defiance of Sceptre's decision.

Decion nodded his agreement, standing up to brook any dissent.

Novan sighed deeply and also nodded. "Let us hear Azure."

Accepting his set back in the argument, Sceptre acquiesced to Astara's request to the dismay of Cirrius' wife and sister. "Fine, what have I missed, Azure, bearing in mind that we need as many of us as we can get to fight both the Amethystians and these so-called Chronossii?"

Timechantress took the slight with a suck of her teeth.

Azure sighed inwardly. Here she was the youngest Starguard defying orders and giving her own opinion, but she had to be heard. Time was not a matter to be messed with.

"Okay, so to which time period do we go back to? Who goes and how do we know we haven't done this before and I or Timechantress aren't saying anything otherwise?" She looked at the others who faces had blank answers. "If you notice, I didn't go back in time to save my best friend, Classia, nor did Novan or any of you ask me to, even for the sake of Novan's feelings and for Elyssia and Astarius. It would have been wrong then as it is now. Also, would we tell Cirrius he died or if any of you had died as you won't remember today as it would have never happened? How could we justify changing your lives? Is one person worth more than another to be rescued if they died? Is. . ."

"There is more than one person at stake. More than Cirrius. . ." Timechantress interrupted, looking at the floor with a vacant stare. "There are the rest of the Astrals," she said in a very quiet voice. She looked at Azure. "The rest of the *other* Astrals," she emphasised.

"Other Astrals?" Novan asked. "What other Astrals?"

Timechantress laughed; an almost hysterical sound. "Cirrius always said he would take this secret to his grave," she laughed again in spite of herself.

Urana charged over and grabbed Timechantress by her collar. "Are you mocking my brother's death?"

"No!" screamed Timechantress, her smile vanishing. "No, never! It is just something we talked about and that we would tell no one else. Only Celestra knows so she can verify my story."

Everyone turned to her orange-haired daughter who had been sitting quietly in the corner. She nodded vigorously.

"She is telling the truth," she said.

"And what truth is that?" Decion drew the hilt of his lancesword from his sheath. There were nervous looks from Azure and Urana.

"Put that away!" Sceptre ordered. "There will be no blood shed between us." He squared up to Decion.

Decion's lip curled back as he defiantly drew the rest of the lancesword out slowly, deliberately, and placed the sword upright in front of him. His large hands rested on the hilt in front of his chin.

"Aerl," he addressed Sceptre gruffly. "We have had nothing but drips of lies and half-truths from her. Enough is enough, she will tell us everything now or the Universe as my witness, I will send her to meet Cirrius and atone for her deceit." His cold voice told everyone he would do it.

"Just stay calm, Decion," Novan said to his brother.

"I agree with Decion," Astara said. "And I side with Azure. We cannot keep changing the past as we see fit. We are not the Great Father and Holy Mother, nor the Storm of Stars."

Sceptre turned from Decion's glare. Sighing, he returned to Novan's original question.

"Timechantress, what did you mean by the *other* Astrals? And what did you and Cirrius keep a secret?"

Timechantress seemed reluctant to talk, but a subtle shift of Decion's hands on the hilt of his lancesword quickly convinced her to do otherwise.

"When Phasia found us back on Ancient Earth we were living like normal humans. We knew we were special, our parents had told us of our heritage, but we did not know about our powers or that we would ever leave Earth." She stared at the wall as if peering into the distant past and her voice grew wistful. "We had joined in Imperial armies, legendary voyages, and great quests all over the ancient world. Men were men, and we all did what we had to do to fit in." Her gaze shifted to another part of the wall as her tone shifted to one of sorrow.

"I knew Lazeron was not always faithful to me even after we had Celestra, but we loved each other. I knew that Cal, whom you called Archron, and Helexius, Spheron and even Xathanius mated with others other than the women they chose as life mates. They could not keep their cocks in their kilts," she smile wistfully. "The only children we brought with us are the ones Phasia found with us at the walls of Troy. There were certainly more. We do not know for sure how many. Even now there could be generations of Astrals on Earth, growing up, not even knowing their heritage let alone that they can travel time," she continued to stare at the wall.

The room fell silent as the news sunk in.

"How do we know this is true?" a sceptical Decion asked.

"Ask Celestra," Timechantress shot back instantly. Her daughter looked nervous, but otherwise gave confirmation with another silent nod.

"Why did the Astrals not mention this before? Why not go back for them?" Urana asked.

Timechantress shook her head. "By the time we knew what Phasia had in store for us and saving Magna Aura. . . we could not return to Earth for long. The Lore could have detected us. So we left Earth for good, building the Chronopolis in another dimension. That is why we sent you Starguards to protect Earth."

"So, I do not understand where my brother fits in," said Urana.

"I told Cirrius about the other Astral children and he made a

. . ." she hunted for words, "a temporal anomaly sensor or an Astral detector." Timechantress smiled as she remembered admiring Cirrius for his work. "He made it seem so easy. As a test, he and Celestra travelled to Earth, as she has a low temporal signature. They spent months on Earth searching, but he was able to find and bring children here as if nothing had happened. . ."

"Here?" Azure asked, a queasy feeling stirring in her stomach.

Timechantress smiled and sighed. She looked straight at Azure. "Yes, Azure, your assumptions are correct: You have already met two of them: Antichilles and Tyran! Xestina *is* actually mine and Cirrius'; our own baby," Timechantress confirmed, half-laughing. "The twins belong to Archron sired in some forgotten village on the way to some battle. Cirrius stole them away while their mother slept and brought them back with him." She paused to let the information sink in.

Urana shook her head in disbelief. "No, Cirrius would never steal younglings. Never!" Her eyes misted over.

"And yet he did," Timechantress reiterated. "Celestra and Cirrius arrived early in the boys' time line. Rather than risk alerting the Lore to their prolonged presence by travelling through Earth's timeline, they took them as younglings. And what is more, the boys do not know they are not ours and not brothers to Xestina. They remember nothing of Earth. We genetically changed their hair to match ours and raised them as our own. Cirrius trained them and doted on them as if he were their father. He *is* their father."

Her face fell. "Was," she whispered. "And that was the secret Cirrius said he would take to his grave." She stared off into the distance again, not wanting to meet the eyes of the Starguards.

Urana twisted and sat down heavily in a chair, trying to digest all the information Timechantress had revealed to them. She shook her head as the import of it all hit her.

"You Astrals are monsters. You think you are Gods roaming time and interfering with lives. And to involve my brother. . ."

"Involve him?" Timechantress shouted back. "It was all his

idea! He contacted us Astrals first. He suggested I send some Starguards to Earth, he created the Astral detector, he stole the children while they slept, he wanted to be as much a ruler as Netherlord and Archron, and he would have been more successful than either of them," she hissed. "He was a great man planning ahead for all our security and lives. . ."

"But now he is dead!" Urana finished.

Timechantress was quiet. "Yes, he is. But he does not have to be and we can be far greater in number if he could continue his work."

"You mean change time and let him steal more younglings from Earth?" Azure asked, exasperation in her voice.

Timechantress nodded. "Yes, but you make it sound so sordid. Saving Astral kin from ancient Earth is not bad. Look, the Astral children will live longer, but look much younger than their human contemporaries. If people found out who they were they could be ostracised or even killed. Worse still they may use their powers for ill. We are protecting future Astral kin from themselves, protecting them from their enemies, and protecting Earth and Magna Aura. The Astral children belong with us. Surely you can see that!" she pleaded.

They stirred uneasily. Youngling lives were at stake either way.

"How many younglings are we talking about?" Novan asked.

Timechantress shook her head. "I'm not sure, ten, maybe more and depending on if they have had children as well." She stood uncomfortably and faced them, exposed, fearful, hopeful.

The Starguards bowed their heads in thought.

Decion's grasp on his sword softened.

"So where is this Astral detector now?" Urana asked the question on everyone's mind.

Timechantress shrugged. "You know Cirrius, always planning, always building something; it is probably in his lab under his island."

"My brother had a lab under the island? Here?" Urana rolled her eyes, "What a surprise," she added sarcastically. "I always wondered where he disappeared to, as if the island was not secluded enough!"

"Typical hermit," Decion scowled.

Urana said. "Where is it then?" She started to make her way to the rear of the room to the transtube which led to Cirrius' lab below.

Timechantress didn't move. "Um, no; his other island. Vavasar." She almost smiled at the revelation. "It is a secure Sky Warrior post in the south given over to Cirrius during the war with the Amethystians," Timechantress explained.

"Another island?" Urana shrieked. Her eyes raked over Timechantress. "All these secrets!"

Novan intervened. "Forget it. We need to move on."

Agreed," said Azure. "So, we find this Astral detector and we won't need Cirrius?" she asked.

Sheer disdain dripped from Timechantress.

"Are you that cold that you do not care for the life of a fellow Starguard, Azure? You, the daughter of the Traitor Synther who the other Starguards took in as family at the behest of Cirrius. Do you hate him for what he did? No matter his faults, he helped save all of us during the first Lore invasion and then fended off the Amethystians until his death. Does that mean nothing to you?" She turned to all the Starguards. "Cirrius deserves a second chance of life..."

"Third chance," corrected Azure with a curled lip, keenly aware that all eyes were on her. "Or did you forget you already changed our timelines once before!"

Timechantress glowered at Azure, her temper rising. "Why you...!"

She made to charge at Azure, but Decion raised the lancesword one-handed stretching halfway across the room to bar the Astral's way.

"Stop it, both of you," Novan shouted. "Right, now, we vote. All in favour of restoring Cirrius to the timeline, say aye!"

INTERLUDE 2

The Continuing Extra-dimensional Adventures
of
Alpha Rion and Chalant

THE HERO SIEGE

"I am Primerion," announced the middle-aged black-haired woman, "daughter of Priorion and Astari." The red-and-black-clad warrior presented herself calmly before Alpha Rion and Chalant. "And I can tell you are kin of my clan."

Her deep blue eyes crinkled in a warm smile as she pointed to Alpha Rion with the large sword in her hand. She sported a couple of short slanting healed scars across her right cheek, but other than those flaws, she was tall, almost as tall as Decion, and a doubtless warrior of the Alpharion clan.

Inwardly, Chalant was surprised. While they looked young, she knew they had to be several centuries old, the eldest, presumably being Primerion.

Alpha Rion nodded, almost feeling the need to bow. Priorion, son of Celennius, had been the leader of the Celestri Knights and progenitor of the Rion clan. Alpha Rion glanced at Primerion's sword and saw it was the precise one which had drawn his attention to the portal in the Fortress leading him and Chalant to this world. He remembered that Primerion's mother, Astari, had been the daughter of Cen Stari. The consort of Priorion able to wield energy in any form.

"We are honoured to meet you," he replied as he and Chalant politely greeted Primerion's companions.

Primerion turned to her right and introduced a young boy, half-hiding behind her. "This is my son, Omrion," she announced with obvious pride.

The boy, perhaps in his early twenties, wore black armour with red trim at the joints. His downturned eyes and dark swarthy features made him look sullen, almost like a young Decion, Alpha Rion half smiled to himself. Omrion solemnly nodded in greeting, but remained silent.

"Hellon," the blue armoured warrior who stood akimbo beside Primerion, introduced himself. "Son of Teo Venga, the son of Haven Mark, and of the Goddess Azurzura the sacred daughter of Helestra and Zen Horol," he boasted with aplomb.

There was something Alpha Rion instinctively didn't like about Hellon, until he realised that with his blue armour, black hair, and dark eyes, he reminded Alpha Rion of Synther in his corporeal form. He banished those thoughts quickly, not wanting to prejudice his feelings toward potential allies.

Alpha Rion could also tell that from his protective stance and her manner toward him, that Primerion and Hellon were a couple.

Holding out his left arm, Hellon then introduced: "Korelestra and Alturi, my cousins, daughters of the awesome Thronen Kor, the son of Hieryon, and the daughter of the soul destroyer of awful beauty, Zen Devestar, twin to my mother."

Alturi and Korelestra smiled in unison, Alpha Rion knowing that they were probably as close as he and his twin sister, Astara, had been. He knew their bond and how formidable it could be. Korelestra, with pretty feminine lines and features unlike Primerion, had short curly black hair and black sparkling eyes. She shimmered with a bright energy, before taking corporeal form again.

Fairer and taller than her sister, Alturi rolled her eyes at Korelestra's display. Smiling widely, she said, "It is good to see others from our world here." Her long brown hair bounced as she talked.

Alpha Rion would have corrected her about Tera's origins, but he waited for the rest of the introductions.

From the Tomes of History, Alpha Rion knew that their father, Thronen Kor, had been Priorion's right hand man in battle. Their mother, Zen Devestar, was a sorceress. Hellon's mother Azurzura was also a mystic, while his father, Teo Venga the son of Haven Mark, was once the wielder of the Havensword, which was lost in time and war.

Chalant stood close beside him, memorising names, impressed by the warriors' statures and their family lines. She now looked at the last warrior to introduce herself.

"Spheron, son of Spheron, the son of Spheron, and of Ulix the hyperpsi, daughter of Ori Archos."

>*Another Spheron*< Chalant psyed to Alpha Rion, suppressing a smile.

The olive-coloured-skin Celestri was crowned with greying hair. He surprisingly bowed to Alpha Rion and Chalant where the others had held a lofty haughtiness. His bright green eyes shone with wisdom and friendship.

"You can call me Uri," he said.

The others laughed.

"A youngling nickname," he explained for the travellers. He smiled as he gazed over at Alturi, Alpha Rion and Chalant understanding now both the nature of their relationship and similar name share.

Alpha Rion's face was a picture of surprise and dumbfoundedness. The Celestri Knights had been lost in battle during the time of the Hero Siege, a Dark Age in Celestri history. It had been these heroes which the Celestian Knight, Zater Jen, had tried to find before he, too, had been lost.

Alpha Rion was about to ask what had happened to them when Primerion spoke.

"So, Alpha Rion, you are a warrior to behold. Are you here to rescue us?" She turned to Chalant, before he could answer. "And who is your consort?"

Alpha Rion almost stammered, not expecting such a question from her. "Er, this is Tera ZaVoir, also known as Chalant. She is from a world called Earth."

Chalant smiled back in greeting.

There was an uneasy stir among the Celestri, though Alpha Rion wasn't sure if in reaction to her name or her origins, but he continued.

"But I don't understand how you are here. Your parents disappeared millennia ago. And how did you know my name?"

Primerion cocked her head at Omrion, Alpha Rion understanding. He was a psi, another sorcerer of the mind, like his own brothers, Novan and Solandus.

"How did you get here?" he asked again. "The Scrolls of History recorded your parents were all lost in battle against a mysterious enemy. And," he hesitated a bit, "there was no mention of younglings."

Hellon guffawed. "Lost in battle? Mysterious enemy? Do not believe everything you read, especially in the Scrolls of History."

Primerion confirmed this. "No, Alpha Rion, there was no battle. Azurzura had felt a strange force emanating from the region where Amethystia once existed. The Celestri Knights investigated as they thought the Great Enemy were trying to open a portal back into our universe. But instead they were sucked into a once-dormant portal and stuck here. There was no escape..." Her voice trailed off in sadness.

Alpha Rion knew he had to ask the obvious question. "So where are the Celestri Knights now?"

"They are dead, Alpha Rion," said a new voice.

Chalant and Alpha Rion whirled as one toward the voice.

"Hallo brother," Solandus greeted Alpha Rion, strolling leisurely toward them. His hair was long and golden-white, ever like his mother's Elysius, with coppery skin. He was leanly built, but he still had his boyish looks about him. The grin on his full lips seemed to mock Chalant.

"Solandus!" Alpha Rion rushed his brother, not sure if he was going to hug him or to strangle him. But as he went to throw his arms around Solandus he passed right through him.

Solandus laughed. "Yes, unfortunately, I am still physically a prisoner, brother, right where your consort left me," he said with a slight sneer toward Chalant. "I never thought to see you again," he addressed her, "much less with my brother, but I must say he has chosen a worthy woman. I salute you, Tera ZaVoir, Archeress, Chalant of the Gravan, imprisoner of Celestians." He bowed to her in mock salute.

Chalant ignored his jibe. "So, you've learned how to project yourself from your physical body. That's impressive," she admitted, silently curious about his accusations against her.

"I have had almost a century to learn. I can explore, as I want to, but without the hassle of being seen by the Gravan."

"A century?" Alpha Rion was more than shocked. "You have not been gone that long from Magna Aura!"

"On Earth it was over nine hundred years since I last visited here,"Chalant blurted out.

"I have been here for close to a century now," Solandus confirmed. "The Celestri arrived at least a millennia ago."

Primerion nodded, looking sad. "Our parents were old when they arrived, now we are old. Omrion could be the last of our line."

She ignored Uri's and Alturi's bemused expressions. She doted on Omrion.

"And the Celestri disappeared millennia ago," Alpha Rion said. "I don't understand how we can all be here together!"

Solandus and Primerion smiled, though they did not elaborate further.

"Whatever the cause," Solandus said, "we are all stuck here."

Alpha Rion and Chalant were silent as they digested this news.

"There is so much to know." Alpha Rion wanted to sit and talk but the room was devoid of furniture. "But first, brother, why did you try to subjugate the Gravan and fight Chalant?" Alpha Rion asked.

Solandus let out a harsh breath in exasperation. "I did not try to subjugate the Gravan. I just wanted the manecrown. It is ours after all."

"Ours!" exclaimed Alpha Rion.

"It is Celestian technology," his brother calmly stated.

"That cannot be!" Alpha Rion raised his arms in disbelief.

"Nonsense," argued back Chalant. "The manecrown has always been in the Gravan possession. Graagan told me."

"Yet, it is Celestian," Solandus reiterated. He walked around the room between those assembled. "I left Magna Aura to explore on my own swordship, along with a crew of fifty. We were meant to return within ten years. However. . ." His voice turned sad, "before we turned back, I cast my mind out as far as

I could to discover if there were any other civilisations out there. I sensed none. We were alone. But at the point of returning, I heard a voice. It called me. It enchanted me and drew me inward. My crew tried to warn me, to stop me, but I did not listen. They all abandoned the sword to return to Magna Aura leaving me alone as I searched for this voice. . ."

"They all died then," Alpha Rion lamented. "None of your crew returned to Magna Aura! We thought you lost too!"

Solandus cast his eyes down, genuinely distraught at the news. "I am sorry," he hung his head. "They were a strong crew and deserved more. But the voice. . . the voice. . . compelling me was so strong that I had to obey it. I followed the course it led me on and I somehow found myself in a new sea of stars, another universe."

"How?" Alpha Rion asked.

Solandus shrugged. "I just did. The voice was like a beacon."

Primerion intervened. "There are many holes in the universe, Alpha Rion. There are beings who can see or sense them and use them for their advantage. But that is not all. We were young when Solandus found us, our parents dead even then, but we were not the first Celestians here," she said pointing at the walls of the pyrathedral.

"Did you recognise the writing on the pyrathedral walls or note the technology?" Solandus asked his brother.

Alpha Rion nodded, "Celestian, but I didn't recognise the language. You didn't build them?" he asked of Primerion.

Primerion indicated not. "No, but it is ancient Celestian script."

"I don't understand." Alpha Rion was about to say that was impossible, but he had said that too many times already. This universe was impossible.

A sly smile twisted Primerion's mouth as she revealed the mystery, "It is Amethystian!" The Celestri smiled in anticipation of Alpha Rion's response.

Alpha Rion snorted. "Amethystians? Here?" He hung his head in resignation. "Impossible!" he said more to himself.

There was an air of amusement as he looked back up at the Celestri.

"How can this be?" Alpha Rion asked. "The Amethystians were wiped out by the Elerae millennia ago. It's in the Scrolls of History! Isn't it too much of a coincidence that they, we, and the Celestri ended up here?" he asked.

"No," answered Hellon. "Our parents discovered many things about this universe. It is a bubble universe. It is finite. Go to the universal horizon and you end up in the same place you started from. And more to the point, time does not run as linearly as it should. There are time pockets and loops, areas of static time, and even reverse time," he explained. "The fact that this universe is a finite bubble, has differing temporal regions, and connects any number of universes, suggests to me that this universe is artificial. Someone made it; someone perhaps experimenting with universal creation."

He looked at Alpha Rion who's mouth was no doubt open in shock. But more was to come.

"And further, I think all the universal stresses point to the fact that this universe is breaking down. There is only a finite amount of time left. We have to escape, but can't!"

Before Alpha Rion could ask why, Solandus continued the Celestri's tale. "This universe at some point connects our original universe with Magna Aura's universe with Chalant's universe and who knows how many more! I think the Amethystians built this universe not just to escape the Elerae attack, but to explore and also experiment, maybe even to plan revenge!"

"Revenge on the Elerae?" Alpha Rion asked. "But that would mean they know where Magna Aura is."

He felt sick to his stomach. Astara could be in danger right now. He sighed heavily. It was a lot to take in.

"So this universe is artificial and was created to nurture some sort of Amethystian colony or civilisation while they planned their revenge?" Alpha Rion mooted. "And what of this experiment you speak of?"

Solandus replied, "We think not only did the Amethystians build this universe and recreate themselves here." He then looked at Chalant, none too easily. ". . . but we think the Gravan might be artificial as well, in a way; they do not act as normal beings. They were part of the experiment, but we do not know if the experiment was by the Amethystians or Sentity."

"What's a Sentity?" asked Alpha Rion.

Again Solandus faced Chalant with a steely gaze. "I learned a lot while imprisoned," he said to her by way of some explanation. "You want to know more about this Sentity and why I blame you for my imprisonment?"

Chalant's dry lips barely moved as she said, "Yes, I do."

Solandus' mouth twitched in barely concealed anger.

"When I arrived here, the voice, a feminine voice, had disappeared. Whatever portal projected me here, I could not find it to escape. I was trapped. I had to find out why. The Gravan were a primitive civilisation arising after the Amethystians left." He pointed helpfully to the script on the walls which told the story. "They were friendly to me when I arrived, but then I discovered the manecrown in one of their temples." His face turned rueful. "The Gravan had forbidden me in their funny psi way not to enter the temple. The buildings were sacred and had been built by Sentity."

"And who is Sentity?" a frustrated Alpha Rion asked again, waving his hands about.

"Impatient," Chalant cracked at him, shaking her head.

"I'll get to that," Solandus said, "but first, as you would have guessed, I ignored their warnings. I was just drawn to the Manecrown. When I examined it, I could clearly see that it was made from original Celestian crystalators. It is really a powerful psychokinetic device, a defensive weapon, the Amethystians must have made it to control or protect themselves from Sentity, whom the Amethystians and Gravan regarded as a Goddess. That was what I was trying to find out. But the Manecrown was too powerful for me and as you know made me a bit crazy. That was when the Gravan turned against me. One of them, Graagan,

I know now, had followed me and raised the alarm. We had fought over the Manecrown and we somehow triggered the portal and off popped Graagan. And somehow he had called for Tera ZaVoir to fight me."

Chalant was stunned. "A group of humans called the Hunters sent me here," she replied. "But now that you mention it, how did I get back to Earth after?"

"That is the question," Solandus smiled at her for the first time. "These Hunters you mention, what type of portal did they use?"

A flash of understanding hit Tera. "The Hunters, or Exmoors to give them their family name, are descended from Celestians. They still have Celestian crystalator technology."

"So their portal was attuned to this universe. I could have used the Manecrown to attune the portal back home, but you stopped me," Solandus pointedly said to Tera. "And in doing so you also entrapped the Celestri. You became the Gravan's Chalant, their champion and Goddess, in place of Sentity. Then you left them. For a long while they felt betrayed. And now you have returned. But during your absence they have deteriorated and I think they are dying with this universe."

"Poor things," Chalant gasped, though she had sensed Graagan's weakness.

"Once you imprisoned me and threw the Manecrown away, I could not help the Celestri nor they I."

"Why not?" Chalant asked, more and more intrigued by Solandus' story.

Solandus smiled wearily. "It is better if I show you."

Solandus concentrated. There was a flash of light.

When the light disappeared, Chalant and Alpha Rion gasped in astonishment. They were greeted by a view of high snowy mountains.

"Another pyrathedral?" Alpha Rion guessed. "We were ported out?"

"Yes," Solandus answered. He pre-empted Chalant's next question. "The whole chamber, the metal panels are the portal power source and threshold emitter." He grinned at the theatrical nature of his announcement. "Every pyrathedral interior and control interface is different as if to seemingly confuse non-users."

"Or Sentity," Chalant guessed.

"Perhaps," Solandus said.

"This is a different world in this universe, devoid of any life," Primerion explained. "The world on which my parents landed, where they resided for centuries, and where we were born. We did not know about Solandus until he reached out with his mind in captivity and Omrion heard him. Then we learned how to use the portals to travel the few worlds left in this universe."

"And so when the manecrown was lost, it was the one object which could have helped us boost our psychic abilities, map the portals, and possibly find the hidden exits from this universe," Solandus added.

Chalant turned to Alpha Rion. "Perhaps Amagesh can help us," she said to him. She turned back to Primerion. "Have you explored the Gravan's world or come across other beings? There was an alien on another continent named Amagesh. He told us we might find others of the mind across the ocean. Perhaps he can help us."

The Celestri shook their heads.

"There was no one else in this entire universe besides the Gravan and us," Solandus confirmed.

Alpha Rion and Chalant looked at each other perplexed.

"How can that be?" Chalant asked, mostly to herself.

Primerion shrugged. "We have never revealed ourselves to the Gravan so they cannot know about us," Primerion replied. "Tell us more about this alien."

A stunned Chalant was sure they would have sensed him. "Amagesh was quite a powerful psi and lived across the ocean with these metal creatures who fed off energy."

Alpha Rion cut in. "Come to think of it, he did tell us not to mention him to anyone else."

"Do you think he has something to do with all of us being

together?" Primerion asked. "We have not sensed him, not even Omrion. Perhaps this is worth investigating." Her mind seemed set.

"Yes, we should visit Amagesh again," Chalant agreed. "I'm sure he has some answers."

"And don't forget this Sentity being. If she's as powerful as you mentioned, she could be behind this as well," Alpha Rion said. "May I ask what happened to your parents?" He eased himself against the wall.

Primerion did not answer, but looked at Solandus. He looked at his brother and Chalant revelling in his showman's role. His eyes dropped to the floor and he traced his right foot along a circular path on the smooth stone floor. At intervals he stabbed his foot in regular taps and swirls. Suddenly, a slab of rock with a star-shaped top rose with a grinding noise. It stopped at waist-height and Solandus twisted his right hand, psychically turning the stone clockwise.

"And here we go," he cried out, as the portal light took them on a journey.

Sure enough, almost instantaneously, they found themselves back in the Pyrathedral on the Gravan world. The metal panels slid back up, revealing the stone underneath.

Without a word, Primerion walked to the wall. She pointed a section of it.

"So, Alpha Rion, to answer your previous question—what happened to our parents? She did." She started reading part of the script on the wall: "'Sentity created all things: She spoke existence into being. Sentity wrote the secret signs and the codes of the universe, she knew the spirits and songs of magic. She is made of the universe. But her words turned against her. And there was war. And the war goes on, forever and forever and ever: The Great Universal War'. Or that is how the script states. Sentity is the Goddess of the universe."

"I'm confused," Alpha Rion said. "Did the Amethystians create Sentity or was she already here?"

Primerion laughed. "Both," she grinned further. "Sentity

seems to have been some form of proto-life sent through a portal to create a universe for whatever reason. Then when the Amethystians had to escape the Elerae attack they used the universe. By then Sentity had developed beyond her programming taken on an energised form by herself or with Amethystian assistance and the Amethystians either willingly or unwillingly worshipped her. Until one of them turned on the other."

"What happened to the Great Father, Holy Mother, and the Storm of Stars? They made the universe!" Alpha Rion cited.

"You're quite the dogmatist, Alpha Rion. This is a different universe," Hellon answered. "The Goddess here is Sentity and she wanted to escape."

A small pit opened up in Alpha Rion's stomach. "I see."

He looked around the room anxiously, focussing on the texts, finding the end where the script turned into the familiar modern Celestian language where the Celestri had ended the story.

"And where is this Sentity now?" he asked.

"For everyone's sake," Primerion replied, "She had better be dead!"

CHAPTER SEVEN

Deep space

". . . Novan of the Starguards, please respond. I repeat, this is Novan of the Starguards hailing the High Commander of the Amethystian Worldfleet. Please respond. . ."

High Commander Amethadaalus' aide looked toward his leader seated on his bridge dais as the Starguard's message came in over the comms system.

Amethadaalus considered the message. Clearly his own crew did not deign even responding to them, but he was willing to hear what they had to say.

"Let them speak," he commanded the Sci-control officer.

His bridge crew tensed, sensing weakness, but he ignored them.

"They are treacherous cowards. They will not retaliate. They can only talk from afar. Listen and learn about your enemy. Now let them speak," Amethadaalus barked his order again.

Halcyon

The Starguards stood crowded in Cirrius' underground island facility on Aqrius, the laboratory and replica of Sky Command's bridge. Here they were shielded from prying Halcyonite eyes and Amethystian sensors.

"I can't believe we're doing this," Urana said. "They killed my brother!"

"A lot more people will die if we do not resolve this now," Novan countered.

Cirrius' death had been confirmed with a vote, much to the violent dismay of Timechantress.

Azure had to render the Astral's temporal abilities void by violently disrupting time around Timechantress, knocking her out. Threatening to do far worse to her had quelled her children's lust for retaliation. From there the Starguards were able to confine them on Vavasar Island.

"Murderers!" a livid Urana had clashed with Novan.

Decion had intervened, his drawn lancesword convincing Urana to stand down. Her glowing fists and anger ebbing away in the face of Decion's and Astara's swords ready to protect their brother.

And it had not helped when Novan had almost provoked Urana again after he had then dared to order that the Starguards try to contact the Amethystians.

"Madness!" seethed Urana. Her eyes were wells of blue pools of tears. She sank into a chair drawing deep breaths, shivering from grief, shock, betrayal and anger.

Azure felt for her, but time was time. She went to console Urana, but a dark glare from her warned Azure off.

"We have to try another tack," Novan had warned them. "There is a way to end this with the Amethystians," he said. "There are references in the Scrolls of History. But it will demand a sacrifice from one of us!" He seemed rather bashful at this revelation.

Decion stepped forward. "Brother, I will challenge their champion in open combat until one of us is dead!" he proudly proclaimed. The other Starguards agreed, except for Novan and Sceptre.

"No, Decion," Novan replied. "Thank you for volunteering your services, but I did not mean combat and I know the Amethystians do not seek one on one combat either. I speak of the old Celestian customs of War Debt and Settlement."

"What war debt settlements?" Urana asked with suspicion, just as the main comms crystalator sparkled into life.

It revealed a striking purple-faced Amethystian. He had a high brow, highlighted by eyes which were wide with black accentuations around them. While his nose was long, his cheeks and lips were wide.

"I am High Commander Amethadaalus of the Amethystian Worldfleet. What is your desire, Novan of the Starguards?" he asked in the Old World custom.

"Hail, High Commander Amethadaalus," Novan responded in kind. "We desire permission to negotiate our war debt."

Amethadaalus smiled appreciably, impressed and nodding to himself.

"You are well-versed in the old Celestian law, Novan. I commend you. Celestian Knight, Starguard, or not, *you* are an honourable Celestian."

"What are you both talking about?" Urana interrupted with a whisper.

Novan turned to her, acutely aware Amethadaalus was listening. "How far are you all willing to go to avoid war?" Novan asked her.

The Starguards were quiet, wary of a catch.

Only Azure seemed alert, a nervous sweat on her brow.

Novan looked at Urana, speaking quietly. "Urana, as the sole family member of the deceased, not withstanding his widow, Timechantress, and also as a descendant of the aggressors, you would be obliged to marry an Amethystian in order to—"

"No!" Urana instantly protested. "Are you mad? I will not marry an Amethystian who murdered my brother, law or no law. I don't care about the history between our ancestors. I refuse to marry." Her thoughts turned to Altair. She wished he was with them.

Amethadaalus' face clouded over in indignation. "It is not for you to refuse. To end the war we will join our lines. You will produce an heir and those younglings will be the guarantors of peace. We accept your proposal, Novan."

Urana looked at him open-mouthed. "Younglings? You want me to breed. No!" Her hands burning in anger. "I cannot and will not!"

Amethadaalus' face broke out into a thin smile. "Treachery even within the Starguard ranks. . ."

He stopped talking as one of his crew approached, addressing him privately with a whisper in his ear.

On board Amethadaalus' ship, Sci-con's station monitors

had picked up a strange anomally approaching them: unidentified energy. He ran the calculations again. Having no luck, he signalled over to Talameth, Amethadaalus' trusted second. Together they studied the mysterious readouts with deepening frowns and then as inconspicuously as possible, Talameth approached Amethadaalus.

"Urana, please understand   how this is for the good of both Magna Aura and the Amethystians," Novan had whispered to Urana during the hiatus with Amethadaalus.

"I cannot. . ."

Novan was about to protest, but Urana persisted with desperation in her eyes.

"I cannot, because I am already with child!" she suddenly blurted out.

Complete silence filled the room. And from the screen.

"Oh, boy," Sceptre sighed.

Everyone stared at Urana's belly. She knew the question on everyone's lips.

"Altair," she quietly answered the unasked question.

Sceptre nodded, absently to the air, understanding her recent 'ailments' and visits to the medtechs. Novan's mouth opened and closed, while Decion wore a big grin.

"Altair?" Astara was shocked. "Altair! By all the Universe, why?"

Urana shook her head. "It just happened on Earth. . . I . . . we. . ." She couldn't finish.

"A forty-year pregnancy," joked Decion. But no one laughed.

"You insult us!" a laughter born of cynicism and hatred spilled from Amethadaalus. "You would give us this soiled woman as a prize?" he shouted. He turned around and shouted orders to the bridge crew. "We will wipe you Starguards and the stained remnants of the Celestians from the memories of the Great Father and Holy Mother!" he vowed.

"Stop!" Azure stepped forward. "There will be no marriage

and there will be no war. I'm tired of this," she said. "High Commander Amethadaalus, how many swords do you have?" she asked.

The question took the Amethystian by surprise, "Who are you, whelping, to ask such a question?"

"I am Azure of the Starguards," she proudly announced. "And I ask you again."

Amethadaalus regarded Azure through the screen. The aide had re-appeared at his side with a small comms pad.

"I will not reveal the totality of the ships that the Amethystian civilisation resides, toils, and battles upon. However, we have more than enough to destroy you. We are not natural planet-dwellers now, so we build more swords as the population grows. Who are you to ask, little one?" he addressed Azure.

"We know your location." Azure looked him straight in the eye on the screen. "And I imagine you already know some of your swords are missing. Check their numbers, now," she demanded.

Amethadaalus looked at her with disdain and a furrowed purple brow, laughter on his lips.

"I do not understand."

"Check the number of your swords," she reiterated slowly for him.

Amethadaalus' aide looked at his crystalator, his lips parting discernibly. He passed the crystalator to Amethadaalus and whispered something into this ear.

"That is not possible," Amethadaalus growled lowly.

Azure walked forward. "Yes it is and I did it; fifteen of your swords are missing. And I will make them all disappear if you do not leave now."

Amethadaalus hesitated, puzzlement mixed with rage on his face.

Azure counted to ten in her head.

"Count again," Azure said through gritted teeth. Her fringe started to mat on her forehead from sweat.

Amethadaalus looked at his crystalator. "Twenty five more!" he grimaced in bewilderment.

"How many more need to disappear?" Azure asked as confidently as she could.

The Starguards gathered around her in support.

Azure felt weak. She had been surreptitiously pushing Lore energy toward the Amethystian fleet. It was diffused among their ships, but thinly. It was taking everything she had to port them away.

Amethadaalus stood defiantly, staring out of the screen at Azure. His chest heaved in anger, his face grew purpler.

"Bring the fleet around. We depart," he ordered.

"Thank you," said Azure, but then she added, "But I can take care of your travel arrangements."

Her eyes flashed a vivid blue and she disappeared in a flash from the lab.

"Oh, Universe!" gasped Urana.

Before she had even finished uttering the words, Azure had appeared on the Amethystian bridge in front of the High Commander.

"Don't come back," Azure advised in a calm voice.

She pushed her arms outward and Amethadaalus and the Amethystian ships disappeared from the screen. The holo-screen in the lab went blank.

Someone behind Novan laughed. He didn't care who.

Azure's portal suddenly opened amongst them. She took a deep breath, sweeping her moist hair backwards. She shook off a tremble and leaned against a bench.

"Well that was impressive," Decion howled with laughter.

"Where did you send them?" a more relaxed Urana asked, grateful she wasn't being married off to Amethadaalus.

"I don't know," Azure said. "I just sent them as far away as possible." She slumped down against a bench top, exhausted.

"Are you all right, Azure?" Sceptre asked. He helped her to a chair.

She nodded; a weak smile on her face. "Just feel a bit light-headed, that's all. Think I moved far in excess of what I am used to."

"How did you do that, even from here?" Novan asked.

"I'm entangled with Lore energy," Azure explained, trying to wrap her own head around the idea. "I realised I don't even have to be in contact with it. I can just sense it, move it, shape it; whatever I want." She caught her breath and sat up straighter, her strength already returning.

Sceptre asked her sotto voce: "What happens when all the Lore energy gets used up, will you powers go?"

Azure shrugged. "Wish I could answer that, but I do not know."

"Well I am glad you were able to help," Novan stated, geeing up Azure's spirits.

Urana rounded on Novan, pulling hard on his shoulder.

"No thanks to you! How dare you try to marry me off against my will," she shouted at Novan. "Why would you do that?"

"Because we have to end this before it really starts and we lose more Magna Aurans or Starguards," he calmly replied. "But now we may have a little time to regroup."

Urana sulked, sucking her teeth. She would never be used as a bargaining piece even if it meant peace. She shook her head in disappointment and walked away.

Novan looked at the other Starguards, their faces a mixture of sympathy and amusement.

He turned and called to her. "Urana, congratulations, by the way," he said by way of conciliation. "I am happy for you."

She sighed heavily offering a weary smile. She felt better, the weight of her secret giving her some respite from the nightmare of Cirrius' death.

The other Starguards gathered around to also offer their praises.

"So, you and Altair," Azure pursed her lips, suppressing a smile.

Urana smiled, feeling somewhat embarrassed. "Yes, I know, a bit of an odd pairing, but I'm happy."

"As you should be," Sceptre said, trying not to sound judgemental.

"A cousin of a predicament for sure," she said.

They laughed at their in-joke.

"No, not at all," Sceptre reassured her. "And I know Altair will be proud when he returns."

Urana hugged him. She backed off, thanking Sceptre with a squeeze of his hands.

"So, what now?" she turned to Novan.

At least we tried to make peace," Astara said.

Novan grimaced. "Yes, but while the Amethystians were seemingly interested, Urana could not be. Her pregnancy... complicated the situation. So not only have her ancestors almost destroyed their race, her descendants will no doubt make peace impossible. That will not go down too well with them," he sighed. "We may have to involve Timechantress."

"No!" protested Urana. "Why?"

The other Starguards also voiced their dismay.

"She knew Cirrius better than we did," he rebutted Urana's unvoiced opinion on that, "at least over the last few years. He may have had a plan. She may help us with it."

"I doubt it," Urana countered, crossing her arms in annoyance.

"If she does not want to, I will make her," Decion happily announced.

Sceptre sighed, Astara shrugged, while Azure nodded in agreement.

"Any other questions?" asked Novan, staring around the room. He felt like he was in charge of younglings again. "No? Let us go then."

Azure ported them all to isolated Vavasar Island. It was a five-square kilometer black blob of a rock rising a hundred meters from the warm southern ocean's surface. Its remoteness and resilient structure had attracted Cirrius' attention as the perfect locale for a secondary lab for his research.

After finding and deciphering Cirrius' specs for the island

and labs following Timechantress' revelation at its existence, the Starguards had discovered the main reason for the secrecy. Cirrius had been experimenting with time. And the irony had not been lost on the Starguards as they had confined Timechantress and her children within underground anti-temporal cells, initially devised by Cirrius.

The dozen prisoner quarters lined a short corridor shielded and sound proofed from each other in closed-off cells. Azure suspected Cirrius had replicated Lore energy with crystalator receptors to create a localised time-loop which jammed temporal travel. The anti-temporal field generator sat above the stellecneum-metal cells in a suspended cone-shaped device pointed downward. Cirrius had prepared for an Astral invasion which had not materialised.

Decion voluntarily fetched Timechantress from her cell, stripped of her winged cape and crystalators, wearing a portable temporal restrainer around her neck, another Cirrius designed device. Her hands has been bound, at Decion's insistence; not that Timechantress would have been able to remove the restrainer as it was partially implanted within her neck. The crystalator was designed to deliver a nasty disabling shock should the restraint be tampered with.

The Astral bristled at the sight of them, until Novan told her what had happened with the Amethystians.

Her laugh was a bitter trill. "It was a mistake to send the Amethystians away," Timechantress drawled.

She slumped down on the corridor bench opposite the Starguards in the ground floor reception office. The domed roof was opaque against the sky, but the ocean waves could just be heard crashing against the island's sheer black cliffs below.

"Now they have time to work out your powers and defences. They know you now, Azure, and what you can do. They will not make the same mistake twice and will be sure to create temporal weapons or counter measures. They are Celestians, after all, and bound to create the same technology we have. They may even be able to create their own Sky Warriors or Starguard equivalents. Did you think of that, Azure?" Timechantress jeered.

Azure stared back in confidence, but inside she was crestfallen. She had not thought about it, but she knew the risk had been worth it.

"I sent them far enough away, but yes, we have around three years, five at the most, before they come back. The scouts could be here in two years. I had to take the risk. I could always spy on them and send them further away or maybe even to a different dimension if I could work out how to do that."

Novan pondered Timechantress' and Azure's words. "Both of you are right. We do not have much time, but we also need to develop ourselves and weapons. Decion, Astara, I am hoping we will be able to recreate the technology which allowed father to naturally open up dimensional portals. Maybe you could visit the weapons' fortress for any clues as to how we can use the portals."

"Enter the fortress?" Decion queried, a dubious face forming. He turned to Astara who had a knowing smile on her face. "Hmm, sounds like an idea Alpha Rion always had," he hurrumped. "Very well, we will try," he grumbled, much to Astara's satisfaction.

"We will have to do everything in our power to resist both the Amethystians and these Chronossii," Novan stated. "But most of all, we need to find the rest of the Starguards and the Astrals. Timechantress, we need more information to follow up on the Chronossii. If you tell us about Cirrius' Astral detector, I will free Celestra as a gesture of good will." He looked at Urana, who started to shake her head knowing what Novan was about to propose. "She and Urana will go to Earth to find the rest of the Astrals," Novan finished.

There were gasps of dissent from the two, but Novan silenced them.

"Urana, we know from our records that Celestra is as good as Lightstream at slipping past Lore senses," he said. "And during that period of Earth's past when the Lore were still a threat, you may need some fire power once there," he finished.

Urana thought about protesting, but Novan's demeanour took the edge off her anger. She inclined her head in confirmation.

"Do you agree, Zasandra?" Novan asked Timechantress, forcefully, arms folded.

Her long icy glare at Novan turned on Urana. Their eyes locked in mutual hatred. Timechantress' eyes flinched first. She looked down.

"Yes," she hissed.

Decion resisted the urge to state how good defeat looked on her. Instead he pre-empted Novan's nodded order and travelled down to the cells again to retrieve Celestra.

A few minutes later, she arrived struggling all the way in Decion's iron grasp. But upon seeing her mother in the room, she relented. She, too, wore a temporal limiter around her neck though her hands were not bound. Decion stood guard over her as she sat on the bench by her mother. The rest of the Starguards stood to the side of Decion. Novan again described to her what had happened and his plans for her and Urana.

He looked at Celestra. "I'm trusting you to not to try and escape. We need all the help we can get to fight these wars."

Celestra nodded and looked at her mother whose return glare was one of betrayal. Celestra ignored her.

"When on Earth should we go search; what time period?" Urana asked Celestra, doubts still in her mind that they could work together.

"There are several options," Celestra said. "The other Astrals are the elder children. I can't guarantee that I can travel to the exact time they lived. So, I can either stay in the ancient world to recruit the first few generations of new Astrals or travel time to collect as many other generations as possible, which would increase our Astral numbers, but possibly also alert the Lore to our presence and thus jeopardise Earth's history. Since you Starguards were on Earth, neither yourselves or the Hunters suspected or discovered other Astrals in the later centuries in

Earth, so either they all died out or we had already discovered and collected them from the past."

"I suppose that makes sense," voiced Sceptre, pondering the logic. "There were no signs of Astrals on Earth when we were there even if they did not know how to use their powers, I'm sure the Hunters would have come across latent temporal signals. I would suggest concentrating your search for them as younglings," he said to Celestra who bobbed her head in agreement.

Novan agreed. "Yes, retrieve them as younglings. They will be able to acclimatise more to Magna Auran life."

"And better to train," Decion added.

From her position on the bench against the wall, Timechantress warned, "Just be careful, Celestra, the threat of the Lore is ever present in the past, so be safe," she added, her stance softening somewhat, though her face was still a storm of emotion.

"I will, mother," Celestra seemed satisfied.

"One more thing," Timechantress addressed the Starguards. "If you did not already know, we discovered that Magna Aura and Earth are in different universes, existing in different spatial and temporal zones. Magna Aura inhabits an old elliptical galaxy, which we named Celestius, naturally. So while the Lore and Chronossii could pose a threat, the Amethystians would be hard-pressed to span universes to attack both Earth and Magna Aura, at least for a time."

There was a bit of a stir as the Starguards digested the information. They had not known if Earth and Magna Aura could be connected, but even if they were, the distance would be too far for humans to travel to Magna Aura, at least for now.

"That is quite a revelation," Urana conceded. Timechantress nodded curtly in response.

"Yes, thank you, Zasandra," Novan said: "With that mission set, I now need a volunteer to help me protect Elysiun and the rest of you will stay here to defend Magna Aura."

Decion and Astara looked at each other. "I will go," Astara

said. She looked at Timechantress. "I could do with the time away. Plus, Decion is needed to train the warriors and keep an eye on Antichilles, Tyran and Xestina."

"Good tactics," Decion agreed.

"Good," Novan replied.

But Decion was not finished.

"It would look suspicious if the young Astrals were not seen for so long. I would consider freeing them on their own recognizance as long as they behaved under curfew conditions and wore portable temporal limiters. They should be easy to conceal under their armour. But Timechantress will remain incarcerated as a guarantee." He looked down upon her daring her to refuse.

Timechantress stared back icily at him. She sighed after a few seconds thought. "Agreed. My children will behave under Decion's command," she stated to Novan rather than to Decion.

Novan considered her words silently. "Very well, we will grant your younglings' freedom."

Surprisingly, there was no dissent from Urana. She was standing over by Celestra, already contemplating returning to Earth. Decion backed away from Timechantress, a grim sneer as a warning.

Novan shrugged inwardly, glad the outright hostility had seemingly died down.

He asked Timechantress his last question, "Now about this Astral detector, where is it and what does it look like?"

Timechantress pursed her lips contemplating her answer. A raised back hand from Decion quickened her reply.

"The device is a crystalator embedded with Lore energy. The crystal sits within a short stellecneum rod, so there's no physical contact with the energy which can react adversely with the bearer."

"How does it work?" Novan asked, intrigued by the device.

Timechantress pulled a face, still reticent to answer. "Upon discovering an Astral or temporal energy it signals you or lights up, whatever you set it to do."

"Ha!" Azure laughed out loud. "I've found it!"

"What?" Urana and Timechantress blurted out together.

"I can detect a small concentrated source of Lore energy beneath the cells. I take it that's where Cirrius' other secret lab is?"

"You couldn't have told us before?" Decion drawled.

"I didn't know what I was looking for before. I have to tune it in, so to speak. Ready to check?"

They all looked at Timechantress. She sighed roughly. "I'll show you the way then."

Cirrius' second lab was located behind a secret door, disguised as a wall panel. Timechantress tapped in an intricate code on the top right of the panel and it dutifully slipped sideways. The lab was identical to the one on Aqrius.

"Definitely a hermit thing," Decion joked.

"Home from home," Azure joined in. She surveyed the room, then walked straight over to another wall panel at the opposite end of the room. "It's behind here," she confirmed.

Decion started to draw his lancesword ready to plunge it into the wall, but Novan stopped him.

"I have this."

Novan paced up to the wall, placing his hands around the area indicated by Azure. He worked his hands in a circular motion and pulled back. A cylindrical section of the wall slid out seamlessly at chest-height; a safe half a meter long. Novan looked back at Timechantress. She stepped forth and instantly a holographic pad appeared as if sensing her specific presence. The Astral entered a code. The lock clicked open. Inside the safe was the temporal anomaly detector. Novan picked it up by its metal handle.

"We'd better test it," Azure said, walking towards Novan to demonstrate.

She had barely moved toward him when the energy signature in the crystalator wavered in reaction to the presence of a temporal field, turning from a white light to blue.

"Well, that works," a happy Azure turned to everyone.

"Thank you, Zasandra," Novan smiled in appreciation.

Looking less than pleased with herself, Timechantress turned and leaned against a work surface. She wasn't ready to be re-incarcerated so soon.

Novan closed the safe's hatch and the cylinder slid quietly back into its carefully concealed hole. He handed the device to Urana.

"You ready?" he asked her.

Studying the detector, Urana nodded. "Give me an hour or so and I will be."

Agreeing, Novan proffered his hand to Timechantress. "Shall we?"

"When will my family be released?" Timechantress asked, her face not hiding her worry for her children. Shuffling to her feet they led her back to her cell.

"Once our missions begin. Celestra will be under Urana's supervision. For now you will be returned to your cell. Decion will remain on guard for the time being."

Decion's face glowered in dark joy, reminding Timechantress that any escape attempt would be most welcomed with severe punishment.

Novan and Timechantress shared a brief look of understanding across the cell's threshold, before he locked her back up.

"Farewell, brother, for now," Decion clasped Novan's arm.

Novan nodded and smiled.

Azure ported them back to Aqrius where they prepared for their various missions.

Once in Cirrius' home, Sceptre spoke up, asking Novan: "And what about me? You have not mentioned my role."

Novan looked a bit anxious, the other Starguards picking up on his mood. He cleared his throat.

"You made a promise to Millennius and Phasia that you would try and find the other surviving Celestian Knights. You must keep that promise and now seems as good a time as any for they may have younglings; more Starguards. I am sending you on a reconnaissance mission to find the Great Seal or another way into the Old Universe. You will attempt to break through or make contact with the other side, if possible. It is a long shot, but are you willing to try?"

There was silence as everyone thought about the implications. Not all of the Lore would have accompanied the Traitor Synther. They might have completely engulfed the old universe. There was a risk of releasing them upon themselves again.

Sceptre, however, had no second thoughts about it.

"I have been thinking about this mission for a long time. It's all planned in my mind. I will go alone for the initial reconnaissance, but if I find the Great Seal then I will return to take a greater force."

"Are you sure about this, Aerl?" Urana asked. "The Lore could be waiting to get through and then overrun this universe. We can't afford to fight enemies on three fronts," she argued.

Sceptre shrugged. "All the better for me to go alone. We have to try. There could be Starguard kin there waiting for us as well."

"That is true, but I would urge you to be accompanied by a small retinue," Novan said.

"Fine, I will outfit a small sword with crew," Sceptre said.

Azure spoke her mind. "Okay, with that sorted, I will help Decion here, but first I'll give Novan and Astara a lift back to Elysiun... Earth saying..." she laughed at their befuddled faces. "Then I will help Sceptre on his way. I might as well make the most of my power while it lasts."

The rest of the Starguards agreed.

"Our missions are set," Novan said. "And long may we survive!"

Deep space

On board the worldfleet flagship, there was stunned silence as the import of their predicament became clear.

"Three point four years to return to Magna Aura at full

velocity," sub-tech Temethis reported, looking at his instruments. "The entire fleet is intact, no damage or injuries reported. Your orders, High Commander?" He glanced anxiously at Amethadaalus. No one liked to deliver bad news to the High Commander. Beatings and/or demotions weren't so uncommon in such situations.

Amethadaalus' rage had subsided somewhat, but his surprise had deepened. Azure could have destroyed them, thrown them into a sun or a black hole. But she had not. And that had been her mistake.

"Continue to Magna Aura, quarter drive," he commanded. He saw the looks of surprise on his crew's faces. "They are not going anywhere so why tax our energy and our ships. Besides, we need to plan for Azure. Talameth, the techs will start on contingencies to counter Azure straight away!"

"Yes, High Commander," he bowed and with decorum rushed off the bridge to carry out the orders.

For a while, all was in order. Having had personal reports from his commanders, Amethadaalus found he could relax. He returned to his duty room just off the bridge. He was joined by his second.

"Would you have gone through with the war debt Novan offered?" Talameth asked as they sat drinking a glass of musky *takann*.

Amethadaalus' mouth twitched, a tell-tale sign he was in good humour. "The war debt is the way of the Universe. I would have been obligated to at least seriously consider it, but Urana was quite unsuitable. That Novan is a wily one. But it reveals their deceitfulness and weakness. They cannot be redeemed now. There is only war. Have faith. We will be rewarded for our patience. And we will destroy them!"

Amethadaalus' eyes gleamed with anticipation as he and Talameth clinked glasses toasting the end of Magna Aura.

CHAPTER EIGHT

"The child is gone," lamented the old woman.

The villager wore a dirty white linen garment and had been pruning the field's olive trees.

She sighed and said, "She was taken in the night, years ago, some say by Zeus himself." The woman chewed her gums. "Taken right up into the air." She looked up into the sky and pointed with her thin skeletal arm. The hills ahead were as sparse and rocky as the ones behind them in the hot dry summer.

East again, thought Celestra. *Same old story.* She thanked the woman and gave her some herbs, as promised. The old woman thanked her with a peck on her cheeks. She walked away to continue tending to her olives.

Now Celestra knew. Someone was collecting the children ahead of her. In her three weeks back on Earth, back in her homeland of ancient Greece, this was the fourteenth village Celestra had visited and the third to have any evidence that another Astral had gone missing, taken by an unknown person.

Coming to an understanding, Urana and Celestra had split up, the Starguard trusting and knowing enough that the search would be executed better if they covered more ground separately. Of course, it only took the implied threat of what would happen to her mother to convince Celestra to be helpful.

But as it was, Celestra was finding herself intrigued regarding the search. Someone had been here before them. The two travellers kept in comms contact, but it was only at night when they dared use their powers of flight. By day, Celestra was doing things the hard way, on foot or on horseback. Their manoeuvre suits had been dialled up to disguise them on their travels and their distinctive hair colours also altered. Urana had chaffed at having to appear to wear the loose fitting ankle length clothing of the day, but Celestra found herself comfortable in her *chiton* and cloak, just like in her youth.

Urana had possession of the detector, while Celestra felt she was sensitive enough to detect any natural temporal fields herself. Cirrius' preliminary results on his first visits had helped to produce a crude map of forty-seven possible sites, but so far she was out of luck. She wondered how Urana was getting on.

She made a note on her own crystalator's map for the next target or rather targets: two children near Argos, two days travel east by horse.

The horse she had practically stolen from an old soldier named Bemos. He had turned to selling the animals and was more stubborn than anticipated. Celestra was a lone woman wandering the mountainside and the retired stableman was indignant that a woman would want one of his horses to travel unescorted. He had waved his *petasos* at Celestra as if trying to swat a fly away. During the bargaining, Bemos' wife had also joined in the argument until he shooed her away. That was when a frustrated Celestra had given him a jolt of energy. He swore she was a Goddess and lo and behold the price dropped to nothing and one of the horses was hers.

Celestra set off just before nightfall and rode the stirrup-less horse just as her father had taught her a lifetime ago. The small, but sturdy chestnut horse was sure-footed and strong, but sometimes had a mind of its own wanting to return to Bemos' village or just stand and graze. However, with strong nudges and frequent kicks from Celestra her course was eventually followed. It was an old war horse, to be sure, but still full of some fire. She named it Decion.

After two uneventful days over bumpy hills, she cantered Decion into what she hoped was the target village in the bright early morning. But she encountered the same story upon her arrival as the previous villages. The boy had been taken at night by lights in the sky. This story had confused Celestra as Cirrius' report had indicated two children should have been here. She mentioned that to the villagers who greeted her.

"Ah, no," breathed a sad Soraclus, the village elder with the longest grey beard of the local elders. "The boy survived, but his sister died in childbirth. Tragic," the man shook his head in memory. "It affected the boy." He touched his head to indicate madness. "Maybe the Gods will look after him now," he seemed to rejoice.

"Maybe," Celestra returned his vacant smile with a weak one of her own.

Celestra was bade to rest and eat with Soraclus' family, which she accepted. She avoided too much talk about herself, though it was simple enough with the bearded man happy enough to talk for himself, his family, and the animals cluttering his farmstead. Three hours later, fed, watered, and ears full of stories of Soraclus' misspent youth, Celestra mounted the also rested Decion and trotted back into the hills. There was one more target left. The trail kept heading north-east and Celestra found herself tracking over vast swaths of land. She knew where she was going—

Olympus, of course, she sighed.

After several days of torturous climbing through the foothills, set back by one sudden storm, and retracing her trail after taking brief shelter, Celestra had to let Decion go. The horse gleefully rejoiced in not having to pick its way up the mountain.

"Good riddance, you stubborn bastard," cursed Celestra watching the receding spot on the horizon.

Climbing higher on foot and feeling over-heated and hungry, Celestra's mind seemed to play tricks on her with visions of being followed along the ridges. Several times she had stopped and listened, taking careful stock of her surroundings.

Then, half an hour later, to her left she clearly saw a woman with long brown hair, seemingly paralleling her path upwards. For an instant, Celestra and the woman stopped and eyed each other. The Astral tried to keep an eye on the other woman as she struggled up a hill in her long *chiton*, but slipped on some rocks, sending them scattering down the ridge. She looked up in alarm anticipating an attack. The woman was gone.

Celestra cursed herself for being careless and distracted. She rounded a rocky knoll and tried to find the woman again. There was no sign of her. She didn't want to have to call Urana over this, but as she raised her crystalator to signal, she felt a presence behind her. Celestra whirled around.

The stranger stood ten meters away further up the trail ahead.

"Who are you?" a shocked Celestra shouted at the woman.

The woman looked back at her with black eyes fringed by her wild brown hair and pretty features. She peered through Celestra's disguise. And then she smiled.

"Celestra," she stated flatly. "Why are you here?"

Celestra hid her surprise, her eyes narrowed in suspicion.

"How do you know me?" the Astral asked, disconcerted that she had been discovered. "But if you do, then you know I seek my kin!"

The young woman, also dressed in the local *chiton* with a long featureless cloak, regarded her as if mulling a decision.

"My name is Vostra. But you are not the Celestra I was told about."

A breezy laughter escaped Celestra's lips. "What does that mean? Who told you that?" Celestra's curiosity was raised.

Surreptitiously, she thumbed a nodule on her crystalator, which was disguised as a bead bracelet.

But Vostra continued to stare at her. "I was told you were different, but I can see your eyes no longer hold fear, suspiciousness and anger. They are mature, wiser, and content eyes. Yet, I still see pain behind them. We have heard stories of strangers seeking the children, perhaps to kill us as unwanted rivals." Her voice was soft, kind, but her eyes held a hard glint. "But now I can sense you need our help. Some great calamity must have befallen the other Astrals."

Celestra nodded, but then Vostra's words struck her.

"You're an Astral?" Celestra uttered in relief, overjoyed at finally meeting one of her lost kin.

Vostra gave a non-committal nod. "Come, we will travel faster if we fly." Without waiting, her athletic body, evident even under the cloth garment took to the air, Celestra having to follow. "We are camped far into the mountains. We have been training," she said.

"Training? Who is training you?" Then another thought occurred to her. "When in the timeline have I appeared?" Celestra asked.

Celestra was sure she and Urana should have been in her own Earthly past. If Celestra had met herself, she would be a toddler.

Vostra turned to Celestra mid-flight, scrutinising the Astral. There was a sad smile.

"You, your mother, father, and Archron have already betrayed your own Astral kin. You have scattered the Starguards on Earth. Not all of the first born of the Astrals will be pleased to see you, nor will they forgive you for abandoning us." She flew on in silence, Celestra wondering how Vostra knew this and what type of reception she would receive.

Suddenly, a thunderous crack shattered the air. Celestra knew what it was as she had heard it many a time, but Vostra lost concentration looking around for the sound and almost fell from the sky.

Celestra laughed. "Relax, Vostra. You're hearing the sound barrier being broken."

Vostra looked confused then realisation dawned on her. "You are not alone!" She looked around for the cause of the sonic boom.

Urana swept in from above carving a wide circle in the air around them. She stopped in mid-air in front of them.

She greeted Celestra. "Thanks for the signal. And who do we have here?" she turned to the stranger, who maintained herself in the hover.

"Urana, this is Vostra of the Astrals," Celestra introduced her.

"You are Urana?" Vostra asked, a mixture of familiarity and edge to her voice.

"I am," the Starguard answered, not sure how to take the question.

Vostra looked her over, apparently satisfied with the information. "Very well, it was so predicted. We will continue on to my village. Come."

She took to the air again, Celestra and Urana exchanging equally perplexed glances before following her.

Celestra was curious about one thing. "Vostra, how was it that one of the Astrals did not survive their birth?" Celestra asked.

At Vostra's puzzled look, she explained about the brother and sister she had been looking for.

Vostra looked taken aback, then her face brightened. "Oh no, his sister did not die," Vostra explained. "Human mothers are weak in this time. They are Fifths after all, primitive and in this case practically giving birth to Gods. Your fathers were almost constantly away at war. I do not think they ever returned or knew they had children in some cases. But no, Dyonus's sister did not quite die. Dyonus was born first, but Syene either by design or expedience transcended into a pure temporal energy form. She merged with Dyonus and resides in his mind. He is now psi-temporal."

Urana titled her head in thought at the term. "You mean he can send his sister's thoughts through time?" she questioned.

"I believe that is what I just said," Vostra answered with mild amusement.

"He can send thoughts through time," Celestra repeated. "That's so cool," she grinned widely. Then she remembered something, an old myth. "Seems rather appropriate Dyonus has this ability. It reminds me of the story of the birth of Athena and how she was born forth from Zeus' head! Dyonus and Zeus both have the same root name, so it is possible that he is the root of the myth. Send his thoughts through time!" Celestra was giddy with happiness. "I can't wait to meet them!"

"They, too," replied Vostra.

Urana thought she caught an undertone to the statement. She caught Celestra's eye, who had the same thought.

They continued flying upwards reaching a camp high up on the mountain. Urana spied a half-hidden village with a couple dozen round huts with pens for livestock dotted under the summit and fortified with ditches and palisades against intruders who would dare climb the already steep sides.

"Olympus!" exclaimed Celestra. "Not what I had in mind for the city of the Gods!"

Vostra directed them down and the three landed near a central hut.

"Vostra, sister, who do you bring with you?" a young man called out.

No sooner had he spoken then Urana and Celestra found themselves surrounded as figures emerged from huts and mounted knolls and ledges to gawk at the visitors.

"I have Celestra, the Astral, and Urana of the Starguards, with me. They have come from Magna Aura, seeking us out. They need our help!" She seemed to almost mock.

There was laughter from the others.

Celestra and Urana looked at each other. It wasn't the reception they had expected. These Astrals knew far more about them and Magna Aura than they ought to.

The laughter died down leaving an awkward silence.

"Hear us out, Astral kin," Urana started. "We do need your help. We are in danger, all of us. We are being hunted..."

"So you have come to save *them* at least," a familiar voice rang out from the centre hut.

Urana couldn't believe her ears. But when the man appeared at the hut's opening, she gasped.

"Cirrius! But, but. . ." she held back tears of relief.

"Did you think me dead, sister?" Cirrius asked rakingly.

The other Astrals converged around him, in protection.

"I heard about your vote; not to restore me to the timeline." Turning to the others around him, he declared, "See, I have told you the truth!" He faced Urana again. "I told them how you would betray me, let me die, and not even try and save me." His voice was bitter. "Well I did die at the hands of the Amethystians, a very painful death. But it was Vostra who saved me after you had all left me to rot in the ground," he sneered. "The humans say 'time heals all wounds'; that is what Vostra does. She is temporalempathic and can feel time, alter it, and even fix anomalies. Death is just a temporal anomaly to her, a temporal matter that can be fixed. So here I am." He held up his hands in triumph. "You expected me to be dead! Do you hate me that much?"

He casually walked down the sloping path to Urana, who silently shook her head, still in disbelief.

Cirrius spoke again. "Well, I had a contingency plan. I knew you would betray me and not let my wife bring me back from the dead. And you of all people," he angrily pointed at her, glaring, "would not fight for me!"

He practically stood nose to nose with his sister.

"That's not true!" Urana defended herself, not sure of her emotions. But she knew she missed her brother. She leaned over to hug him, but he drew away.

She looked for Celestra, asking for her favour. Celestra stared back at her, features unreadable. Urana pleaded with wide eyes.

Celestra's mouth quivered. "It's true. She fought for you like a sister would." She ignored Urana's look of gratitude.

"No, they are my family, now," Cirrius bellowed, indicating the young adults around him. "We look after each other and I train them."

"Train them in what? Are you training them with the Scrolls of History?" Urana asked.

Cirrius laughed. "Scrolls of History? This is the Ancient world, there is no reading or writing. This is the time of oral tradition, when myth held sway. There are centuries to go before writing is adopted and by then we'll be long gone and our exploits forgotten in the mists of time. No, we do not have the Tomes. I am teaching from memory."

Urana scoffed. "Your memory? I hope it is as good as you remember!"

"You mock me." He paraded around the cleared area on the small plateau. "She mocks me even now," he declared to those around him "We are in the distant pre-Astrals era," Cirrius continued. "Phasia has not yet taken Xathanius and the rest at Troy to become the Astrals. We are all alone here. And here there are no Astrals. There is only the Chronossii!"

Celestra started in recognition.

"The Chronossii?" Urana repeated, more to herself, before realising where she had heard that name. "But Timechantress told us they are the ones that attacked and took the Astrals!"

She realised what that meant.

"She was lying! Lying to us all this whole time." Urana's stomach felt empty, sick, and she wondered how much her unborn baby was affecting her emotions.

"That cannot be," Celestra's shock mirrored Urana's.

"What kind of person is she?" Urana turned to Celestra, trying to fathom both mother and daughter's motives.

"A great one," Cirrius answered. "A great actress. Did you know that before Phasia found the Astrals, Zasandra was an accomplished singer? She sang the old stories for the warriors before their wars, recounted the heroics of ancestors for kings, and beguiled foreign ambassadors with the prowess of their hosts. In another lifetime it would have been Zasandra who would have composed the Iliad and Odyssey instead of another poetess. Be that as it may, we planned this, Zasandra and I. The elder children of the Astrals should have been the true heirs; had their recognition been announced, but they were forgotten."

"That's a lie," Urana blurted out. "The Astrals never knew about them." She half-hoped to herself that that was the truth.

"No, Xathanius, the so-called Lord Aeon, made the decision and left their other children behind. He and Zasandra talked of it often. But only she constantly remembered them. Xathanius literally had all the time in the universe to return for them, but he did not. He was the liar, the deceiver, the abandoner. He would have left the Chronossii ignorant of their heritage and legacy."

"And Tyran and Antichilles, what about them and your lies?

Do you intend to tell them you are not their true father... or was that a lie as well?"

Cirrius looked at his sister. No love in his eyes. "They *are* my sons," he countered with venom. "But let me tell you about the Chronossii."

He turned to each one as he introduced them.

"You already know, Vostra, lost daughter of Helexius."

She waved back at Urana maliciously.

"Over there. . ." Cirrius pointed to a tall, bare-chested athletic male honed like a warrior, with brown hair and eyes, and a youthful beard, ". . . is Dyonus and within his mind, is his sister, Syene, the lost children of Lord Aeon."

Urana could see the resemblance in Dyonus to Xathanius even before Cirrius announced it. Dyonus for his part folded his arms and stared at her with mild interest.

"Spheron, the son of Spheron," Cirrius stretched his arm out to his right. He laughed, leaning forward to Urana as if to emphasise his words. "Yes, Spheron named his son Spheron. How traditional. Fortunately, Spheron here has taken on the name Phasion."

Phasion smiled as if enjoying his own private joke. He was dark skinned, bald and tall with large arms like his father.

"I hear I have a sister," Spheron said. "Does she still survive?"

Urana shook her head. "I do not know, but she is a credit to the Spheron lineage."

Spheron seemed to dismiss her. "Shame," he said.

Urana made a face at him.

Cirrius added, "And as for Antichilles and Tyran they are Archron's twin sons, but I have raised them as my own. And when we return to Halcyon we will free Timechantress and take over Magna Aura." He looked satisfied with himself, but took a conciliatory tone. "In the interests of the truth, the Chronossii had nothing to do with the disappearance of the Astrals. We truthfully do not know where they are. All Zasandra sensed was an alien energy, nothing like a temporal signature. Nothing else. So, we are now the guardians of time. That is it. And we are leaving."

Urana looked hurriedly at Celestra, who seemed rooted to the spot.

"Did you know about this?" an anxious Urana asked.

Celestra shook her head. "No." Her eyes were wide with surprise.

Nonetheless she took a step closer to the Chronossii. Urana didn't have to wonder where her loyalties lay.

Cirrius spoke to Urana again. "I, we, want you to join us, sister. We want you to help finish what our father wanted us to do, what Netherlord and Archron failed to do."

Urana shook her head vociferously. "You're crazy. The Storm of Stars are gone, Cirrius! They defeated us at the beginning of time, then disappeared. What more do you want? The Knights Destina path is dead!" she shouted at her brother.

Cirrius shook his head. "You do not understand all we have been tasked to do. This is not just about the Storm of Stars," Cirrius raised his voice. "We have our own galaxy now, yet we are hemmed in to one system, two, counting Novan's world. We can explore and become a conquering empire, an empire of time. The whole universe could be ours. It is what our parents wanted for us Starguards, Astrals, and Chronossii; to re-establish the Celestian worlds," his eyes gleamed at the future that was possible, fists clenched around a palpable reality. "And now we know about the Amethystians. They have played their hand and we can crush them as our ancestors intended!"

He regarded Urana with neither compassion or anger, Urana not recognising the person who stood before her. Had death really changed him or had she just been blinded to his ambition? As if sensing her thoughts he walked forward closer to her.

"And in the end, we Knights Destina will return." He chuckled. "I hear Aerl and Novan want to return home to our own universe and take it from the Lore. Well after they do we will take it from them and rule both universes as Gods! That is the destiny laid out by the Storm of Stars!" He looked at Urana expectantly who stared back defiantly.

Urana's laugh was a coarse choke of disbelief. "You're mad! All of you! No, I will not join you. I cannot!" Urana protested. "I will return to Magna Aura or the Ribbon System in peace. I am with child, Cirrius—Altair's child! And I will have no part in this!" Urana chopped the air in disgust with her arm and the other held her stomach. "Return me to Magna Aura. Now!"

"Altair," Cirrius spat his name, shaking his head. Hands on hips he looked at her with disdain. Turning his back on her, he motioned Dyonus over. "No, sister, you will not be part of this!"

Urana backed away from the group. "What do you mean? What are you going to do?" She braced herself for battle, summoning forth energy to her hands.

Cirrius looked at her. "I cannot have you and the rest against me. Not all of you together, at least." He shook his head as his meaning became clear. "You cannot go back. You are exiled here."

Urana looked around at the desperate terrain; at the Chronossii and saw no mercy in either one.

"But my baby!"

"Your baby will be safe," Cirrius assured her. "Your baby will ensure the cooperation of the rest and the seriousness of my intent!"

Urana grasped for words. *What did that mean?*

"Vostra," Cirrius nodded at her.

Vostra raised her hands towards Urana.

Urana felt strange. She tried to raise her arms to blast the Chronossii, but she could not move. She was held tight within temporal eddies. And then she felt a strange temporal affect not unlike a portal, but just surrounding her. It gave her vertigo.

"You see," Cirrius started, his voice sounding like an echo to her, "Vostra can also control localised time. And right now she is ageing you through seven months, give or take."

A horrified look materialised in Urana's eyes as she realised what was about to happen.

Vostra rotated her hands clockwise and Urana felt time twist savagely around her. She cried out in pain.

This cannot be happening, she thought. But she could feel her baby growing abnormally fast within her. She could hear herself scream, the sounds echoing away as time rushed around her. Another scream formed behind that and another, the sickening sound sucked away as if down a well only to bounce back at her.

Her view of the Chronossii was blurred and ultra slow, like living statues, expressions of aloof righteousness sculptured on their faces. The vertigo made her sick, and she stumbled in slow motion onto the ground. Her baby kicked inside. She retched within her own time bubble, the roil circling her.

"No!" Urana managed to scream at Celestra, not knowing if she could hear her. "Don't. . . don't let them. . . do this to me! Please!" she cried.

Celestra's face was a mask, only her eyes betraying the calmness she projected. She said nothing.

Urana's vision blurred as the baby continued to grow. And then all was still. She took a deep breath. She tried to calm herself, gather her strength, and try to escape. But in that split second as she marshalled her energies, her contractions started. Wave after wave of spasms recoiled through her vagina. She cried out in pain again and again.

"Celestra, Vostra, help her," Cirrius ordered.

Vostra released Urana from her temporal grip, Urana too weak to mount an offense. She had no choice now.

Celestra hesitantly followed Vostra's eager steps forward.

Without knowing Urana's crystalator command code for her manoeuvre suit, Celestra helped hold Urana still while Vostra manually unfastened Urana's uniform. Vostra then placed a crystalator over Urana's abdomen.

"It is coming," she said.

More contractions made Urana scream, her breath coming in shallow rapid puffs.

Vostra performed the procedure as Urana pushed. All Urana could do was look up into the bright sky, breathe, and pray to the Universe. There was one last push. Urana felt hands pulling, her lower body being tugged. There followed silence for agonising seconds. And then there was crying.

Vostra placed the newborn on Urana's chest.

A boy, she rejoiced. She hugged him, thinking of Altair and their joy. She was still mesmerised by her son, when Vostra leaned over, cut the cord with a knife, and carefully prised the baby from Urana's arms taking him away.

"What are you doing?" an angry Urana panted. "Give me back my son!" She made to get up, but was still groggy.

Celestra still held her down, her eyes wide with emotion—*guilt!* Urana realised.

Cirrius sauntered over to her. "I am taking him," he announced. "I will raise him as a true warrior and as insurance against you or the Starguards acting against us. You really should have joined us." His voice was thick with emotion.

He carefully received the baby from Vostra and cradled the boy gently, looking down on his nephew with fondness. The Chronossii had gathered around him and the baby. Cirrius gave Urana one last look.

"Goodbye, Urana."

Phasion initiated the temporal portal and then they were gone. The portal flashed closed with a finality not lost upon Urana.

She lay helpless, shattered, upon the ground, disorientated from both the post-temporal effects and the birth. She was all alone in the mountains. Night was approaching. She was hollowed out physically and emotionally. She had nowhere to go and no hope of escape to Magna Aura. And her son was gone, forever.

Trying to raise herself up, Urana collapsed to the ground in pain, sobbing uncontrollably.

Universe, help me! Urana's tears beseeched the cosmos, her sobs softly echoing around her.

INTERLUDE 3

The Continuing Extra-dimensional Adventures
of
Alpha Rion and Chalant

SENTITY

"So what happened to the Celestri Knights?" Alpha Rion asked Primerion, after her dire prognation concerning Sentity.

She looked at her son, Omrion. "Our preserver of memories."

Her son reached out his hands towards them. Images began to form in Alpha Rion and Chalant's minds.

Then they heard the soft voice of Primerion's father, Priorion.

Six hundred years ago

We had fallen through an undetectable dimensional portal orbiting the ruined Amethystia. Yet, while we may have been dead to our own universe, we managed to live here in peace for some time. And after a time we bore our succeeding generation here.

Alpha Rion and Chalant saw the Celestri as they were. Priorion was resplendent in the now-typical red and black armour of the Alpharion clan. Long straight black hair fell past his shoulders, a thin pointed beard framing his long chin, focussing his deep blue eyes. He was tall, thickly muscled and carried his famous protonic sword.

By his side stood Astari, a blonde warrioress in her gold and white uniform, beautiful speckled eyes like flint steeled against any injustice. High cheek bones, full lips, and a slightly pointed chin lent her an elfin look.

The brown-skinned Thronen Kor also had long thick black hair, tied in a top knot. He wore his beard short. Whether his bellowing voice or the thundering of his hammer-sword was louder in war was a source of amusement or fear. His malevolent demeanour was enhanced by his black armour and crested helmet with silver-lightning-bolt trim.

Zen Devestar, his wife, had deep green eyes amidst her light-brown skin and long wavy blue hair, being half-Elerae on her mother's side. She was an energy devourer hence her soul destroyer sobriquet. A touch from her could turn her victim into a soulless slave with a prolonged touch resulting in death.

Her identical twin, Azurzura, spoke the secrets of the universe to weave her cosmic spells and dances. Her light armour was red, wrapped in a red silky filament fabric. A thin gold chain connected her nose piercing to her left earring of five dangling silver stars.

Her consort, Teo Venga had short silver hair, dark eyes, and wore silver armour. A thin silvery nimbus about his head bore evidence of his psychokinetic abilities.

Spheron wore the typical green armour of his clan, adorned with a shield motif. Unusually for his clan he was clean-shaven with neither a moustache or a beard, and he was bald.

Ulix the sci-tech and the philosopher of the group was a petite waif with straight long blue hair. She was the doted-on only daughter of Ori Archos the Elerae. On Earth, Alpha Rion would have called her look Chinese.

Seeing them all in his mind's eye, Alpha Rion realised that apart from Priorion and Astari, the rest of the Celestri were of colour. He had never differentiated between people like that before. Celestians were either Galatian, Elerae, Trinari, or whatever. Like his brothers Novan and Solandus, their colour did not matter. He wondered if that was a good thing he had now noticed or had Earth changed his racial views on people? He didn't like that, but for now he focussed with some comfort knowing that the Celestri had lived beyond the Scrolls of History's account.

Priorions' voice had continued...

But Azurzura had always felt a force here, watching us, following us from world to world. This universe held many secrets.

On one world, we found a pyrathedral; startlingly like the Galatian Qors. We investigated, finding symbols etched in obscure places like they were hidden. Until this time we had seen no other living beings, but here, in one of the courtyards, a small girl approached us. We had not detected her nor did we know from whence she came.

She looked like a Celestian, save for her purple skin, purple hair and eyes, and translucent purple armour which shone from within. She seemed lonely.

"I am Sentity," she introduced herself.

"What does that mean?" Priorion asked.

The girl surveyed us Celestri, uttering, "I am that born of this universe. And that from which the universe was born. I am the mother of all beings, the matrix of all that has been, is, and will be."

Hesitantly, I introduced myself and my companion Celestri. After a time we befriended her. She played with our younglings.

We told her of our plight, lost from our home worlds and desperate to return. She told us of the portals within this universe on the differing worlds, hidden within the pyrathedrals, which only she could use between worlds but not without. There was no way out from this universe she had told us. She was guarded and coy with our questions concerning her. But the more she learned about us and heard our stories of our worlds, she changed.

This is what happened.

We were gathered in the pyrathedral in our make-shift quarters, which Sentity had allowed us to prepare. Azurzura had collected fruits from the surrounding forests and we were enjoying our meal with the younglings. Sentity suddenly interrupted, appearing among us in a flash of light. She looked concerned, agitated. Her face was clouded with dark emotions.

"I have heard all of your words concerning your worlds, its people, their customs and your powers. Excepting your presence, they are as told to me by my people. They left me here." She looked at us with fearful eyes. "You will not leave my universe."

Priorion looked at the rest of the Celestri, wary of the implied threat, then back at Sentity.

"Your people? You have never told us about them."

"And why cannot we leave?" asked Astari.

"Because I will not let you," Sentity said in her little girl voice. "And my people are not your friends. I know you."

Puzzled, Priorion countered, "We are not of this universe. We do not know your people." But he had suspected. They all did. "We only desire to return to our kin in our own universe. Will you help us?" he pleaded.

Sentity laughed, her girly trill sounding incongruous from her as she seemed to age before their eyes. A young woman now stood before them.

"If I help you, I will go with you," she stated bluntly.

"What?" Astari cried out.

"Why?" Priorion asked. "Do you intend to hold us here against our will forever?"

Sentity ignored their questions. She walked toward us. For whatever reason we could not fully discern we Celestri retreated slowly. Ulix ushered the children behind us, keeping the table and chairs between us and Sentity.

Sentity turned glum. "I have grown lonely since my people abandoned me." She swayed innocently, her purple eyes pleading for acceptance and sympathy.

"Who are your people?" Priorion asked intrigued. "The ones who made these pyrathedrals?" He pried to satiate his theories. "Who were they? Were they Celestians like us?"

Sentity was silent.

"Priorion, we should discuss this," Astari said, eyes wide, motioning with concern over to the younglings, who had stayed remarkably calm.

The rest of the Celestri nodded their agreement knowing full well that by discussion, Astari meant how they could escape or destroy Sentity, if necessary. She was not a trusting sort.

Priorion turned to Sentity. "I must confer with the others," he said.

Sentity tilted her head in assent, smiling confidently. Though she had matured into a young woman's form she turned around and walked playfully, unbalanced, along an imaginary line on the gold-coloured stone-paved floor.

"Speak!" ordered Priorion, once Sentity was out of earshot.

Astari started, "We know nothing of Sentity and what she is capable of. We cannot allow her to come with us! Destroy her!" she ended darkly.

Thronen Kor concurred. "She is dangerous, I can feel it. If she is a Goddess then she can leave her own realm. The Storm of Stars did. I do not trust her."

Zen Devastar and Azurzura agreed, Ulix adding, "We must get her to show us how the portals work. Perhaps one leads from this universe."

Weighing in with his opinion, Teo Venga said, "We strike now or we will be trapped here forever!"

Spheron was silent, watching the girl-universe play shadow games against a wall. Behind him, Alturi had corralled the younglings trying to make them feel safe, distracting them with a glimmering light show of her own.

Priorion stroked his beard, his smile grim. "We are leaving this universe," he decided.

He took a few steps forward and motioned Sentity back. She approached, humming a tune, the melody of which he dimly recognised.

He did not wait for her prompting. "We cannot take you, Sentity. We will not."

There was no answer, no reply, just a stare of revulsion from darkening purple eyes.

"We don't trust you," Priorion continued. "We think you are not telling us everything. Who are your people? Give us a reason to trust you." He looked at her earnestly.

Sentity looked at them with venomous eyes. Energy began to swirl in them.

"My people are the creators of this universe through me. I am a universe come to life. My people escaped their destruction and vowed revenge through me." She smiled and her eyes glowed even darker purple as she said, "My people are the

Amethystians. And I am their Goddess!" she screamed.

Thronen Kor did a double take. "Is she about to. . .?" he began, just as a torrent of purple energy flashed from Sentity's eyes. "Priorion, look out!"

"Father!" screamed Primerion.

Purple energy lanced from Sentity, splitting Priorion's head apart. His lifeless body toppled sideways, blood spewing from the gaping hole of a head over the golden stones.

Astari dropped to her knees in shock.

Sentity screamed again as she discharged more purple bolts from her eyes.

Everyone ducked for cover in the pyrathedral's hall. Spheron drew his right arm about him, throwing up an energy shield enclosing them all as Thronen Kor dragged Astari to safety. The younglings shouted in fear and confusion, their screams echoing around the enclosed pyramid. Primerion tried to run to her father, but Ulix held her back.

"Get them out of here!" Thronen Kor yelled at Ulix, who looked for the nearest exit.

The light in the hallway shifted to a purple gloom. Sentity stood in the middle of the room, her eyes smouldering hatred. She raised her hands.

Craaaack!

Purple lightning snapped across the room flaring off Spheron's green oblate shield. The noise from the energies tearing at each other threatened to crack the walls down upon themselves.

Having forced back the shock of losing her consort, Astari shouted "Azurzura!" over the din of the lightning still flashing at them. No other order was needed.

The sorceress started to chant, slowly at first, an ancient Neb prayer for deliverance entwined with the Equationless Poem of the Potentiality of Quantum Coherence. There was a coldness in the air as her chant increased with speed. Atoms swirled out of kilter binding themselves to the word of Azurzura.

Spheron's shield filtered Azurzura's cosmagic spells through *his shield while shutting out Sentity's.*

Sentity looked around her. Space broke up around her as a myriad of micro-dimensional holes warped over her. The girl shrieked in pain as pin-pricks of nothingness swept over her. Sentity felt herself being pulled apart and out of existence. Her feet disappeared from view as a bright orange dimensional plane clashed against her purple skin swept in from below. Her lower torso and left arm were trapped in a cold arid state of limbo. Her shoulders and head swam in a sea of shredded energy shards. She felt herself being stretched to the limits. But she knew the Celestri had forgotten one thing.

She wasn't corporeal. She was energy; energy of and from her own universe.

She fought back, first with a swirling microwave-string shield to disrupt the micro-spatial tears and then with a wide field of spiralling dark dust to obscure the sorceress' sight.

But Azurzura continued chanting her cosmic spell, interspersing gravimetric enchantments interweaved with passages from the venerated thirteeen-lined verses of the Tomes of Destruction.

Sentity countered with her purple energy, letting it be buffered by the waves of disruption from Azurzura, trying to anchor herself to this reality.

From behind Spheron's shield, Thronen Kor and Teo Venga skirted the field to the left, while Astari and Zen Devestar stalked to the right. Ulix held the children back behind the shield. She found and worked on the previously unlocked stone door to the chamber behind, which was now jammed somehow. The young Primerion and Hellon also pounded on the wall producing large stones with which to batter the door.

Sentity started to claw herself back. Other space, her escape conduit through space, was closed to her by the infernal sorceress. She clung on to her universe attuning its matrices, building, creating a field of dizzying quarkite mites. She sent them forth with a wave of her hand.

Azurzura instantly felt the mites eating through her shield, which she dispelled with a Hierarchical Prayer of De-coherance, her fingers contorted to reinforce the bonds. The mites exploded with little pops of energy.

Sentity could feel a force pulling at her from somewhere else, another space, but it wasn't strong enough to hold her. She concentrated on Azurzura and her spells. But her eyes shifted wavelengths and through the energy glares she coud see the other Celestri sneaking up on her.

She loosened her own physical bonds again and began transforming into her natural energy state.

The flanking Celestri froze as the body of Sentity broke down and melted into energy.

Azurzura invoked a Prayer of Guardianship, verbally twisting together a super-string chain of containment. Her wrists and forearms danced in unison in Blended Symmagictry. A dark form loomed in front of her. She pushed her arms out forward. The obloid entanglement cage shot forth enveloping Sentity.

But Sentity coalesced into a ball of purple energy.

Azurzura silently cursed. Her strongest spells weren't enough.

"Get the younglings out of here, now!" Astari ordered Ulix, shouting over the cacophony of spells and energy fields, as the four flankers fell back behind the shield of Spheron.

And just in time to avoid being incinerated by Sentity's flaring purple lightning.

They were thrown back as Spheron's shield buckled.

When the air cleared, Sentity hung in the air before them.

The shield held, but they knew Spheron and Azurzura's spells had little time left.

"Help me, Teo," Ulix called for Teo Venga, "the door won't move." They could see the purple energy around the door frame, trapping them in.

Teo Venga shoved at the door with his mind, but it remained unmoved. He looked at the door again, psychically feeling for a weak spot. The younglings were frightened, but none dared respond to it. Fear was normal; it was how it was used which was important.

Thronen Kor charged angrily at the large stone door. He hefted and pounded the door with his hammer-sword. Dust and small bits of stone shrapnel fell off, but the door remained intact.

"Universe above!" cursed Thronen Kor. He spat on his hands, gripped the long-shafted T-shaped, bifurcated blade and kept on hammering. The stone rang to the physical blows while Teo Venga also fought to bore a hole through the barrier, telekinetically.

Azurzura sang an Ode of Stellar Anguish, conjuring a microscopic singularity behind Sentity, whose ball shape warped into an oval as it was dragged toward the spiralling hole of infinite density.

Sentity morphed back into her little girl form. She looked back at the rapidly rotating singularity. It was frighteningly simple in its complexity yet the most mysterious of entities in any universe. She bathed the primordial hole with a constellation of her own purple singularities, siphoning off the central maw, which began to shrink.

Her voice still strong, hands clasped together before her, Azurzura combined an Aria of Truth, an ancient gospellic refrain from the Last Tomes of The Lost with an informational dark quark dump from an upper dimension.

Sentity's sense of reality faltered. Noise, the cosmic background of life and energy, was ripped apart by the Celestri sorceress leaving Sentity blind and deaf to her universe. Sentity admired both the Celestri's power and elegance in execution. The informational quark flares felt like solar plasma burning away Sentity's self. But still she hung on. Her little girl form was leaning forward away from the reforming singularity and into the face of the brutal energy rapids enforced by the vengeful incantations of Azurzura's worded energy. Sentity could still manage to fire off purple energy bolts, but the countering energy flow made them fall well short of and disperse before Spheron's shield.

"Almost there," grimaced Thronen Kor. He struggled to disengage the hammer-sword from the door where the weapon had lodged fully two-thirds into it. Teo Venga poured on psychic fire. A large chunk of the stone door fell away. And on they pounded.

"Get the younglings through," Astari shouted over her shoulder, trying to keep an eye on Sentity through the haze of Spheron's forcefield and the energies of Azurzura and Sentity.

The scene before her was like looking out on the universe itself with micro stars, black holes and naked energy emerging, flashing, twisting, careering, and vanishing around the pyramid's interior.

Astari made herself look at the body of Priorion laying on the cold floor between them.

I swear on our universe and the next, Sentity will die! she vowed.

She drew her sword, Gliri. And though loathe to, also crouched down and drew Priorion's sword, Wroughtwar. It shimmered in the purple light. She caught the eye of Zen Devastar. They knew what they had to do.

The hole in the door grew as a manic Thronen Kor chopped stone chunk after stone chunk out with wild shouts of anger, his top knot loose from the effort, his long dark mane also seemingly striking the wall for extra power.

An Incantation of Exponential Extolation was uttered in a mad whisper by Azurzura, the atomic field obeying her cellular scream attacking Sentity, pulling her out of her alter-state.

Sentity once again sought to attach herself to the fabric of the outer extremities of her universe for stability. She hung on for dear life, purple streaks grappling for shredded tethers which existed in an Underverse. She could feel the threads tearing. Through the dimmest of shimmering lights she could see the Celestri young escaping. She could not let that happen. Slowly, she started to claw her way out of the Underverse.

Azurzura began to dance. A Pirouette of Existentialism. Hips swayed, fingers interlaced, as spells of vibrational energy shimmered along her verbal prayer lines. The undertone of the combined quantum frequency shattered reality around Sentity.

Sentity blinked out of existence.

Azurzura caught her breath.

All the Celestri looked back in relief.

Thronon Kor broke through the door; a hole small enough to crawl through created.

"Alturi, take Omrion through with you!" Ulix commanded her daughter, the smallest of the children after Omrion, whose eyes were wide, taking in the battle—remembering.

Alturi, aghast at leaving her mother, refused, shaking her head. She cradled the younger Omrion in her arms and would not budge.

"We stay to help you," she said, steel in her little voice.

"No!" Ulix responded in anger. "Go, then the rest of the children will follow you. We will hold off Sentity!"

"We will follow," Teo Venga assured her.

Hellon turned around, rebelling against his father's wishes. "Father, mother, no! You must come with us!" he shouted at his father.

Azurzura was too deep in her enchantments to hear her son, ensuring Sentity's disappearance.

"Leave Sentity behind and escape!" Hellon demanded of Teo Venga, rage rising in him.

Teo Venga refused. "Son, we are Celestri. This is our duty, not just for this universe, but for ours. Go, go now, for it will take all of us Celestri to hold Sentity back. And pray she does not escape!"

Hellon looked back at his parents. "Mother, father, I will not forget you," he bravely shouted his last salutation.

From within her entropic prison, danced into life by Azurzura's frentic Dance of Cosmic Magnificence, threaded with streams of dark fluidic plasma, Sentity looked on in anguish as the children began to escape.

"Noooooo!" she screamed, from the edge of oblivion. "Nooooo!"

Energy flooded from her mouth erupting from the void, engulfing the Celestri, Spheron's shield faltering for a second.

Thronen Kor looked back at the children to make sure they were entering the hole.

"Farewell, Korelestra, beloved daughter," he shouted over the din. There was no fear in his eyes.

Korelestra hugged her father then dived through the hole, leaving only Primerion.

The oldest of the children watched in grim determination as Thronen Kor, Zen Devestar, Astari and Ulix prepared again for a frontal assault on Sentity, who still surviving Azurzura's sorcery, continued to grope her way into reality all the while pouring energy against the Celestri, Spheron's shields weakening.

"This is my universe!" Sentity was screaming, purple tears streaking down her face.

Astari gave her daughter a silent look, Go! But Primerion only wanted to be with her parents, feel her father stroke her hair one last time, spar with her mother who would never let her win. Primerion smiled in memory and returned her mother's gaze.

Azurzura was tiring. Her cosmic spells would have vanquished anyone else, but Sentity was living up to her Goddess of the Universe status.

She had one last shot, never attempted by her before, but talked about by her grandmother, Nyghra. Azurzura invoked the Song of Anguished Uncertainty, pinning the tones to chaotic sub-atomic vortices, further enshrining them within tachyonic pulses creating a trans-temporal surge. The spell was tricky with specific wording, notions of faith, and movements involved, but in her eyes opened to the universe, she could see it all coming together.

So could Sentity. Her little purple eyes widened in shock as she realised what was being created. She would be adrift in time, lost in the unfathomable depths of temporal uncertainty. She looked behind her. Azurzura's initial singularity still lingered, half spent, but powerful enough. If she could reach it and project it at Spheron's shield...

Sentity reared backward using her energy to repel and sidle around the singularity.

"No!" an aware Azurzura shouted a warning, sensing what Sentity was about to attempt.

The Celestri, alerted to the danger reacted.

"Now!" Astari commanded as she, Zen Devestar, and Thronen Kor rushed Sentity through Spheron's shield, weapons drawn.

Ulix threw Primerion through the hole and blocked it with the unturned table. Teo Venga melded the table to the stone; a crude, but effective barrier created. The two turned to face Sentity.

"You are mine! I will escape! I will hunt you down and destroy you!" was the last thing Primerion heard from Sentity.

And then there was an explosion. The pyrathedral shook violently. Then it was all black.

The voices and scenes faded and Alpha Rion and Chalant found themselves once again with the Celestri.

Silence was a strange sensation after the psi-images they had heard and witnessed.

"Universe, we are sorry to experience what happened to your parents," Alpha Rion said.

Omrion's visions had chilled him. And this Sentity was a mad Goddess.

"What happened to your parents? To Sentity?" he asked.

Primerion shook her head. "We went back, to exact revenge or die with our parents. We found our parents' bodies. Sentity had disappeared, hopefully destroyed, but she has not returned, here or anywhere else in the past few centuries. I think her destroyed. We buried our parents in the pyramid. Over time we worked out how the portals work. We've been to many worlds, but came across the Gravan on this one. We avoid them, but study them. As subjects of Sentity we thought it best not to interact with them lest they encourage Sentity to return and attack. We have managed to forage our own food and live comfortably on this world."

"And then we discovered Solandus," Hellon took up the story. "Imprisoned."

"Wait a minute," Chalant beat Alpha Rion to the punch. "You mean you were here when we battled? Why didn't you say anything? Contact me? Or help either of us?"

Primerion almost smiled, a wicked twist of the lips. "No, we were half a world away. Only when we were exploring more did Omrion sense Solandus' psi-presence. We intended to release Solandus after your departure, but he declined."

"Why?" Alpha Rion asked his brother.

"I found out something about the Gravan. They may have been created by Sentity, but the raw material, the beings she used were Amethystians. The Gravan are devolved Celestians!"

"Mighty Ra, no!" Chalant was shocked.

"But it is so. I have searched their minds, such as they are and we have examined an old dead body. Whatever happened between the Amethystians and Sentity left a lot of dead bodies. She had reconsitiuted those bodies into the Gravan. And that is why the manecrown is Celestian."

There was silence for a few seconds as the newcomers took in that information.

Alpha Rion smiled, almost chuckling.

"What are you smiling for?" Chalant asked.

He shook his head. "They are Celestians. Whatever life they may have now they have survived. They are resilient. They are like us. We should try and return them home with us and restore what we can or at least keep them safe."

But Solandus shook his head. "We cannot. The process that created them, however long ago that was, is breaking down; their bodies are destabilising. It is why they appear more animal-like generation after generation. They will degenerate into non-sentient beings and become unstable and wild. They cannot procreate. Have you seen Gravan younglings?" Solandus asked them.

Alpha Rion and Chalant shook their heads. It had not occurred to them.

"They are practically dead already as a race," Solandus said. "Whatever experiment Sentity was running has failed."

Alpha Rion acknowledged that, but Primerion reiterated Solandus' words.

"Alpha Rion, we have been through this many times amongst ourselves. We regrettably have to leave our kin behind. Solandus and Omrion have recorded all we can about the Gravan and their culture, but their end is near. All we can do is leave them in peace. We will leave a beacon here to note our passage and warn of the dangers on this world and in this universe as others may come across Sentity."

Alpha Rion agreed. "So I guess it is time to plan how to escape this universe?"

No one disagreed.

"Primerion," Alpha Rion addressed her, "Chalant and I travelled here from the fortress. I was able to enlarge the portal that your sword created and follow it here. Perhaps we can reverse the process to return to the fortress. At least from there we can find the map room and figure out how to get to Magna Aura from there."

Sombre, Primerion said, "It could work. I had never thought of using my swords' portals to travel. You are lucky you saw Gliri. I had only drawn her for training."

"Lucky you did," Chalant remarked.

"Is it safe?" Alturi asked.

Primerion nodded. "Yes, it should be. Gliri should be able to direct us to the fortress. She is a trusted sword." She held out the long black metal blade.

For the first time, Alpha Rion summoned his swords, his portals flaring into life. "And with these," he said of his bright energised blades. He stowed them back in their dimensional sheaths, their hilts still visible by his side. "Are we ready?"

"What about the surgeship?" Chalant said. "We can't just leave it here. The Gravan or someone else might discover and use it. It could come in handy for us."

"A ship?" Hellon was incredulous. "How big is it?"

Chalant laughed. "You will love it. It's as big or as small as we want. The Surge are living metal. We only need to take part of the ship then we can grow a bigger ship."

Hellon looked at her dubiously, wondering if she was being truthful.

"Fine, let's get the surgeship," Alpha Rion said.

They all moved for the door, except for Solandus. Alpha Rion looked behind and saw the strained look on his brother's face.

"Come on, Solandus. We cannot wait around," he urged his brother.

Solandus shook his head. "I cannot." He waved his hand, letting it pass through a wall. "In this psychic form I cannot leave my body behind indefinitely. And if I were to escape the Gravan would break out into civil war."

"You cannot sacrifice yourself for them. This is not your world, brother," Alpha Rion told him.

Solandus hesitated. Chalant reassured him. "Solandus, you did not start this conflict; their Goddess, this Sentity did. And we are no longer enemies. We need to leave, for I feel that once we leave, we will never be able to return and save you."

Sighing, Solandus nodded. "Fine, I'll be back in my cage. Come get me," he smiled, then disappeared.

Alpha Rion then turned to the Celestri. "And of course you're coming back to Magna Aura with us?" Alpha Rion said.

Hellon and Primerion looked at each other.

"We would be honoured to join you and to be back amongst our own kin," Primerion said.

"She speaks for all of us," Korelestra said.

Alturi and Spheron nodded in agreement.

"Okay," said Alpha Rion. "No time like the present."

They walked toward the long hallway entrance and back across the courtyards, past temples, ponds, elegant stone buildings, and wide avenues. Finally they reached the great gates which were closed. As they neared them, Chalant and Omrion psionically pulled open the gates. The seven of them walked out together, Chalant and Alpha Rion stopping so sharply that Primerion almost bumped into them.

"What is the matter?" she asked.

"That!" Alpha Rion said of the scene before them.

It was full of Gravan. All of them.

"Um, what's this?" Alpha Rion turned to Chalant, who shrugged, looking as shocked as he was. "Goodbye party?"

"I don't know," she answered.

The Gravan were huddled on their knees en masse in uneven rows stretching back as far as the eye could see into the forest two hundred meters away, their manes ruffling in the wind like large fluffy purple cauliflowers.

As Chalant walked forward to greet the Gravan, they shuffled out of the way, a low grumbling emanating from their throats.

Chalant felt an overwhelming sense of animosity from the Gravan. It welled up in her mind, the malcontent and feeling of grievousness flowing through her. She was able to see Omrion who was shaking his head as if to force out the noisy feeling grabbing at his mind. The emotional turmoil crescendoed and the hum of hostility became a furious rant, Chalant seeing the hate behind the word that formed in her mind:

Them!

Chalant turned to the Celestri and understood. The Gravan somehow knew them. Sentity must have imparted this hatred to her people, blaming the Celestri for Sentity's disappearance. Now their new Chalant was with the enemy. The Gravan felt alone and betrayed once again. They did not understand.

Chalant faced the Celestri, "They resent me for being with you!"

"Tough!" Alpha Rion replied.

"Are we safe?" Primerion asked, sword hand by her side, ready.

"Doesn't matter," retorted Alpha Rion, "Tell them we're

leaving, say we're taking them away to punish them," he said with a relished mischievous grin.

Chalant tilted her head. That was a good plan. She turned cheerfully around to the Gravan, seeking out Graagan. She psyed out to him. Fifteen or so meters away from the second row, Graagan stood up dutifully and bobbed his way to her. He got within five meters and then he stopped as if scared of Chalant or the Celestri, despite Chalant beckoning him on. He would not come closer.

>*Graagan*< she psyed. >*I discovered these intruders in the pyrathedral of your ancestors. I am taking them away to be punished, along with the prisoner-god*< she added as an after-thought. >*Allow me passage!*< she commanded.

Chalant's head pitched back as if she had been slapped. Graagan's answer, with the force of his people's will behind them had been emphatic.

A dark shadow had seemed to coincide with Graagan's reply.

Chalant spun around, "Um, he said 'no'," she told the group.

"You're their Champion for Universe sake!" Alpha Rion said, more than a little agitated. "Tell them!" he motioned Chalant forward.

"Or we will make them move," Hellon snarled under his breath.

She sighed. More glumly, she turned back to Graagan. >*Graagan, we are coming through. Do not try to stop us!*< She stared down the Gravan leader.

"Walk slowly," she told her group.

The low growls continued all around them, a howl or two sounding in the background. Though they moved apart, the Gravan still pressed in around the Celestri, making it difficult to move freely. Teeth were bared, hisses and snarls could be heard. One Gravan snapped at Alpha Rion, whom he shoved away back to the ground.

"Tera!" he snapped at her in turn, urging her to do something.

Chalant looked into the wide-eyed Gravan's faces. They were

ready to attack, their faces contorted into rage, saliva dripping from jaws.

"Oh, stupid me!" she berated herself. She had forgotten the one asset she could control. "When I say run, run," she said over her shoulder. >*Ship, to me!*< she commanded.

She controlled the speed and direction, the surgeship shooting like a black bullet through the trees.

The Gravan turned in surprise at the sound of tree branches and trunks breaking, many running away. But Chalant wasn't through yet.

A psychic shock wave burst from her mind, all the Gravan falling to the ground holding their heads.

"Run!" Chalant shouted.

The surgeship touched down ten meters away, Chalant already commanding the door to open. They all bundled in. The ship lifted off before the doors had even closed, Chalant directing the ship to the Citadel of the Eternal Ruins on the Fire Island of Vrame, Solandus' erstwhile prison. She made the front section transparent so they could see.

"We'll have to break him out," Chalant said.

>*No, you will not*< came Solandus' surprising reply. And sure enough as they neared the island they could see him on the external rock-hewn steps waving to them. >*I could have escaped at any time, Tera*< he psyed, a playful tint in his voice.

Chalant shook her head as she edged the surgeship toward the rocky ledge, Solandus hopping in once the door formed. It was only when he entered and took off again that Chalant saw he was carrying something.

"The Manecrown, Solandus? You stole it after all!" she was shocked, disappointed even.

Solandus shrugged. "Years ago, I made one of guards bring it to me and hide it under my cell." Seeing Chalant's disapproving look, he elaborated. "It was not because I wanted it for myself. It is Celestian technology after all, but now we can be prepared in case Sentity survived and is still out there. This either controls her or protects the wearer from her. We have to study it and find out."

Chalant had to reluctantly agree with him. "Okay, makes sense, we keep it."

"We?" Solandus said, suspicious. "You still do not trust me?"

"I trust you," responded Chalant with a smile, "But the more of us who know how the manecrown works and how to use it the better. You're in charge of it," she confirmed for him.

Solandus smiled and half bowed to her. "Thank you." He then went and hugged his brother, Alpha Rion, pleased to physically touch him. "It is good to be here, brother," he said, holding in his emotion. He then greeted each Celestri in turn. "Thank you all. Now let us get home."

Primerion looked around the cramped quarters of the ship. "How long will we be in this ship?" Her voice worried thinking of living in such crowded conditions.

"Oh," Chalant turned around. "Hold on."

Quite gradually, the back of the ship expanded out and five discreet compartments formed aside from the ablutions areas.

"Better?" she asked of Primerion, who smiled and walked off to one of the compartments for an impromptu inspection.

"Where are we going?" enquired Alpha Rion.

He could see that they were already at fifty-thousand feet and rising, courtesy of the altimeter reading on his crystalator. Seats had risen from the floor, which the Celestri took up. Alpha Rion, in his own co-pilot seat, was surprised that they had hardly felt the acceleration away from the ground.

"Take your pick," Chalant answered in the pilot's chair. "We can head back to Amagesh for answers and shelter or somewhere else on this world?"

Alpha Rion didn't particularly want to see Amagesh again, but they were indebted to the alien for their unexpected reunion. But not everything was up to him.

"Primerion, any preferences?" Alpha Rion swivelled in his chair to ask her, as she returned from her brief tour.

As if voicing the joint thoughts of the Celestri, Primerion leaned forward and said, "Just land somewhere away from the

Gravan and we can get off this world," her frustrated tone showing through.

Chalant heard her and studied her sensor screens. "Landmass across those mountains, Gravan free, ETA in. . . twelve minutes," she announced like a seasoned pilot.

The rest of the flight went uneventfully. Chalant landed the surgeship on a white sandy plain in the shade of the low sinuous mountain range. They disembarked breathing in fresh air.

No sooner had they taken in the views of mountains, trees, sand, rock and the deep blue horizon when Primerion pushed for them to leave.

"Fine," Alpha Rion said, looking around. "This will do."

He unsheathed his swords, their brilliance almost outshining the white-hot sun. He concentrated on his swords and held them out before him with outstretched arms. Primerion did likewise, the jet-black Gliri seemingly absorbing the sun's light.

A nebulous black opening slowly formed in the air before them, Alpha Rion wedging his swords in slowly to gradually widen the portal. Primerion advanced, staring at the rent in dimensional planes.

"I never thought the portal would look this way. Are you sure it is the portal to the fortress?" she asked, trying to peer beyond the darkness of the portal.

Alpha Rion grinned. "Yes, it's all pitch black, but it leads to the..."

He turned swiftly, as they all did toward the far end of the plain. A roaring sound echoed off the mountains. Then out of the trees on a slope, a little over two kilometers away, Gravan emerged rushing toward them.

"How can they move so fast?" Alpha Rion was flabbergasted.

"There was nothing on the screens," Chalant defended herself when everyone looked at her. "Nothing, no life registered!"

"Perhaps they do not register as recognisable life, but now we have to hurry," Primerion said.

Chalant psyed the ship, increasing its size to hover in the way of the fast-approaching Gravan.

Alpha Rion had carefully widened the portal, rounding off its wavering edges propped further apart by his swords, while Gliri widened the horizontal axis under Primerion's directions. She was amazed at the size of the portal as normally it would only be as big as the weapon required. Alpha Rion was essentially tricking the portal into processing a larger weapon through.

"Someone go," Alpha Rion encouraged the first entrant. "Primerion and I have to be in contact with our weapons to maintain the portal."

Hellon exhaled deeply. "I will go," though he didn't sound too sure. "What is this fortress like?"

"Stony, dark and cold. Just go!" Alpha Rion smiled grimly, urging him on.

Hellon grabbed Primerion by the waist, almost loosening her grip on Gliri, and kissed her. "Do not be too long," he said. He then gave a final look at the other Celestri and ran and dived through the portal.

Primerion called the order, "Omrion, go!"

Her son vanished into the portal next.

"Alturi!"

She wasted no time in jumping through at Primerion's instruction.

Korelestra didn't wait for her name to be called as she barrelled past the portal's rim, quickly followed by Spheron.

The Gravan were now a couple hundred meters away raising black dust about them. Chalant swung the surgeship toward them and the onrushing vanguard swerved away, but the second and third waves were undaunted.

"Primerion, go!" Alpha Rion ordered. "My swords can support this now and I'll see Chalant through. Tell everyone to stand away from the portal for when the ship exits." He commed Chalant, "Let's go Tera!"

Primerion clutched his shoulder, looked back at the closing Gravan and then grabbed Gliri as she dived through. Alpha Rion took up the slack. Even as he did so, Chalant had pointed the ship at the portal. Several Gravan were clinging to it, but a few barrel rolls by Chalant and off they flew into other pursuing Gravan, clearing the way. Chalant and the now shrinking surgeship zipped through the portal.

Alpha Rion grinned at the Gravan, feeling some pity for them, but not enough.

"Later suckers!" he yelled, diving backwards through the portal with his swords.

The portal disappeared. The Gravan arriving at an empty location.

No one had noticed the black dusty shadow which had followed the Gravan attaching itself to the underside of the surgeship.

The fortress was as Alpha Rion had left it as described to Hellon: stony, dark and cold. Excepting of course the back wall of the stone corridor where Chalant had crashed the surgeship, leaving a large dent in the otherwise intact fortress. The ship and Chalant were undamaged.

Collecting themselves off the floor, Alpha Rion led them through the fortress. Primerion and her Celestri admired the weapons collected on the walls from past kin. Upon reaching the map room, they rested, sitting on the stone chairs tired, hungry and needing a plan to return to Magna Aura.

Solemnly, Alpha Rion looked at Solandus. "Father's here!" he said.

Solandus rocked in his chair. "Father? Alive? Where?"

"No, not alive." Alpha Rion stood up motioning his brother to follow him.

He walked with Solandus, recounting the story of his and Chalant's time in the fortress. By the time he had they were at Alphatronius' burial chamber.

Solandus ran his hand along the stone tomb. "I hardly remember him." He paused as if trying to recall a memory. "Nor mother! I remember travelling through father's portal as a child. Then we searched for a suitable home until we found

Magna Aura. And then I waited until I had come of age and left. I wanted to make my own way in the universe. To prove myself to you all. Now look where I am, under father's arms again." He laughed to himself.

Alpha Rion regarded his brother. He knew the pain he was in and the relief at being free and almost home. He put his arm around him in support.

Hellon entered the chamber, niggling Alpha Rion with his interruption.

"Alpha Rion, Primerion has an idea of how we can return to the Magna Aura system." For Hellon, he sounded excited.

"Great, I'm all for listening."

They jogged back to the map room.

Back in the map room, the others gathered around as Primerion began to speak. "I think. . ."

A sudden shift in the air caught their attention. The fortress began to rumble.

"We're moving," Chalant cried out.

"Impossible," replied Alpha Rion, even as the floor lurched.

"What's that noise?" Primerion asked, hearing an escalating loud-pitched whine.

Chalant looked at Alpha Rion. He shook his head.

The steady piercing whine suddenly crescendoed and they all cupped their hands over their ears, the noise by-passing their manoeuvre suit's defences. It grew louder, cutting through to their very cores.

"We are under attack!" Hellon shouted.

Looking around they could not see their attackers.

Then Chalant saw a shadow; a tall dark figure approaching.

"Amagesh?" she smiled in greeting through the din.

But her smile disappeared quickly from her face as she realised it was not Amagesh, but another rangy all-black alien entity.

It raised its hand; an eructation of dense black energy exploding over the Starguards and Celestri.

Everything was blackness.

"Threshold complete," Nexionon announced.

CHAPTER NINE

"I will kill you with my bare hands!"

The oath was met with laughter.

"I have already died, Decion! And now I arise." Cirrius splayed his arms out theatrically. "The Amethystians are gone, the Starguards and Astrals gone, you are my prisoner, and my family and the Chronossii are by my side, safe." Cirrius laughed again at Decion.

Vavasar Island was Decion's prison now. He pulled uselessly at his chains.

"And I will rule as the King, forever!" Cirrius' last word was inflected with a flourish. "Now I must leave you, speeches to make." He smiled again, backing out of the cell.

Dyonus closed the heavy metal door as he left.

Decion was left in the semi dark, his arms and legs bound together. Even without his manoeuvre suit, which had been switched off by a crystalator Cirrius had crafted—*more deviousness on Cirrius' part*, Decion cursed—Decion should have been able to break free. But he knew it would be no use as demonstrated by Cirrius earlier in his incarceration.

He was trapped in a temporally-recursive cell initiated by Vostra. The cell was surrounded by a temporal field in that even if Decion managed to find a way out through the door or a window or a hole in the wall, the path led straight back into the cell.

"Focking time travellers!" He sat against the wall, his eyes boring into the door, contemplating his fate.

And his day had started so well, he had thought.

Hours earlier.

"I must admit, Ilis, Vista Oscendant is much superior than Vista Mare," Decion conveyed his admiration of the construction of the newest of the orbiting Star Warrior bases.

It was the last of twelve new stations built around the system, a lesson learned from the Lore attack. Each was a natural asteroid captured and hollowed out and inhabited by Star Warriors, Meccun techs, and visited by Swords on a regular basis. The stations were manoeuvrable and capable of defending any part of the system thanks to their awesome array of fire power.

"Thank you, Decion," Star Commander Ilis Rona replied. She was a tall, lean, sharp-angled woman with her long black hair tied up atop her head, accentuating the starkness of her features.

A pleasing view, Decion decided.

"Cirrius was very prescient in having the bases constructed..."

Of course he was, Decion thought, *he had Astral help in glimpsing the future!* Decion wondered how far in the future he had seen.

". . . just before the first attacks forty years ago. He is a great Celestian and Starguard. . ." she continued.

And dead! Decion wanted to say. But he resisted.

The rest of the Starguards had delayed announcing Cirrius' death until Urana and Celestra had returned. Then the Starguards would break the news to the populous and try to maintain order. And then there was the matter of their own missions as instructed by Novan, only a few hours before. Sceptre had already left to search for the Great Seal leading back to their original universe.

"Indeed he is," Decion responded flatly to Ilis' praise.

". . . though it is certainly a pleasure escorting you around this base," continued Ilis, her black eyes sparkling at him.

A true Xarian beauty, Decion decided.

Ilis was the niece of Yons Mona, the former Captain Councillor of Placia's military council and tough ally of Urana until his retirement. He was now a resident initate of the Neb following his full conversion to their faith. Decion wasn't too bothered by that, but he was disappointed Ilis seemed to be another Cirrius worshipper. Nevertheless, he was entranced by her. And she seemed to welcome his pointed gaze.

Suddenly, the Star Commander's crystalator buzzed, interrupting the moment. Decion's comms also sounded and he looked down at his forearm screen in annoyance. Until he saw the message. It left him dumbfounded.

His hand clenched into a fist and angrily and automatically reached for his sheathed sword.

"Huh, the King has an another announcement," Ilis said, in a curiously less-than-cordial manner. "Tonight!"

Ilis' voice broke Decion's action and the lancesword remained in its dimensional sheath. Through his anger, he had the distinct feeling that Ilis felt differently toward Cirrius than she had let on. But that had to wait.

"I have to depart," he said, trying to think of a reason why, besides telling Ilis he had to see if Cirrius was really still alive.

"Me, too." Ilis saved his excuses. "I look forward to speaking with you more in the future," Ilis said.

Decion's heart leapt. "Of course." He bowed with a courteous nod of his head.

They gave each other a final look and then proceeded in opposite directions. Decion almost whistled a tune before noticing that his route to the hanger led him past numerous Star Warriors who greeted him in awe. He maintained his customary scowl.

Decion wasn't a natural flier like most of the Starguards. And while his manoeuvre suit would protect him in the harsh vacuum of space, he preferred a personal craft. He set the controls for the place he knew Cirrius would be, if indeed he was still alive, Aqrius. Clearing the flight with Dock Control, the small ship darted out of the station and toward Halcyon dead below.

He had audio feeds on his crystalator catch all the references of Cirrius, but Cirrius himself had not yet been heard or seen. Decion dared hoped he was still dead.

Minutes later, he was dropping through Halcyon's atmosphere steering toward Aqrius. But as he approached the island, he could see a group of younger people outside. He landed the craft expertly in the softly rippling water next to a pier. Getting out, he briskly marched toward Cirrius' abode, but half way there, he was confronted by an unexpected sight.

"Hallo, Decion," Timechantress practically sang at him.

She stood defiantly before him, her blue hair and manoeuvre suit wings upon her regal purple uniform fluttering in the stiff breeze. Her hawkish face regarded Decion with hate.

"I do not care how you escaped Vavasar Island, but I can cleave you in half and see who's in there!" Decion held out his hand to indicate Cirrius' dwelling.

He could only assume one of the younglings had defied their orders and freed their mother. He half-hoped Timechantress would challenge him, but she stepped aside, a little too eagerly.

Decion willed himself to stay wary as he passed her with a glare. He made his way up to the dwelling. Again, as he ventured forward, other figures, younger Celestians exited the house and stood by the entrance.

No, not Celestians, Decion realised. Their clothes were stylised, but not in a Celestian style. They dressed like humans of Earth, like. . . he remembered seeing Antichilles and Tyran for the first time; their helmets, robes, and other garb.

"Astrals," he growled. His hand instinctively grabbed for his sword. But the group stepped aside, as had Timechantress.

Decion eyed them warily. Then he noticed Celestra and Xestina by the door.

"Where is Urana?" he snapped at Celestra.

Her eyes dropped.

There was no answer. At least from those outside.

"Come in, Decion," came Cirrius' voice, clearly from inside.

The voice chilled Decion. He had seen Cirrius' dead body himself; shot by an Amethystian weapon.

Lips tightly pressed together, Decion strode up to and into the house, the wind sighing softly across the threshold. He watched everyone around him holding back the instinct to draw the lancesword and slaughter all of them, starting with Cirrius. Warily entering the room, Decion stopped short.

In the centre stood Cirrius.

He stretched his arms out in greeting. With a wide smile in his face, he said, "Welcome, Decion. Let's talk!"

"How are you still alive?" Decion started, bluntly. "And where is Urana?" he asked again.

Cirrius smiled again, almost a sneer. "My friends, outside, saved me. You thought them Astrals? But they are not! They are related, but they are the Chronossii!" he introduced them. A soft sigh followed with a look at Decion as if weighing up what he was going to say. "And as for my sister, she is not coming back! Urana is dead!"

Decion did not think he heard correctly. He looked behind him at Celestra, the only other at the threshold of the door, but her downcast eyes told him all he needed to know.

"How? When?" he asked, his body aching to take the lancesword to Cirrius' neck.

Cirrius shrugged. "Details!" he whispered sadly. "She opposed me and she is dead."

Decion was quiet, not wanting to think that a Starguard could kill another, no matter what he had thought and done in the past and his feelings toward Novan and Sceptre. But Cirrius, out of all of them? No, this had to be the work of Timechantress, the Astral manipulator. Then Decion remembered something.

"Urana was with child!" he felt his anger rise. "You would not kill a child? Your unborn kin?"

Shaking his head, Cirrius let out a short laugh. He held up his left hand to stop Decion from advancing, while stifling his laugh with the back of his right hand.

"Apologies, I do not laugh at you, Decion. I am amused, but insulted, you think I would kill a newborn."

"A newborn?" Decion was confused. "Urana was not due for birth!"

Cirrius stared Decion hard in the eye. "We made her so. The son of Urana and Altair is safe here on Halcyon. He will grow up under my care..."

Decion had heard enough. He reached within himself to open up the dimensional sheath and draw his lancesword and swipe Cirrius' head off in one stroke...

... But nothing happened. He was frozen.

Decion tried to move, but found his arms wouldn't obey. Nor his legs. He found he could only move his eyes. And they watched as Cirrius drew closer to him.

"I am protected by temporal sorcerers, Decion. Did you think you could kill me, here?" he shouted, spittle hitting Decion's face.

Cirrus motioned someone into the room.

"This is Vostra," Cirrius presented Decion to the young woman now in front of him. "She can slow down, speed up or stop time locally. You are in one of her fields." Cirrius looked at Decion with dark purpose. "And your cell will be in one of her fields. You will never escape it!"

And Cirrus had been true to his word. Decion had been ported to Vavasar Island. He had been stripped of his crystalators, his manoeuvre suit switched off and he wore only his black under-armour. Even if he could draw his lancesword it would be no use to him in the time-loop cell.

After a while, the chains released themselves via the timer attached, though it was of no use to Decion. He was trapped.

And would be forever.

"I promised you security," Cirrius declared to the Sky Warriors in the hanger and to the millions of Magna Aurans watching on vidscreens across the system.

"I promised you more allies," he pounded a fist to his chest, as he paced back and forth along the stage set up on the hanger. "So I have been searching for our lost kin amongst the stars." He smiled widely as he proclaimed triumphantly: "And I found them!"

There were cheers of surprise and joy over the announcement.

Antichilles, Tyran, and Xestina already stood behind him on the stage. The Astral youths awaited their de facto kin to arrive.

"They are the Chronossii," Cirrius proudly announced, "Lost kin to my wife, Zasandra, and our children!"

He held up his arms and Timechantress ported in with three younger warriors. There was a hushed wave of awe as the light faded.

"May I introduce to you: Dyonus, Phasion, and Vostra," Cirrius announced.

Raucous applause erupted as each stepped forward in turn, smiles and waves offered to the crowd. Surrounded by his family and young charges, it reminded Cirrius of when the Starguards all last stood together when Novan had made his own announcement forty years ago before he had left for Elysiun to find his mother. And now the King of Magna Aura had a few words to say about the rest of Starguards. Cirrius let the adoration swell for a few minutes and then let the clamour die down. He took on a sombre demeanour.

"However, amid the victories there have been set backs and there is some regretful news. The rest of the Starguards have elected not to return to us."

There were gasps of disbelief and anger from the crowd.

"No, never!" someone cried out.

Cirrius ignored them.

"Upon their return from a distant planet called Earth following the Lore war, we had a disagreement about the course of action I was taking. I will not lie to you," he lied, "But they have not abandoned us again. Novan had convinced them to settle on his world of Elysiun. And while it hurts me they left in our time of need, I have, with great risk to my personal safety discovered who our real enemy are!" He paused for effect. "They are the Amethystians!"

There was a powerful wave of disbelief and fear.

Whether voluntary or not eyes sought out Eleare faces and hair.

"Yes, you heard me correctly," Cirrius continued. "The

legendary Amethystians are still alive." He looked about the hangar, singling out the Elerae Sky Warriors with their blue hair, like his own. "Still alive! We know the Amethystians were famed for their technology. Yet we had no idea they had constructed great portals in secret. Several millions escaped the destruction of Amethystia and they have roamed the universe since, looking for revenge!" Cirrus shook his fist in anger, remembering the moment he was killed. "But thankfully their last attack was repelled by the Starguards before they left to join Novan. They fight for our survival on another front!"

Cirrius did not care where the Starguards were, as long as they were away from Magna Aura. He waited for the cheerers to subdue themselves. Of course, he was not going to state that Azure had sent the Amethystians away and they would not be back for at least five years. An active enemy on the celestial door step was a handy one.

The thunderous cheers almost made his lies and half-truths worth it. He smiled to himself.

"The treacherous Amethystians are still out there but being fought by the combined forces on Elysiun of the Starguards and Novan and your journeyed families—blessed by the Universe!"

There were a few chants for Novan, Cirrius waving them off. He didn't need any more sympathy for Novan building up. And besides, he had more news, the most important—personal news. Cirrius summoned up his serious face. The crowd picked up on his downcast demeanour and waited.

"But worse news concerns my sister, Urana," Cirrius' voice broke as he bowed his head in sorrow. "Urana is dead." There were cries of astonishment and heads turned to look at each other in shock. "Yes, she had tried to negotiate peace with the Amethystians and they attacked her! The Starguards rescued her, but too late!" he wept.

A young female Sky Warrior cried and almost fainted, having to be carried out of the hangar to medbay. Cirrius let the emotions swirl around the hanger.

"I will avenge my sister!" he shouted, to returning choruses of "Vengeance! Justice! Urana!" from the Sky Warriors. After a few minutes, Cirrius calmed the crowd.

"But from that sorrow, there has been joy!"

He turned to his side and from off stage, Celestra who joined him, cradling a precious bundle, her eyes downcast and wet. It didn't go unnoticed by Cirrius. He took the bundle and turned back to the Sky Warriors.

He said, "Unbeknownst to me, Urana was with child; Altair's child!" There were more gasps of shock, a few claps, and cheers. "And upon her death bed, she gave birth to a son!" he held up the baby. "Urrius!" shouted Cirrius, "Son of Urana and Altair!"

"Urrius," came the hallowed whispered greeting, ushering Urrius into the Starguard fold.

"And with Altair also lost after the war with the Lore, I claim my nephew as my own son, who will be as bold and as strong as his parents!"

The Sky Warriors cheered wildly as Cirrius held up the boy again, who cried loudly at all the noise and surrounding hullabaloo. It had been Timechantress, who had suggested the name to honour both Cirrius and Urana. A very fitting name at that.

Cirrius smiled at the ovations and chants of his name remembering to tinge it with sadness and gratitude. The King of Magna Aura was in control and the Starguards could not interfere any more. The Chronossii would see to that. They were his family now. Again, he let the triumphant mood sway the crowd, until it reined itself in, ready for him to speak again. He gave Urrius back to Celestra who joined her mother's side, her eyes still shaded.

Victoriously, Cirrius declared, "My fellow Sky Warriors, Star Warriors, friends, and to all Magna Aurans, I and the Chronossii will defend you with our lives. We will keep you safe for all time. This I promise! May the Universe bless you all!" He ended with his fists in the air.

And at that, there were adoring cheers and chants of "Cirrius! Cirrius! Cirrius!" as Cirrius, the Astrals, and Chronossii made their way down the launch tubes to disembark for his island.

Even as they were out of sight of the crowds and histographers, someone in the ranks started singing the Sky Warrior hymn, everyone joining in, the song reverberating down the tube launches.

Several flashes of portals heralded their exit, Cirrius feeling proud as the song echoed in his ears, just as Timechantress ported him to Aqrius.

Once on his island, Cirrius requested Tyran, Antichilles, and Xestina take the Chronossii to their quarters he had built for them in the rear extension of his home. They needed the time to bond with their kin.

Only he, Timechantress, and Celestra remained and they talked in his private office at the rear of the main lounge. He had one more request to make.

"Altair and Alpha Rion are the only Starguards unaccounted for. I cannot have them returning! Find them!" he asked of Celestra.

"Yes, Cirrius," she replied, "And when I do find them?" She feared the worse. Cirrius' methods were hard to fathom.

Cirrius sighed. "Altair will naturally want to help his brother. And when he hears about Urana, well. . ." He threw his hands up in askance. "I'm sure you can find somewhere, somewhen to strand him. But first, find him," he repeated, with a wave of the hand.

"And Alpha Rion?" Timechantress asked.

Cirrius drummed his fingers on the chair arm. "I am less concerned with him. I believe he was killed on Earth when the building collapsed. Sceptre and Urana were clear on that. There's no need to worry about him." He looked at Celestra again. "But Altair, he could survive such a thing. Just find him," he reiterated.

Celestra nodded and winked out of existence.

"Temporal stranding?" Timechantress asked, her voice purring with admiration.

Cirrius half-smiled. "Altair is dangerous. He will oppose us, especially if he hears about Urana and his child." He sighed deeply. "I didn't want to do what I did to Urana, but it was necessary." He looked at the ground and rubbed his face.

"I know," Timechantress approached him and cupped his face in her hands, raising his eyes to hers. "But we have the greater good for Magna Aura to think about! Our legacy!" she spoke softly.

"She is still alive." Cirrius half-believed it himself.

"Of course she is, Cirri." She didn't believe it.

They looked at each other, then she kissed Cirrius softly, their lips opening in passion. They worked at each other's clothing before Cirrius led Timechantress to his bed chambers.

But nothing Timechantress could do could erase the memories of what he had done to Urana from his mind.

Sky Command

"Did you believe him?" Deputy Sky Commander Aphene asked.

There was a beat of silence followed by a humorous snort.

"No," Tol Valar replied. "Some things did not ring true."

They were in his command office, the Sky Commander careful to place crystalators around to jam any listeners of the King.

"I know it is not true," MedScholar Iesse Ede spoke up.

Everyone looked at her expectantly. She looked around the room, still expecting eavesdroppers.

"I knew Urana was with youngling," she half-whispered. "She visited me soon after they returned from Earth. But. . ." she hesitated, trying to fathom a mystery, "she was not due for months. I cannot believe this is her youngling or what Cirruis claims is true."

Tol found his face slack with surprise. "Oh."

"Universe," uttered Camtrin, a mixture of both pleasure and grief on her face. Urana had found happiness, but at a tragic time.

"Urana swore me to secrecy," Ede confided.

"No matter," Tol replied, gathering himself. "Do not feel guilty over this. We respect your loyalty to Urana."

"Tol is right," Camtrin spoke for the others. "This is not your fault. Cirrius is to blame."

Tol nodded. "Agreed. What we need to know is where is this Earth? And where are the Starguards?" he asked the other four in the meeting, two seated in his office. "Even Decion has disappeared. I never thought I would miss him."

There was muted laugher at his admission.

"And do not forget the *Star Ode* incident. The stories from my informants on the *Exthereal* do not add up with the explanations from the Captain," Star Commander Ilis Rona said, her holo presence from Vista Oscendant radiating from a crystalator.

"Hmm," Tol Valar mused, agreeing.

The destruction of the *Star Ode* was never completely resolved with Ilis Rona's hands having been tied by the King's twin sons being placed in charge of the follow-up investigation.

"And like you, Tol, I do not understand Decion's disappearance," Ilis continued. "I had the impression he did not support Cirrius, but I did not envisage him leaving Halcyon. In fact," her holograph image showed them a crystalator padd, "when he left here, he took a personal craft straight to Aqrius. And never left!" Her face was a hard mask of resoluteness.

"You think he is being held prisoner or worse?" asked Tol Valar.

"I do," came the Star Commander's reply. "Decion has not returned any of my hails and after some discreet inquiries, his craft was brought back to Vista Oscendant by Celestra who offered no explanation why Decion had abandoned it."

"Perhaps Decion was exiled to Elysiun with the other Starguards," Aphene said.

Ilis twisted her head in thought. "Maybe." But they could see she did not believe it.

"So, we cannot expect help from Decion," Tol Valar summed up the situation.

"Nor Urana," Camtrin from the vidscreen put in sadly. "Now I know why she had not responded to my coded signals. Even Astara is incommunicado."

The Trinari councillor looked tired and stressed from long days of no sleep. Now she was in mourning over Urana.

"The longer the Starguards are not here, the more it will give Cirrius opportunity to take over everything completely."

"And the Starguards are somewhere we have no charts for," lamented Ilis. They all rued not finding out where Novan and the Ribbon System were. It had been a closely guarded secret to protect them, Cirrius had announced, and now they knew why.

"So, we need to find out where this Earth is," said Aphene.

"Not quite," Tol Valar steepled his hands in thought. "We can find the Starguards, first, ally ourselves to them and let them know what is happening here. We need help or we are on our own in dealing with the King."

"And what of these Chronossii? Who are they?" Ilis Rona pressed on. "Cirrius claims they are kin, but he does not name their ancestors. Nor do we know their powers, besides teleporting. I do not trust them!"

"Maybe I can do something," Iesse said. "I'll bring them in for medical checks as they are new to our worlds and try to observe and record their powers."

"That would be useful," Tol Valar commented. "That is if Cirrius agrees. But our main goal should be to locate and warn the Starguards."

Aphene nodded. "But how will we find the Starguards? We do not even know where the Ribbon System is."

"That may be a problem. Though I may know someone who can help," the Sky Commander smiled.

Any questions were rudely stifled when all the command alarms screamed into life. It took Tol Valar seconds to realise the cause looking at all the office screens.

"The storm! Something's happening!"

Aqrius

Cirrius still lay in bed, Timechantress sprawled beside him. He propped himself up on his elbows and looked down at her face with its contented smile as she slept. He wished he had the same carefree conscience she did.

Earlier, Timechantress had given Antichilles orders to fill in for his father on Sky Warrior base tours, while Tyran was on Placia with the Chronossii training in the remote Trishangashi mountains. Later they had planned for all of them to head into space for more temporal manoeuvres away from sensor probing.

Cirrius was sure the Chronossii would be able to help him fulfil his ambition of ruling Magna Aura. They were young, but willing to learn, and to trust in him. They had grown up on a cruel backward Earth, deprived of their heritage, and were grateful to be hailed as lords in a new world. They had been trained as warriors and knew what had to be done to gain and keep power. They had backed him over Urana and now they would back him when he started his quest to defeat the Amethystians, and to bring Novan's Elysiun under his rule, and any other civilisations. Perhaps even Earth. His lips formed a smile at that notion.

A flash of a portal interrupted his thinking.

Celestra had returned.

"Back so soon?" Cirrius inquired as Celestra casually walked into the room.

She ignored his naked torso and her mother's naked body beside him. Timechantress stirred into wakefulness.

"What news of Altair," Cirruis wanted to know.

There was a grim look on Celestra's face, her orange hair hiding a slight flush of embarrassment.

"He has disappeared!"

"What do you mean?" Timechantress was now fully awake and drawing on a gown.

"As you surmised, he survived the building's collapse. There was no word on Alpha Rion, but Altair definitely survived. I tracked him after the explosion in the Twenty-first century. Can you believe he actually exiled himself from Earth!" she scoffed.

"What!" Timechantress puffed from her lips.

"He left Earth, mother!" Celestra stressed. "But I lost him in space. I searched for him century after century, but nothing, until he returned in the Twenty-fifth century to save Earth from an alien creature. But no sooner had he arrived and saved them, he disappeared again. I couldn't trace him. It was like someone covered his tracks spatially and temporally. He's gone!"

Cirrius sat up in bed. His head hurt. What was it with Starguards not staying dead.

"What you say is impossible!" Timechantress said.

"I'm telling you, mother, I cannot trace his trail. It was like he was never there!"

"Then there is another force in play," Cirrius deduced, feeling a headache coming on. "Altair would not be able to do this by himself." He thought more on the subject. "Have Tyran return the Chronossii. Take them with you and search again."

Celestra half-bowed. "Yes, Cirrius." She left the room.

"What are you thinking, my dear?" Timechantress stroked Cirrius' arm.

He turned from where Celestra had stood. "First, it would not hurt for her to call me father."

A shadow crossed Timechantress' face. "I'm afraid she never will. Lazeron will always be her father, despite his faults. But she respects you."

"Are you sure?"

"I think she feels guilty over her actions with Urana," Timechantress admitted.

Cirrius' eyes narrowed. "Not too guilty I hope."

Timechantress smiled. "She'll get over it."

"Of course." He nodded absent-mindedly. "Of course."

Silently they both knew Celestra would have to move on. There was no place for disloyalty or second thoughts in his command. Cirrius smiled into her eyes, distracted by his wife's beauty.

"What are you thinking?" she asked him.

"I am thinking how much I love you," he said, even surprising himself with his forthright emotion.

Timechantress laughed. "I love you, too," she playfully grabbed his lips and kissed them. "But you know what I meant! What are you really thinking?"

Sighing, Cirrius answered, "The Astrals. I think the Astrals helped Altair. And if, when, they return him here, it will be war!"

Timechantress laughed, "Do you really think they would?" she asked. "I am sure they have disappeared or been killed. I would have sensed otherwise. Their temporal signatures just aren't there."

"Yes, I think they would. Perhaps you can check yourself. . ."

But Timechantress shook her head and rolled onto Cirrius. "No, I cannot!"

Cirrius looked at her curiously, anger rising. "Why not?"

Timechantress smiled; a tiny smile, but one of unadulterated happiness. "Because. . ." she looked uncertainty at Cirrius, "I am not sure of the effects of time travel upon a baby!"

"A baby?" Cirrius' face creased in confusion, before it suddenly dawned on him. His face lit up in joy. He half turned so they were on their sides facing each other and he touched his hand to her belly. "A baby!" he grinned. "When?" He wanted to know the birth date.

"Oooh, about. . ." She stopped, startled.

A loud noise interrupted from outside the bed chamber. And within the room, it turned considerably colder and darker.

Cirrius and Timechantress looked at each other, sitting up in bed.

"Celestra?" she called out.

There was no answer, but a shadow seemed to move across the open doorway.

"Universe!" Cirrius cursed.

A tall alien being as black as dead space had solidified from the shadow and entered the room.

It raised its arm and fired.

CHAPTER TEN

Urana lay on the ground, for days it seemed to her. The manoeuvre suit slowly healing her; her strength returning. Whatever Vostra had done to her had also affected Urana's powers. She had no energy, but she couldn't be bothered to move anyway, not after what had happened.

She felt empty, ripped apart; violated, by her own brother.

Besides, she had no idea where to go. She was hundreds of years before Millennius, Destina, and Spheron would arrive, which meant there would be no contacting them, Phasia, or the Astrals for rescue. But Urana had kept her manoeuvre suit's comms on, sending out a repeating signal, a harmonic melody, a song from times past on Galatia. She hoped that would attract a Starguard's attention more so than a voice signal as she couldn't talk much anyway.

Urana pushed herself up. She half-crawled into one of the crude wooden shelters erected by the Chronossii. It was cool by day and kept out the cold of night. Her powers hadn't returned enough for her to self-start a fire so she did it the old-fashioned way with kindling and flint they had left behind. There was a little food left behind, but Urana couldn't eat. Her stomach and throat were sore from retching; feelings of unrelenting grief overwhelming her into sickness. She slept most of the time and dreamed of a rescue by Phasia. If Phasia did not come, then once her strength had returned, Urana had resolved to climb down the mountain and seek any help or maybe live some kind of normal life on Earth. Still hurting, Urana drifted off to sleep.

She was awakened by an object poking her in the abdomen, a painful action to say the least.

Her heavy lids eventually obeyed her and opened. She was surrounded by five men. They had somehow sneaked into her hut without her crystalator warning her. Despite being unarmed, she was sure she could still kill the men if they tried anything. She tried to stand, but couldn't.

One of the men held up his hands, palms facing her. He shushed his way closer to her and said:

"I am Atton."

He was the tallest of the men and was wearing what seemed to be an old patched up tunic and trousers uniform, which Urana thought strange for a native of Earth. He was lean with shoulder length brown hair and striking blue eyes within a handsome face.

"We received your signal," he said.

Urana tried to smile and raise her head to look at them, but she fell again, unconscious.

Furtive whispers wove into her dreams.

"So he brought her here?"

"She is one of us. Look at her, her hair, her uniform. . ."

"The sample will tell us. . . ..."

"It is a ruse by them. He should have left her to die!"

"No, she is not of this world!"

"But can we trust her?"

"We take her with us!"

There was a tense pause between the speakers. Urana made a noise to signify she was awake, the whispering stopping. She opened her eyes and was greeted not with the shelter fabric on the mountain, but to a metal cabin; clean lines, functional, cramped but comfortable. She had seen the type of design before, but this was an older kind.

Urana looked at her rescuers? Captors? She was not sure by their demeanour as they stared back at her. There was a group of two men and two women staring at her intently.

One of the women had purple hair. It startled Urana.

More puzzling was their clothing, tattered uniforms patched up with leather and other cloths. Her mind clicked, the pieces falling together as she realised then that she was on a swordship.

A Celestian ship!

"Who are you?" she croaked, keeping her excitement to a

minimum, less her hopes be dashed. "Where am I?"

She sat up on her cot uneasily, just as the man who had identified himself as Atton entered the cabin. Looking in mild annoyance at the crowd in the room, he swung around to all of them.

"Go! I said she was not to be disturbed!" he ordered the group.

Urana realised they were younger than she thought; just out of teenaged years. They obeyed, leaving the room with last glances at her.

"Hallo," Atton's friendly greeting made Urana smile. "I see you are awake. Are you feeling better?" He picked up a crystalator and walked toward Urana holding it out toward her to examine her wounds.

Urana sat up straighter. The pain wasn't as intense and nauseating. She did feel better, at least physically. Emotionally, she would never be the same.

"I am fine, Atton, thank you," she remembered his name. "Where am I? And who are you?"

Atton stood a little straighter, Urana noting his posture and authoritative bearing.

"I am Star-Captain Atton of the Sword *Zen Stellarion*. I am the direct descendant of Orizel who commanded the original crew and elected to remain on this world, Destinia, millennia ago. . ."

". . . In the Antiqchronals Quest!" Urana finished for him.

The surprise and relief on Atton's face was evident. "You know of us?" he asked tentatively.

Urana nodded. "Olesseus eventually returned home, but no one believed him," she added. And now came the hard part. "This happened countless millennia ago to us. Adantus and the Antiqchronal Quest are all myths! No one knows you are alive here."

A beat of irritation crossed Atton's face. "You are not here to return us home?" A harshness came into his voice.

"No, I was stranded here by my treacherous brother and his

followers!" She laughed out loud. "My infallible brother made a mistake!" She laughed again.

"Why would your own brother do this to you?"

Urana shook her head. "I would not follow him as a false god."

Atton smiled as if understanding completely.

"He would dare?"

"Yes, he would. He has changed," lamented Urana.

"Where is he now?" asked Atton. "If he is still on this world we will take action against him," he vowed.

"He is no doubt back on our world playing false god to our people."

Atton's head shot back in non-comprehension. "He was here on Destinia days before we found you, yet he is back on our worlds? How?"

"He has powerful allies who can travel time, the Chronossii. They are the ones who. . .who did the deed." Urana rubbed her abdomen and turned her face away from Atton in shame.

"Ah, yes, we had noticed you had given birth in unusual circumstances. He took your youngling?" Atton asked with sympathy.

Urana could only nod reluctantly. She tried to hide her inner pain.

"Gods!" Atton cursed. "I am sorry to hear of your woes when ours are relatively paltry."

They were silent for a while reflecting on Urana's ordeal. But she had enough of feeling sorry for herself. It was time for action. She drew in a steady breath, letting it out

"Where are we now?" she asked.

"Several days away from where we found you. We have a small sky skimmer and came for you when we heard your signal; an odd Celestian song."

Urana smiled. "My mother used to sing it to me. Strange how I remembered it while near death." She looked at Atton with gratitude. "Thank you for saving me."

Atton waved her away. "Ah, it was not easy. We were wary

about you and thought you to be a Lorespawn, a trick to lure us out even after we took a sample..."

"You took a sample of my DNA?" Urana was outraged. No one touched a Starguard.

"Yes," Atton said matter-of-factly. "We determined that you were not temporally-tainted by the Lore, but also indeed not of this world. So who are you?"

Still angry, she forced herself to calm down. "I am Urana, a Starguard, daughter of the Celestian Knights Hyphon the Sky Warrior and Ultra Ari," she said proudly.

Atton shook his head. "These names mean nothing to me."

Urana knew the Antiqchronals Quest had pre-dated the rise of the Celestian Knights, but it was still strange to hear this crew still existed.

"But you are pure Celestian," Atton continued, "if not an enhanced one, which is good enough." He paused as if mulling something over. "You could rule as a queen here!" he half-joked.

Urana's face darkened. "I am no queen!" she spat through gritted teeth, more out of anger toward Cirrius' claim of Kingship. Her anger caused a stab of pain and she lay back down.

"Are you in pain?"

"I'll be fine," she answered. "So you thought I was a Loremaiden? If you know about Loremaidens, I take it you are an Exmoor? But I see you have female crew. Are you not fighting the Devouts?"

Atton's face was a blank. "If a Loremaiden is a female spawn of the Lore, then yes, we are aware of them," he replied darkly. "But what is an Exmoor or Devout?"

Urana looked hard at him. He had the same looks as an Exmoor, but his face betrayed no dishonesty. She explained the Exmoors to him.

Atton was silent, worry on his face. "I suppose I am an Exmoor then." He didn't seemed too pleased by it. "Some of us males do live much longer and some of the females have started to exhibit strange abilities. We tried to confine the more disruptive ones, but some escaped. We do not know how this happened. . ."

"A Lore stone," Urana interrupted. She explained that to him.

Atton hesitated in thought. "We had thought it was this world affecting us naturally or a consequence from the war, but a Lore stone?" He was quiet again, pensive.

Urana had the feeling he knew what she was talking about.

"And they still retain such power millennia from now?" Atton was pained by the suggestion when Urana nodded.

"Is there something wrong?" she pushed him for more detail.

Atton sighed heavily. He looked around him, Urana following his gaze at the insides of the ship.

"This is the last of Adantus' sword ships, buried for millennia which has also served to hide our presence" Atton looked at the hull fondly. It has been my home for over six hundred years."

He was pleased by Urana's surprised look at his youthful appearance.

"After the original crews fell to the Lore upon this wretched Fifth world over nine thousand years ago, my ancestors searched for centuries gathering up all the remains of their swords, dead comrades, crystalators, power sources, and materials. Then centuries ago we . . . Exmoors and Devouts," he looked at Urana affirming their newly-named status, ". . . started to evolve apart. I do not think it was a natural occurrence and that we were subjects to an experiment. We have survived, but the consequence of that experimentation is that we can no longer produce offspring."

Urana understood his pain, but there were more besides him on this ship. "Your crew must all be hurting," she said.

"They are, yes. And there are divisions about how to live on Destinia; whether we should rule or unite with the Fifths. For a while we had a precarious peace, choosing to guide. However, the Great Father and Holy Mother seem to be testing us again as now we have a new enemy."

Urana leaned forward, wondering who this enemy could be.

Atton paced the room. "Over the past three thousand years, there has been a selective infection of Fifths by Psi-beings who have been shoring themselves upon this world. They pleaded mercy from extinction and we gave them the benefit of the doubt. But then they merged with thousands of Fifths driving most of them crazy. These Fifths are not ready for such power." He punched one fist into his other hand, clearly frustrated.

"We have hunted and destroyed many of the psis and their hybrids as they upset the balance of the good we have created. But many of the Devouts have allied themselves with the Psi. Some Devouts also advocate mating with the Fifths and to subjugate them. More still want to experiment on them to raise them to our level and to fight against us Exmoors. They seek to remake this world in their image. And you say this will continue unabated for millennia?" His pacing had practically turned into a frentic dance, his arms waving in frustration.

"We want no part in that," Atton reiterated. "We just want to go home. And we now have the capability to do so. All we needed was a sustained energy source. And here you are," Atton pointed at Urana. "All you would need to do is power our escape. Then it will not be long now. We will be going home. Sword *Zen Stellarion* will carry us home!" His eyes burned with hope.

Urana didn't know whether Atton was mad or delusional. She wasn't a Sword engineer, but she knew this sword would never fly again. She felt a weariness coming upon her as she prepared to tell Atton more hard truths.

"Atton," she looked him in the eyes, "the Six Worlds are gone! The Lore attacked and destroyed everything. The Celestians who survived moved to other worlds in another universe. I come from one such world." She saw the shock on his face.

"That is not possible. . ." his voice trailed off. If that were so, then all was lost and he had failed his crew. He sat down heavily.

"The Lore!" Atton grieved, a bitter laugh escaping his lips. "Always the Lore. We sought the other Antiqchronals across the stars, but the Lore destroyed us here. And now they have destroyed our homes!" He looked up to the ceiling, Urana knowing he was crying to the Universe.

Urana detached the crystalator from her forearm comms panel. "Here," she offered it to Atton. "These are the Scrolls of History. They detail the events after you left on the Antiqchronal Quest; the birth of the Celestian Knights, the return of the Lore, and the destruction of the Six Worlds. . ."

"There are Seven Worlds," Atton corrected her.

"Um, yes, about that. Atton, you'd better read the Scrolls in private. You can then decide whether to show the rest of your crew. In my time, there were only Six Worlds!" She kept the rest of the story to herself.

Atton gave her a dubious look, but took the crystalator.

"I will return soon," he said, his face still somewhat crestfallen.

Urana bade him farewell and could only hope that her crystalator was compatible with the *Zen Stellarion*'s technology.

She decided to get some sleep, but fitful swirling dreams filled with baby screams tormented her. She felt herself being surrounded, her insides torn out. . .

She awoke with a start from a nightmare.

Atton had returned. He was seated across from her at the small desk. His face looked haggard as if he had discovered a deep dark secret. Urana sat up knowing she felt as lost as he did right now.

"So, it is true." He chucked the crystalator back to Urana who caught it and attached it back to her forearm comms panel. "Our worlds disappeared millennia ago." He sighed through his nose. "And you are one of our descendants. I built a crew from Six Worlds here," he looked around at the bulkheads. "All, but the Elerae led by Xal. And Universe knows what happened to them!" He shook his head in dismay.

"Did you see the rest of the updated crystalator archive files?" Urana asked. "About the Amethystians surviving and now attacking their former kin?"

Atton nodded solemnly. "They and the Elerae are two sides of the same coin."

Urana nodded. "So, now what?"

"We are leaving this world." He left it at that, Urana wanting more information.

But Urana thought she could try a plan of her own.

"Do you understand how time travel works?" Urana asked Atton.

"No, not really," Atton confessed. "The crystalators don't have all that knowledge."

"Well, I'm stranded here on Earth in this time. There are no Astrals to rescue me and my brother's Astrals won't be back for me unless to kill me. This ship cannot fly, you must know that!" she tried to emphasise gently, ". . . and a signal from us could alert any surviving Lore to our position and kill us all. So my only option is to send a message through the Exmoors. Tell each generation of Exmoors about me, that I am trapped, and need help from the Astrals or the Starguards. And they will come and save me, any minute now!"

Atton looked around as if expecting someone to suddenly appear from a portal.

Urana followed suit. "Well, I guess it will take time to work." Her shoulders sagged in despair.

She was devastated inside, but this was no time to look even more vulnerable in front of Atton.

"We can do this," she said more to herself. "If only we knew the way to Magna Aura from here."

For the first time, Atton smiled. Urana thought it to be quite a grim smile, but it made her feel reassured that they would get home.

Atton said, "As I stated, we have been building. The *Zen Stellarion* herself cannot fly any more, you are correct. She is a broken wreck buried half under a lake from when she crashed. We were going to construct another sword and fly her to the four great galactic constellations which we identified as leading to the Sea of Voices."

At Urana's confusion, Atton brought out a cylindrical crystalator from which a holograph of the universe appeared.

"Here," he pointed out to Urana. "The Northrider, the Helmsman, the Crested Archer, and the Crooked Mage."

Urana looked at the star charts. She didn't recognise any of the four constellations. "That would have been a long shot. What had you in mind?"

"Let me show you," an enigmatic-sounding Atton said.

He's enjoying this, thought Urana. *And so am I.*

"Are you able to walk?" he asked her, Urana nodding affirmative.

Even though she was in pain and hobbling a bit, Urana just wanted to be doing something.

Atton led Urana through the sword, followed by a two-guard detail, Urana knowing she was still not quite trusted.

As if the guards could stop me anyway.

She passed more crew, male and female, who stared back at her with smiles to her face and whispers behind her back.

"Some of the females are unaffected," Atton commentated off the cuff, though Urana had wondered at their continued presence on the ship.

Zen Stellarion was truly on her last legs with huge patches of metal knitting the millennia-old ship together. Even rock showed through at some points, though Atton had assured Urana that the ship was fortified enough from the lake above and from any attack.

"Can you believe the Fifths did not even know how to make metal when we arrived?" Atton scoffed. "Truly primitive!"

"They call themselves humans," Urana corrected him, remembering her conversation with Zane at the night club so many thousands of years ago in the future. "And some of them are quite capable. They have potential," she defended them.

Atton smiled. "But only if we are not here to interfere and breed war." He gave Urana a raised eyebrow. They descended more decks, each more ragged and built up than the last. "We are on the engineering deck. It took a hit as we came down. We have managed to keep the core crystalator running now on back-up fusion reactors and solar power."

Even before they had reached the engine core, Urana's manoeuvre suit pinged an alert to her: temperature rising from a power source ahead. Knowing nuclear energy was not a Celestian energy source, Urana queried its origins.

"Oh, this world has plenty of raw materials so we searched for what we needed and built from there. We are very self-sufficient," he smiled with pride.

Urana was impressed, but there was something else as well, a familiar yet warped energy signature reading on her comms padd.

There were three guards in front of a large thick square metal door. Atton acknowledged them with a nod and they cranked the door open by hand. Their own escort waited just inside the door.

Urana stopped short on the threshold of entry. The object within was huge, but unmistakable.

"A portal!" she gasped.

Atton breathed in himself. "It is a remarkable feat my engineers have achieved after centuries of toil. The Amethystian scientists devised it, perhaps it is the forerunner of the technology *your* Amethystians used to escape their world," he emphasised.

The dimensional portal filled the frame of *Zen Stellarion*'s aft engineering section; twenty meters high and wide. A rounded section of metal was welded and wired together with other instruments powered by crystalators. A faint hum rose from the apparatus, but even Urana knew it was still not fully functional. The rear wall of engineering stared back at her through the middle of the portal.

Then Urana's eyes fixated on a sight which horrified her. Gathered around the bottom of the portal were seven translucent stones, half glowing from flowing crystalator energy.

"Lore stones!" snarled Urana. She looked at Atton angrily. "These are what infected you! You created the DNA alterations amongst yourselves!" She was disgusted by them.

Atton was unrepentant. "We did not know at the time. We ran tests, but by then it was too late. The Lore stones have enabled our survival. . ."

"And war," Urana shouted. "For millennia."

"Yes, and war, but this is what we need your energy for," Atton said. "The Lore stones will be destroyed, drained of energy, once the portal is activated. But," he sounded uncertain, "now that we know our Worlds are gone, where should we go? What of your worlds of Magna Aura?"

Now it was Urana's turn in the realm of uncertainty. If Cirrius and the Chronossii returned to Magna Aura they surely now controlled it. And even if the Starguards knew where she was they would have a hard time finding the exact time period she was in. She would have to find her own way out. She thought for a while and happily remembered her crystalator would have the location for the Ribbon System where Novan resided, but from Earth, the dimensional coordinates would be different.

"Can you view or scout the way ahead before entering the portal?" Urana suggested. "I have coordinates in my crystalator, set from Magna Aura, not Earth."

"That can be done, but it takes more power; your power!" he stressed.

"But can anything travel the other way?"

"There is that possibility," said Atton. "But again, the risk is to you and your power if you cannot shut the portal off in time, should Lore, Amethystians, or your brother and his allies try to enter the portal."

"We will just have to chance it," Urana made up her mind. "I have to return home!"

Atton let out a breath, a simple heavy sigh of relief. "Then we should prepare. I have not told you that our intelligence reports we are under threat of an imminent attack by the Devouts and the psis. They somehow know we are building something and want the *Zen Stellarion* and the portal. But we have scouting parties out shadowing their positions. We intend to destroy the

Zen Stellarion and thus the portal after we enter." He gave Urana a stern look. "There will be no turning back!"

A question popped into Urana's mind she hadn't thought to ask before now. "So where are we on this world? How far from Greece did you take me?"

"Greece?" Atton replied, shaking his head. "We just know local names. Here, we are surrounded by mountains and a large lake high up on a plain."

Urana tapped a command into her crystalator. She placed it on the nearest work station and a hologram beamed out from the opaque crystal. Landmasses of mountains, valleys, plains, lakes, seas, rivers appeared forming into the familiar continent Urana knew.

"This is Europe," she pointed out to Atton, "Or will be called that in the future." She pointed out the rest of the world as the hologram revolved around. "So where are we?" she repeated. There were no satellites or GPS to instantly guide her.

"Let us take a look," Atton smiled.

He walked out of the room, Urana following behind, in turn followed by Atton's two guards.

They travelled up five decks and across a section of crew quarters and then what used to be a hanger bay, now a food growth and storage facility. At the far end of the bay, past rows of stored wheat and refrigerated goats and lambs, they came to a working airlock.

Atton keyed in a code and the heavy doors slid opened. Without the vacuum of space as an encumbrance there was no need to equalise pressure. The doors were now simply large grey physical barriers to the outside.

Urana was surprised to see a large cavern around the sword, thinking she would see the surrounding countryside. There were steps carved into the wall upwards.

Atton explained as they started to climb up the cavern.

"*Zen Stellarion* was one of the smallest swords in Adantus' fleet; one kilometre long, half so wide. We crashed into the side of a volcano, like a blade cutting through flesh, collapsing part of its flank and taking a sizeable bite of the ship with it. Earthquakes and volcanic eruptions caused further damage to us. We were buried even as we altered the landscape. There was no hope in repairing her.

"And as we explored east and south, we became the subject of many ancient stories concerning comets, harbingers of death, giants, the descenders, the shining ones, and the such. They thought we were gods, but we have tried to avoid them since, but eight thousand years of oral traditions have turned it into dogma. Why not just worship the universe?" he shook his head in exasperation.

Urana grinned. This was far different to what Decion and Altair had once thought. But not her brother. Her grin subsided.

Thoughts best left alone, she told herself.

Ten minutes later, they were in a cavern mouth through another hatch disguised as a boulder. It was guarded by two more men, Amethystians, Urana saw by their purple hair even under their hooded cloaks. They politely ignored her. It was cold and windy as they finally walked out of the cave.

The view was amazing, a green valley sloping majestically down from a towering extinct volcano. Urana could see the shining surface of a large body of water in the far distance. She tapped at her comm pad and a stream of data crossed the screen from the reams of stored data from twenty-first century Earth.

"Lake Urmia," she said, looking at Atton, who studied the screen on her forearm. "This will one day become a land called Iran," she explained.

"Iran," Atton repeated the name, liking the notion of having learned something new. But he said, "Boring, like Earth and humans. These Fifths are so unimaginative!" They stood for a moment admiring the view as colours shifted in the coming low light. "Shall we return?" Atton asked.

But Urana was transfixed by the sight. "No, I'd like to watch the sunset."

Atton acquiesed. And they sat for another half hour, just past the sunset. After Urana retired to her room rejuvented.

In the morning, feeling slightly more rejuvenated after a surprisingly restful sleep, Urana had breakfast from the stock of food which had been stored in her med room; cold meat, fruits and water. Wondering what she would do for the day, there was a knock on her door.

"Enter."

One of Atton's Lieutenants greeted her, pleasantly, but succinctly.

"Captain Atton has requested you meet him in the primary medlab." She promptly turned and left.

"Okay," Urana said to herself, confused.

The main medlab was only two corridors away, though her med room was nominally being used as a guest quarters.

Hastily finishing her breakfast, Urana made her way there, noting only one security officer followed, though his demeanour was less sterner than the other escort detail. Once at the medlab, Urana entered.

Atton smiled, but looked strained and pensive.

"Urana," he began, "thank you for coming. Please sit. I, rather embarrassingly, have another request and also a confession to make."

"Oh?" Urana's sense of foreboding and pending betrayal from his tone arose within her. She could feel a rise of boiling energy surge through her. Her fists clenched and she felt reassuring heat swirl within them. She sat on a work bench.

Atton spoke. "After pondering the information from the future, I came to the decision. We cannot allow the Devouts to destroy this world once we have left. So I developed another plan," he considered her somewhat warily. "And again, you may be able to help us, if you are willing," Atton said.

"What more do you need of me?" Urana asked, suspicion creeping in her mind. She wasn't about to become a weapon for them.

"As you know, we Exmoors and Devouts cannot produce

offspring together; the result of the radiation from the war with the Lore, further complicated by the Lore stone energy altering our DNA. And of course, the offspring of those Celestians who did mate with humans will have a corrupted lineage making future procreation with other Celestians impossible. We will all die off without a future generation."

"What do you want?" Urana rapped off impatiently.

"We want to use your genes, your energy, to bridge the gap." Atton looked at Urana somewhat apprehensively.

Urana knew the look of devastation on her face hurt Atton. Though it was not his fault.

His voice grew softer, sympathetic. "Urana, what the Chronossii did to you, you will never have younglings, naturally, again."

Urana's eyes brimmed with tears. She hadn't been sure of the physical damage up to now.

"This is another thanks I owe my brother," she swore.

It was too much to bear. She punched the work top, the angry strike almost breaking the top surface in two.

"But," Atton looked decidedly embarrassed and fearful at the same time, "We may have a. . . solution." He paused, a fearful look in his face. "We. . . umm. . . when you arrived we did not know who you were and . . . umm. . . did not know if we could trust you. . . we. . ." He stood up straight. "We saw an opportunity to survive and took it. . ."

Urana stood up, braced for whatever Atton was about to say.

"I am sorry, Urana." Fear laced his voice. "We removed your eggs. . ."

"What!" Urana screamed.

Her arms automatically raised and fired plasma.

Atton flew across the room, the energy knocking him over equipment and against the wall where he crumpled to the floor. He coughed in pain, his hands instinctively patting the burn areas across his torso.

The door slid open and two armed guards rushed in seeing their commander down, the lab strewn with damaged equipment, and an angry Urana's glowing hands ready to lash out again. They aimed at Urana.

"No!" Atton wheezed. "Get out. It is under control." He waved off the guards, who looked at Urana and their leader. "Go," Atton ordered.

The guards looked at each other, reluctantly lowering their weapons. They slowly backed out of the medlab, the door sliding shut.

Urana stared at the prone Atton, uncontrolled fury in her eyes.

"You really think this is under control? That you can control me?" she sneered through bared teeth. She got ready to shoot again.

Atton raised his hand again. "Please, no, let me explain."

A seething Urana waited a good half minute before relenting.

What good would it do to kill Atton or the whole crew? she thought.

"How could you do this to me?" was all she could say.

Atton stayed slumped on the ground nursing his wounds. Urana didn't care.

Then she remembered something; dreams, dark visions of people standing over her while she slept.

"How long have you been doing this to me?"

Atton looked confused. "How long? Only once, when you first arrived. We did not know if you would survive and after we got to know you it was too late to say anything."

"So why say anything now?" Urana asked.

Atton backed himself up against the wall. He winced in pain, blood on his face. He lifted his tunic revealing burn welts from his chest to his belt line. Urana sighed heavily. She marched over to a cabinet searching for medical supplies.

"Top cabinet on the left," Atton directed her.

Urana gave him a warning look, but grudgingly reached over to the next cabinet. She came across jars and containers of unfamiliar ingredients.

"The blue ceramic jar," Atton said, still wincing from the floor. "Burn treatment salve."

Retrieving the foot-high stoppered amphora, which Urana could see and smell consisted of some fatty residue, she set it down beside Atton. She then filled a bowl with water for him and soaked a few bandages which she threw down to him.

"Treat yourself," she said compassionless as she sat on the floor by him. "Now explain."

Atton started dabbing his wounds and burns. In between winces and ouches, he started talking.

"We meant no harm," he said. "At first we were ensuring our survival, but we knew, I knew, we had done something wrong especially after we got to know you and the sacrifices you had made. We were selfish, but I am now telling you because we have a plan. Not only can you save us, but you can have younglings through artificial means." He smiled in hope, his swollen lip threatening to open up.

Urana tried to contain her feelings drawing her body inwards feeling subconsciously over-fertile. The emptiness gripped her inside again. Her emotions were still too raw. She knew unleashing her energy here would have burned the whole ship out. Clenching her fists, clamping down on her emotions, Urana fought back her rage and tears.

She turned to Atton. "What do you want of me?" her voice full of anger.

Atton knew he had to reply carefully. "We want to produce younglings from you..."

"Universe, what?" Urana fumed, not believing her ears. "Have you not listened or cared about what Cirrius and the Chronossii did to me? How could you think I want this?"

"Urana, I have listened. The younglings will be part of you and us, the crew, but matured here in the lab," he told her. "You can help heal us and our DNA; perhaps even bring the Exmoors and Devouts together."

Urana was unimpressed. The thought of conceiving another youngling, let alone with strangers terrified her. The lab may have been one of the only intact rooms on the sword, but it did not seem adequate enough to protect a youngling.

"No," was all she could say.

Atton inclined his head, respectfully, gauging Urana's reaction before continuing.

"Look, if we do this, the younglings will be created to balance the power struggles and also counter the Lore stone's effect. With our genetic technology and your energy, such younglings will have the Exmoor's longevity and a Devout's power. They will be your legacy and our saviours."

He looked at Urana, desperate for any sign of approval.

Urana had her doubts. "Jesus Christ!" she blurted out remembering the human curse.

Where had this child been when the Starguards had been in the future? she thought.

"What?" Atton finished dressing his burns, looking at Urana in confusion.

Urana raged at him. "You are not a God. And I am not the Virgin Mary."

"I do not understand," Atton wiped his forehead with a cool cloth.

"Never mind. Earth myths," Urana replied tersely.

"I see."

"Do you?" Urana asked. She needed to be understood. "I am not a breeder for you."

"I know," Atton replied.

He grimaced as he pushed himself up to stand. Holding his side he shuffled over to another metal cabinet. He reached inside withdrawing a small cylindrical metal canister. He unscrewed the top and pulled out a sliding inner padded sleeve which held in its centre a tiny oval crystalator.

"Your legacy," he said.

Urana was taken aback by how quickly things were moving.

"How long have you been planning this?" she asked.

"Oh," chuckled Atton. "You are not the first we have tried. We have been trying to conceive younglings for centuries without success. The crystalator is a prototype. I am just adapting the plan and you are our best hope for this world's future."

Making a face to show her understanding, Urana let Atton continue.

"This," he held up the almost transparent crystalator with fine runes carved on it, "will be implanted into the youngling's brain. It will help the youngling to process new languages and cultures, to blend in. In an ideal scenario, the youngling will regenerate every few hundred years. And while they may remember fragments of their former lives, they will not know their origins, as the implanted crystalator will have to delete selected data over the millennia to function or to re-set when the youngling regenerates. The younglings will be bulwalks against the Devouts and Exmoors becoming too powerful, able to detect, resist, and absorb the Lore stone energy. That should help to defeat the Devouts and bring peace," Atton explained.

"This crystalator will also have another function. It will be a guide. Once there is peace or the younglings are worthy the runes will reveal themselves to them, unveil their legacy, and guide them to us wherever we are." He stared at Urana, finished, awaiting her verdict.

Her face was full of a hundred questions.

"Yes, there are lots of things that can go wrong," he pre-empted her unasked questions. "But it is the best option we have."

Urana was quiet with thought. And trepidation.

"You're serious about this?"

Atton nodded.

She went back into her thoughts: *A youngling? Younglings? Younglings to be lost and abandoned by me! Would it be fair to them? Will I risk changing the future? The younglings could become powerful enough to rule the world. Or save it.*

Her anxieties kicked in and she thought she would panic. She regarded Atton. He was patient. And she suddenly realised he was taking a risk as well. He wanted to save this world. He was acting where the Starguards and Astrals had not. They had abandoned humanity, but a Celestian was here now to save the Earth.

Urana needed more time. "I hate what you have done to me and I will never forgive you." She looked at him pointedly; his naked guilt making her angry again. "I need time to think."

Atton, despite his bid to hide his disappointment, bowed his head in acquiescence.

"Tomorrow?" he asked tentatively.

"Tomorrow," she affirmed.

Urana left Atton alone as she went back to her room, the trip seeming to take longer than normal as she thought. She noticed the fragile state of the *Zen Stellarion* more and even its crew. They may have been Celestians, but the strain of living in a broken, grounded star ship on a world like Earth for generations was taking its toll. Morale was low.

Inside her room, Urana collapsed onto her bed. She lay still for many minutes trying to take it all in.

Who am I to have another youngling only to abandon it to Earth? She thought again. *For what – to save Earth with eggs stolen from me? Do I care about humanity or the Zen Stellarion's crew? Would I ever see the younglings again?* That hurt Urana. *I will be a mother to more younglings and never see them.* That made her angry.

But then she thought - *This is Cirrius' fault. If I ever escape Earth and have a chance of seeing my son again then having another youngling now who could potentially survive into the far future would be the best revenge I could have on Cirrius. I must survive; put this behind me. I must live. And give myself the best chance of surviving through this ordeal and for my children.*

Urana had made her mind up. But she would tell Atton her decision tomorrow. She needed to take her mind off this. She decided to explore. Leaving her room she walked around the ship for exercise. She didn't see Atton, but she ran into his second-in-command Dener, and other crew members Nary,

Lelek, and Jamev. The latter three had been the crew whispering in the medbay when she had arrived. They were quite friendly now and Urana found herself enjoying their company while they ate in the forward galley.

"Atton told us about the Elerae destroying Amethystia," Lelek said. She was the pretty Amethystian with long purple braids.

"I am sorry," Urana spoke meekly as if personally apologising for the whole of Elera. She all of a sudden felt very subconscious about her own blue hair.

But Lelek seemed to hold no grudges.

"When we return to your worlds, I will speak to the leader of the Worldfleet and tell him of the experiences our ancestors had while on the Antiqchronal Quest and of their descendants while on Earth. We are all Celestians. Fighting amongst each other is wrong. My sister also agrees."

Urana smiled at her youthful earnestness, but could only reply, "I only hope they listen."

They had drinks, the closest thing Urana had tasted like Wolobean juice. Nary, the best food forager and *Zen Stellarion's* best chemtech had found a combination of eight local berries, herbs and nuts which approximated the taste. And it was fermented, a rare treat, but Urana declined, sipping the fresh version. She wanted all her senses ready for tomorrow.

For the rest of the day the three crew showed her around the ship, through broken corridors, patched up crew quarters, observation atriums, and personal farms and gardens, but not the bridge. Urana wondered if it was for security reasons or if Atton was avoiding her and had ordered them not to. After their evening meal, Urana retired again to her room. She noticed she was unaccompanied by security. That and the long day had made her happy, secure, and tired enough to fall asleep as soon as she got into bed.

Waking up the next day, Urana dialled her manoeuvre suit into softer attire and headed straight for the labs. There was no need to comm Atton. He was waiting for her at the medlab.

Urana didn't return his knowing smile.

"Despite your theft, I am ready to do this," she stated calmly, adding, "But, if I am betrayed again, I will burn you all to hell. Understand?"

Atton nodded. "We will not betray you again, you have my word."

Urana looked him in the eyes seeing only trust, and more than enough fear and guilt that she believed him.

"So, how do we start?"

"We need to take some samples," he stared at her apprehensively.

Urana's breath caught, but she nodded.

The door to the medlab opened.

Walking in, Atton gestured to the room's sole occupant.

"Medtech Tyeca will perform the procedures."

Urana regarded the Meccun Tyeca. "I suppose you were the one who took my eggs?" she said too harshly for her own liking.

The medtech had the good grace to look as guilty as Atton, her dark features flushing.

"Please accept my deepest apologies. . ."

"I know," Urana cut her off. "Let's get on with it."

"I take my leave," Atton announced.

Urana watched him leave without a word.

Tyeca turned briskly walking to a refrigerated unit at the rear of the room, glad to have the distraction of work. From the fridge she took vials and canisters spreading them out along a bench with crystalator instruments.

Next she took blood and tissue samples from Urana's arm, the Starguard not thinking about the procedures, letting her thoughts stray into revenge and survival.

Tyeca was methodical and quick, the crystalator sensors allowing for an efficient procedure.

"All complete," Tyeca confirmed calmly, placing the samples and fertilised eggs removed from Urana into a silver canister and that back into the cold storage unit.

Urana nodded her thanks. She almost felt like a new woman;

whole somehow, with a new chance to create a new life. With a curt nod to Tyeca, Urana departed and returned to her room.

For the next few hours, Urana rested. At times she desperately wanted to be alone, but she knew it would be counter-productive. Besides, she owed Atton in one matter. And she could feel her powers returning. Either Vostra's temporal effects had worn off or her psychological wall had dropped. Urana didn't care either way. She left her room. It was time for action.

"I'm surprised," Atton startled Urana upon his entry.

For the past few hours, well into the night, Urana had been in the sword's engine room running golden plasma energy from her arms to recharge the two huge circular crystalator portal engine coils. She made sure she avoided the Lore stones.

"Atton," Urana looked over to him still pouring energy into the engines.

Her slight smile, while warming Atton's heart, stabbed at him all the worse for the news he had to give her. Urana caught his subdued reaction and stopped her flow.

"Atton?" Urana's heart thumped harder. "The youngling? What's wrong?"

"Nothing, but you had better come with me!"

"What?" Urana asked as they walked through the corridors. "Is there a problem?"

Atton shrugged. "We do not know, yet." He didn't say anything else along the way until they were with Tyeca.

There, in the corner of the Tyeca's lab the medtech showed Urana the birthing tank. It had been covered by a light-weight siler tarpaulin before, now tucked away at the tank's side, so Urana had not been aware of it. But now, in the middle of the blue liquid, what Urana saw astonished her. She turned back to Atton.

"How is the youngling so big? And why is it glowing?" Urana stared at the foetus in the tank with a bright yellow glow around its body.

"So this is not normal for a Starguard?" Tyeca asked.

"Err, nope!" Urana stared back at her. "Are you sure you carried out the procedure correctly?"

"Umm," Atton had no words, so turned to Tyeca standing by him.

Shaking her head, she said, "Of course we did. But, quite clearly we did not compensate for the power of your energy mixed with Celestian DNA and we detected some previously unexpected excess energy which must have caused an unusual reaction." Tyeca looked pleased with her explanation.

"Excess energy?" Urana was confused. "This isn't normal." She pointed at the tank.

The medtech nodded in understanding. "Were you ill at some point? There are several unusual markers in your DNA."

Urana thought of her time on Earth. "Yes, when I was on Earth in the future, I was ill. It was diagnosed as some form of temporalosis, from my forced transport from Magna Aura to Earth by the Astrals, but the Exmoors tried to cure it. I guess they weren't able to do anything before the Universe chose a different path for me and the Starguards. And of course there was Vostra's power. . ." She didn't finish the thought. "So what does all of this mean? Have I harmed the child?" She was concerned for its life.

Tyeca smiled and shook her head.

"No, he is fine."

"He? A boy?" Urana grinned. "Another son." A sudden wave of guilt hit her as she thought of what she had already lost.

But Atton was at her side. "Do not think of the loss, only the gain. The new life," he assured her.

"Your energy and the residual temporal energy also enriched the other donor DNA, enhancing the youngling's lifespan."

"Whose DNA did you use?" Urana asked, already knowing the answer as she looked at Atton.

"I am the captain, of course, so yes, my DNA," he answered, casually.

"So our DNA was mixed with each other," Urana pursed her

lips and exhaled noisily. "We are the parents of a new Celestian boy."

"Yes, he is pure Celestian and part Starguard! He will pass for human, though will not get ill, will be stronger, live longer, and have great power hidden within him," he beamed proudly.

Urana smiled. "The last Starguard on Earth; my legacy!"

"How long before he matures?" Urana asked.

Tyeca replied, "At this rate, it will be three weeks before he is born. We will arrest his growth at age two. Then he will be given to a human family to raise until adulthood."

"What? Why?" Urana was aghast at having her son raised by humans.

Atton explained. "We had to change our plans. We are leaving soon; through the portal. So the youngling will have to be left behind as planned. But do not worry, we have selected a human couple already who will take care of him. He will be able to counter the Lore stone and balance the forces between the Devouts and Exmoors."

Urana nodded thoughtfully. Though it was a good plan she wasn't overly keen to leave another child behind. She counted the Universe's graces, glad she had a healthy child.

"But he will never know us," she lamented.

"In time, he will. The implanted crystalator will do its work over time." Atton seemed confident enough.

Sighing, Urana stared longingly at the tank "Just let me know how the rest of the process goes," she said, before leaving the medlab. She knew if she had stayed longer, she wouldn't be able to let the child out of her sight.

For the next few days, Urana deliberately stayed out of the med labs. She didn't want to jinx things so she received updates from Tyeca and Atton. That somehow made the 'pregnancy' seem normal to her. Urana didn't want to see him until he was born, albeit at two years old. She busied herself charging up power supplies around the ship, gaining her strength, and making friends amongst the crew. She was now a trusted member of *Zen Stellarion*.

She met up with Atton and Tyeca in Atton's quarters. Even though Urana would not forget what they had done to her, she couldn't help still warming to them. The topic fell on the youngling.

"Perhaps we have given Earth a chance to survive," Atton conceded. "There will be a balance. And once he completes his mission, there will be peace between the Exmoors and Devouts, and our son will return to us."

"How?" asked Urana, curious as to how her son would span the reaches of the universe.

Atton only shrugged. "He is our son, Urana; He belongs with us, among the stars and not on Earth. Besides, he will have many questions and we will be the ones to answer them, wherever we are. And as to the how," he smiled again at Urana. "Once he has countered any existing Lore stones, the only way he can do this is to absorb its energy. . ."

Urana was shocked. "What? What will that do to him?"

"That is the best part," Atton said. "Upon accomplishing his mission, the crystalator will activate and send him a message. His absorbed energy from the Lore stone will enable him to generate a portal to our location wherever that will be. He will be with us!"

Urana tried to look like she understood what he said and just smiled.

"What message will that be?" she asked.

"The one you will record for them now," Tyeca said. "I can set the crystalators up for you."

Urana smiled joyfully. "That sounds great."

At that moment there was a knock on Atton's door. They all looked around as they had not been expecting anyone else.

"Enter," Atton said.

The door slid open. Lelek poked her head in then entered the room, purple hair bouncing about. She was followed by another woman.

Urana had never seen her before, but noted her beauty under her red hair.

Atton's face clouded over for an instant before he forced a smile on his face.

The red-haired woman bounded over to Atton and kissed him full on the lips, Urana feeling a little awkward watching, while Tyeca scowled, cross-armed.

Lelek was all smiles. "Urana, this is my sister. She is just back from her wanderings in the far north."

Atton cleared his throat. "She is also my wife."

Wife! Urana's thoughts ran wild.

"Pandra," she introduced herself, holding out her arm for Urana.

Urana clasped her arm in greeting.

Urana took in Pandra's wild auburn hair accenting her remarkable beauty, with wide lips and cheeks.

She smiled at her. "Hallo, Pandra, I am Urana and I am glad to meet you. If you'll excuse me, I was just about to record a message."

"Ah, yes," Pandra looked between Atton and Urana. "I had heard of my husband's plan for younglings." She glared at Atton mischievously, who stared away.

Urana tried to ignore Pandra's pointed remark as she followed Tyeca to the far wall to begin her message into the crystalator which also recorded her image.

"Hallo, my dear child. I am your mother... Urana of the Starguards!"

Behind her, Pandra smiled to herself. Yes, she had heard much of Urana's and Atton's growing friendship. But she was not threatened by it. Her own plans were almost complete. And no one, not even Urana or Atton could stop her. Nor would they be around when she took their precious youngling.

CHAPTER ELEVEN

Elysiun

"Sacred Universe!" Astara cursed. "He's betrayed us, again!" she shouted at the holographic message sent to them.

"He and Timechantress, both," Novan reminded them, incensed.

"Urana can't be dead!" a shocked Azure cried. "He wouldn't kill his own sister!"

"We don't know him anymore," Astara said. "And my brother. . ." she couldn't finish the sentence, thinking of Decion's fate.

First had been the shock that Cirrius was still alive. He had Timechantress port a crystalator to them with a personal message:

"Hallo, dear Novan, I hope that dead rock of a sun-less world is enough for you because you and your people will be there for the rest of your lives. No more will Magna Aura be your home and source of comfort.

"You left me to die permanently at the hands of the Amethystians," he spat angrily. "You imprisoned my wife!" he shouted. "And you insulted my children!" He controlled his anger breathing in deeply. The Starguards could see the décor of his island cabin around him.

"Well, regretfully, Urana is dead. Left to die on Earth in the past. I do regret that, but it was necessary. She did not want to join me. But not to fear for her new-born youngling, a boy, for I have him and I will raise him as my own!" he sneered. "And as for Decion, he is my prisoner. He was never going to train my boys; they are too good for him. Do not attempt to rescue Decion or launch an attack or he will die.

"I am protected here. You see," he laughed, "I had actually found the lost Astral kin long before you had returned. Timechantress and I had anticipated your return, your

233

reactions, and planned this long ago. And you fell for it. The Chronossii, they are not called Astrals," he stressed, " were extremely grateful when I had found them, revealed to them their true heritage, and rescued them from Earth. They are totally loyal to me and will help me expand my empire. They are my eyes, arms, and shields, throughout time.

"We are ready for the Amethystians. And when we are finished with them, we are coming for you, Novan." He smiled thinly. "You, Sceptre, Astara, and Azure; the Starguards and Astrals are finished. Long live the Chronossii!" he held up a tall translucent glass of nectar and saluted them, before the holographic winked out.

Anger sliced the silence which followed.

"Next time he is dead, I will make sure he stays dead," Astara snarled.

Azure almost laughed; with her jet-black hair crossing her face sporting a contemptuous growl, Astara had reminded her of Decion. Almost.

"Well, Cirrius has played his hand," Novan said, somewhat over-cheerfully. "He is over confident. You will get your chance, Astara."

Astara harrumphed and sat in a chair. They were in Novan's office, the original bridge of Sword *Celectral*, intact and mainly for his use when he needed solitude. Now what was left of the Starguards were there, but it gave him no comfort.

Novan, foolishly, he now knew, had been over confident, too. He regretted letting Sceptre leave so soon, after Urana and Celestra had left for Earth. He had been confident that Timechantress and Celestra had turned a new leaf and that Cirrius' death would unite the people. Cirrius had seen to that, but on his own terms.

Azure turned to Novan who had remained quiet for a long time as if debating an important decision. She wondered if it was now time to broach what she had been feeling regarding his rather surreptitious actions recently.

She approached him. He turned to her as if her presence

seemed to spur him into action, though his smile was not one of confidence.

"Both of you, come with me. It is time I revealed a few truths to you!"

Azure and Astara peered at each other. *What now,* they thought.

Without another word, the three Starguards, alone, walked through the city. Entering one of the hangars they had embarked on his personal craft and lifted off out into the system. He busied himself with duties, without a word to his two passengers, which made them uneasy under the colourful ribbon-like strands of star dust surrounding them.

Azure hadn't seen a normal star for a long time now. But she could definitely feel the tingle of Lore energy mixed in with the dust. She let it brighten her mood.

An hour into the journey Novan said: "Because of the Lore attacks and damaged swords, we did not get to explore much," he explained. "But after Azure saved us and after the Amethystian attacks, we were able to explore and we found this..." he pointed out the view port. "We call it Tessara."

The gaseous world spun in a sea of orange and yellow. It was a large world, deep red with no visibility beneath its scarlet veil.

"Elysian is actually one of several moons orbiting it at long range." Novan said, steering the ship to starboard.

But Astara and Azure had fallen silent. Novan grinned without saying another word. For what gained the Starguards' attention was not the world, but a very unexpected sight.

"Are those. . .?" Astara began to ask.

"Yes, they are," Novan replied proudly.

The five swords were shorter, broader and more angular than the elegant classical sharp crisp lines of the older Celestian or Magna Auran swords, but beautiful in their own way nonetheless. They were deep purple with four curvy protrusions nestled over propulsion nacelles in sleek lines around the aft section. From their viewports, Azure and Astara could see new repair and modifications being carried out on the swords by

Elysian ships and crews.

"Amethystian swords," Novan confirmed. "We captured them during their last attack, though we did not know who the crews were then."

"Where are the crews?" Azure asked. "Are they prisoners?"

"No," Novan answered, sombrely. He stared at the planet. "We gave them a choice. To renounce their animosity against us and live in peace among us or. . ." he pointed his chin at the planet. "To the last Amethystian, they never surrendered. To the last member they jettisoned themselves in pods or individually down to the planet. They will not return." His face reflected the red glare from Tessara as they closed in on a sword.

They flew on in silence until they docked with one of the swords.

"Welcome to Sword *Aurajena*," Novan announced. "The other swords are similar, though we have managed to rebuild one ourselves from salvaged parts of the *Relentance* and other wrecked Amethystian swords."

After docking, Novan walked them through the sword's corridors, crews of Star and Sky Warriors manning stations, testing installed equipment, or repairing damaged sections. Novan gave a running tour, explaining this section or that, introducing them to various officers and crews. They then reached the bridge.

"Who commands your swords?" Astara asked, interested in the job.

"I do," a long unheard male voice said, as he walked onto the bridge behind them.

There was a stunned silence as Azure and Astara saw who it was before them.

"Altair!" breathed Azure.

She rushed over to Altair and clapped him around the shoulders. She just about held back her tears only noticing the changes to him.

Altair beamed back at her. "Hallo, Azure, Astara. Good to see you both again. I see you still need my help," he laughed.

He stood there as if nothing about him had changed.

There was a sudden awkward silence. Seeing their eyes taking in his lack of a left eye covered by a gold-fabric patch, a trimmed blond beard complimenting his aged visage, and his left arm with the empty sleeve pinned from the elbow to his manoeuvre suit, Altair smiled, though not sadly.

"I've been in the wars myself."

"What happened to you?" Astara asked, trying and failing not to stare.

"You should see the other guy!" he grinned, deflecting the question.

"And how are you here?" Azure wanted to know. "When did you get here?"

"And why did you not tell us, Novan?" Astara asked, with annoyance in her voice. She took her eyes off Altair.

Altair calmed the clamour as he told them of his adventures after their supposed deaths on Earth; his lone galactic wanderings, his losing battle with a creature called the Infinitus, his arrival back to Earth in the Twenty-fifth century, to his return home by Adam Finitum of the Zater Jen.

"Or rather here," Altair raised his good arm. "I arrived three years ago in the heat of the battle with the Amethystian fleet. I didn't know where I was, but I instinctively sided with the planet being attacked by unfamiliar swords. Adam Finitum must have somehow known I was needed here. I didn't know who the Amethystians were at the time, but they retreated. After the battle, I was surprised to see Novan approaching me in space."

He grinned at Novan, who still seemed bashful at having kept his secret for so long.

"Anyway, we formulated a plan should the Amethystians attack again. Myself and a sizeable force would hide around Tessara with the five captured swords and train. And if the Amethystians did not return we could always use the swords to get back to Magna Aura. Or at least that was the plan until Cirrius screwed that up with his Kingship. And then you were returned by the Astrals." Upon mentioning that, Altair suddenly went silent and looked around the bridge. "So where are Urana, Decion, and Aerl?"

Eyes turned grim as they looked everywhere, but at Altair.

Novan sighed. "That is why I brought Azure and Astara here, Altair. There has been news." He then turned to the two female Starguards, explaining, "We operate in communications silence so as not to alert the Amethystians and now Cirrius. The swords are in very low orbit and obscured by the atmosphere." Turning to Altair, Novan continued, "There has been a message from Cirrius. We do not know the whole truth, but Urana apparently did not return from Earth with the Chronossii. Cirrius says she is dead! To the Magna Aurans he blamed it on the Amethystians! But he. . . killed her himself or as good as." Novan almost choked on the last words.

Altair face grew dark with anger. "Killed her? I don't understand! Why?" He felt as if his heart had been punched.

"She wouldn't follow him," Novan explained simply. "And he wanted revenge for us leaving him for dead at the hands of the Amethystians."

Right fist balled up and starting to glow red, Altair swore, "When I get my hands on him. . ."

"There's more," Novan said, knowing this part would be harder. He held Altair at the shoulders. "Urana was with youngling," he breathed in deeply, "Your youngling. A boy!" he exhaled. "And Cirrius forced Urana to bear the youngling so he could possess it, raise as his own, believing you to be dead."

A choked agonised sound grew in Altair's throat. "A youngling?"

He shook his head, a brief smile of pleasure lighting his eye. Then he reared back from Novan's embrace, his smile growing dark across his face as he realised what he had lost.

"We will get my son back!" he swore.

"Yes, we will," Novan promised, as Astara and Azure drew close to comfort him.

"And rescue Decion," Astara reminded them. "Cirrius claims he is their prisoner!" she scowled.

But Altair smiled, "Decion a prisoner? Then I feel sorry for his jailers!"

This at least derived a grin from Astara.

Novan answered the last part of Altair's question.

"And as for Aerl, I commanded him to start his search for the Great Breach. We need to find out if there are any Celestian kin on the Old Worlds! But we could not have predicted Cirrius' actions," he lamented.

"Ah true," Altair held his forefinger up. "But there are some out there for sure, as I discovered a lost Celestian colony!"

"What?!" all three others uttered.

"Why did you not tell me this before?" Novan asked, incredulous. "Out of all the things you told me when you first arrived you never mentioned this!"

"I was busy with the swords and I wanted to tell Aerl first," he shrugged. "It was his mission, so I was saving the news for him."

"So tell us about them," Azure was excited.

"Another time," Altair promised, smiling sadly this time. "Besides, I do not think I could ever find them again even though I was there for two hundred years." A haunted look flickered in his eyes as if in memory. "But when we Starguards are all together and telling tall tales, as the humans would say, I will tell you a truly amazing tale!"

"Agreed," Novan said, eager to hear the story. But they had other business to attend to. "Back to the matter at hand. . ."

But Azure interrupted Novan with a look that made him stop talking. Something in her mind had just fallen into place, while they had been walking around the *Aurajena*. Novan's whole demeanour had changed as soon as he had stepped aboard and she was sure it wasn't just to do with Altair.

An exciting thought bubbled in her mind, and she saw the mutual look in Novan's eye. She shook her head in amusement.

"No memorial, Novan? Really? Are some of those Sky Warriors you said were dead really here?" she asked, her excitement growing.

"Most of them," Novan replied coyly, his smile growing.

Azure's eyes pleaded for answers. "Please tell me. . ."

Novan activated his comms. "Captain to the bridge."

"What is happening?" a confused Astara asked, looking at Altair who also had a grin on his face.

The door at the side of the bridge opened.

"May I present to you the Captain of the *Aurajena*, Deputy to Fleet Commander Altair, the Sky Commander, and my wife," Novan replied, a broad grin on his face.

Classia came bounding onto the bridge toward Azure.

"Hallo, my Little Star."

Azure just stared. She wasn't sure how she would react upon seeing her supposed dead friend alive. It had been hard enough trying to accept her death, but now. . .

Looking at Classia, Azure could see the same young girl with curly brown locks, deep brown eyes, and full lips. Even now, forty years since leaving Magna Aura, Classia was still youthful, beautiful and more womanly. She was a worthy wife to Novan, rising a touch of jealousy within Azure.

Classia stopped short of Azure, bemusement on her face, looking at Novan, confused.

"You are glad to see me, are you not?" she asked Azure. Her skin crinkled around her eyes in a smile.

Azure smiled. "Of course I am." Though she felt stiff with emotion. "I just hadn't thought of what to do if you were alive!" She walked toward Classia. "I wasn't even sure I had actually been here the first time, and then to hear you were dead made me feel this place was cursed. But. . ." She hugged Classia with all her might and felt the sincerity returned. "Welcome back from the dead. You look amazing for a dead woman. But don't ever do that to me again!"

She squeezed Classia's hands. They felt older.

Classia laughed. "Now you know how I felt when you did not tell me you were a Starguard and then you disappeared." She stuck her tongue out in jest.

"We are sorry for the subterfuge, but we could not let anyone know what we were doing or the swords could have been discovered and destroyed by the Amethystians or even that coward Cirrius. We were not ready for battle, but now we are." Her dark brown eyes shone in excitement taking Azure back to the days when they played in the skies over Halcyon.

"We have five swords here in orbit, the *Aurajena*, the *Exmoor*, the *Infinitus Rex*, the *Arrowsun*, and the *Destina*," Novan proudly announced the names.

"Some familiar and strange names," Azure said.

"I chose them from my travels and adventures," Altair added. "Plus there is this. . ." He held up a palm-sized blue pointed shard of crystal. He passed it around.

"A crystalator?" Astara asked, turning the sharp-sided artefact around in her hand.

"No, it's a piece of Adam Finitum. He told me to use it when I was in trouble. I think it will summon the Zater Jen army to our cause."

"Cool," Azure breathed.

She took the shard from Astara. rolling it around in her palm. Azure could feel the temporal energy eddy around inside. It felt different to a Lore's energy; warmer, sweeter—she licked her lips involuntary—and its pulsing rhythym was pleasing to her soul.

"You've really been on an epic adventure." Azure gave the shard back to Altair who tucked it away in a hip belt pouch.

"We could use the Zater Jen's help now!" Astara said.

"I'll save it till later!" replied Altair. He patted the shard for luck.

"We have a lot to catch up on," Novan said, looking at his wife and Azure. "And much to plan. Let us. . ."

BOOM!

The *Aurajena* rocked violently sideways. Alarms starting blaring and comm pads came to life in a cacophony of bewildered voices. For a second, the anti-grav dropped out before kicking in again rising and dropping them to the floor.

The sword, however, stayed pitched at roughly sixty degrees; twisting, creaking, burst pipes and ripped cables adding to the stressful chorus of damage and complaints.

Just as Novan was about to issue orders an ominous black light blanketed the room clawing back in the explosive sound like a smothering hole. Even the alarms seemed severely muted.

Azure tried to move but could not. The darkness was cold, morbidly so, clinging to her in a death-like caress. The mordant stage seemed to last forever. There was no sound, no screams or movement. She could only scream within her own mind. But she could feel something; a presence, dark and malevolent.

It moved through the darkness and Azure had the sense the presence was moving toward her. She tried to ward it off summoning any power she had. The reaction was strange; a strangled sound, sudden movement, and just as she had given up hope, the black light disappeared as suddenly as it had appeared. The alarms were deafening.

Everyone was still standing, except one.

"Novan!" cried Classia. She dropped down at her husband's side. "Novan, what is wrong? She reached out to touch him, only to snatch her hand away as if in pain. "Universe, he is so cold!"

She put her hands to her face, over her mouth in shock, as tears welled up.

"He is dead!" She looked frantically at everyone. "He is dead," she screamed again. "Deb do something!" she stared wild-eyed at Azure. "Someone do something!"

The lights about them flickered in mad sequences, throwing dancing shadows which kept them on edge.

Altair was first by Novan's side. He tried to cradle Novan in his arm, but he too jerked his good arm back in shock.

"Gods, he is cold!"

Classia raged. "What happened?"

Astara cried out above the alarms, "Azure, can you do anything?"

Azure was frozen to the spot. She had felt something in the dark, an evilness.

Classia shook her hard, bringing her back into reality.

"Something, some. . . being was here, Class," she told Classia.

"I felt its presence in the dark. It was cold." She shivered. She couldn't bear to look at Novan's body.

"Can you track it?" Altair snarled.

"No," Azure whispered, still half in shock. "It hid itself well. There's no energy trace."

"Amethystians? Chronossii?" Astara snapped. "Lore!" She paced around in a circle, fists clenched.

Azure shook her head, her voice barely above a whisper, "No!" She tried to concentrate on what it felt like. "It felt. . . wrong!" She tried to put it into words. "Like it was not from this universe."

Everyone stared at her.

"Seriously?" Altair couldn't contain his anger. He looked back down at Novan.

Is he doubting me? Another universe? Azure wondered if her instinct was right.

"Whether it is or not, they could still be ready to strike again!" Astara said, focussing herself. "First Urana, now Novan. Someone will pay for this," she vowed.

Suddenly, a flurry of activity spilled onto the bridge with the arrival of a half dozen Sky and Star warriors.

They stopped short upon seeing Novan on the floor, dead. They looked around at the Starguards and their commanding officer.

"Keep a look out!" Altair ordered to no one in particular. "The attackers may return. Remain on high alert." A few of the officers disappeared, barking orders (and the news) into their comms. One remained behind, panic on his face, wanting to speak, but not.

Azure crouched down by Novan's side, Altair running scans with his suit's crystalator.

His brows creased in deep worry. "I don't understand this!" his voice hard. He tapped into his crystalator pad again, re-running the readings. "I do not understand this!" he shouted louder, "These readings look. . . the energy is unknown, but. . ." He looked up at the group. "Azure?" he invited her to have a look at his data.

"Why her?" Classia piped in a high-pitched voice of contempt.

Azure ignored her. She looked at Altair's readings.

"Temporal. Yes, I think the energy is temporal, but nothing like I have seen or experienced before."

"Another universe, indeed," was all Altair said.

"Most likely. " She looked at Classia. "I am sorry, Classia."

"But you can help him?" Classia's eyes pleaded, fighting back tears

"No, Classia, I cannot do anything!"

"What do you mean? Change it! Change time!" The lines on her face creased making her seem older than ever.

"I cannot!" tears started to roll down Azure's Cheeks. "I can't, I swore I would not. We swore we would not!" She looked at the other Starguards.

Classia's voice and face were fraught with despair. "Astara, he was your brother!" she screamed at her. "He would have done the same for you, anything to have you alive again!"

Astara shook her head, her voice stuck in her throat. "No. No, Azure is right. We are not Gods. We cannot!"

The two of them stared at each other, each determined in their own way.

Classia made a noise of disbelief. "You would betray me?" she started to cry. She turned to Azure. "You would betray the man I loved and his younglings? Are you that jealous that you did not want to see me happy?" She threw her closed fists against Azure's body.

Azure grabbed Classia's hands and held them. "You know that's not true, Class. I loved Novan as well, but we decided this action over Cirrius. We are not gods. When our time comes, we will not extend it, will not live beyond our time. No matter what we do time will run out. It will unbalance the universe's nature if we changed time to our will. What Cirrius and the Chronossii are doing will forever damage Magna Aura. We have to save our people."

Classia shook her head vehemently. "No, you are wrong," she whispered, looking into Azure's eyes. "You have to leave. Leave now!"

"Why?" Azure asked, but she knew why.

Classia's face glowered harshly in the flickering lights as she faced Azure.

"I will not live without Novan. His younglings will not. His people will not. He is our leader. Our heart," she yelled. "Cirrius understands that." She left the sentence hanging.

"Classia, what are you saying?" Astara asked, trepidation in her voice.

Classia turned to them. "I will plead with Cirrius for his help."

A noise behind them, an almost audible whimper above the continuous alarms made the Starguards and Classia turn around. The lone officer had been standing, waiting for their attention.

Classia struggled to remember is name. "What is it, Henga?" she hissed. "Why are you still here?"

Normally Sky Leader Henga was a reliable Sky Warrior, but now he seemed rattled, scared.

"It is Cirrius, Sky Commander," he bowed. "He. . . he is on Elysian. With the Chronossii!"

The dense silence which greeted his words converged around Henga, seemingly paralysing him.

"What? When?" Classia forgot her grief for a second, a flicker of a crooked smile crossing her face.

The Sky Warrior stood unable to talk.

"Henga?" Classia shouted at him, making him jump.

"We. . . we had a coded message from Elysian just before the attack. . ." he stated.

"Cirrius arrived just before the attack?" Altair interrupted.

Henga nodded quickly, almost afraid to speak.

Classia retreated into the recess of a corner where she slumped along a wall, her back to them.

Altair looked back at Astara and Azure, their faces also grim in the flashing lights.

They all had the same thought: lure Cirrius aboard and make him pay for the attacks and deaths of their families and fellow Starguards.

"Classia, we have a plan!" Astara said.

Classia remained silent in the corner, muttering to herself.

"Classia!" Azure shouted, trying to get her friend's attention and snap her out of her stupor.

Classia ignored them from her corner refuge in semi-darkness, her hands fidgeting together.

Her voice was harsh. "I will do everything I can for my family!"

"What are you doing?" Azure realised too late Classia had not simply withdrawn in grief.

Classia stood up and faced them from the corner, finished with her comm pad.

"What have you done?" Astara shouted at her.

Classia tried to smile confidently, brittle nervousness showing through. "I sent a message. . . to Cirrius. They should be here any. . ."

A portal showered the room in white light, delivering Cirrius, Celestra, Antichilles, Dyonus, Vostra, and Phasion.

Astara tried to draw her nexus sword from its dimensional sheath. Nothing happened. Empty-handed and shocked, she managed to pick up a fallen slender metal pipe from the floor and hold it out in front of her.

"Murderer!" she spat at Cirrius, ready to charge the group.

There was a moment of confusion as no one moved. The Chronossii's eyes were focused on Novan, dead in the middle of the bridge.

"Novan?" Cirrius' voice faltered. The fight seemed to go out of him and he staggered back a few steps. He pointed at Novan. "What is this?" He looked lost.

"What do you mean?" Altair snarled back.

Cirrius' head snapped back as if he had been hit. He then recognised who had spoken to him.

"Altair? How are you here? I thought you were..." he tailed off as he looked at Novan's body again. He swallowed hard and sank to the ground, sobbing.

The Starguards looked at each other in bafflement, the Chronossii breaking formation with baffled looks on their faces.

"What's going on here?" Azure asked, not quite believing what she was seeing.

Still sobbing, Cirrius raised his head. "She is dead!"

He abruptly collected himself as if remembering himself, as if the words had brought him back to reality. He wiped his face with his palms and sniffed away the last of the tears. He stood up and smoothed out the non-existent wrinkles in his manoeuvre suit.

"We know Urana is dead! You killed her!" Astara shouted at him, ignoring his minor breakdown.

But Cirrius shook his head. "No," he seemed to refute Astara's claim. "I did not mean Urana." He hung his head and seemed about to cry again. "Zasandra," he said, "... is dead."

No one spoke for a few seconds.

Azure recovered first. "Really?" Sarcastically thrown at him. But something about him had changed. "Dead? How?"

Cirrius pointed at Novan. It was the only explanation he could give.

"Novan? He didn't kill her. He's been here all the time," Astara defended her dead brother, affronted at Cirrius' accusation.

Cirrius shook his head slowly, mournfully.

"Creatures," he replied. "Black cosmic creatures. They somehow stole onto my island, it seems from the storm on the other side of Halcyon. And they killed Zasandra." He swallowed hard again, his eyes clouding in pain. "I think they meant to kill me, but Zasandra, she tried to protect me. After, we fled. . ."

"Here?" Astara finished for him. "Why? To warn us, get help? You idiot, they followed you. This is your fault. My brother is dead because of you!" she fumed at him.

She threw the pipe at him, just missing his head.

Cirrius did not move; did not speak. He didn't want to provoke anything.

But Classia took her moment to speak. "Cirrius, I am sorry to hear about your wife, but, please, if you can save Novan, please save him!" Her eyes were full of pleading and barely held back tears. "Change time!"

Cirrius shook his head, his face contorting in anger. "You do not think we tried that with Zasandra?" He pointed at the Chronossii youth. "Nothing worked! Whatever this being was, our powers have no affect on what they have done, temporal or otherwise. They are dead!" He balled his fists up. "Dead!"

"All will be forgiven," Classia promised, ignoring Astara's sneer.

"I cannot!" Cirrius screamed. "It is impossible."

Classia was not about to give up. "Please try. You cannot deny me this. And if you never try, the people will always wonder why you never tried. And you would be no King!" she sneered, "least of all mine. And the Elysians will fight you!"

Cirrius glared at Classia. He turned to the Chronossii and motioned to Vostra, who reluctantly went forward to Novan.

She gave Classia a glower of her own. Kneeling over Novan, she held her hands out just above him, careful not to touch his body. She closed her eyes and concentrated. A sheen of energy radiated from her hands, but it flowed around Novan, never touching him. For a few minutes Vostra stayed in that position.

"Aaaaargh!" Her head jerked back. Eyes shot open looking at her hands. She worked her fingers, shivering.

"What is the matter?" Classia asked anxiously, coming to her side.

Vostra shook her head, her hands wavering, as if of their own free will. "There's. . . there's nothing!" she exclaimed in a stammer. "There's no energy about him. There's no time, just like Timechantress!"

"Huh?" Altair was baffled.

Azure looked over at him and then at the young Chronossii. "That is not possible. Everything has a time field around it, flows with energy, even dead things so they decay but lose energy or entropy."

"That is what I am saying," Vostra spoke in a halting sentence. "There is no temporal energy around Novan. Nothing!" She seemed as if she wanted to scream at the incomprehensible.

Azure tried to understand what she was saying, but she knew instinctively what had happened. She tried a trick Zane had told her about, shifting her temporal sight and there it was. . .

"Oh, universe," she whispered. When everyone turned to look at her, she tried to explain what she was seeing. "Chronossii, shift your temporal sight into, I can't explain it," she threw her hands up, ". . . another phase!"

The Chronossii looked at each other. Vostra stared, but to no effect. None of them could replicate Azure's feat

"Okay, must be a Loremaiden thing," she said.

"So?" Classia was impatient, momentarily forgetting her anger towards Azure.

Azure gave her a look back. "And, so what I can see is a sheen of black energy around Novan. I don't know what kind of energy, but it's encasing him."

"So we remove the energy and we can save Novan?" Classia's anger dissipated as her hope rose, brown eyes brimming with tears.

"No. I don't know." Azure knew the truth of the situation and as she looked at Cirrius and Altair, they knew it too. "No, this was a message from whatever that being was. They killed Novan. They killed the leaders of the Starguards and the Astrals. Their laws of physics are different. Novan has been altered by their black energy, as it seems Timechantress was."

Cirrius' look at her confirmed her thoughts and his thinking.

"Technically, I do not think Novan is part of our universe anymore, but theirs, our energy will not revive him, they may not work upon them, and probably not in their universe. But as we've seen they can operate with impunity in our universe. They're telling us we are powerless against them!"

"That is just great," Altair said. "And who are they?"

Azure shrugged.

Cirrius looked downcast, bereft of a plan for once.

Classia looked at Azure in disbelief. "Novan cannot be dead!" she shouted at Azure. She rushed past the Starguards to Cirrius. "Do something," she screamed at him, who couldn't find the words. "Go back in time, save him!" Classia was still sobbing and shouting. "Save him!"

Azure stood, mute, no words would come.

But Cirrius spoke. "We cannot go back in time. Whoever these being are have seen to that. We tried, but there seems to be an anti-temporal field blocking transit..."

"My sword!" Astara blurted out. "I could not summon my sword when you arrived. The weapons portal kept collapsing."

"Perhaps an anti-dimensional field as well," surmised Cirrius.

Altair aimed his good arm at the wall behind him. Red energy lanced out scoring the wall.

"Well that works!"

"But I bet it does not work against them," Astara surmised.

"They just seemed to be worried about or threatened by temporal and dimensional powers. Could be a weakness," Azure pondered.

Azure had not told them her powers still seemed to work in some fashion in warding off the presence from her. She thanked the Lore for that. But at the back of her mind, a small voice was telling her that she had been the target and that Novan had died trying to save her. She couldn't tell them this. What they had to figure out was who the enemy were and would they return.

Through the discussions around her, Classia's thunderous anger had been growing and it exploded. She rushed Azure, pounding on her body.

"Save him! Save him!" Azure stood still offering no resistance. Classia suddenly stopped and looked Azure in the eye.

"You did this on purpose! You did not want to save him. You

always wanted him for yourself!" she accused Azure who stared back, tears welling in her eyes. "You are so jealous that you would rather Novan die than let me have him. Is that not so, *friend?*" her last word was an icy stab. Classia drew up to Azure's face and whispered. "You are evil, Deb, a traitor, just like your father!"

Azure clenched her jaw, suppressing a gasp and went to stroke Classia's arm in sympathy, but the Sky Warrior pulled back sharply.

"Do not touch me, traitor," she spat through gritted teeth. "Leave!" she pointed to the door. "Leave, all of you, and never come back. You are no longer welcome on Elysian."

She stepped back from the Starguards and the Chronossii.

Azure looked down at the floor. She had failed as a friend and nothing she could say or do would change anything. Novan was dead. Her friendship was dead. Her heart was dead. She was her father's daughter.

Not waiting to see what the others would do, Azure fled the bridge storming past the rest of the Starguards lest she broke down and fell apart in front of Classia.

She headed for the nearest airlock. She needed room, space, to think and recharge. Cycling through the double-doors she took off into space. Once above the swirly-clouded red planet, she could grieve, her tears escaping her immediate protection in the darkness of the cosmos and crystallising into tiny crystal droplets. They floated away into the night of nights.

Even the universe weeps for you, Novan. Goodbye!

CHAPTER TWELVE

Deep Space

"It is confirmed, Sceptre," comms-tech Vinge reported. "Contact with Magna Aura has been lost." There was little concern on his face, but his fingers tapped the console in staccato fashion.

Sceptre's lips pursed. They weren't far enough from Magna Aura to have lost contact. Sword *Altairion*'s crystalators had been diagnosed and re-analysed as working to maximum capacity. The problem was not with them.

And now the bridge crew, the whole complement of thirty on the small scout sword were waiting on his orders:

Turn back or forge ahead?—he pondered.

Sceptre desperately wanted to succeed in finding any remnants of the Six Worlds and Celestian Knight offspring. It was why he had named the Sword after Altair, so he felt as if his brother-cousin was by his side on this important mission.

Precisely as he was about to issue his order, Vinge's station burst to life in ear-shattering pulses.

"What the. . .?" Sceptre began, just as the bridge competed with the noise with its own assault upon the eyes.

A portal opened and a blinding flash of white light coalesced into a woman's form. Sceptre's eyes took a while to filter the light before it faded to reveal who it was.

"Zane?" Sceptre asked, smiling in surprise.

The black-haired Zane smiled at Sceptre, but said nothing. She held out a hand. Sceptre stepped forth to take it in friendship. But a finger of angry white energy fizzed from Zane's hand biting into Sceptre.

He howled in pain and tried to snatch his hand back, but the energy engulfed him within a portal.

"Back in a sec!" Zane chirped to the astonished bridge crew.

Elsewhere

The flash blindness dissipated. Sceptre found himself in pitch black space.

"Hallo," he shouted, but the blackness seemed to swallow up the sound.

"Shhh!" The sharp hiss was right at his ear.

"Zane, is that you?" he asked, confused.

"Not so loud," Zane whispered. "They'll hear us."

"Who will hear us?" he raised his voice.

"Would you shut up!" her eyes blazed hot white in the darkness.

"Not until you tell me. . .!"

"Ego Byss, would you please keep him quiet?"

Sceptre sensed a force behind him and turned in time to see the big red Zater Jen approach from behind.

"Oh, hallo. . . ack!!"

Ego Byss' right-hand palm eye still glowed from zapping Sceptre unconscious.

Zane sighed. "Told you to be silent," she whispered.

Deep space

"How long do we wait?" Star-leader Kersa asked in her crisp Xarian accent.

Everyone looked at Star Commander Qalcris who had taken command after Sceptre had disappeared ten hours ago.

"As long as it takes." He turned to Vinge.

The comms tech shook his head.

"No signals, sir," he reported. "No messages or energy readings to trace. It is all quiet."

He hated reporting such negative news, but it was all he had. They had searched every frequency and spurious energy source to no avail.

Qalcris tapped a tab on his chair arm. "Qalcris reporting," he announced to the ship in his hourly report, "Sceptre has not yet returned. All off-duty personnel will hold stand-by positions."

He looked steadily at the bridge crew.

"Sceptre knew this person. We all heard him greet her in friendship and even though she took him unawares she announced they would return." There was fidgeting among the lower ranks and shifting eyes. Qalcris face creased into a weak smile.

"You think me naïve and trusting," his grin widened. "Perhaps. But I have faith in Sceptre. We were briefed to expect the unexpected, indeed hand-picked to join Sceptre." He set his jaw; this was going to be hard. "We also know that the beings known as Astrals took the Starguards from Magna Aura. And we waited forty years for them to return. Well, I am willing to wait another forty for Sceptre to return." He waited for any dissenting voices. There were none.

Vinge smiled with his approval and tapped out calculations at his station.

"Forty years," Vinge repeated. "Well, at least the replenishments will last that long."

Elsewhere

Sceptre was aware he was still alive and awake by the dull pounding in his head. He stifled a groan, remembering the cost of noise.

"Good, you're awake," Zane whispered by his ear again.

"What do you want?" Sceptre kept his voice so low he could barely hear it over his throbbing head. "Why did you knock me out?"

"I am sorry about that, but you weren't listening and I needed your attention."

"Well you have that now. Where are we?"

He could hear laughter in Zane's voice. "We're in my own personal space-time," she answered. "As a Loremaiden, I can create little pockets of independent space-time. This is my hideaway."

"Hideaway? From whom?" He almost raised his voice.

"Don't worry, Scept' baby. I need your help. We have powerful enemies out there, again!"

"I know," Sceptre forestalled her announcement. "The Amethystians!"

"What? Who are the Amethystians?" Zane asked, annoyance in her voice.

Sceptre couldn't tell if he was looking up or down at her voice.

"The Amethystians. They are our kin." He quickly explained who they were. "Cirrius, who by the way has proclaimed himself King of Magna Aura in our absence, confronted them and they killed him. You did not know all of that? Where have the Astrals been?" He was exasperated himself.

Zane sighed. "A lot has happened to me, too. But that's another story. However, suffice to say, I was captured. . ." her voice was even softer.

"Captured, by who?"

Zane shivered. "The Omenuum."

"Who are they?"

"Think of them as another universe's version of the Celestian Knights, but not nice!"

"Oh, Universe!" Sceptre cursed, laying his head down or up in the blackness. He'd had enough. "So why are the Omenuum after us? I've never heard of them. What have we ever done to aggrieve them? How did you get away?"

Zane sighed again. "I didn't get away. They let me go, but wiped my mind of the capture. They put me back on the temporal path I was originally on and that's when I rejoined you all on future Earth, all aged. But I've started to remember the torture they put me through with Ego Byss' help."

"Hallo again," Sceptre greeted Ego Byss through the darkness.

>*Hallo, Starguard, Sceptre*< the Zater Jen psyed in reply.

"So what happened?" he asked Zane.

"When I tried to go to the Chronopolis, after the war on Destinia, I saw Astrals there. I meant to leave them as it was in my future, but one of them followed me. When she found out who I was she told me what had occurred." She was silent for a while.

Sceptre's patience grew thin. "So what happened?

"I cannot tell you that part, future data protection and all that, but I can tell you the source of the problem."

"And that is these Omenuum? What did we ever do to them?"

"It's not us who wronged them. We never did anything to them; it's the Celestian Knights—again. When Alphatronius opened that portal, he didn't just open it between your old and new universes, he opened one into all the universes—*every* universe, Aerl!" she emphasised. "Some closed on their own, some had them closed by beings who didn't care, but others spilled forth like fountains inviting invasion and death. Some beings blame us, some praise us, others want to destroy us: The Omenuum, the Forethere, the Gogma, more Lore, you name it. They are looking for us for answers, revenge, power, and destruction."

Sceptre felt space twist and a horrifying vision greeted him. And it was cold. Even for him.

"This is the Malverse," Zane continued. "This is the home of the Omenuum!"

As far as Sceptre could see dark expanses of space lay dead before him. Zane's vistas shifted through system after system, galaxy after galaxy. He could not see a whole intact world or lit star.

"But it's empty," he observed. "Dying." He shivered involuntarily.

"Not quite," Zane said. "The Malverse isn't dying. It is a broken cosmos, dark and cold, and timeless——literally. It is dead. It is a horrible place. And the Omenuum blame us, or rather the Celestian Knights, for it."

"Why, for Alphatronius' mistake?" Sceptre couldn't get his head around it.

"Partly, but I also think there is a darker story to this. And the Omenuum hate us for it. But I also had the sense they were interested in me, or Loremaidens. I don't know why." Zane's voice was low with concern. "We have to do something about it, Aerl."

Sceptre grunted in agreement.

"Let's go," Zane said, to Sceptre's relief.

The scene faded out and the absolute black and coldness tingled for a while around Sceptre until Zane's sparkly phase space surrounded him.

"Were we really there?" He looked around in amazement.

"Yes, I opened a tiny portal; not enough to travel through, but enough to pierce the veil for a peek. It's not nice. And it's what the Omenuum want to escape from."

"Why not let them? There's room enough in this universe, surely!"

"No, we have to stop them. They will invade and destroy this universe! Luckily, they cannot travel directly to our universe as the Great Breach was closed on this end, but they are powerful enough to take advantage of other conduits elsewhere to invade for short periods. From what I have seen, the longer they stay in a breached universe, the better they can adapt and remain."

"You have seen them invade other universes?"

Zane nodded without further elaboration.

Sceptre sighed. "What can we two, three," he remembered Ego Byss, "do about it? The Starguards are back on Magna Aura and I am searching for more Celestian Knight progeny. Surely you could seek the former, while I confirm the latter. And you never did answer regarding the fate of the Astrals."

Zane made a face. "I don't know. Well, I don't know where they are exactly, but I do know they are in hiding from the Omenuum. It was the Omenuum who attacked the Chronopolis..."

"What!" Sceptre raised his voice a little too loudly for Zane's liking. "We were told it was the Chronossii who attacked the Astrals!"

"What's a Chronossii and who told you that?" Zane looked unsure of herself.

Sceptre was silent for a moment. "We never learned who the Chronossii were, but Timechantress specifically told us that the Chronossii attacked the Chronopolis. She couldn't enter it, but overheard the Chronossii gloating over the Astrals." He looked for Zane in the darkness. "Are you sure it was the Omenuum? Are the Chronossii in league with them?"

"I don't know, but whatever Timechantress told you about the Chronopolis attack was a lie." Zane paused, thinking. She made a decision. "Aerl, we have to continue to the Great Breach."

"But, don't you think something is going on, if not with the Omenuum, then with Timechantress? Her story does not add up!"

"Yes," Zane agreed, "If she had been within the Chronopolis when these Chronossii or the Omenuum attacked then she would have known the Astrals were not killed or taken. They escaped and sealed off the Chronopolis so no one else could enter, not even another Astral! Perhaps that act sealed off a way for the Omenuum to enter our universe. You have to go, for whatever the Omenuum are up to we'll need allies."

"You mean because the Starguards cannot be our allies." He regarded Zane closely, her features barely seen in the darkness.

She shrunk a little from his gaze.

Sceptre cursed himself. "You're not my Zane, are you? I mean the one who brought us back to Magna Aura? You're an older version. You've seen the future. And something has happened to the Starguards. You're trying to warn me without actually warning me!" His eyes were now fixed in a hard glare upon Zane.

"I couldn't possibly answer that," replied Zane, her chin jutted upward, her eyes nervelessly returning his stare. "You have your mission from Millennius and you swore to complete it. I'm just helping you out." She looked away into the distance of her micro universe.

"Ha," Sceptre almost laughed. "Okay, have it your way. So how are we going to break the breach?" Sceptre whispered harshly.

A smile was in her voice. "With me! The Great Breach can be opened by a Loremaiden of course."

"I should have brought Azure with me," Sceptre deadpanned.

"Well you lucked out with me," Zane feigned hurt feelings.

Sceptre grimaced. "So how are you going to open the breach?"

"The Great Breach is like an infinity-way street. You just have to know how to apply your senses to see, hear, smell, feel and taste the Lore energy to open it."

"And you can do this?" Sceptre was impressed.

>*I will aid*< came Ego Byss' voice from behind him, startling Sceptre.

"Forgot you were here!" he blurted. "When do we go?"

"Now!"

"And my swordship?"

"No, we won't need them; no telling how long we'll be in the old universe and what we will encounter. We can swing by and let them know?" She asked for his permission.

Sceptre nodded. Zane stuck out a hand and energy glowed from it. The portal opened and they were swept in.

Seconds later, he and Zane were on the bridge of the *Altairion*.

"Blessed Universe," Star Commander Qalcris spilled out of the command chair in shock. He held his chest for a moment.

Sceptre suppressed a smile. He gave a little cough.

"Apologies for the surprise return," he offered to his crew. "This is Zane," he introduced the Astral to them, though he was not forthcoming with more information about her. "She will take me onwards to the Great Breach and beyond."

There were sharp intakes of breath.

Before there was any dissent, Sceptre carried on.

"I know you all volunteered for this great honour, but this is now my burden to carry on. You can return to Magna Aura with honour."

"Well, actually," Zane interrupted, with a bashful glance at

Sceptre, "Please continue to these coordinates." She stepped forth and placed her forearm crystalator against the comms console.

Comms-tech Vinge's eyes lit up. "What star system is this?"

"You'll see when you get there," was all Zane said, stepping back. "Toodles!"

She waved at Qalcris, grabbed Sceptre's hand, and the familiar flash of light engulfed them.

"Toodles?" Qalcris repeated.

The crew looked at him with the same wide-eyed demeanour.

"Have those coordinates set, Kersa," he ordered, bringing the bridge back to order.

Vinge transferred the coordinates to Kersa helm.

"All set, Star Commander," she reported after inputting the data. "Speed?"

"I would say we have time," Qalcris half-said to himself. "Half drive, Kersa. Let us see what this toodles is."

Deep space

Sceptre and Zane emerged once again into the searing blackness of space. It took Sceptre a moment to orientate himself after the brightness of the Sword's bridge. They were joined by Ego Byss.

"Where did you send my crew?" Sceptre asked, not happy about not being told they were being sent to an unknown destination.

"Somewhere safe," Zane replied. "I can't say more than that."

Sceptre sighed. He knew he wouldn't get more from Zane. He followed Zane's gaze and almost gasped himself.

The three of them were facing a rotating dark disk the size of a small moon; a scarred knot of space and time.

"The Great Breach," Sceptre breathed in awe.

"It sure is," Zane replied, getting immediately to work. "Okay, let's go!" She flew up against the gargantuan portal.

Her hand glowed as she reached out, touching the Great

Breach. Zane felt icy cold even through her temporal forcefield. She found herself slowly rotating with the portal.

"Now, wait a minute. . ." Aerl protested, looking up as Zane drifted away upward in the Breach's direction of travel.

"Ego Byss," Zane ignored the Starguard, instead requesting the Zater Jen's assistance.

The two time travellers held hands, their free hands touching the cosmic skin of the Great Breach.

The Glorious Ego Byss, former Captain of the Zater Jen's Light Guard, lit up bright red. His palm-eye blazed against the Breach. Zane glowed, her white energy flowing throughout the Breach's body. Their combined energies pulsed, sometimes in synchronicity, other times in complete random patterns, but it seemed to Sceptre that a communication pathway with the Great Breach was being sought and navigated.

Sceptre had no time to finish his thoughts as he suddenly felt Zane reach out to grab him again. The stars spun and streaked away into oblivion as Zane' portal banished reality. The familiar wrench of space-time washed over Sceptre, churning his insides to bursting point, as his skin burned. Just as he began to scream in pain, he was thrown out into normal space, spinning end over end. He did just have enough time to void his forcefield as his stomach in turn voided it contents. His vomit splattered across his native universe like a spiralling chunky starscape of multiple colours.

But the stars had changed. Or rather, most of them were gone. It was a barren universe.

It was not the home he remembered.

"We're through!" exclaimed Zane, taking in the surrounding cosmic gloom. She politely ignored the spewed projectiles on a trajectory to nowhere. "A portal through a portal. Amazing!" she raved.

Sceptre wiped his mouth and glided over to Zane and Ego Byss. They looked around. No Lore. No attacks. No nothing.

"There're no stars," remarked Zane in surprise. "Where do we go?" she asked Sceptre.

>*There is something here*< Ego Byss psyed. His gaze was piercing the galaxy around them.

The space around them seemed to thicken; nebulous filaments and gas clouds converging.

"Stars!" Sceptre shouted. He pointed vaguely around them.

Zane noticed it, too. The barren waste of space suddenly warped and the stars were upon them.

Too close and too well-patterned.

"Are we at the centre of them?" she asked.

>*It would appear so, young Astral*< answered Ego Byss. >*Outside of this cluster of lights there is nothing. No life or stars or planets*<

"Only this galaxy?" Zane asked.

>*This is not a galaxy. There are no stars. Just a conglomeration of lights*< he paused. >*It is not a natural formation. These lights were brought together*<

Sceptre was impressed Ego Byss could see and sense all of this. They looked like stars to him.

"Are you sure there are no signs of life here?"

Before he was answered, the glittering multi-coloured points of light suddenly rocketed around them. Sceptre made out they were small balls of light, approximately two meters across. Sceptre tried analysing them, but the lights darted too fast defying his crystalator's attempts to lock on and study them.

"What are these things?" Zane asked, totally taken in by the lights, but not daring to touch them.

Ego Byss psyed >*Bio nodes, millions of them forming a sensor colony. This is very sophisticated for Celestians*< His golden eyes were flashing, sensing details Sceptre and Zane could not.

Someone laughed. It was not any of them.

"Did anyone else hear that?" Zane had frozen to the spot, all senses on alert.

>*I hope you heard me*< psyed an unfamiliar female voice.

"The lights!" Zane exclaimed. "They're alive!"

The laughter rang out again. >*The lights alive! Funny! You* *are a funny one. Let me show you alive!<*

And just as they were getting used to the mesmerising lights and voice show, the lights sped toward them, enveloping them in pulsating kaleidoscopic light.

The trio disappeared from space...

... and found themselves on a planet's surface. It was not exactly a paradise, but the red and blue forests in the distance framed by mountains of black were all hunkered down under a dark sky, with only dim stars to illuminate them. A somewhat tepid breeze wrapped around them.

"I thought you said there were no planets," Sceptre muttered to Ego Byss, more smugly than intended.

Sceptre may have imagined it, but for a Zater Jen, Ego Byss indeed looked confused. His red head was more animated than usual taking in the surroundings.

"Welcome," said a new voice, almost startling Zane and Sceptre. It was male and assured, though the person it belonged to was either invisible or hidden.

They looked around for the voice's owner, before Zane replied, "Hallo?" She looked at Sceptre and shrugged.

Sceptre continued. "There is no need to fear us. We are not here to harm you. My name is Aerl, the Sceptre, of the Starguards, son of Celestian Knights Sola Venga and Iria..."

>We know who you are, Aerl, Zane, and Ego Byss< psyed the returning female voice, almost sarcastically. *>Why have you returned here?<* There was just a hint of excitement in the cold voice.

Sceptre and Zane exchanged perplexed looks. "We are here to search for survivors; our Celestian Knight kin," Sceptre replied.

There was a slight pause as the voice's owner pondered this.

>And the Lore? Will you rescue them? Abandon them? Destroy them?< asked the male.

Sceptre immediately replied: "We will destroy them. They cannot return."

"Why, are there Lore here?" asked Zane with trepidation.

There was a self-satisfied chuckle.

>*Yes*< came the reply.

Thousands of stars materialised and descended in energised-humanoid forms around the trio.

>*We are the Lore!*<

CHAPTER THIRTEEN

The cell door suddenly opened.

Decion was ready to rush the door, but the sight of Astara stopped him.

"Sister, you have rescued me!" He reached out in delight to hug her just as another person entered.

"Cirrius!" Decion sidestepped Astara, grabbing Cirrius roughly by the neck. He dragged him across the room, holding him high against the wall. "I will crush your life away!" he yelled.

"Decion, leave him be," Altair ordered.

Decion dropped a spluttering Cirrius to the floor, astonished to see Altair. Then he noticed his injuries.

"It is good to see you, Altair, but what battle deigned to honour you?" he smiled sadly.

Altair twisted his lips into a cheerless smile, knowing Decion was serious. "Long story, I will tell you later. But first we come with sad news. Come," he beckoned to Decion out of the cell, "We are returning to Aqrius."

"No!" Decion declined, "Not there. Don't you know what happened there? And the Chronossii. . .!"

"Brother," Astara held Decion's hand, lightly.

The gesture was totally unfamiliar to Decion. He looked searchingly into his sister's eyes encountering a depth of sadness only a death could bring. He then noticed the other faces, the same haggard looks, the same sense of grief.

He returned to his sister's eyes and followed her wordlessly out of the cell.

Outside the cell, the Chronossii called Vostra, if Decion remembered correctly, gave him back his core crystalator. Patching it to his underarmour, his manoeuvre suit once again coalesced around him. He unnecessarily smoothed down the hard red and black armour and resisted the urge to draw his lancesword.

Altair, satisfied Decion had controlled himself, led them outside to where a sky skimmer awaited. Decion thought it odd they did not port to Aqrius.

Minutes later, en route Astara told Decion the news. He sat, trying to come to terms with it.

The twenty-minute flight became a seemingly endless voyage. Decion wished at that moment he could fly and get away from the chaos.

"And then the beings disappeared," Astara explained as the skimmer began its descent. "There was nothing we could have done."

Cirrius had stayed silent, trying not to think of the death which had occurred in his own abode. They landed with a gentle jolt, but enough to bring Cirrius' mind back into focus. But as they disembarked the skimmer, he stopped. He stared at his front door unwilling to move.

It was only when his children came to the doorway Cirrius found the courage to move.

He and Decion exchanged looks, Decion giving him a brief nod of condolence. Cirrius turned forwards and entered his place.

Inside, Decion found Azure and Celestra already seated at the table in the middle of the room. He could see Azure had been crying. She gave him a smile, but otherwise stayed seated with a youngling in her arms. Celestra's eyes remained glued to the table.

Azure brought the meeting together. "There have been no further sighting of the aliens. We still do not know why they attacked or where they have gone."

"We have lookouts posted," Tyran added.

"Pah! Lookouts," spat Altair. "Recall Dyonus and Phasion. They have no temporal powers anyway, not with the alien energy shield up."

Tyran relented coding a message into this crystalator.

Decion looked up in anger. "Novan, Urana, and Timechantress dead! Two by unknown aliens and one by your hand, Cirrius. Why?" he asked specifically about Urana.

The intervening silence was punctuated by a baby's soft mewling. Altair, having retrieved Urrius from Azure, held his son, having fed him small sips of *tingil* juice. Urrius, wrapped in a blue tunic, dabbed happily at his father's chest with his small hand and kicked his feet, content with his juicy supplement. Altair rocked him gently. It would be time for Urrius to sleep soon.

Cirrius tore his eyes away from father and son. He shook his head in sorrow. "I was angry, angry at you for leaving me dead. You *voted* for me to stay dead!" he bared his teeth. "Do you know how that feels, after all I have done for you?" He was quiet for a while.

"Tell them," Celestra quietly pleaded with him.

Cirrius gave her a hard look. He relented, looking each Starguard in the eyes, deciding to confess.

"We did not kill Urana. I ordered Vostra to speed up Urana's pregnancy and I took Urrius. We left her stranded in Earth's past, alive." His eyes had been on the floor until the last word.

"Truly?" asked Altair, somewhat gratified Urana could be alive. But anger still tinged his mood.

"Yes," Cirrius said.

"It is the truth," Celestra backed him up.

She sat by her siblings, comforted by Xestina. Tyran and Antichilles fidgeted with anxiety. Cirrius had had to quell the twins' vengeful natures after Timechantress had been killed. But they still itched for a battle.

"Did you intend to return for her?" Azure tried to tease out some redeeming notion from him.

"No," Cirrius answered, truthfully. "It was her punishment."

If there was any shame in his manner, he did not show it.

Decion growled his displeasure.

"If I did not have my child with me," Altair stated, "whose name I will be changing to a more suitable one, by the way, I would kill you, again, Cirrius!"

There was no reaction from Cirrius. "Be that as it may, we

cannot go back now due to these beings closing off the temporal paths, somehow, perhaps by corrupting my temporal field." He sat in silent thought.

"I believe those beings also inhibit my ability to draw my swords," Astara said. "Decion, can you draw yours?"

Looking chagrined at the prospect of not having his lancesword, Decion flexed his arm, but no dimensional sheath opened and no sword.

"Fruk it!" His arms dropped to his side.

Astara sighed, clearly as frustrated as Decion without a weapon to hand. "I have been thinking about this and we may be able to enter the fortress and take our swords that way."

"How?" Altair asked.

"Hey!" Azure's loud cry interrupted their plans. "Enough about your weapons! Novan is dead! Timechantress is dead! Urana is lost in the past. We have the Amethystians to think of and now these other aliens still at large! What do we tell the rest of Magna Aura?"

Everyone looked at Cirrius.

"I do not know," he said, dejectedly. "I have already told them the Starguards are fighting the Amethystians and the Chronossii would keep them safe."

"Can you keep it together for another speech?" an exasperated Azure asked, disgusted at Cirrius. She was worried about his frame of mind. Someone needed to lead who was clear-headed.

Cirrius shrugged then nodded. "I will have to. I know now what I must say. . . and then we will have to discuss what we know about these new beings and what they want with us. They clearly attacked specific targets, they could have killed us all or more people, yet they did not!"

"They had or have an agenda!" Altair surmised.

"Exactly," said Cirrius, slowly feeling more himself.

"Hmm, we will, indeed, discuss this," a disgruntled Decion agreed.

Azure nodded. "Now, to your speech, Cirrius."

Sky Command

"Another speech? What now?" complained Aphene as she entered Tol Valar's office.

She stopped short as she saw who was with him.

"Deb! I mean Azure!" She flushed, giving Tol a you-could-have-told-me look, but smiled for Azure. "I meant no disrespect to you or to the King," she apologised quickly with a curt bow. She turned and made to leave.

"Stay." Azure laughed. "It's okay, Aphene. I'm not a big fan of Cirrius, either, but regrettably he bears rather sad and important news." She did not elaborate further.

Aphene and Tol shared a glance. Curious, Aphene nodded and took a chair on the other side of the desk from the Sky Commander. It felt decidedly hot in the office. Tol Valar sat while Azure stayed standing. They all looked at the vidscreen on the wall.

It came to life.

Aqrius

Cirrius, sitting at his desk backed by large paintings of the Celestian Knights, identifying his location as his island said:

"There has been news. The Starguards have returned from Elysian. They bring with them Altair, who had been returned to the Ribbon System fighting against the Amethystians." His smile was brief, grateful, but sad. "And while, not totally victorious, I am pleased the Amethystians have been pushed back availing us time, years, to prepare for their next attack." He licked his dry lips.

However. . ." his mouth twitched with emotion, "there have been grave developments. A new enemy has appeared. Possibly from another universe!" He went silent for a few seconds, not wanting to, but having to state the inability of the Starguards to counter them. "An enemy we were unaware of. . . and had no defence against. They. . . they killed my wife, Zasandra, here in this abode." He closed his eyes and took a deep breath. "And on

Elysian, they murdered. . . Novan!"

There was a shocked gasp from Aphene. Tol Valar's lips parted, horrified. He said a silent prayer to the Universe. Even Azure's heart still pained when she heard Novan's name. She was sure the whole Magna Aura system was in shock.

"There was nothing we could do," continued Cirrius, trying to sound as if it was not an excuse. "The attacks. . . these murders. . . were sudden and unprovoked. To that end, I am empowering the Starguards to take charge of the defence of Magna Aura. With Sceptre away on a mission of great import to Magna Aura, Altair will take command of the Sword fleet, Decion will command the Star Warriors, and Azure the Sky Warriors. Astara will resume her Protectress of State duties, and the Chronossii and I will provide a constant vigil for the enemy." He looked directly, fiercely, into the camera. "We will avenge these atrocities. Magna Aura will stand and fight. This will not be our End!"

He stood and walked away out of view. The screen went dark.

Sky Command

There was stunned silence in the office. Then frantic motion.

"Supreme Commander!" Tol Valar immediately shot up and addressed Azure. He walked briskly to the other side of the desk and waited for Azure to take the command chair. He stood to attention, Aphene likewise.

"Oh, Universe, don't treat me like a stranger!" Azure mildly admonished them, with a wave of the hand. "Sit down. Tol, you will still run the day-to-day as you have. I'll just be around to run over-arching strategy with Cirrius, Decion and hopefully the Ribbon System." Though Azure was not quite sure what state of mind Classia was in.

"May we ask what the strategy is?" Tol asked.

Azure smiled to herself. *Universe if I know!*

Aloud she said, "Cirrius and Decion are working on plans now, which they will present in due course."

I hope! She smiled at them.

Tol and Aphene looked at each other. Azure had the feeling they wanted to discuss something, but a non-verbal message seemed to pass between them and the moment could have disappeared, but Azure wanted to know.

"Is there anything else, Tol, Aphene? You can speak freely," she tried to will it out of them.

Aphene seemed certain to open her mouth, but Tol spoke before her.

"The storm!" he blurted out. He looked at Aphene, who seemed relieved she hadn't spoken.

"What storm?" Azure asked, puzzled as to why a storm would cause this much consternation. Though storms were rare on Halcyon, they were allowed to occur for study and to regulate planetary cycles. "Explain!" she ordered, as Tol appeared to hesitate.

"I do not think the Starguards were briefed on the storm on the other side of Halcyon. Cirrius ordered us not to say anything. When it was discovered twenty-two years ago we sent probes in and tried to study it, but the storm seemed to resist all those efforts. We did think it was a weapon somehow sent during the war, but now we know the Amethystians did not create it..."

"A twenty-year storm?" Azure interrupted. "Show me!"

Tol stood and toggled a tab on his forearm comms and from the centre of the desk a hologram blossomed into life between them.

Azure studied the storm. She let out a low whistle seeing how it had grown and stabilised now at thirty miles high and fifteen miles wide. But what drew her attention were the dense black clouds, fanning out like an immense cone, almost as black and sinister as...

Could it be? she thought.

"Even Cirrius' powers to alter the atmosphere enhanced to its limit by his father's meta-staff could not affect the storm. It almost broke him," Tol added.

"That was a bad time," Aphene said. "Cirrius disappeared for a while. Some say he secretly met with the Neb on Placia. . ."

"The Neb?" Azure peered through the storm at Aphene. "Why?"

Tol made a face. "No one knows, but when he resurfaced he was different, more settled and rejuvenated," he said. "That is when his strategy changed."

"Exactly," piped in Aphene, looking rather anxious.

Azure straightened up from staring into the holographic storm. She had been listening to the two Sky Warriors, but she knew she was hearing something else beneath their words.

"Some of the Meccun techs claimed the storm could be a dimensional breach, but Cirrius ordered everyone to stay away and to contain it as best we could," Tol explained.

"Cirrius deliberately kept techs away from it?" Azure asked, suspiciously.

Of all the Starguards and Magna Auran techs, Cirrius was *the* most ambitiously-curious and infovore-minded of anyone she knew. Either Tol was lying or Cirrius knew something about the storm and had decided to leave it alone. And knowing how Cirrius felt about protecting Magna Aura, he couldn't have seen the storm as a threat. She realised Tol was still talking to her disrupting her thoughts.

". . . on threat of death," Tol said. "There is a fifty-mile security perimeter around the cloud and automatic defences set up to prevent entry but not exit. None of us understand the tactics or strategy in this. Either he created it or it is as if. . . if. . ." he did not want to finish the sentence.

So Azure did, understanding what was happening now between Tol and Aphene. "As if Cirrius was leaving the system open to attack from something in the storm. And you were plotting to. . ."

"Wait a minute, Azure!" Tol pointed at her in shock. "We were not plotting anything!" His wide eyes stated otherwise.

"Okay," Azure said, calmly. "I understand," she smiled. "I will talk to Cirrius of this storm." She looked at Tol and Aphene, the latter's eyes also wide with guilt. She tried to reassure them. "I know Cirrius. He may be blind to others' emotions, but he does want the best for Magna Aura. I cannot imagine he would endanger that. . ." *unless it got out of control*, she thought, ". . .so I would suggest he is fully aware of the nature of the storm and for some reason is keeping it secret. I will find out." She walked through Tol's still-rotating hologram of the storm. "I'll find out," she reiterated, staring each in the eye. "Resume your stations," she ordered as she left the room.

There was a moment's silence as Tol and Aphene looked at each other rather guiltily.

"Think she will tell him?" Aphene asked, eyes on the ground.

Tol shrugged. "No, she is not like that. She was always the honest one." He smiled at some fond distant memory.

"All the same, we should warn the others. Get our stories straight," Aphene said.

With a sigh, Tol nodded. It would not matter anyway, there would be no hiding from the Starguards if their plot to kill Cirrius was revealed. But he had faith in Azure.

Aqrius

"Tell me about the storm?" Azure demanded immediately upon entering Cirrius house.

There was complete silence. The remaining Starguards and Chronossii were gathered for the evening meal, a time to reflect, grieve and make plans, but Azure's words had stirred up more emotions.

"What storm?" Decion asked gruffly. He had only just begun to trust the new company he was keeping. Now he eyed them warily.

Cirrius sighed. "Who told you?" he directed at Azure. "Ah," he smiled, "Tol Valar, of course. He always had a weak spot for you!"

Azure suppressed a twisted smile.

Cirrius rubbed his neck, set aside his plate, and spoke to the air. "Show current storm footage," he verbally keyed his crystalator and as in Tol's office, a hologram sprung into being over the dining table. "There, over the Astral Islands," he pointed.

"The storm began almost fully-fledged with dense black swirling clouds which have defied all analysis. Za. . ." he looked around the room for his wife, then realised. "Zasandra tried to reverse-time the storm and glimpse the interior, but that failed. My powers and the meta-staff also failed against it. But Celestra did detect a dimensional rift within the storm, plus the gravitational mass of one of the islands had increased. Either the clouds are super-dense or some artefact or structure has been placed on the island."

"Why didn't you tell us?" Azure shouted. "Why haven't you allowed anyone to enter to investigate?" she asked.

"Because he is selfish," Astara joined in. "Urana knew that. We all did. Always your secrets to keep," she accused Cirrius.

"No," Cirrius rejected their accusations. "They were not my secrets to keep!" he blurted out. His eyes shot away as he realised what he had revealed.

"What do you mean?" Azure interrogated him.

Everyone else moved closer to the table.

"I could not tell anyone," Cirrius replied.

Azure shook her head, not believing what she was hearing. "Why not? Pride? Scientific secrets?"

"Religion," stated Cirrius simply.

"Pah!" laughed Altair, pacing the room; Urrius having been placed in the bed chamber, doted on by Xestina. "You don't have a religious bone in your body."

"No, I do not, but the Neb do," Cirrius spat out.

There was confusion amongst the Starguards.

"What has this to do with the Neb?" Azure beat Astara to the question.

"Everything," Cirrius said. "They had a prophecy, messages from the storm; some ancient God connected to the Great Father and Holy Mother. They were told to wait for the arrival of emisaries from Bood."

"Bood?" Altair asked. "Who or what is this Bood?" He looked

around the room, confused.

"Some new God, some Celestians have been worshipping for the past twenty years," Decion filled Altair in, "Well, according to what Cirrius told us when we had returned," he glared at him.

"And you think the Neb are right?" Altair asked Cirrius

Cirrius shrugged. "That is what they told me. The storm is a sacred sign for them. The Neb Higher Assembly of Law Gatherers forbade me from taking action. I could not interfere."

"But I'm sure you did, I bet," Azure replied.

Cirrius smiled. But he glanced over at Decion and Astara, with mild trepidation, before continuing.

"Of course. With Celestra's aid, I was able to ascertain a frequency for the dimensional rift."

He pressed a facet on his crystalator and over-layed within the storm a red oscillating line appeared along with a strange rhythmic hum.

"Dimensional spectrums" he explained. "Each dimension, universe, galaxy, even planets have their own frequency and characteristics. And I happen to know this frequency!" He licked his lips almost nervously as he looked at Decion and Astara again. "It is the fortress!"

"Fortress?" asked Tyran, intrigued by a military mystery.

"*The* fortress? As in our fortress?" Astara asked.

Cirrius nodded solemnly. "Yes, your fortress, the weapons depository for Alpharion's descendants. I have checked the Scrolls of History and countless of Spheron's descriptions of natural and Celestian-made frequencies. The fortress is within an artificial dimension so the frequency is known. And it is a match. I do not know how, but someone or something has brought the fortress here."

"Twenty years ago?" Decion asked dubiously.

"Yes," Cirrius replied.

A thought dawned on Astara. "Alpha Rion?"

Cirrius shrugged. "Perhaps. But I am guessing with this unnatural storm and with little knowledge of the aliens' nature, it was not of his free will!"

Decion's frown increased. "But why would the fortress appear over twenty years ago and only become more active now?"

All eyes shifted from Decion to Cirrius.

Cirrius obliged them. He manipulated the holograph bringing up more data.

"As you can see from the collected data, the storm built up swiftly and then stayed stable for twenty years, and then this. . ." he switched displays and the storm's readings changed dramatically. "This is the day you all returned to Magna Aura. It did not change when the Chronossii arrived. It is like the storm was keyed to intensify output when the Starguards returned. Your arrival may have triggered the attack by these aliens."

"So they have been watching us!" Astara surmised. "Waiting to invade."

Azure added, "They can attack and counter us, but we cannot even detect them. Who knows what's inside the fortress."

"There's only one way to find out," Decion interjected. "I think this is an invitation. They want the Starguards, they get the Starguards!" He punched one heavy fist into another.

"I agree," Astara joined her brother's side. "We will not know anything until we try to enter. We do not have our weapons, but I am sure you would not have told us all this if you did not have a plan, Cirrius!" Her last words and looks to Cirrius were almost sarcastic.

"I may have a plan," Cirrius smiled sheepishly, "but it will involve the Starguards and Chronossii working together!"

There were low groans as less-than-cordial glances were shared between the two groups.

Cirrius tapped his forearm crystalator padd again and another display shone to life in front of them.

"A schematic of the fortress," he announced. "Or what is known of it!"

Decion was aghast. "How do you possess that?" he growled. "It is sacred to us and can only be entered by the Alpharion clan!" He wished he had his lancesword to painfully interrogate

Cirrius further.

Cirrius rolled out his put-upon world-weary sigh. "The information comes from painstaking studies of both the Scrolls of History and the Knights Destina's Tomes of War." He looked scornfully around the room. "Pity none of you read between the lines or sought out the deeper meanings and hidden tales and passages. There are books hidden within books and references leading to more. All of it to save us, in times such as this." He looked more pleased with himself, though Decion still wanted to knock the smirk off his face.

The others looked mildly aggrieved and abashed at the admonishment, but said nothing.

"So, this plan of yours. . ." Decion prompted, before Cirrius gloated himself up to the Universe again. "When do we go?"

Cirrius stared at Decion, a rather churlish smile on his face. "We do not," he said plainly. Before Decion exploded from his chair to strangle him, Cirrius deftly raised his hands in deference. Checking his smile, he explained. "Organic matter does not survive the storm clouds, not even in our manoeuvre suits. And we dare not port in not knowing the conditions. There is only one who can enter unharmed. . ."

"Syene," answered Dyonus, somewhat sceptically. "You want my sister to enter and form a psychic bridge into the fortress."

"Yes," Cirrius replied, pleased someone was following the logic of his conversation.

Puzzled, Decion, Azure, Astara and Altair looked at each other and along the Chronossii line. There were knowing smiles amongst the latter.

"Who is your sister?" Azure asked the question on their minds. "Haven't we met all of the Chronossii?"

Dyonus laughed and tapped his head. "Of course, you have not had the pleasure to meet my sister!" He closed his eyes and shivered a little as a fist-sized stroboscopic silver ball of psychic energy fizzed from his head. He shook his brown locks as the ball hovered in front of him. "Meet my sister, Syene!"

"Frugging Universe!" Decion gasped, half-rising from his chair in awe.

"That is your sister?" Astara struggled to understand.

Dyonus told them the story of his sister's birth.

"Amazing," Azure said. "A temporal psi!" She realised what she said and looked at Cirrius just as he looked at her.

Cirrius shot up and started pacing the floor. He ignored the others, deep in thought, silently talking to himself.

A babble of confused voices rose as Cirrius' antics continued. But Azure voiced both her and Cirrius' thoughts.

"Do you think the aliens killed Novan because of his abilities and not because he was our leader?" There was concern in her voice and a little fear.

Or were they still after me? she asked herself again.

"I am beginning to believe so," Cirrius conceded. There was a strange, yet perceptible smile on his face. "I knew they were after me, but Zasandra threw herself in front of me." He stared at the floor, still thinking.

"So they have a weakness?" Astara asked.

Azure shrugged. "Perhaps. Maybe they are susceptible to psis."

"Perhaps," he said. "We may yet find out." He turned to Syene, not sure how to address a disembodied psi. "Syene, we need to know what is happening in the fortress. Can you do that?" He looked at Dyonus for an answer.

"She says 'yes'!" her brother reported. "*Kalí tíhi!*" he wished her.

Syene flashed brightly twice then disappeared.

"Tracking!" Cirrius ordered his crystalators. Images appeared of the storm, remote vids searching for Syene.

"You will not see her," Dyonus chuckled. "She chooses to manifest as a silver agglomeration, but in reality she is a thought in time, as untraceable as the wind. I can sense her, here, though," he touched his temple. Sitting down and gazing inward, his eyes drifted off. "She is at the storm's perimeter. So far no reaction or resistance. She is going in!"

His head twisted this way and that fighting off some mild pain.

"There is a structure in the storm!" He raised his head, in the direction of Cirrius, but his eyes were now clouded over. "It is the fortress!" he confirmed. "You were correct, Cirrius!"

The Starguard took no comfort in that. "Where is she now? Can she enter?"

Dyonus turned his stare away from Cirrius. "She already has entered. It is dark. . . aargh!" He held his head in pain.

Vostra leaned over to help him.

"Guhhn!" he grunted in pain. "I can. . . barely. . . hear her. . . she. . . What? Where?" he asked her. "No, no do not! Syene? Syene? Where are you? No! She is gone!" he thumped the arm of his chair in deep frustration.

"What happened?" Cirrius asked frantically. "What did she see?"

Shaking his head, Dyonus could only muster, "She said she saw someone, something, but then she was gone. Not dead, I would feel that, but I just cannot communicate with her." He sighed heavily, covering his aching eyes. "She is on her own!"

CHAPTER FOURTEEN

Ancient Iranian Highlands

"They are just so inferior," Pandra lamented again.

Urana hated her disdain for humans. It was an every day littany by Pandra.

"They will be better in a few thousand years," Urana replied tiredly.

"We do not have thousands of years. We are stranded here, but we will not die here. If we cannot leave, we will stay and survive, breed or conquer and rule!"

The condescension in her tone made Urana bristle. She didn't trust Pandra's intentions. And she knew Pandra's feelings toward her were reciprocated.

Atton interceded. "I think we should come to an agreement that what is best for us is to leave." He gave his wife a hard look.

Things between Atton and Pandra had been strained the last few months. Atton spent more time with Urana and the youngling growing in the tank. Pandra had increased her patrols though closer to the ship. Atton's attempts to find out what Pandra actually did on those patrols was a useless mission in itself even when he sent out embedded spies within her group or tracking her from afar.

She is up to something, Atton knew. He reminded himself to post more guards around the ship, especially around the labs where the youngling was maturing.

"Fine," Pandra conceded. She gave Urana a sour look before leaving the room.

"She does hate me doesn't she?" Urana commented drolly.

Atton frowned. "That is my fault. Over the decades we have grown apart and now I am having a youngling, where others, especially Pandra cannot. I put myself in an impossible position. But I know we have to keep the Celestian civilisation alive, either here or back on the home worlds."

"But you do know it is not here?" Urana tried to explain again. "In the future, the only remnants of you and your crew are the Exmoors and Devouts. They knew nothing of this ship or you. We must have left this world. So you succeeded in keeping us alive," she said.

"Perhaps. But maybe if we stay here, we can change the future for the better. No more wars. We elevate humanity. Make this world better."

"You sound like Pandra," Urana accused good-naturedly.

"Oh no," he smiled back. "We can do all of that without conquering or ruling. We can stay by humanity's side and guide them."

Urana puffed out air between her lips. "Maybe or that might just change the timeline. I might not arrive back in this time and then nothing changes."

"You and your temporal causalities." He shook his head. "Fine," he parroted Pandra, "For now we will continue work on the portal. Progress is still optimal?"

Urana nodded. "Yes, it is tricky balancing my powers without triggering the Lore stones, but your engineers have done a brilliant job."

Atton acknowledged the praise. "Dener is not only my second, but a great engineer and I believe you have also met Jamev who is also skilled. Pandra's sister, Lelek, coordinates between them and the other system controllers making sure the crystalators are all functioning correctly."

Urana wasn't sure she liked anyone associated with Pandra being around the portal and Lore stones, but she didn't voice her concerns.

"Well we have about a week to go and we should be ready for trials." She stopped as she saw the grave look on Atton's face.

"We will not have enough energy for trials. Even with your energy, Dener has projected the portal will be able to open for around forty-five minutes then it closes, forever. We send through crystalator probes and then we go or do not go depending on the readings. There is no other option. And when we go, the *Zen*

Stellarion will be destroyed taking the portal and Lore stones with it."

Urana looked at him solemnly. "I understand."

A dour smile crept onto Atton's face. "Do not worry. In a week's time the youngling will have matured to around two years old. We will birth him, name him, and he will be ready to travel."

The Starguard smiled back, approving of Atton's preserving the old Galatian custom of not naming younglings until they had been birthed. Appearance and personality played a hand in names.

"Thank you," she replied much more calmly on the outside than her insides felt.

It had been weighing heavily on her mind recently. Now she felt as if she had a future worth fighting for and to forget even about Cirrius.

"I'd better get back to work then," she said, relieved and feeling energised.

"That is a good idea," Atton said, but he hesitated, prompting Urana to stop at the door and turn around.

"You wanted something else?"

Atton almost waved her away, but caught himself. "We can check on the youngling together tonight, if you wish."

Urana almost laughed. If this had been future Earth, Atton's tone would have been construed as a come on. Urana regarded Atton. He had an easy manner but with depths to be explored.

But he is married, Urana reminded herself. *But to Pandra.*

"Sure," Urana responded. "Let's do that." *Date night it is.*

With a tilt of his head, Atton acknowledged her as Urana left the room. She didn't see Pandra scurrying around the corridor's corner in the other direction.

Urana made her way down to engineering, meeting Jamev along the way.

"Jamev, hallo, ready for another day at the office?"

Jamev screwed his face up. "What is an office?" His face lightened up as he realised Urana was making a joke. "More human humour." He grinned back at her.

Urana laughed. "Yes, it is. It means we're going back to work."

Jamev laughed as they headed below decks together, the young Galatia Jamev regaling Urana with stories of engineering training on the sword.

"And luckily I still have my fingers," he finished, sending Urana into fits of laughter.

They reached the engineering section. The chamber seemed unusually dark even with the overhead lighting repaired. The large outer door to the portal chamber was open. Slowly, the two stepped past the entrance and stopped.

Dener was stood in front facing them, hands by his side. His expression was grim. He was the only person in the room when Urana knew there should be at least six others helping to tend to the . . .

Urana stopped. She looked around at the portal and then at Dener. His expression confirming her fears.

"There's a Lore stone missing," she exclaimed. Her mind raced with the implications of what this meant.

"That is correct," came a voice from behind them.

Lelek stepped into the room, a bulky type of pistol aimed at Urana.

"What are you doing?" Jamev asked, surprise on his face. He tried to activate his wrist comms but Lelek aimed at his head, Jamev getting the message. He lowered his hands.

"It is time we took charge. Pandra will lead us the way here, on Earth. You can all run away back home, but we have found ours." She sneered at Urana. "And with your younglings, we will rule. . ."

"Younglings?" Urana asked.

Lelek laughed. "Oh, yes, we have a surprise for you..."

No! Urana's heart punched within her. *No, not again!*

Urana lashed out, twisting her wrist as plasma energy twisted across the room like a staccato whip. Lelek fired just as she was slashed in half by the raining trail of energy.

There was a shout behind her. Dener had been hit in the shoulder by Lelek's shot and gone down. Jamev raced to his side just as other figures started flooding into the room weapons raised.

Females only, Urana realised.

The Devouts had started the war. Urana faced them defiantly. No one was going to take her children away.

Her hands lit up.

As Urana had left the lab, Atton had made his way to Pandra's quarters down the corridor. It was time to reassess their relationship. He didn't bother to knock, using his Captain's override pass.

Pandra looked around in surprise as the door to her lab opened unexpectedly.

For a while, the visitor stood, looking in shock around her make-shift lab in her quarters.

"What are you doing?" Atton asked as he walked in, the door sliding closed behind him.

There was no time for Pandra to hide her work.

Atton moved forward into the room observing dozens of vials held in hand-made wooden racks on the shelving units lining the back wall in stacks of ten.

But in the corner of the lab was the unmistakable form of a birthing tank, not a regulation one, but made by Pandra, Atton suspected. And complete with a suspended youngling inside.

"What is that?" he pointed to the tank and equipment.

Pandra knew she could have spun a lie, but the time had come for hard truths. She steeled herself.

"Are you not you tired of hiding or being stranded here on this pitiful world? I am!" She gave him a hard look gauging his reactions.

Atton looked momentarily confused. "And what has that got to do with what I think those are. . . Urana's and my biological samples?" He gestured to the glass vials. "And *that?*" He pointed at the tank again. "Is that what I think it is. . . "

"Atton, I am a medical. . ."

"No!" he shouted at her. "This is beyond that. I can see that now." He smiled as Pandra's face fleetingly lost its hauteur before regaining composure. "Yes, Pandra, I have known you have been up to something. So tell me!" he demanded.

Pandra blinked slowly framing her thoughts around Atton's accusations. She could only tell him the truth.

"We are stranded. We might not make it home with your far-fetched portal plan. So I am creating an insurance policy, one where we control this world."

Angry, Atton just stared at his wife. "What have you done?"

Pandra pouted. "I experimented. It is what I do."

"On the youngling?" Fists clenched, Atton stepped toward Pandra.

"No, of course not. I would not harm her. . ." she stopped.

It took a few moments for Atton to understand. He drew closer to the tank. He saw a rose-like birthmark on the youngling's shoulder.

"This is another youngling?"

Pandra smiled. "A twin."

Atton whirled on her. "You stole samples from Urana, her eggs, and my samples to create this youngling?" He was horrified at her actions.

Unrepentant, Pandra shrugged. "Tyeca seems to have succeeded with Urana's samples where I failed with all the crew. I wanted to see if the experiment could be repeated, with an extra ingredient," she teased

It took another moment for Atton to comprehend her words again. "You added your own DNA?"

Grinning from ear to ear, Pandra said, "She will be our legacy; the best of us. I will be our saviour."

Atton shouted at her. "All your experiments have cost us our Celestian heritage. Urana has saved us."

"We lost our heritage when your ancestor stayed on this forsaken world. I tried to save us, but. . ."

"But it went wrong. Of course." Atton was beginning to

realise what had happened.

Pandra's tongue loosened. "At first I did not know what had happened. I wanted to create Celestians capable of surviving this world. To heal our genetic structure. But my formulae did not work, so I used a new source; the Lore stones, as Urana calls them. I experimented on myself first. . ."

"What?" Atton cried out.

Pandra laughed. "Atton, I was the first Celestian to have powers; ever!" she lauded herself. "The experiment has endowed me with abilities. Have you not noticed I still stay youthful." She sounded hurt Atton had never noticed.

Undaunted, she carried on. "But while I could not recreate the effect for everyone, I later learned that my experiments with the Lore stones had somehow created long-lived males and super-powered females."

"You did this?"Atton shouted at her. "It was you all along? Experimenting on us? My own wife poisoning us against each other! Why?"

"Because I hate you!" she calmly spoke to him. "Even before Urana arrived, I hated you!" she spat through gritted teeth. "It was your cowardly decision to not take this world as our own. You have stranded us here. You have made us prisoners on our own ship. We have to live, yet we are barely surviving on this ship for fear of desecrating some primitive life out there." She stared at him with loathing in her eyes. "And then you betrayed me!" she accused him.

There was confusion in Atton's face. "I betrayed you?" he half laughed. His mouth was still half-asking the question Pandra finished for him.

"How? Are you really asking me that?" she shrieked. She looked at him with rising anger and raised her arms as if taking in the heavens. "This," she indicated the ship in general, "was ours. This world was ours. I was going to makes us gods on this world. I was almost there! And then Urana arrived from nowhere," she screamed, pointing at the samples. "She charmed my own husband, took you away from me and . . ."

Atton smiled, throwing Pandra off. "She did what you could not. I see now! You made yourself this way, you made all of us impotent. You are the real reason we cannot have younglings. So now you want revenge on Urana's and my youngling?"

"These younglings. . ."

"These younglings were genetically engineered without your help, without your expertise." He laughed, slowly understanding Pandra's anguished look. "They will have the powers you crave. What have you created?"

"What have I created?" Pandra repeated, sighing heavily, a half-admitted sign of defeat. "A line of long-lived males and females with untold powers. But I cannot recreate the traits in the other gender." She sat down on a chair by the lab workbenches.

The look on Atton's face shocked and intrigued Pandra. There was something written on his face she couldn't quite read. She stared at him, looking deeply into his eyes. He tried to out-stare her, but averted his gaze. He looked behind him, seating himself in a chair opposite her.

The lips of Pandra curled into a sly smile.

"What did Urana tell you. . . of the future?" her breathless voice on the edge of excitement.

Atton shook his head. "Nothing that involves you," he said, hoping his lie threw his wife off the trail.

Pandra stood up and walked slowly around the seated Atton. Her uniform was a patchwork of older Celestian uniforms and local leather. Pouches of leather on a leather belt were slung around her waist, Atton knowing some contained herbs for her medical administrations to the humans, specimens of various crystals, minerals, and animal cells. But the large leather pouch slung over her shoulder resting on her left hip was new. She saw him looking at it.

She made a sound of amusement. "What did Urana tell you?" she repeated slowly. Her left hand reached up to caress the bag.

Atton made to leave the chair, indignant at the questioning

and not entirely trusting where Pandra was leading? But he couldn't move. Was it his imagination or was he just tired? He shifted again, uncomfortably in the chair, pushing away but he was indeed stuck. He looked up at his wife, mild panic in his eyes.

"What... is... this?" he growled. He struggled to stand.

Pandra looked up directly above him, Atton following her gaze. He saw the beam projector. He had been manoeuvred to sit in this chair.

"A forcefield?" he spat. "Universe help you, Pandra, let me go!"

Pandra laughed. "Or what?" She reached into the shoulder-holstered pouch and pulled out a dull blue stone. She held it out to Atton's face.

"A Lore stone? What do you want with that power source?" he asked.

"Power source?" huffed Pandra. "You really believe these will power a portal back home." She shook her head in pity. "These Lore stones will only power my experiments and create the next Celestian race. What do you think their presence on this ship have been doing all this time. Ha!" she laughed. "If we cannot go back home then we will rule this one, starting with our younglings!" Her eyes shone with glee.

Confusion clouded Atton's eyes, not knowing what Pandra meant. Until she caressed her abdomen.

"You had samples left over, so. . ." she left the sentence unfinished.

Atton roared in fury, frantically trying to free himself from the chair. The force field was a light medical restraining field adapted by Pandra and as such was not adequate for a forcible reaction. Slowly, Atton was able to push himself upright.

The forcefield wavered, straining to contain Atton's mass as he shifted upward.

Pandra watched in eerie fascination as the slow-motion Atton forced his body against the forcefield. She knew the field would collapse releasing Atton.

"Pandra," came his angry snarl.

She looked at the Lore stone in her hand. Then at Atton emerging from the forcefield's edge. And back at the Lore stone.

Atton slipped through the forcefield just as Pandra slammed the Lore stone upon his head, but he held out his hand to stop it.

"Aghh!" Atton was thrown back against the chair crashing to the ground. He held the back of his hand; a small burn scar already searing into it. "What was that?" his shocked face contorted in pain.

Pandra's brow furrowed. She was as surprised as Atton. She had only meant to short the forcefield, but the Lore stone seemed to have reacted to Atton's touch.

"I do not know," she confessed.

She instinctively proffered it tentatively forward toward Atton who recoiled away, sliding across the floor.

"What in the Universe are you doing?" Atton continued to retreat as Pandra slowly advanced, the Lore stone stretched out in front of her. She was beginning to understand.

"You have power," she whispered, mind calculating. "Both of us always had the potential. I just never realised that about you before."

"Power? What power?" Atton tried to put chairs, benches, and cabinets in the way between them, but he was running out of room, backing into a corner.

"The younglings," Pandra continued to reason, "It was not just Urana with power, the energy. It was you, too. With this!" Pandra looked at the Lore stone fascinated by the new discovery. She flicked her eyes up at Atton. "This made you. The Lore stone has been passively creating mutations." She got excited. "You cannot be the only one," she said as she realised the import of her words. "I did it! I created a male with powers. And now..." she placed her hand on her belly again.

Teeth gritted in anger, Atton prepared to strike, not wanting Pandra to finish her thoughts.

But Pandra stared Atton in his eyes. "We are going to have a youngling, husband," she smiled.

She made to put the Lore stone away, just as Atton launched himself at her. He grabbed her arm and they wrestled for the blue object tumbling over furniture, the stone crashing to the ground.

There was banging on the door from outside, repeated loud thumps as blows rained down trying to knock it down. The two ignored the noise, concentrating on each other.

Pandra clutched the stone close to her chest, Atton trying to prise it out even though he could feel it burning on his fingertips.

"Atton, no, you will burn yourself," she screamed over the din at the door. "You do not realise what you are doing. . . your power could disrupt the stone. . ."

"That . . . is. . . the plan," a grimacing Atton sneered as his fingers gained purchase over Pandra's.

"Nooooo!" Pandra screamed.

Atton ripped the stone from her hands, his own practically welting up in red boils from the energy within. But still he held it, half aloft over his head, out of her reach. He rolled on top of her, his knees pinning her chest and arms down beneath him.

They realised the position they were in, the violent pounding on the door failing to match the raging pace of their hearts.

Atton shook his head. "I am sorry, Pandra. I cannot let you do this. Ever!"

He raised the Lore stone above his head and stuck down with his might upon Pandra's head.

She managed to raise her arms in defence, but the pain against her forearms was enough to make her cry out.

"No, you cannot. It will know. . . ahh!"

Another blow caught the side of her head.

"No!" she repeated

A top corner of the door was folding over; laser cutters toiling away.

Atton hefted the Lore stone high over his head again. He had to end this. His wife was evil, uncaring, unrelenting in her quest for power. If he did not do this now then he would never get another chance.

He hurled the stone down. He expected to crush Pandra's head. But something stopped him, a weird force, inches from her face.

He looked, wild-eyed, closely at the stone. Chest thumping, sweat dripping down onto Pandra's face. Something was swirling within the stone. It transfixed him, a bright blue creature sporting sets of seemingly unending array of teeth almost impossibly too big to inhabit the stone.

Atton stared at it. It suddenly turned. And looked back at him.

A look of horror rippled over Atton's face. The blue form in the Lore stone seemed to get brighter.

"Drop the stone, Atton, drop it now!" a panicked Pandra hissed. She reached out desperately to grasp the Lore stone, but Atton snatched it away.

And just as he did a creature's sleek head, blue and crackling of energy darted, lightning quick, out of the Lore stone, rapacious teeth burying themselves deep into Atton's upper torso and neck and ripping away.

Atton screamed in agony as the energy head disappeared in a vortex of whispery swirling wings back into the stone. He fell over sideways, his upper body jerking violently and smouldering in wispy smoke, the gaping wound of jagged muscle, bone, and hissing blood cauterised, his eyes wide open in shock and lifelessness. The Lore stone dropped from his hands and rolled closer to Pandra who swiftly curled an arm around it pulling it toward her. The creature subsided from view within the stone.

The door finally burst open and soldiers clambered in. They juddered to a stop on seeing their captain dead on the ground with his wife lying beside him in a half foetal position.

Behind the soldiers, Tyeca arrived.

"J'valla's Cry," she cursed in Elerae. "What happened?"

Then she saw the birthing tank.

She turned to Pandra, speechless. Her face billowing rage and disgust.

Pandra didn't want to speak, but she had to, and it would be only her story that mattered. She pushed herself up to her side, one of the soldiers helping her to her feet and onto a chair.

"It was an.. . . . . accident. . . an experiment went. . . wrong. And. . . and Atton was. . ." she couldn't finish.

She realised she was telling the truth. It had been an accident.

Hadn't it?

Even though Atton was trying to kill her, she did not wish her own husband dead. And whatever that creature had been, she had not summoned it. She looked at the Lore stone.

Did I? she asked herself.

"Take her," Tyeca ordered, coldly. She had to tell Urana before the rumours spread.

The soldiers dragged Pandra to her feet, roughly. The room spun and her foot slipped on blood. She almost dropped the stone but managed to keep it in its pouch. In a half daze, she was led out of the room, other soldiers entering behind her.

Pandra looked back at Tyeca who was staring down in shock at Atton. She motioned two guards to help her with his body. That was the last Pandra saw of Atton.

"Where are you taking me?" she demanded to the silent soldiers.

They were all male, Pandra noticed, marching her off in the general direction, she knew, of the ship's confinement units. Chirps and other signals were being relayed through comm units. She wondered who was ordering what to whom.

The ship corridors were eerily quiet and it seemed just lined by males. A little voice starting to form in her head.

Something has happened. They know.

By now she knew where they were going. And it was not to the cells. It was to the bridge, or what was left of the bridge after centuries of decay and repair cycles.

The guards at the door were male, Pandra still wondering where all the females were. The doors were opened.

Pandra baulked entering, inviting the guards to hold her tightly and force her onto the bridge. The scene on the command deck was the very last thing she wanted to see.

Urana sat in Atton's command chair.

No, I will not be judged by her! Pandra vowed. *Not by the interloper; the destroyer of my family.*

"What happened?" a stern Urana questioned Pandra. "Why did you kill Atton? And how dare you steal my genetic material for your experiments," she raised her voice.

Tyeca, Pandra thought darkly. *That did not take long for her to change sides.*

The command chair was slightly raised above the bridge, Pandra having to look up to the seated Urana.

"How dare you question me. You do not belong here," Pandra screamed back. She turned to the soilders around her. "Do you follow her now?"

There was no response.

"Cowards!" she shouted at them. "You will all be punished when this world is swept clean by my. . . "

"Devouts?" Urana finished for her. She smiled seeing Pandra's face falter. "You forget, I've seen the future. I now know what caused the wars. I know who created the Devouts and Exmoors." Urana sat triumphantly in the command chair staring down upon Pandra. "And it ends now!"

All of Pandra's resentment for Urana seared into one moment. She would destroy Urana no matter what. She wasn't defeated. She still had a chance.

"Your sister and all the Devouts on board are either dead or locked up," stated Urana.

Pandra screamed in fury straining against the soldiers holding her back.

"And you will never ever harm my younglings," Urana promised as she rose from the chair.

I can end this right now, Urana thought.

And she could see that Pandra knew that as well. There was fear in her eyes. She had lost. She had lost everything due to her own machinations.

It also meant she had nothing left to lose.

Pandra stared aghast at Urana. But she had one chance left, if only to spite Atton and Urana. Destroy the portal and take the younglings.

Pandra slumped in the guard's arms as if ill taking the soldiers by surprise. As they lightly loosened their grip she threw one of them off to the ground. The other raised a pistol, but Pandra had unshouldered her pouch and crunched his head in the full-blown swing.

That was the moment Urana fired at Pandra, a rain of plasma streaking upon the Celestian, who held the pouch out in front of her. Urana's plasma energy was absorbed irradiating the Lore stone. The stone glowed a menacingly blue within the pouch.

Urana's breath left her chest as she saw the glow. Time seemed to skip a beat.

No, not again! her horrified thought sent shivers to her core.

There was an unearthly shriek. It echoed around the bridge, the crew searching for the source of the ear-splitting assault. There was no cracking of the translucent stone's surface, it just dissolved as the lorelet's sleek scaly head followed by its sinuous buzzcut body, at least five meters in length, and large blazing energised wings emerged from the stone, its long thin tail thrashing about.

A crew member screamed, the lorelet attracted to the sound, darting over in the blink of an eye, devouring the top half of the crew member. The bottom half fell over in a slosh of blood.

Pandra watched in fascination, seeing the whole creature for the first time.

"Haha, by Great Father, that is a beauty!" Pandra delighted.

Her gaze raked over Urana, who stood transfixed, not able to use her energy to defend herself and the others lest she turned the lorelet into a bomb as Altair had.

But that did not stop Urana from firing on Pandra again. The Celestian ducked out of the way in time, diving behind a bridge console.

And Urana ran.

The bridge crew were busy entertaining the lorelet with their fire power and lives soon finding out the creature was not only impervious to their energy but was also feeding it.

Urana sped from the bridge. She grabbed the doors manually shutting them with a crash, welding the doors shut with her energy. She knew she was condemning the crew inside to their deaths, but she had the rest of the crew, her younglings, and even Earth to think about.

Hell, she thought in a human moment, *even the timeline was at stake.*

She ran down the corridors almost knocking over the injured Dener helped by Jamev and Tyeca.

"The younglings, take them both and leave now," Urana ordered them.

"Both?" Dener questioned.

Urana looked behind her down the corridor, flustered. "There's no time to explain now, Pandra has to be stopped and there's only one way to do it."

The determined set to her face and body almost convinced them.

Tyeca was about to protest, but Urana said, "Go, I will follow. I promise. But I have to stop her!" she reiterated.

Behind them, an awful crash of metal rang through the ship like a bell followed by an eerie shrill call.

"She's coming." Urana looked around in fear.

The faces of the other three followed Urana's gaze.

"Please go. Save the younglings," she implored.

With a final look down the corridor to see what was causing the noise, the trio took off towards the labs. Urana knew the birth tanks would have to be drained and the younglings administered with physical and health checks to ensure the auto-nutrition feedlines and immuno implants had worked, then they would be considered viable. All that would take around half an hour. Urana had to buy them time.

As she ran she made sure every door was welded shut or barriers of debris strewn across the corridors and blocking the way towards the lab. A burst of energy from her destroyed all the lights behind her. Pandra and the lorelet had to be led downwards. Wherever she encountered crew, male or the few remaining loyal females, Urana directed them to follow Dener off-ship then she secured the doors behind them. Dashing through corridors, crossing decks, ever downward through the hulk of the ship Urana descended.

Urana could hear Pandra and the lorelet closing in. An eerie blue glow preceded them in the distance. She had guessed correctly that the lorelet was not so autonomous that Pandra could control it, so she had to follow it or vice versa, and the only direction they could go was where Urana directed them.

Yep, keep following me, Urana thought.

She remembered the tales of Theseus and the maze he had negotiated to kill the Minotaur. But this time the beast was hunting her.

She reached the engineering deck, the large square door looming ahead of her. Surprisingly, she found it still guarded.

"Lerkoz, Kitrotrin, what are you still doing here?" she called out to them, remembering their names.

The two guards looked at each other perplexed.

"Dener ordered us to stand guard after he was taken away injured," the Trinari guard answered. "He said not to let anyone in until he ordered us otherwise." He stood a little straighter and taller.

They had laser pistols and a compound-adjustable weapon Urana thought looked like a cross between a blade and an axe.

"Guys, Pandra is coming and she has a monster with her. Only I can defeat them, but I need to get into that room. Dener, Tyeca, and Jamev are leaving the ship with my younglings," she explained, even as the lorelet's shrieking got louder.

Lerkoz, a tall Meccun, looked anxiously down the corridor.

"Comm Dener if you don't believe me," Urana pleaded.

"There's no signal," Kitrotrin stated. His hand slid down his hip to rest on the leather holster around his waist holding the pistol.

There were distant screams and another shriek from the lorelet sounding even more satisfied, if possible.

"You really have to go," Urana said, "Save yourselves. . ."

Lerkoz ran. He unholstered his pistol and dagger-axe for protection. Sprinting halfway down the corridor a blue light wriggled right through him, lifting him up and then smashing him viciously into the wall, before he crashed to the ground, his weapons spilling from his grasp.

Urana realised the light was the lorelet's tail which had skewered him. She looked behind at Kitrotrin who was already manhandling the door trying to pull it open in open panic.

Good boy, thought a relieved Urana.

She turned back and faced the oncoming lorelet, Pandra sauntering behind it. In one movement she reached down and collected Lerkoz's dagger-axe. As a smile snaked across her face, the lorelet seemed to also grin with its multitudinous teeth.

"There you are," Pandra said, her airy tone belaying the anger on her face. "Trying to run away are we, like a coward?" Her lip curled in a smirk.

Kitrotrin hauled the door open and ran in. Urana backed in after him and pulled the large square door shut just as the lorelet pounded into it. She blew out the controls with her energy to lock the door and quickly sealed the surrounding edges with welds, but Urana knew the door wouldn't last long against it.

"Now what?" Kitrotrin asked. "We are trapped."

"I did tell you to leave," Urana silently muttered to herself, but to answer him she just pointed at the portal.

The pounding on the door increased. A faint blue glow spilled around the edges as the lorelet started melting the metal.

"We don't have long so start it up," she told Kitrotrin.

"No, no, no, no, no, I am not going through that," he countered. "It has not even been tested. Where will we end up?"

Urana shrugged. "Either way we are dead when that lorelet gets in, so you have a choice." She could see he was scared. "You know, back on Magna Aura, my aide and best friend was a Trinari; Camtrin. She was brave and offered me great advice. I miss her a lot," she confessed. "I need you to be my Camtrin now, brave, fearless, and ready for an adventure. Can you do that for me?"

Kitrotrin just stared at her. His head turned toward the door, back to the portal then back to Urana.

"No," he calmly said.

"What?" a stunned Urana replied.

The door was glowing red hot. Any second now and they would be through.

"You do not belong here," Kitrotrin spoke plainly. "This is my ship, my home for decades. I may be scared to death, but I will stay with the *Zen Stellarion* until the end. You go," he lifted his chin to the portal. "You belong out there in the stars. Go!" His face was a fierce mask of determination.

Urana nodded her head. "But you know what happens when I go through the portal." Stated not queried.

Kitrotrin closed his eyes and smiled. He was at peace. He faced the door and raised his weapon.

"I will give you as much time as I can," he shouted over his shoulder as the lorelet's shriek grew louder.

Urana ran over to the portal and shunted energy into the control coils avoiding the other Lore stones. A piercing cry outside announced the imminent arrival of the lorelet, sensing its stone-bound brethren inside.

The portal flared into life just as Pandra and the lorelet broke through the door.

Kitrotrin started firing, he dived for cover behind a large control panel to avoid the lorelet. He kept firing keeping Pandra at bay, fury in her eyes as her prize was about to escape.

Urana stood at the threshold of the portal, a shimmering vortex of dark blue energy.

She turned. "Here, kitty," she yelled at the lorelet, enticing it toward her by energising up her hands.

Pandra screamed. "Noooo!" She was pinned down by Kitrotrin's covering fire, who grinned and gave a thumbs up to Urana.

Pandra saw her chance. She hurled her arm back, throwing and lancing Kitrotrin through the top of his chest with the dagger-axe she had taken from Lerkoz's body. He toppled over sideways his dead eyes willing Urana on.

The lorelet rushed Urana who unleashed a frantic jolt of energy at the creature's head. It turned away in momentary blindness. The moment gave Urana time as she aimed at the Lore stones around her and gave it everything she had in one outburst of plasma energy.

Pandra was floored, covering her eyes.

"Urana, I will kill you!" she screamed.

Back on future Earth, Altair had merely touched a Lore stone releasing a lorelet, but Urana had already calculated with Atton when attuning the portal's energy with the Lore stones, that a massive energy injection would create a cascade effect within the Lore stones causing energy to loop upon itself and then. . .

Urana leapt backwards through the portal.

. . . *Zen Stellarion* exploded.

Ripped apart, the mountain around the ship erupted like a volcano hurling rocks miles away. Earthquakes shattered surrounding lands, the fleeing inhabitants believing the Gods were ending the world. The underside of the ship collapsed existing faults pummelling the ground even deeper until separate parts of the remaining Swordship lay almost five kilometers down, twisted, broken, finally slain by the power of the Lore.

The dust took days to settle, the days were cooler under the shrouded sun. Some brave returning inhabitants were unwittingly joined by new villagers, apparently refugees from the mountain tribes settling in new domains on the lower fertile plains between two large rivers.

Among them were a couple with two young children, and others with new skills, which greatly benefitted their lands.

Months later in the dead of one night, the newcomers had met together in one of the homes of another.

"What do we do now, Dener?" asked Jamev. "We have waited long enough, Urana is not coming back."

They had left clues in the landscape and in villages as to their whereabouts in signs only Urana would have known. Furtive patrols had been taken back to the area. No one had survived the explosion.

Now Dener looked at the faces of his one-time crew, all male, except for Tyeca. But she, too, knew what had to be done.

They all looked at the two younglings asleep in cots behind them.

"We must protect the younglings of Atton and Urana," he said. "Pandra's experiments made us long-lived. Urana called us Exmoors and that is what we will be. We know some of Pandra's followers escaped, so we must be sure these Devouts do not persist. They must never find the younglings or be allowed to create humans with abilities. That is our solemn duty."

Jamev nodded. Others grunted approval.

"To that end, we must split up."

"What?" The decision took Jamev by surprise, his high-pitched yelp almost waking one of the younglings.

"Yes, we must separate the younglings as no doubt the Devouts will be searching for siblings." He searched out Tyeca. "Tyeca, you, Jamev, Fal, and Kuin will take the boy. Name him when you are far away. Teach him our ways and to use his powers responsibly. We," he pointed out Qortrin and Hantar, "will keep the girl and do the same."

"Yes, Dener," Tyeca accepted.

"We will need to help Qortrin hide his shiny face, though," Jamev said with a smile.

The Trinari was the cause of much amusement having to cover his silver complexion with scarves and hats.

"I have some skin transformer which will help," Tyeca replied.

Qortrin sighed. "The most beautiful of us all and I have to hide my features. They had better be worth it," he said of the younglings.

Dener laughed. "They will be. We will make it so."

They all stood in a circle, arms clasped with each other.

"May the Great Father and Holy Mother look down upon us and bless our destinies," Dener prayed.

Dener watched that night as Tyeca, Jamev and Urana's son left the village, never to be seen in any of their lifetimes again.

I only hope Urana returns to see her younglings, he heartened himself.

It was dark.

Her skin was crawling like millions of needles were stitching her back together. She ached all over. Opening her mouth to cough she sucked in enough dust to make her choke violently.

So, I am still alive. How?

Pandra laughed to herself.

So that is my power, regeneration not longevity. She squeezed her limbs to make sure she had her fingers and toes.

She couldn't see much, but lower down to her left was a faint blue glow.

An intact Lore stone, she rejoiced.

Inching it up her thigh, she realised she was naked, her clothes disintegrated during the explosion. She half rolled over to gain a more comfortable position on the ground beneath her and abruptly cried out in pain. She reached out under her and dragged out the offending item she had rolled over.

Dagger-axe. Great.

With drawn dagger-axe and toughened Lore stone, Pandra dug her way up. After hours of gruelling crawling, climbing and clawing, her skin ripped and bruised in several inconvenient places, Pandra emerged from the bowels of hell.

She barely had time to survey her surroundings, a chaotic melee of rock under a moonless night, before collapsing from exhaustion on the cold rocks.

Something pecked at her head alarming Pandra into full awareness. She instinctively brandished the dagger-axe in one fell swoop. The vulture died from the blow, sending two others flying into the sky with loud angry squawks.

The dim sun dazzled her eyes. Pandra stood up slowly testing her limbs, which felt strong enough for the journey. She needed food, shelter and clothing. She had barely walked ten meters down the ruined mountain when she saw them.

A dozen cloaked figures stood in the distance. Pandra crouched in fear that they had seen her. They had. And they were approaching her. Pandra looked at the Lore stone. She rattled it, but nothing stirred. She knew only certain energy would activate it. Her only defence was the dagger-axe and the myriad of rocks around her.

She stood up again in defiance bracing for a fight, but stopped in her tracks. The figures had lowered their hoods.

The women stared back at Pandra in disbelief.

"You are truly our chosen leader, Pandra," announced one of the women.

"A miracle," cried another.

Pandra smiled, recognising her crew mates who had been off ship when she had returned to the *Zen Stellarion* for the last time. It felt like a lifetime to her now.

They all sunk to their knees in worship and gratitude.

Pandra basked in the adoration for a while. Her skin prickled and she looked down to see her cuts and bruises healing before her eyes. She was indeed a Goddess to be worshipped. And a victorious one at that.

"Atton and Urana are dead," Pandra proclaimed, not knowing if the latter was strictly true.

One day Urana would appear in Earth's future. And Pandra would be waiting for her.

"But I am sure her younglings are still alive somewhere out there," she pointed to the horizon. "The so-called Exmoors have them. And we will find them and use them to avenge our fallen sisters and defeat our enemies. Our destinies will be forged as the Devouts!"

"Vengeance and victory!" shouted one of the women in ecstasy.

The others joined in, arms in the air in salute to Pandra.

Vengeance and victory, indeed, thought Pandra. *Wherever you are Urana, vengeance and victory will be mine.*

Urana awoke.

The lights were bright above her; round artificial lights attached to a white metal ceiling. She had a vague case of *deja vu*. She was on another ship, not the *Zen Stellarion* nor a recognisable sword from Magna Aura. Her head felt groggy but she managed to raise it and look around.

Ah, she noted to herself, *another medbay.* But she wasn't alone this time. About two dozen others lay around her in medbeds within the circular medbay. But they were not *Zen Stellarion* crew, which puzzled her.

Three medtechs busied themselves on the wounded crew until one of them realised Urana was awake. The Trinari medtech, silver skin flashing under the lights approached Urana with a smile on his face.

"Hallo," he greeted her brightly. He brought up a crystalator to examine her.

Urana didn't object much, she was just tired.

"Where am I?" she asked.

The medtech looked uncertain as he passed the crystalator over her several times.

"Where do think you are?"

Urana shook her head.

The medtech looked behind him, toward the medbay doors. They opened and in strode a half dozen warriors. Urana would have thought them to be Celestian Knights such were they garbed in uniforms and capes.

The large black man who led them spoke.

"I am Procyon. This is my sword. Who are you and how did you come to be in our space?"

Urana stared back not sure what to say.

"She has energy-abilities," said the medtech, showing Procyon his crystalator results.

Procyon studied them with a frowning brow. He looked over Urana then back at the readings again.

"You may be Elerae," he said observing her blue hair, "But you are not one of us," he concluded. His tone was suspicious.

Before Urana could ask what that meant, Procyon proclaimed to the others:

"She is a Celestian Knight spy!" He directed his hard gaze at Urana. "And you are now a prisoner of the Knights Destina."

Urana stared at him dumbfounded. And things tumbled into place.

Not just where am I, she thought. *But when am I?*

CHAPTER FIFTEEN

"What happened?" Alpha Rion asked the dark room in general as he raised himself off the cold stone floor. He rubbed the back of his neck.

"We were attacked by that alien," Primerion grumbled in reply, sounding as groggy as Alpha Rion felt.

They could see they were all alone. No alien in sight.

Primerion spoke to the others. "We have to secure this room, formulate a plan, then find, interrogate or destroy the enemy!"

"Sounds like a good plan to me," Hellon said.

He turned to make sure Omrion was fine, his son sitting on the floor with his back on the wall. He indicated his good health with a cursory wave of his hand.

Then Hellon remembered something. He turned back to Chalant who had only just got to her feet as the others had.

"Did you know our attacker? You called out a name." His demeanour darkened.

Chalant shook her head, as much as to try and clear it for memories to seep back in. "No, no. . . at least not this alien. Back on the Gravan world before we found you, we met an alien, similar——tall, all black, but this was not he. The alien who attacked was different." She looked at Alpha Rion for confirmation.

"That is true," he corroborated. "The alien we met was called Amagesh. He was our host and directed us to you in a surge ship. He was nothing but helpful. But, be that as it may, it looks like a member of his species has attacked us for whatever reason. Primerion is right, we need to prepare for any more attacks."

"Oh, for Universe sake," Korelestra sulked.

"Do not be like that!" admonished Primerion. "We have to defend ourselves!"

Korelestra shook her head, a little smile on her face. "No, I know that. I meant we have replaced one prison with another. Where will it end? We cannot hide. We have to go on the attack!"

"I agree," Alturi said. "We have lived behind walls for too long. We should find this alien and destroy it!"

"I also agree," Spheron joined in.

"Why attack us?" Hellon glowered once more at Chalant, the human getting the feeling he did not like her for some reason.

"Why keep looking at me? Is there something wrong?" she asked him.

He turned away with a scowl.

But Primerion laughed. "I think he is suspicious of your non-Celestian nature." She seemed to be mocking him, Hellon turning his glare upon his wife.

Chalant cocked her head. "My non-Celestian nature?" she repeated. "Because I am human or at least a Chryri?" She turned to Alpha Rion. "Is he being racist?" she semi-whispered to him.

"Oh Universe!" he rolled his eyes.

"What is a racist?" Hellon asked.

"Someone who doesn't like someone culturally different to themselves." Alpha Rion explained to them.

Hellon was just about to protest, but Alpha Rion's gaze around the room noticed an oddity.

"Where's Solandus?"

Everybody suddenly looked around, checking corners and behind the pillars, but only they were in the room.

Hellon did a double take, his face clouding over.

"Did anyone see him when they came to; He was definitely with us when we were attacked," Alpha Rion recalled.

"You don't think. . . ?" Chalant began.

"He has gone looking for the alien himself?" finished Alpha Rion. They looked at each other, knowing the answer.

With a grin, Korelestra said, "So, we go looking for the alien after all!"

"Yes," Alturi said. "And we should stay together."

Primerion sighed. It had been much easier to command in the pyrathedral, but it seemed Alpha Rion's and Chalant's appearance had changed the dynamic of their group. In a way she was glad, she did not have to be responsible for everything, but in others respects, she knew it took away her authority. But for now, all she wanted to do was to find her son.

Syene had infiltrated the storm and into the fortress without incident. Her silvery presence threw shifting shadows as she flew through the dark corridors, like a pulsating glowing ball. She skittered to a stop.

She could sense something, someone, coming toward her around the corner. Whoever or whatever it was, it was radiating its own psychic force searching, methodically, but stealthily.

Syene shrunk back. She was pure psychic energy. She couldn't see or hear or touch as such. Her world was the psiscape and thus whatever approached interfered with her psychic environment, which reflected back to her. But she couldn't suppress herself enough. She must have been detected. She waited for the presence to approach.

>*Then I will attack*< she thought to herself.

The presence stopped.

>*Did it hear me?*<

Suddenly, the presence disappeared. Syene scanned the area.

>*Nothing!*<

She edged forward. And came face to face with a male at the intersection of the corridors.

There was a brief shocked silence. The stranger recovered first.

>*Hallo*< he greeted her.

Syene could sense he was Celestian, thus not the enemy. But he had somehow hidden his presence from her. She was impressed.

>*Do not be afraid*< she psyed.

>*I am not afraid*< *he replied with humour.* >*Just relieved you*

are not the enemy. At least I hope you are not< he psyed back to her. >*Who are you? And where did you come from?*<

>*You, the fortress, I mean, is back on Magna Aura. Cirrius sent me to investigate why*< She felt an odd sensation when he answered her.

>*On Magna Aura? I do not understand*< He looked at her... at her... Syene realised.

Solandus laughed. >*Yes, I can see you. You are a beautiful spectral form*<

>*But no one can see me. Not even my brother. I am a ball of psychic energy to everyone*< She felt a thrill of excitement tingle through her.

>*Well, I see the beautiful woman you project in front of me*< Solandus admired the lithe, brown-haired woman in front of him. >*And whom do I have the pleasure of meeting?*<

Syene felt herself stand up straighter. >*I am Syene of the Chronossii, daughter of Xathanius, Lord Aeon of the Astrals*< she proudly announced. >*And you?*<

>*Solandus, son of Alphatronius*<

>*Solandus? Solandus?*< she repeated. The name was familiar. Then she remembered. >*You were lost, the others said*<

>*And yet, here I am*< Solandus held out his hands, palms out. >*With my brother, Alpha Rion, his betrothed, and the Celestri*<

Syene shook her spectral head. There was too much information to share between them. She looked at Solandus and could see he knew the same thing.

Time was of the essence. Something else was coming for them.

>*Quick, inside me!*< Solandus pointed to his head.

An affronted Syene rocked back on her heel.

>*No!*< came her sharp retort.

>*They cannot find you here. I can hide you!*<

A wide-eyed Psyene viewed Solandus. She did not know this Celestian, yet he was trusting her in his head. She had never been in anyone else's head before. She did not know even if she could. It might have been just the bond between her and Dyonus.

>*Come on*< Solandus willed her; half panic in his voice and face. >*Quickly, I can hold you!*<

She gave him a dubious here-I-come look and her spectral form broke up replaced by a shining psychic ball.

>*Beautiful either way*< Solandus approved.

The psychic charge shot into his head, Solandus stumbled backward hitting the cold hard stone wall behind him. His head felt like it had exploded. His vision was blurred, his balance was off as he staggered along the corridor. His mind wanted to jump out of him.

No, it was more like Syene wanted to jump back out.

>*No*< he gasped. >*Stay. I can do this*<

He clamped down on his thoughts, but there was a psionic bleed from Syene. He could see her world from the very disturbing vantage point of being inside her brother's head. Almost alien thoughts and emotions flooded through him as he lived the life of a woman trapped in the head of a man in ancient Greece, the hardships, the nomadic life of an outsider considered a madman with his only company being his sister whom he could never see.

How lonely you must have been, he thought. As lonely as he had been trapped in a prison on an alien world.

>*Not as lonely as you*< replied Syene. >*At least I had my brother!*<

Solandus smiled. The psionic link was wide open and they could see each other's life.

>*You will have to teach me that spectral projection trick*< she said.

>*Deal*< Solandus' head still ached like the fortress had fallen on it, but it was getting better. He was a couple of corridors from the others now.

>*So why are you here?*< he asked her.

>*Oh, you have not seen that part yet. Here*< Syene dropped a cascade of psychic images into his head.

>*Invasion!*< Solandus was shocked. But he fell to his knees when he saw the next image. >*No, not Novan! No!*< He slumped to the floor and cried.

Novan, as his eldest brother, with psychic abilities like Solandus had tried to teach the youngster everything he knew. They were not warriors like Decion or like the twins, Alpha Rion and Astara, who shared a deep bond. It had been Novan who had encouraged him to explore beyond Magna Aura to earn himself some respect among the Starguards. And now, instead of returning triumphantly to tell Novan all he had seen and experienced, he would never see him again.

>*I am so sorry*< Syene psyed.

It took Solandus a while to recover his thoughts and emotions, anger foremost.

>*Thank you*< he psyed back. He quickly processed the rest of the information from Syene.

>*So the fortress has been back on Magna Aura for over twenty years. It only seemed like a moment to us. And now we have been awakened when the Starguards returned. Why?*< he asked more to himself than to Syene.

But she answered anyway. >*I think they want us to be all together. They want us all in one place...*<

>*To kill us?*< Solandus shook his head. >*No, they could have killed us in the fortress, but kept us alive for this long. They have a different agenda*< But he could not see it. >*We should get back to the others and find a way to leave here*<

Syene smiled. >*That is why I am here. You may not be able to leave, but I can. And with our combined psychic abilities, we may be able to free the others as well*<

Solandus nodded. >*Let us go then*<

The Malverse

"Comprehend the nature was psychic," reported Nexionon. "An added presence of a temporal element was spun within the anomaly."

The cavernous crater had been hewn into the side of the

once-planet and left open to the depths of space; a bleak, starless, unmoving tapestry. On the other side of the worldlet, the wormhole generators were still holding the portal open to the fortress. And the auto-sensors had detected the unusual readings.

"Messaging system?" asked Techmoses, "from the Starguards to the fortress!" His face was a mask of blackness, but the frown could still be discerned in its features. "Responses?"

Nexionon's head tilted left on his slim shoulders. "Negative, the signal comprised a one-time pulse. No response. Contrary expectation, my storm is not as impervious to psychic phenomena as calculated!"

"Agreed. Expectation sub-optimal," a perturbed Techmoses replied. "An alternative outcome is desired. Understand, I will investigate!"

There was a slight hesitation from Nexionon, Techmoses understanding the dilemma. But if the Starguards could change tactics then so could he.

"Expectation altered," he told his subordinate. "Understand, we will make direct contact. Understand, we will make the Starguards fathom their place in the forthcoming changes to their universe. They will witness the death of their gods!"

The Fortress

The introduction of Syene to the Celestri and Alpha Rion and Chalant, with her popping from Solandus' head in all her silver-balled glory went well considering, a cheerful Solandus had thought.

"It is a silver ball of energy," a fascinated Chalant reacted.

"Observant, as usual," Hellon mocked her.

Chalant ignored him.

Solandus looked from Syene to Chalant. "You cannot see the woman Syene has become?" he asked, concerned neither Chalant or Omrion could see her as he could.

"Woman?" Chalant's voice was edged with a touch of curiosity.

There were shakes of collective heads. Syene shrugged.

>*Guess it is just you and me, then*< she sounded dejected.

"It might just be a case of psionic tuning," he said aloud for all to hear. "But we will worry about that another time!"

He told them all he knew from Syene about Novan's death, the return of the Amethystians, the arrival of the Chronossii, and the invasion.

"So as you can see, much has changed since we have slumbered." He looked at his brother, Alpha Rion.

>*We will grieve for him when we can*< he psyed to him privately.

Alpha Rion nodded, trying to put Novan's death to the back of his mind.

"So what is the plan for now?" he asked.

Chalant was by his side, her sympathetic energies calming him.

"Obviously we have to leave the fortress and join the rest of the Starguards and. . ."

"Expectation agreed," a new voice joined the conversation.

Syene disappeared in the blink of an eye.

The collective energies of Solandus, the Celestri, and Chalant snapped on, directed at the black humanoid being in the stone-arched doorway flanked by Amagesh and an even larger muscular black being behind them. Alpha Rion and Primerion found they could not harness their swords.

Though his face was obscured in blackness, like a haze of swirling cosmic dust, the sense of smile emanated from the being.

"Understand, I am Techmoses of the Omenuum," he announced in a calm, cold voice. "Understand, I acknowledge Alpha Rion and Chalant acquaint themselves to Amagesh," he looked over his left shoulder. "Urvursur is our third," he introduced the massive individual to his right.

Alpha Rion recovered first, reconciling the alieness of the intruders.

"We know Amagesh, or thought we did," he replied with a

surliness. "And what does the Omenuum want on Magna Aura? Why are you attacking us?" Alpha Rion asked before Primerion could.

There was a snarl in the voice, a rasp of accusation as Techmoses replied. "You reason yourselves the victims? You reason you have experienced merciless existences or even that your lives compare to the suffering my people have endured from yours! It does not. And you will find out what it is like to live in a dead universe!"

"What is he on about?" Chalant whispered to Alpha Rion, resisting the urge to laugh in the obvious face of death.

Alpha Rion pulled a face. "I have no idea." He turned to Techmoses, smiling to present a friendly face. He walked slowly toward him, hand out-stretched to shake his hand.

A streak of black energy exploded from Amagesh's arm knocking Alpha Rion off his feet and flying through the air. He collided with a crunch along the back wall, blood spurting from his mouth. He stayed down, but managed to look up.

"Fire!" yelled Primerion.

Hellon, predictably, was the first to fire.

Alpha Rion had never seen Hellon use his powers before and he was astonished at the ferocity and uniqueness of them. Hellon controlled various energy spectra, but channelled differently from several body parts. Twisted blue plasma energy snapped from his eyes curling around the intruders like livid wraiths. More blue energy pulsed from his hands in tight vertical circlets like cosmic holes of decoherent radiation. But it was the scream Alpha Rion would never forget. Hellon's mouth was a sparkling froth of more blue energy from which a quantum-string splitting scream sundered the air around them, everyone holding their ears...

...except the intruders.

The plasma bursts rolled off the invaders, who stood unperturbed. No forcefield had been used. The energy just had no effect.

Aghast, Hellon terminated his assault and looked at his

hands, helpless. He kept his hands and eyes lit expecting retaliation, but the three beings stood nonchalantly.

Korelestra had shimmered into white energy. She was a soul destroyer, like her mother, and she would delve into the alien's being ripping out whatever nascent conscious energy held them together. But one wave of a hand from Techmoses and Korelestra's energised form coalesced back into a corporeal form. The surprise on her face was mirrored on everyone else's.

And even before Hellon's energy had rippled off them, Chalant, Solandus, and Omrion had launched concerted psi attacks on the three invaders. But as the others had found out there was no effect.

A strange noise gurgled from Techmoses.

Alien laughter, Alpha Rion realised as he raised himself to his feet. His armour had protected him somewhat, but he had still felt the force of hitting the stone wall. His back ached and his suit told him more than one rib was broken.

"I was not attacking you, Techmoses," he half-wheezed, "I was extending the hand of friendship." He slowly approached Techmoses again but stopped when Urvursur flexed a large shoulder. Alpha Rion held up his hands. "Okay, I do not know what is going on here and I do not know about any attack on your people, so tell us and perhaps we can start talks about peace."

There was a long silence from Techmoses and Alpha Rion thought he had got through to him or at least he was considering it, but his hopes were pitifully dashed.

"Starguard, this waged war upon my people started long before you were born. My people were civilised, exploring starwrights, and aged long before the Celestians were born. But you killed them just the same."

Alpha Rion looked at the others in despair. Techmoses wasn't making sense. He could see the others were at a loss as well.

"I do not understand," he replied. Surely he must have had this wrong.

A sound of disgust played in Techmoses' throat.

"Enough!" he rasped. "We visit the rest of your decrepit families."

He raised a hand and the inhabitants of the fortress disappeared into his black portal.

Aqrius

>*We have to go now. Right now!*< Syene was barely back in her brother's head before psying.

"What's happened? Where are the others from the fortress," Dyonus asked aloud for the benefit of the Starguards and Chronossii in the room.

>*No time to explain. We Chronossii have to leave now*< Syene tried to urge her brother to portal. He felt his powers trying to charge up.

"What is going on?" Cirrius stalked over peering into Dyonus' eyes as if he can see Syene inside his head. "Syene?"

Dyonus listened internally as his sister flashed memories at him. He made the decision.

"Chronossii, we are leaving now. The enemy is coming and they cannot find us here. They do not know us. We will be their only hope but only in the future." He stood apart from the rest.

"Dyonus!" Cirrius shouted. "No! I rescued you all. You serve me. I am the King!" He glared at the youth.

With a wordless order from Dyonus, Vostra, and Phasion stood up.

"You are really leaving?" Azure was alarmed at the prospect.

The rest of the Starguards, Celestra, the twins, and Xestina looked on in shock.

"Yes, Syene has a plan. We have to portal out to escape the anti-temporal field; transition to Earth maybe then we will be back. Promise. Goodbye."

And with that, the Chronossii ported out as one.

"Traitors!" Cirrius cursed them. "Traitors."

He slumped into a chair and promptly dropped out of it as the group were felled by a shock wave of black energy from a portal.

A dense coldness rolled through the room as dark forms emerged from the portal. Ahead of them other figures were thrown down onto the ground. It took a while for the two groups to realise what had happened.

"Alpha Rion!" Astara screamed as she rushed and hugged her brother tightly.

Then she saw who was beside him.

"Solandus?"

Solandus looked up at his sister, then to Decion.

"You two grew older!" he quipped with a cheerless grin.

Decion growled with humour. "You are still a whelp! Come here, boy." The two drew closer and Decion gave his youngest brother a bear hug, Solandus' white hair tangled with the black of his brother's.

"We will mourn Novan together," Solandus promised. Decion nodded firmly in agreement.

Chalant stood between the three brothers, wary of the presence of the aliens behind them who seemed content to let them settle in.

Alpha Rion introduced her to Astara. "This is Tera ZaVoir, known as Chalant. She is my betrothed,"

Astara laughed with surprise and hugged Chalant. "Welcome to the family. If it lasts," she stared warily at Techmoses.

But the attention soon turned to the new group of Celestians. Solandus looked over to them as they stood taller after their conspicuous ungainly entrance.

"On my travels to places far and wide enduring many adventures and trials," Solandus said with a wink to Chalant, "I came across our fellow kin. May I introduce to you the offspring of the lost Celestri Knights: Primerion, Hellon, their son Omrion; Spheron, Korelestra, and Alturi."

"Get out!" Azure blurted out.

Astara turned on her. "Azure, how dare you insult our honoured guests and kin! They cannot leave."

Azure laughed. "Sorry, Astara, it's an Earth expression. It's one of disbelief and surprise. Believe me, I am happy about this," she grinned. "You guys are legends, literally," she addressed the Celestri.

"Thank you," Primerion replied. "It is a great pleasure to meet you all, especially you Decion and Astara, my kin."

Decion bowed. "I would be honoured to spar with you when we have the chance." He eyed the dark beings with displeasure.

"Granted," Primerion answered back.

Cirrius held the corner of the room with Celestra and his children. His sons, their helmets off, watched on as their father was ignored.

For his part, Cirrius had warned his children not to demonstrate any temporal abilities. The aliens might have moved against them otherwise, though he would never forgive the Chronossii for abandoning him.

"Altair?" Alpha Rion saw the blonde Starguard at the back of the group. He stared at his missing eye and arm.

Altair grinned. "Don't worry about me. You should see the other guy. I'm fine. I'd like to know more about the friends who brought you here though," he sneered. "I think I met and killed one of their kind. Is that so, friend?" his only eye boring into Techmoses.

A violent purr spurted from Techmoses' mouth. "Your prattlings are but the nonsensical murmurs of mewlings," he spat back.

He turned around the room to each in turn, returning to address the original group on Aqrius.

"Understand, I am Techmoses of the Omenuum, servants of Bood of the Forethere, Vanguards of the Godscended. We attend your universe to slay your creators."

"Our creators?" Cirrius stirred at the back of the room, his interest piqued. "The Great Father and Holy Mother?"

"Veti and Lega," Techmoses spat the words out with venom.

"Who are they?" Alpha Rion asked, desperately trying to make sense of the situation.

The Celestians looked around, shrugging, vacant of ideas.

It was Amagesh's turn to gurgle in laughter. "They are

unaware," he said in a tone of surprise. "They are ignorant..."

"Inexcusable," retorted a bitter Techmoses.

An exasperated Alpha Rion had had enough. "So tell us!" he shouted, risking his healing ribs popping out. "Stop this piecemeal torture and tell us! What have we done!"

"You were born!" Techmoses sneered sharply, sending cold air across the room. "Born in sin. Born from death. Our death!" he hissed.

Keeping his temper, Alpha Rion, wanted more information. "Explain."

The air about Techmoses seemed to grow colder and the Celestians mentally shuddered.

"We were once like you," Techmoses began, "Young, blissfully ignorant of the universe, beloved of the gods," he growled the last word. "We were the Phanor, the children of Bood, the neuter god. Aeons ago, Bood's chosen, Shahalavahunti, the hermaphroid god acceded to the Godscended. And in that moment, in their lust for glory Veti and Lega murdered Bood, dooming our universe to an everlasting cold death, while they escaped to their own hidden realm. And there," Techmoses rasped rawly, "there they dared create their own beings, against all the decrees of the Godscended, the Forum of All. They re-imagined themselves as the Great Father and Holy Mother and begat the Storm of Stars who begat the Five Peoples. Your lives are abominations of the universe. Your lives drink of the blood spilled in our universe, consume the lost souls yet to be born. You are the hell we were born to destroy!" Techmoses proclaimed with venom and relish in equal amounts.

Deathly cold air deepened around them like an expectant death shroud.

"Shit in a hand basket!" Chalant whispered.

Primerion grimaced in scant understanding.

"So you are going to kill us, like you did Novan and Timechantress?" an annoyed Alpha Rion asked without trying to provoke a quicker end.

The rest of the Celestians looked at him, imploring him not

to speak further.

A raucous noise toiled around Techmoses' throat. Amagesh and Urvursur also shared in the amusement.

"You are already dead to us. We merely exercised an element of fear and control. No, we are not here to kill you all. We hold you hostage for the Storm of Stars and for Veti and Lega. We have been chosen by the Godscended to avenge them and to destroy the errant gods. Then we will take their children to our universe as slaves until the end of their days. And the slate will be wiped clean."

Primerion balled her fist, her anger giving way to fury. "No!" she screamed rushing Techmoses.

The force that hit her, shot her across the room against the wall. There was a sickening crunch of bones. Her neck at the wrong angle. She slumped over, not moving.

"Mother!" cried Omrion, running to her side. She was still alive, barely, the Celestri reading his mother's mind and vitals over his suit's crystalator comms.

Hellon joined his son, hand on shoulder to calm him down. Turning, he glared at Urvursur who had been the one to flex some invisible force against Primerion.

Omrion's rage boiled over and he rushed the aliens. Scant meters away, he was intercepted by Solandus who held him tight as the youth kicked and screamed.

"Let go!" Gritted teeth spat the words out, but Solandus held tight.

Techmoses' impassive face stared steadily and wordlessly back at Omrion, almost mockingly.

The room was already tense. No one else moved.

"This system, this world, and you Starguards are now under Omenuum control," Techmoses' cold voice announced. "There is no escape."

Then he, Urvursur, and Amagesh vanished into a cold black portal.

Solandus looked at the Celestri Knights with a sour expression. "Welcome to Magna Aura!"

TEMPORAL INTERRUPTUS

The Chronopolis. Some time ago.

"Father, I found Alpha Rion and portalled him to the other Starguards on Earth. What was so urgent as to call—" Lightstream stopped dead as she exited her portal and entered the Chronopolis' columned main hall.

Syene watched as Lightstream stopped and followed the gaze of her father, Helexius, and Spheron's daughter Sola looking at her. She hovered like a small very shiny silver ball, in the center of the temple. This was her plan. She had to make it work.

"Father? Sola?" Syene heard Lightstream call out. "What is that?"

"Don't move, Lexa," Helexius whispered to his daughter. "It just showed up and it seems to be searching or waiting for something."

His eyes never left Syene who smiled within at the slightly portly man. Though Syene didn't like Sola's response.

"I think it's from the Lore! Some form of energy probe. We tried blasting it, trapping it in temporal fields, everything, but it's too fast, anticipating our moves. It stops when we stop. Thought you might have something up your sleeve."

I'd better make my move, Syene thought. And before anyone else could react, she streaked toward Lightstream.

"Look out!"

"Noooo!"

Syene shot straight across the hall plunging into Lightstream's forehead.

>*Don't panic, don't panic*< Syene tried to assure Lightstream.

Syene could see out of Lightstream's eyes. She was flat on her back, staring fixedly at the domed hall's ceiling. It was an odd and noisy sensation for her with Lightstream's confused thoughts flooding in. Syene continued to pour out calming notions.

Helexius and Sola rushed over by her side. Still prone, Lightstream held up her hands to say she was okay. Syene allowed her autonomy as the Astral gingerly felt her forehead. Of course she wouldn't have physically damaged Lightstream, but now she had to get to work.

Lightstream tried to get up.

Sorry, but you need to know this. We don't have much time.

"Raaargh! Lightstream screamed in agony.

Syene flash-streamed visions at Lightstream; the origins of the Chronossii, their discovery by Cirrius, his death and deception of the Starguards, the pain of betraying Urana, the deaths of Novan and Timechantress, and the invasion of the cold-black aliens.

Syene could feel Lightstream resisting, arching and writhing wildly on the floor, screaming incomprehensible words. She couldn't breathe. She tried to take over Lightstream's body, to make her listen. She felt Lightstream's eyes turn silver and her body closed in on itself. She convulsed and shuddered as Lightstream tried to portal from under the influence of Syene, the Chronossii feeling as if time itself would crack her open. For Syene if only lasted a few seconds; it was all Lightstream could take. Then. . .

She felt it. A foreboding coldness. They had somehow found her.

>The aliens are coming for you Astrals. You have to leave now! Meet us here< she imprinted coordinates into Lightstream's mind. The depths of nothingness wracked her.

Frrriiish!

Syene emerged from Lightstream's head, hovered high in the hall and then vanished.

Panting for breath, Lightstream lay on her side, dull eyes staring straight ahead.

"Lexa, Lexa, are you okay?" Helexius frantically shook her.

"Get off me," Lightstream brusquely pushed him away, wiping drool from her mouth. She stood up groggily.

I have to remember everything.

"You were attacked!" an alarmed Sola cried out. "We need to check you out in the med bay."

"No," Lightstream declined, holding her hands up again. "I wasn't attacked. I was chosen!"

"Chosen?" Helexius and Sola shouted together.

A portal flash caught their attention. Their alert defenses were raised this time, but it wasn't the sphere.

It was Aristedes.

Oblivious to the traumatic events in the hall, he shouted:

"Zane's alive! Did you know?" shouted in frantic, angry, desperate tones. "Did you know?" he yelled again.

The three Astrals stared back at him, paralysed with emotions.

"What's happening, Helexius?" Sola asked, trying to grasp the train of events, fear creeping across her features. She turned to Aristedes. "Aristedes, we were just attacked, or Lightstream was. . ."

"I said I wasn't attacked. I was chosen!" repeated an annoyed Lightstream, breathlessly.

"Attacked," Aristedes repeated. "By a red crystalline alien?" His anger was returning.

"What? No, a silver glowing ball of energy!" Sola sounded confused.

There were a babble of voices as Sola and Aristedes tried to tell their stories at the same time.

"Stop!" Helexius ordered. "Just stop, both of you! Aristedes, you first. What's happened?"

Aristedes told his story. "My friend, Lynn Kellis, in the twenty-third century just told us that Zane is alive in the twenty-first century, with the Starguards we placed there!"

"What?" Lightstream momentarily forgot her own mission. "But I sent Alpha Rion there, too! Let's go. . . " She was intent on returning to Earth, but Aristedes stopped her.

"No, you can't! After Kellis told me this, I tried to rescue Zane myself, but I was actually prevented from doing so mid-temporal stream by a red crystalline being with a third eye in his hand! He then told me to return to the Chronopolis and transported me here itself. He knew of the Chronopolis *and* its location!" he emphasised the last part.

He saw their shocked reactions and knew they had not encountered this being.

"Another time-travelling race? A powerful one!" Helexius pondered.

"And that was my warning," Lightstream said, gaining everyone's attention. "I was chosen by that silver sphere. It was a messenger."

"From who? Where? When?" Helexius demanded.

"I don't know, but it showed me things. A war far greater than we can imagine. Greater than this war Netherlord wanted. It spills through universes and eternity. We have to leave!"

"What? Leave here, but. . ." Sola choked.

Lightstream held her friend's hands softly. "We're not abandoning your father, Sola, but we're not safe here. I've been told where and when to go. And we have to go now!"

She looked earnestly at them all.

"I mean now!" she repeated more harshly.

"You believe this messenger?" Helexius was anxious.

"Yes, father, we're in grave danger. We have to leave!" She was ready to portal out.

"Give me a minute," Aristedes said, suddenly. "I have to get someone."

"Now?" Helexius gasped. "Who?"

"Yes, now. I'm not leaving her behind. Her name is Starshina." He portalled out.

They looked at the empty space, before Helexius sprung into action. "Grab the core crystalators, disable the Oracle, destroy anything else, shut the Hades thing down, and erect the temporal shields. No one enters but us four!"

Lightstream and Sola obeyed, dismantling crystalators and pocketing the critical crystals. Then the three of them began weaving temporal fields: overlapping fields of reverse, null, chaotic, fractal, asymmetric, dense, and shredded time, interlaced with an impenetrable barrier of energy, plasma strands. They also back-timed the field so no one could trace them once they had left—the paradox field would prevent a temporal incursion into their immediate past but still allow events that had occurred, to happen, ensuring their escape.

Aristedes portalled back in with a snow-white-skinned woman.

"Starshina, meet my uncle Helexius, my cousin, Lightstream, and Sola. Now we can leave!"

There wasn't much time for Starshina to react, except with a brief smile and wave.

The Astrals took one last look around the Chronopolis.

"Follow me, closely," a resolute Lightstream commanded.

Four flashes of light disappeared into the timestream; their portals sealing off the Chronopolis.

Almost at the same time as the Astrals ported out, six black portals dispensed six tall shadows on the outskirts of the Chronopolis. Dark coldness radiated from them in ethereal wisps.

They surveyed the enshrouded Chronopolis, empty and protected by its myriad of energy fields.

Amagesh, Degena, and Voddodon searched for hidden weaknesses, finding none. No Threshold would be completed here. They rejoined the other three.

"They were forewarned!" Antrameda stated tersely.

"It seems!" Urvursur, his whispery voice seeping dread.

Techmoses promised, "They will not escape, they cannot hide, they will die!"

"Where are we?" Sola asked, quietly.

"Hera's buggerhole!" Helexius cursed into the pitch blackness. Even their portals had not pierced the depths as they flashed in.

"Hush!" Lightstream hissed.

There was an echoing quality to their mystery surroundings.

Lightstream stepped forward. "I came as your messenger requested," she shouted into the void with a little trepidation.

"Show yourselves."

A slight change in the air to their right caught their attention.

"You are safe here," said a male voice emanating from that direction.

"Who are you?" demanded Helexius, prepared to battle for his life, as figures advanced toward them.

There was humour in the voice when it said:

"We are you!"

"Hades you are," Helexius replied caustically. "We are the Astrals, unless..."

"We are not your future selves," the same voice said with even more humour.

The figures stepped forward as light began to stream into the room.

The Astrals looked up at familiar surroundings.

"The Chronopolis," Sola remarked, seeing the walls of the temple around them.

But Helexius was more observant. "No, this is not our Chronopolis. Look at the extra rooms and that corridor is different. Where are we?" he addressed the newcomers.

The male who had spoken was tall and athletic. His beard was still light. But most curiously, they were dressed in all black manoeuvre suits. No capes, helmets, or weapons.

"I had expected to see my father here, Uncle Helexius," Dyonus spoke. "Is he still alive?"

Helexius' mouth worked up and down wordlessly.

"What?" Lightstream asked before her father did. "Who are you? And why did you invade my mind to warn us?"

"They're Astrals," Aristedes smiled. "They are us."

"We prefer Chronossii," Dyonus replied, "Brother," he emphasised.

The Astrals stared at each other and then at Helexius.

"Father," Lightstream tried to prompt her father. "Is this true?"

"Yes, it is, little sister," Vostra walked toward Lightstream. "We are your long lost, and conveniently *forgotten* kin," she sneered. "But we won't hold that against you, much." She stood nose to nose with Lexa who stared back into black eyes trying to see any resemblance to her.

"Father." Vostra greeted Helexius, coolly. "I am Vostra. I was from a little village close to Demes, quite forgotten now as well, and my mother was called Henna." She stood expectantly before him.

Helexius made a funny nervous noise, a half chuckle-cough. "I can see her in you," he said with some embarrassment.

Lightstream scoffed and backed away. Vostra haughtily stared at the rest of the Astrals.

Sola looked at Phasion. "I take it you are my brother, Spheron."

The youth laughed. "I grew tired of living up to the Spheron name, so unimaginative, so I changed it to Phasion. I am pleased to have a sister. Looks like we are both rebellious in our own way." He grinned, Sola finding herself charmed at his way. She turned to find Lightstream scowling at her.

"Where's the silver ball?" Lightstream changed the subject quickly. "That's the reason we are here, isn't it?"

The Chronossii turned to Dyonus who tapped his head. "My sister, Syene," he said. "She is a pure psi-temporal entity. She normally resides in my head." He waited, but nothing happened. "She's a bit shy now. All the excitement." He smiled ruefully.

"That sounds both awesome and painful," Aristedes said.

"And not so private at times," Dyonus humoured him.

"I have a sister, too?" Aristedes said, thinking of Zane. "I hope they get to meet one day. And father as well." He walked forth and took Dyonus' hand in acceptance.

Dyonus took his brother's arm firmly.

"Do you know if father is still alive?" Aristedes asked.

Dyonus turned to the others as if seeking a silent permission.

"Yes, they are alive. From what Cirrius told us, the Starguards were somehow transported to the furthest future of Earth where they fought the Storm of Stars with the Antiqchronals. . ."

"Hahaha," Helexius roared, until he noticed no one else was laughing. "You're serious?"

"Yes, I am. The Starguards told their story upon their return."

"So we can see my father and Zane?" Aristedes asked.

"Once their participation in that war is over, yes, we can find them. The Astrals were not involved so you will have to wait for the timeline to resolve itself."

Aristedes nodded his understanding, happy in the knowledge that they were still alive.

"Fine, we will need their help," he told his brother.

Dyonus smiled in agreement. He noticed Starshina standing beside him, the snow-white-skinned human taking in the proceedings quietly.

"And which Astral are you?" Dyonus inquired with curiosity.

Starshina smiled. "I am human. You may call me Starshina."

"Oh," Dyonus looked between her and Aristedes. "Interesting. Well, welcome to our Chronopolis."

"And how did you know how to build this fortress? I also assume we're in a pocket dimension?" the engineer in Helexius asked.

Dyonus pointed to Lightstream.

"Ahh," Helexius understood, "your sister learned everything and transferred it to you. While I'm not too enthused about the invasion of my daughter's mind, still, this feat must have taken years as it did us."

"Three in all," Dyonus replied proudly, "relatively speaking. Now here we all are."

"Indeed," Helexius agreed. "Impressive."

"So what is this dire warning about—invasion and death." Lightstream asked, not wanting to remember all she had been showed. It had been a deeply compressed temporal experience even for her.

Dyonus stood between the two groups addressing the Astrals.

"We have come from Magna Aura. Long ago, Cirrius found

us in Greece as children. He told us how our kin had abandoned us; left us on Earth when Phasia took you from the Battle at Troy. Naturally we felt less than nothing. We were the eldest, yet you were the favourites. We were deprived of our destiny. You took that from us. So when Cirrius returned and outlined the plan to take the Starguards to Earth and have us replace them and then to keep you Astrals away from Magna Aura, we agreed.

"But things did not turn out the way Cirrius had planned. The Amethystians miraculously returned and tried to invade. Cirrius held them off for over thirty years. Next a mysterious storm on Halcyon appeared defying all efforts to discern its nature. Then we found that the Starguards had returned and that the storm was caused by another invading alien force. They were waiting for the Starguards to return. They killed both Novan and. . . " he looked at Helexius, ". . . and Timechantress."

"No," was all Helexius could say, not knowing how to mourn news of his sister's death.

Lightstream rubbed her father's shoulder, leaning on his back more out of sympathy for her father's loss rather than any feeling for Timechantress.

Good riddance, she thought.

Dyonus spoke. "From what we have seen on Magna Aura and heard from Timechantress about the Chronopolis, it seems these aliens cannot cross directly from their universe to ours. They need an intermediary dimensional breach like the fortress and the Chronopolis.

"And they may be susceptible to temporal or psychic abilities," he added, "which is why they tried to take you out at the Chronopolis. That's when my sister came up with the plan to warn you. She warned us on Magna Aura and we fled. We left the others behind." If he felt ashamed, he didn't show it.

"Live to fight another day," Lightstream retorted coldly.

She wasn't sure of Dyonus' intentions and loyalties. If he could abandon Cirrius, who had allegedly saved the Chronossii, to his fate, then who knew how he would treat the Astrals who had abandoned them.

"That's right," Dyonus replied, not picking up on Lightstream's slight barb. "And fight we will. We need a plan and when we do we will return to Magna Aura, destroy the aliens and save the Starguards."

"That seems to be our job description nowadays," whispered Sola, drawing a sharp look from Helexius and a roll of the eyes from Lightstream.

"So, Astrals, are you with us?" Dyonus asked.

The Astrals looked to Helexius.

He grinned. "By Zeus' bulbous cock we are!"

Epilogue

Deep Space. Two and a half years since Magna Aura.

"High Commander, I, I. . . " Sci-controller Xemetheed looked down in shock at his instruments unable to speak.

"What is it, Sci-con?" Amethadaalus asked.

Xemetheed shook his head again, almost afraid to speak. "There's a strange energy signature directly in front of the sword. I think, it looks like. . ." he turned toward Amethadaalus. "I think it's *Her!*"

"Azure? Here?" He almost panicked in front of his crew.

"No, High Commander. . . *Her!*" His eyes were wide with fear.

Amethadaalus shot from his chair. "*Her?*" He quelled the rising fear inside him.

This is not going to go well, he told himself.

But Talameth was far more exuberant. "Sentity returns to us?! We should rejoice, High Commander?" He looked at his commander in askance.

"Rejoice in death?" Xemetheed replied.

But before Amethadaalus could say anything, a message came in.

"Amethystian World Fleet, this is Sentity. I request permission to come aboard."

The bridge all looked at Amethadaalus, confusion and the same questions on their faces.

Why would she request permission? She was their Goddess; the deity they had spurned and hidden from.

Amethadaalus nodded to Comms to return her request.

"Sentity, I am High Commander Amethadaalus of the Amethystian World Fleet. We rejoice in your return and your request is accepted." He motioned to the bridge to standby for the Goddess' appearance.

Moments later, a bright purple light pervaded the bridge. When the light subsided, a woman stood before them, not the little girl image Sentity had previously taken.

Talameth fell to his knees, followed by many others on the bridge; Amethadaalus knelt from his command chair.

"We worship you, Goddess!" Amethadaalus intoned as piously as he could. "We kneel before your justice. We... "

"Stand up!" Sentity commanded softly, with a smile. She turned to Amethadaalus. "Look at me. I am not your Goddess. I am not anyone's Goddess."

There were gasps around the bridge, Talameth's mouth wide open in shock. Sentity knelt before Amethadaalus.

"Amethadaalus, I have been away from my people for many centuries. I have lived on an alien world and experienced all the emotions Amethystians do; love, hate, anger, joy, jealously, and vengeance. I have seen how other beings have treated each other and I now know what the Amethystians endured. I could not have empathised with Amethystians before that time. I was not made for that. I was a weapon of vengeance. I was created by your ancestors. I failed you. I erred and lost my path."

She looked down upon the crew with compassion.

"I am here to beg your forgiveness. Your ancestors were right to escape me. And I am glad for I would not have learned about loyalty, duty, and trust. I may be pure energy in a mortal form, but I am an Amethystian. Your enemies are my enemies and I will protect you from them." Her soft voice belied her intentions and intensity of purpose. She stayed on her knees, her head bowed.

Amethadaalus wasn't sure what to do. This was totally unexpected.

"Rise, Sentity," he said softly.

She did so and looked at him. He did not know whose form she had taken, but she was short, pudgy, and not too pretty.

Sentity observed his disapproving look at her new form and laughed.

"I am not in a familiar form, I know. It is a form I have become accustomed to." At his puzzled look, she laughed. "As I stated, I have learned a lot over the years; mercy for one. You do not need vengeance. I have learned how not to hate. Yes, your ancestors were wronged, but seeking revenge will not bring them back. You do not have to war with the Six Worlds. Go your own way, remake the Amethystian world and live in peace. In time, your anger will be assuaged and you may even want to re-contact the Celestians, in peace."

Amethadaalus listened in complete shock. How could this be the same Goddess who had cowed them into submission, leading them to abandon her out of fear?

"What has become of you, Sentity? Your words are. . ." He couldn't bring himself to say it.

"Weak?" Sentity finished for him.

Before Amethadaalus could reply, Xemetheed suddenly screamed, clasping his ears, the implanted crystalator comms unit glowing red behind his ears as it burst open. He collapsed to the floor.

A ragged ear-splitting laughter rang through the sword. The bridge looked around for the source, Sentity seeing it first.

A searing flash of blue light invaded the bridge, crushing the senses of the Amethystians, setting off alarms all over the bridge. Only Sentity remained unaffected. The twisting light coalesced into a female form.

Amethadaalus waited for the blue spots to clear before barking orders, but his voice was an unintelligible snarl. And then they all noticed there was someone extra on the bridge.

"Greetings High Commander Amethadaalus."

An unfamiliar woman stood on the bridge. The blue had disappeared and the woman had flaming red hair and dark eyes.

"I am the Archwitch, Elisabeth van Tager!" she announced with a wide smile.

Amethadaalus was momentarily frozen with fear. He could see the shimmer of energy beneath the woman's skin. And he took her for what he thought she was:

"A Starguard! Kill her!"

Van Tager shook her head and threw up an arm. Everyone froze on the bridge.

"Oh, *please,* do not insult me! I am not a Starguard or even a Celestian. Sentity, here can tell you that, right, darling? I have been following you everywhere." She looked at Sentity for substantiation, but Sentity's eyes were a blaze of purple.

"Van Tager, what do you want? How are you even here?"

Van Tager grinned. "Now that is a long story! But what I will tell you is that I will fulfil your every desire, your destiny, and help you destroy your enemies—the Starguards and their peoples. What do you say High Commander?"

Van Tager stepped forth, hand held out in friendship and promise.

"No," Sentity bristled. "Stay with me, your kin and protector!"

She, too, held out her hand aloft to clasp Amethadaalus' forearm.

Amethadaalus looked between them as his crew watched him at this momentous event in their history. The fate of all Amethystians lay in his choice. His mind whirled.

Choose our Goddess Sentity and peace or choose to go forth with a stranger on a path of vengeance?

Amethadaalus stepped forward, raised his hand, and made his choice.

APPENDIX A

THE HERMETICA GALACTIC

Welcome to the holo site of
Hermes Daracales

I am the Greatest Exoarchaeologist in the Universe

And I present to you

My Greatest Works...

Awarding winning author of Three Book Mars: *Of Mars to Come, This Island Mars,* and *Extinction Mars.* Author of *Biography of a God, Once Upon a Time in Outer Space, The Herographica,* and *The Phoenix Society.*

Working with assistants Ranch Stegson, an unreconstructionist archaeologist ('Everything he did was very much 20th century!') and Mass Morgon—veteran of the End World Wars, Hermes Daracales travels the galaxy in search of archaeological mysteries.

So, here lie the works of me, Hermes Daracales. The truth of my words will stand the test of time as I swore oaths to gods and angels to hold true to their chronicalisations, and I am but a humble man of my word.

From the Pages of *Once Upon A Time In Outer Space* - A story told by Hermes Daracales, based upon excavations and ancient texts.

"...Our civilisation was a failure. We had groped our way out of primitivity, mastered the nuclear fire, and lived among countless stars for over five hundred years. Yet we had nothing to show for it! For the universe is a cruel place, condemning us to oblivion. Even after we had thought we were saved by our technology, we were not the same people and our civilisation spun into decline. And no one cared. Except me. I could not live to see such failure in man and all he had achieved. So I left. I left Earth to find the light of life and bring it back for all mankind.

I am exoarchaeologist, explorer, and author Hermes Daracales, searching for that within the universe, those splendours, which I hope will re-awaken the spirits within my fellow man. But I had found something else, or rather he had found me. He, who I stood before, trembling. A God. A God who took me on a path of enlightenment and awakening.

I never knew! Never knew such wonders. Of course not, how could I? I had never knowingly met a God before. Until now!"

I was dropped upon a world unknown to anyone else, hidden, forgotten. But here I stood. And in my first few days on this unparalleled orb, I discovered a city, a wondrous ruin of vast beauty. And then I witnessed the unearthing of an incredible story carved in stone. It took me a further two years to decipher.

"The first carvings on Stela I, I deciphered were..."
    'One day, bold men will write epics about what they saw today!'

"It seems to be a story about a God who fell from the sky. The translated name is Alatair, but I think the best interpretation is with the honourific which renders the name as Alatarius..."

Stela IV
    "Who are you?" the man asked. *"Are you a God? You fell from*

the sky and yet live, despite your injuries."

Alatair remembered a humorous saying: "You should see the other guy!" he grinned.

The people looked around at each other. "We saw no one else with you," the man said.

Alatair shook his head. Some humour was an acquired taste!

"But I get ahead of myself. The main back story concerns a curse upon a young hero and the quest he has to undertake for vengeance. . ."

Stela III

Emperor-Sorcerer Warlon, the Dark Lord from the Land of Phanor, loved a woman who spurned him and married a lesser lord, older than herself. Warlon was livid. He killed the newly-wed husband on his honeymoon night, but the woman escaped, aided by a mysterious sister. Later the woman found herself pregnant and it was proclaimed by her sister that she would bear a great son.

But Warlon cursed the son-to-be prophesying that the son would only live to an age equal to the age difference between the boy's mother and father: fourteen years.

The mother swore that by the living stars which burn and die that her son will be great by his 14th year and destroy the curse which hung above him! But she would never know his fate for she died in childbirth.

Raised by a mysterious sisterhood, the young boy was led to destiny by angels, Alatair, and motley adventurers. So begins the saga of Coley Arrowsun.

"The name of the planet's inhabitants are the Celesterians—A mysterious and powerful race of humanoid beings left stranded on a distant world after a war with their evil arch enemies the Lora, beings of dark light."

"There are a list of characters on a stela, designated Stela II, some of whom are related to the story, but it is difficult to tell as the lower left corner is damaged."

Pallan Dach - Celesterian warrior. Paragon of virtue, but full of dark thoughts. Never was there a braver soul than the one which died from fear. He who wished could have borne a braver soul.
Auri or Aura-Jena - a Celesterian Angel - Part of a mysterious sisterhood with special powers who aid Coley Arrowsun in his cause.
Araya - a Celesterian Angel
Adara - a Celesterian Angel
Pritti – Coley's childhood friend - a serving woman.
The sentient ship Sunstrand. Her crew: Cohort the android, Moment - a flickerer or apparitional entity.
The Above, a military force commanded by General Trad.
The Grand Slines – Coley's mountainous homeland.

"The Celesterian Angels seem to be women who had mysterious powers. The male warriors seemed to have longer lives. Was this true of all Celesterians? I do not know."

Stela V
   The man from the stars [Alatair] came with us. He had powers like the angels, but he bore red lights from his hands, while Auri bore yellow.
   Twelve great battles would have to be fought as prophesied by Warlon, who had disappeared from sight years ago.
   On the eve of the first great battle against Warlon's army:'Remember what I told you Coley.' Auri put a hand on his left shoulder. There was an inner light in her face, her hair like gold-spun sun rays, her eyes like fiery diamonds. She was an angel.
   'Yes, Auri,' he answered. He took a deep breath. 'To those of you in the city,' he shouted up the valley slopes, 'know that the very scourge of heaven shall fall upon mine enemies' souls.

Leave this place, for it shall be no more come the morning.'

He waited.

Pallan shouted a warning.

An arrow loosed from the citadel walls lodged itself in a nearby tree. Then another. And then more came raining down. Coley had his answer.

He stood in the hail of missiles and shouted, 'I shout your deaths. I shout the end of your world!' And from his mouth he screamed a tremendous and continuous torrent, the likes of which had never been heard.

Pallan covered their ears, for they could not believe the sound that came from within one so small and young. And then they could not believe their eyes as the valley slopes trembled, the roar of bricks and stone hurtling down the grassy sides as the castle disintegrated. The screams of the dying.

Alatair had taken to the air. We had seen him fall from heaven, but we did not know he could return. But he stopped in mid-air and vented forth red energy from his hands down upon the city. We were amazed.

Auri continued to hold Coley's shoulder. She could see her army, the arrows of angels, slaughtering thousands, arrows like raining death, a rain of blood, rivers of blood, the blood of the world. Angel arrows screamed like the end of the world sundering the bonds of life, until nothing was left.

She let go of Coley's shoulders. He stopped screaming. The dust and noise settled, to reveal a completely levelled valley top.

Aura-Jena, Coley, Pallan, and Alatair made their way up, skirting great chunks of broken castle walls and hundreds of dead bodies.

'Gods of the Universe!' Pallan said incredulously. 'What have you done, Coley?'

'He's destroyed the city. Warlon's army are no more.' Auri said.

Coley stared at the carnage. There were dead everywhere.

'You have a very powerful voice, Coley,' said Alatair.

'I shouted the end of the world. I shouted their fate. They

died at my word!' Coley said.

'They all will,' Auri said.

Coley collapsed to the ground on his knees and cried. He was only 12 years old and conquering a world. What else could he do?

Auri comforted him. She felt a hand on her shoulder. It was Pallan, as usual. His heart yearned for her. He tried to kiss her.

'Don't you ever try and kiss me again, or I will kill you,' she warned him.

'But I've never kissed an angel before,' he pleaded.

'And you never will!' She pushed him away.

'One day I will,' Pallan promised himself.

Stela VIII

"From the context of this fragmented stela, the next surviving one, there are more battles, but Emperor-Sorcerer Warlon is never found. However, on the eve of the Battle of the Chasm Castle, Pallan senses a change in Coley...

Pallan could see the evil in the boy's eyes. It grew stronger with each battle cry. Auri sensed it too, Pallan saw even as she tried to remove her hand from his shoulder, Coley kept it there with his little hand. He was too powerful for her to act.

Alatair watched from above. He had known evil, fought the dreaded Lora, and could sense all was not right in Coley. Yet, he was an outsider and he did not want to interfere.

Pallan drew his bow. His last arrow sat in the quiver and was now laid across the string. He aligned his sight and drew the string back. And fired.

The arrow pierced Coley's heart in mid-shout, a horrible sound croaking from his throat. As Coley fell to the ground, a dark shadow emerged from his mouth; evil flowing from death.

It was the spirit of Emperor-Sorcerer Warlon. He had transcended life years ago and secretly inhabited Coley. It was an angel's touch which had empowered him within, infecting Coley's soul.

Auri released herself from Coley, who sunk to his knees. She drew her knife to attack, but the Shadow-Sorcerer Warlon reeled back to escape.

But in one fell swoop, Alatair swooped down and with the fearsome red light from his hands rent the dark form in half, which disintegrated.

Warlon was dead.

Coley lay very quiet on the ground. His blood streamed from his body in droplets like red tears.

All eyes fell on Pallan.

He walked over to Coley, the boy's eyes upon him. He tried to tell Pallan something, but while his lips moved they were soundless. His eyes darted about.

'Don't speak, boy,' Pallan said. He picked Coley up, the boy's eyes clouding over. He knew what he had to do.

Coley couldn't hear a thing. There were angels everywhere. Singing; a cosmic chorus in unison. Heaven itself.

Stela X – The Song of Stars
"What I wouldn't give to hear this song—the lament of the Gods, the rendition of Kings, and the epi-dirge of heroes. I weep for you Coley Arrowsun.

What is it about the stars,
that shine so brightly upon your face?
Protect you from the veil of darkness.
What is it about the stars?

The stars, that burn so bright,
like a halo dancing 'round your head,
shining forth the way to paradise
What is it about the stars?
What is it about the stars?

The stars, embrace your soul,

*spreading wondrous love, the sunlight radiant
from above, for all your days
What is it about the stars, the stars,
What is it about the stars, they love you so
What is it about the stars, the stars
What is it about the stars?*

*The stars, that grant you heaven's will.
No host of angels can compare
in all the starry fields.
What is it about the stars, the stars,
What is it about the stars, they bless you so
What is it about the stars, the stars
What is it about the stars?*

*The stars, they sing your praises
to all of those in highest places.
A cosmic chorus in unison.*

*What is it about the stars, the stars,
What is it about the stars, they shine for you
What is it about the stars, they burn for you
What is it about the stars?
The stars, the stars, the stars, the stars...*

Stela XI

Pallan walked; walked to the chasm, its endless depths whistling to the winds of time.

'Goodbye, boy'. With tears in his eyes, Pallan flung Coley over the edge. A fitting tomb of infinity to one so great.

Pallan turned to see Auri behind him. The look on her face disheartened him.

'Tell me Auri,' he said, 'are you an angel?'

Pallan walked closer to her. She did not move. He got closer. She stayed still. He leaned over to kiss her.

She didn't warn him this time. But he knew. He didn't see

her hand move like a blur to her hilt. But he knew. Their lips touched. His eyes closed. She was fast. And he felt bliss.
Pallan fell to the ground.

"That is the end of the story—unsatisfactory, I know. I was fortunate to excavate at the Chasm Castle. It sits in the mountains on the edge of a five-kilometre deep chasm. The ruins are magnificent and there are signs of a huge drawbridge which spanned the seventy metre chasm gap. We could not excavate in the chasm itself for health and safety reasons. Could Coley Arrowsun's infinity tomb really be down there?"
"There are a few broken stelae, but a couple of surviving ones, perhaps XIIII or XV, of a much later date carry on the story that Alatair purportedly lived among the Celesterians for perhaps a century or two, possibly married, but had children. He promised he would return to the Celesterians and take them away, perhaps to his own homeworld, but the dating is imprecise. We will never know if he did. It all might be fancy romantic tales abut him!"

"Some commentators, wrongly in my opinion, have stated that this fallen god Alatair and the Starguard Altair are one and the same, but this cannot be corroborated on the archaeological evidence presented. However, we do know from written records that Alatair possessed both arms and eyes, but by the time Altair returned to Earth he only had one of each. There is no mention of Alatair in the Celesterian records after this, so one must assume he returned to the stars or died, or lived the life of a hermit. If the other commentators are to be believed then this is the event which emboldened Altair to take on the Infinitus and then return to Earth two hundred years ago to save humanity. I think not!"

Disclaimer:

This interviewer wishes to clarify the fact that the works of Hermes Daracales do not express the views of myself or this holographic site. Professor Daracales has claimed for a long time that on a sabbatical tour of the outer solar system, he was abducted by a God and taken through time and other dimensions to witness the beginnings and ends of great civilisations. In fact, none of his stories have been verified and all his staff, including his assistants Ranch Stegson, who has a criminal record, and Mass Morgon deny ever setting foot on another planet, let alone shaking hands with a God over story contracts. And none of the worlds in question have ever been found. Despite this, Professor Daracales promotes his post-Mars series as true stories. Beware reader, though I do not wish to cast dispersions on the good professor, please read on, but with informed caution.

RB.

APPENDIX B

FAMILY LINES – The Starguards

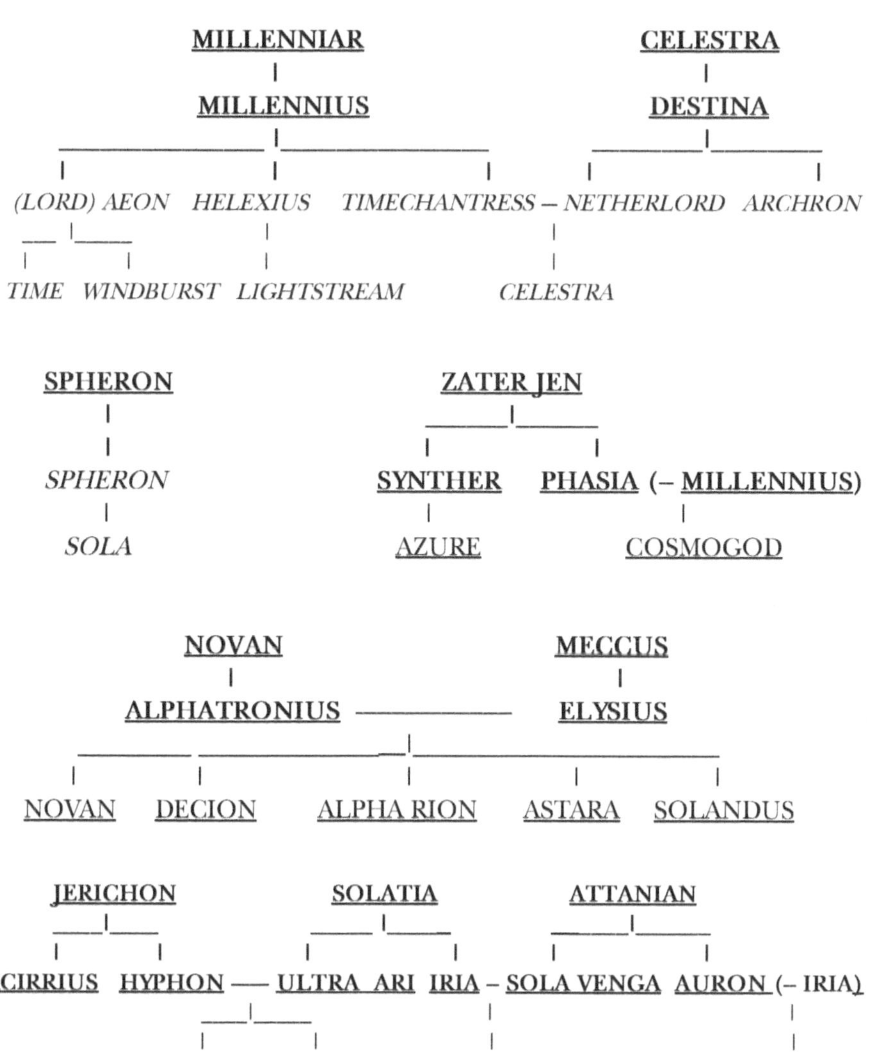

CELESTIAN KNIGHT
STARGUARD
ASTRAL

APPENDIX C

FAMILY LINES – The Celestri Knights

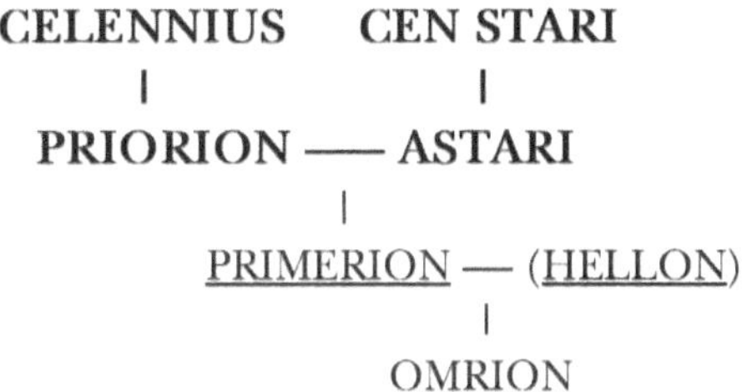

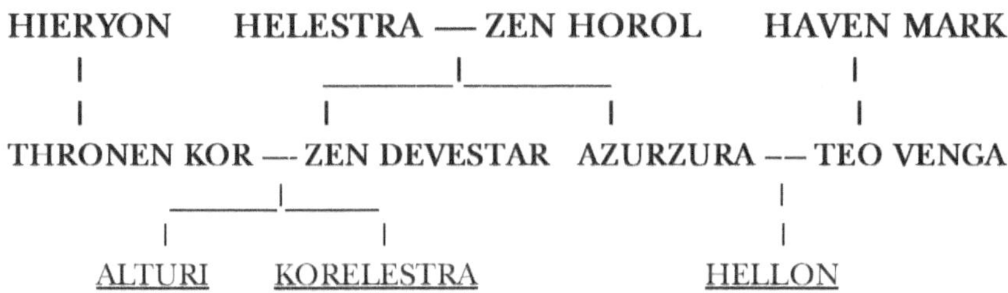

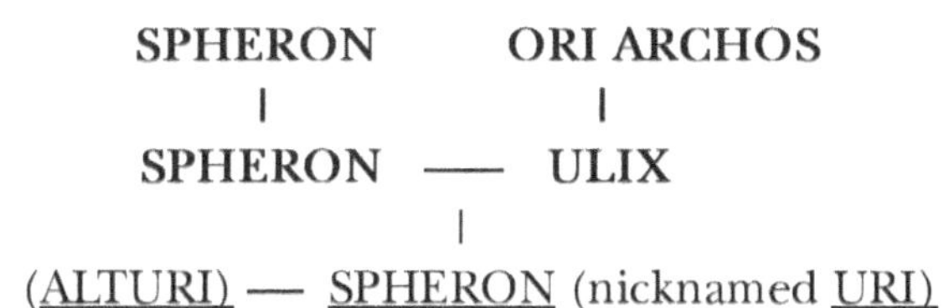

APPENDIX D

FAMILY LINES – The Astrals and the Chronossii

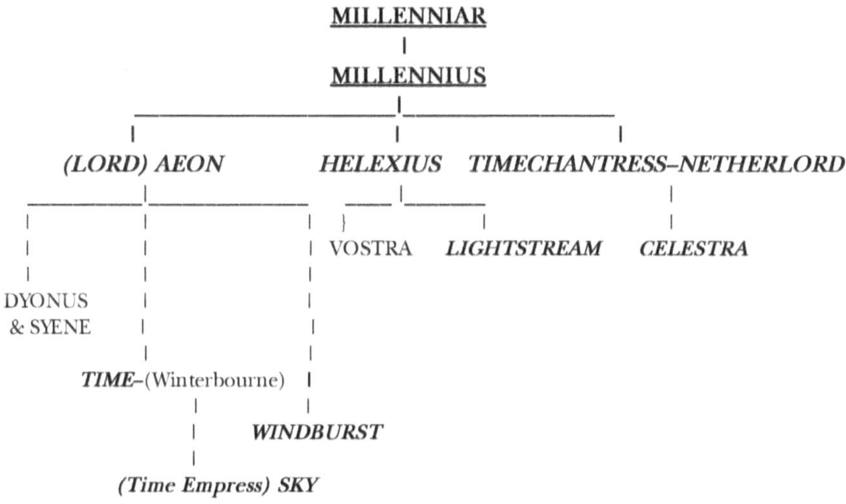

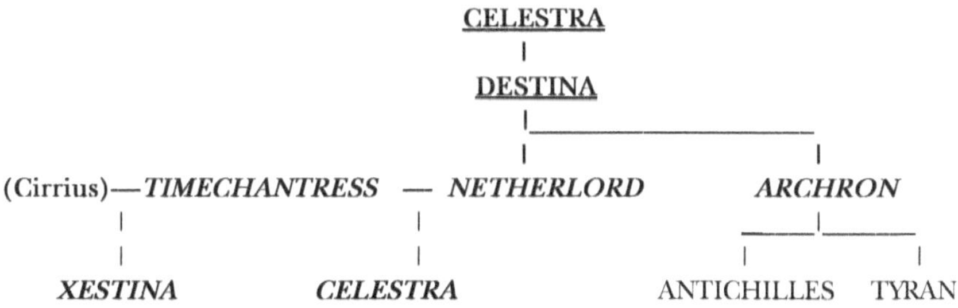

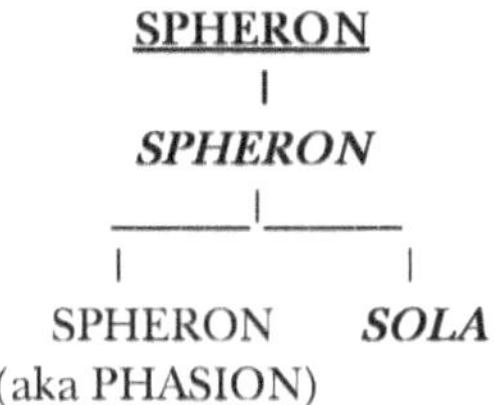

<u>CELESTIAN KNIGHT</u>
ASTRAL
CHRONOSSII

APPENDIX E

CELESTIAN SCRIPT

Lowercase

Capitals

Numerals

Have you enjoyed this book?

If so, why not write a review on your favourite website?

THE STARGUARDS

continues in

BOOK 6

The Exmoor Horizon